EROTIC SCIENCE FICTION, FANTASY, AND HORROR

Edited by
David M. Fitzpatrick

Illustrated by
Aleksandar Žiljak

Epic Saga Publishing
Brewer, Maine, USA
www.EpicSagaPub.com

SALACIOUS TALES

This anthology is dedicated in memory of

Janett Larue Grady

July 12, 1943 - Jan. 6, 2013

Janett was a writer's writer, always writing no matter the topic, the genre, the purpose, or the idea.

*She inspired, educated, and entertained with
her flexibility,
her dedication,
her perspectives,
her creativity,
her stories,
and her friendship.*

She was taken too early, for there's no doubt she had much left to give — as a writer and as a person.

Contents

Introduction

"There is hardly anyone whose sexual life, if it were broadcast, would not fill the world at large with surprise and horror."
— W. Somerset Maugham

I always wonder how many people skip introductions and just get straight to the meat of the book. In this case, the meat of the book consists of twenty-two stories which combine two things that typically aren't combined.

You're about to read erotic speculative fiction — that is, science fiction, fantasy, and supernatural horror tales with erotic themes. That merger is one thing that sets this anthology apart, because there doesn't seem to be much of that sort of thing (at least, not much that's particularly good).

The other thing that sets it apart is the quality of writing. Erotica frequently suffers in that department, often not rising very far above the kinds of stories you're apt to find wrapped in plastic at the magazine stand. Not that there's anything wrong with porn stories; they serve a purpose. But they're rarely written well, and tend to be entirely about the sex act — nothing more.

The sexual elements are vital to the stories in this book, but their plots go far deeper — if you'll pardon the pun. They run the gamut for erotic fiction, from teasing and tantalizing to explicit and hardcore. But they have engaging characters and strong plots and real resolutions; while eroticism is key, the stories are inherently about other things.

It's tough to find quality erotica and, in an age where everyone is publishing everything, it's getting harder to find quality speculative fiction. Mixing the two has been a fun experiment. As an editor, I always insist on obvious things: good writing, strong characters, solid plots, engaging storytelling, believable settings, vibrant imagery, and so forth. But for this project, I had to add a new condition to acceptance: Did the submission, to put it bluntly, turn me on?

The original plan was to have four *Salacious Tales* erotic anthologies — one each for science fiction, fantasy, horror, and adventure. After eighteen months of reading submissions, I wasn't close to filling any of them. I received a gazillion subs, but most seemed to be the wrapped-in-plastic variety. When I did get quality writing, too often the sex was an afterthought, as if the writer had an existing unsold story handy and merely added a sex scene that had no bearing on the plot.

I decided to merge the accepted stories into one volume of sci-fi, fantasy, and horror. This was risky, because fans of one of those genres wouldn't necessarily enjoy the others. But with the unifying erotic theme, I suspected readers would be more willing to explore outside their comfort zones.

The result is a unique cross section not only of diverse genres but of varied settings, innovative themes, original styles, and imaginative ideas. If that weren't enough, I was lucky to partner with a stellar artist who has been a game-changer for this project. Aleksandar Žiljak's cover art and his twenty-three full-page interior illustrations are an incredible visual showcase that has brought another dimension of creativity to this anthology.

Some writers you'll recognize from other venues, and some you won't. Some are new to being published; some have been in print before. Many are old hats, such as John Grant, who has won, among other things, two Hugo Awards. So when you're done enjoying the stories herein, please turn to the final pages and read about the authors who have made this anthology possible.

For those who care about such things: The stories are arranged in order of length, not by any special formula of what works and what doesn't. Each story is preceded by a title page with a hint of the artwork to come, along with some small-print information letting you know just what the story is: its genre and even subgenre, but also what sort of erotic aspects it contains.

From the annals of amazing coincidences: Three stories by three different authors who don't know each other all have characters calling other characters by the pet name "bunny." I swear I never noticed until the final proofreading before publication. I don't think I have a thing for rabbits, but I'll try to consciously avoid "bunny" stories for *Salacious Tales 2*.

And there will likely be a *Salacious Tales 2*, because this has been the most fun I've ever had putting together an anthology. Plus, I still have submissions coming in from prospective contributors who are happy to let me hold them until I begin reading for a follow-up. With that much interest, I guess it's almost required that we move ahead on it. It would be nice to sell a few copies of this one first, but I'm not one to demand profits when a fun creative project is at hand.

So—happy reading! Whether you do so with the lights down while alone in your bed or discreetly during your lunch hour in the employees' break room, here's to hoping you have to fan off the sweat or squirm a little where you sit. But, more importantly, here's to hoping you come away with some insight into intriguing perspectives you might never have otherwise considered.

David M. Fitzpatrick
Brewer, Maine
March 2013

Opal Heart

by
Frances Pauli

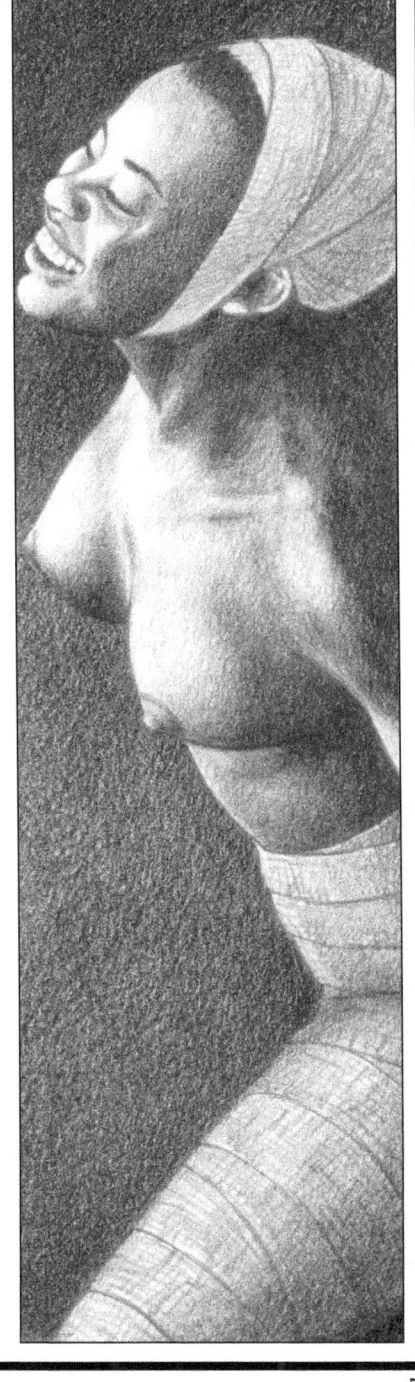

Can an woman wrapping herself in bandages in order to preserve her undead body be sexy and erotic? Can an entire society of such people even exist? They do in this tale, which will make you believe in magic and immortality, and in the power of desire and passion, and in a woman who only wants what many little girls dream about: to become the queen in a fairy-tale kingdom. Only in this fairy tale, our heroine's body is slowly rotting away — yet, somehow, this story brings us real eroticism nonetheless.

Fantasy
Undead/Zombie
Heterosexual teasing
Desire
Romance

They claimed her own vanity killed her. Anji snorted and shuffled her bound feet a touch faster. Her new wraps restricted movement but held the dead muscles firmly in place—gave her a pleasing shape and kept the ravages of time at bay for another sunset. It hadn't been vanity. She sucked in her breath and allowed her mummified midriff a reprieve from the constant pressure of the bandages weaving around and around her abdomen.

Their jealousy had finished her. She touched her ribcage absently. That and a well-placed dagger.

Today, however, she almost doubted her decision to rewrap. The fresh linens looked much better, but they slowed her considerably. No matter how fast she shuffled, she was going to be late. If she missed the trays, Majel would make her scrub the kitchen floor again—or, worse, do the mountains of filthy pots and pans. She strained against her own handiwork and leaned forward, weaving a jerky path toward the servants' entrance.

The kitchen lay toward the center of the complex. A clay wall segregated the temples and the palace from the more functional buildings, and a less imposing twin walled off the servants' quarters and the rows of rubble that housed the legions of undead who served the Zombie King.

Anji scowled at the line of creatures parading from the back door. They carried trays laden with the flat loaves of bread and pitchers of foamy drink. She shuddered at their decay, at the protruding bones and the ragged, curling flesh. Shouldering her way through the press, she lifted her feet as high as they would go and prayed something might be left for her to carry.

Inside, the night softened against the glow of torches burning. The warmth of the kitchen fires hung thick in the air. Anji stopped for only a second to let her eyes adjust before ambling to the back of the work line. She sighed as a few more trays passed by. It would be pot scrubbing for her today for certain. At the line's head, Majel passed out the night's chores. Anji felt her heart sink with each tray the woman handed over.

At last she stood at the front. Anji waited while the old kitchen woman picked at her receding face. Majel's skull showed more bone each evening, but her devotion to her task never faltered. She dropped the bit of flesh into a can tied at her waist, shrugged, and flashed an ever-widening grin.

"Anji." Majel looked her up and down. "You've added new wraps again?"

"Toshi spilled wine on the old ones."

Toshi worked closer to the palace, and he heard things. Anji had been forced to bat away his advances at the cost of her bandages, but his stories made up for the inconvenience. She sniffed and brushed at the clean linens sheathing her body. A little flirtation was worth the things Toshi could tell her about the Zombie King—the things he'd whispered to her about the Opal Heart.

Anji couldn't help that she'd been preserved by experts. Whatever Majel thought of her, she intended to keep her flesh as long as possible. Unlike some people, she refused to succumb cheerfully to the ravages of time. That fact had earned her more than one scolding from the decaying woman, but today Majel gave her no reprimand. Instead, the balding head nodded, and an unfamiliar look crossed the remains of her features. "Good. Take this, then." She pushed a tray into Anji's bandaged fingers.

Anji stared at it. The golden goblet encrusted with gems, the alabaster plate—she knew exactly who they belonged to. Still, she turned a question toward her mentor. "To him?"

"Yes, silly girl. To him. And I'd hurry my foolish steps if I were you."

Anji had only seen the Zombie King from afar, had stolen glimpses as he'd toured the palace grounds surrounded by his private guard. She'd listened to the whispers, and she'd felt the power in the man even across the wide courtyards. She'd seen the Opal Heart, flaring rainbows as he passed along the roof-top promenade. Anji had paid attention.

To stand before him now? Her knees might have quaked had they not been bound so snugly. As it was, her mummified body tingled and tried to shiver as she stumbled back out of the kitchen. The night seemed darker after the torches, and she struggled not to let the tray rattle or, heaven forbid, spill. Her fingers seemed thick and suddenly unreliable carrying such a heavy burden. The thin strips she'd wound between them pre-vented any kind of proper grip.

Still, Anji clung to the tray with sheer determination. Her chance had come at last. She stood taller, stepped more lightly on her way. She passed through the inner wall, carrying His Majesty's evening meal as if it were spun of glass. She flexed inside her cocoon, strode with just a hint of the grace she had known in life, all the way to the throne-room doors.

She found Toshi standing guard, his good leg supporting the majority of his torso and his better arm holding a long spear. Anji leaned her tray against his shoulder bone and ad-justed her bandages.

"What are you doing?" he hissed.

"Can you see my eyes now?" Anji's eyes had always been her prettiest feature, and she still had both of them.

"Yeah."

She took up the tray again and turned sideways. "How do my wraps look?"

"New. Majel's going to—"

"Toshi!"

"They look good, sexy."

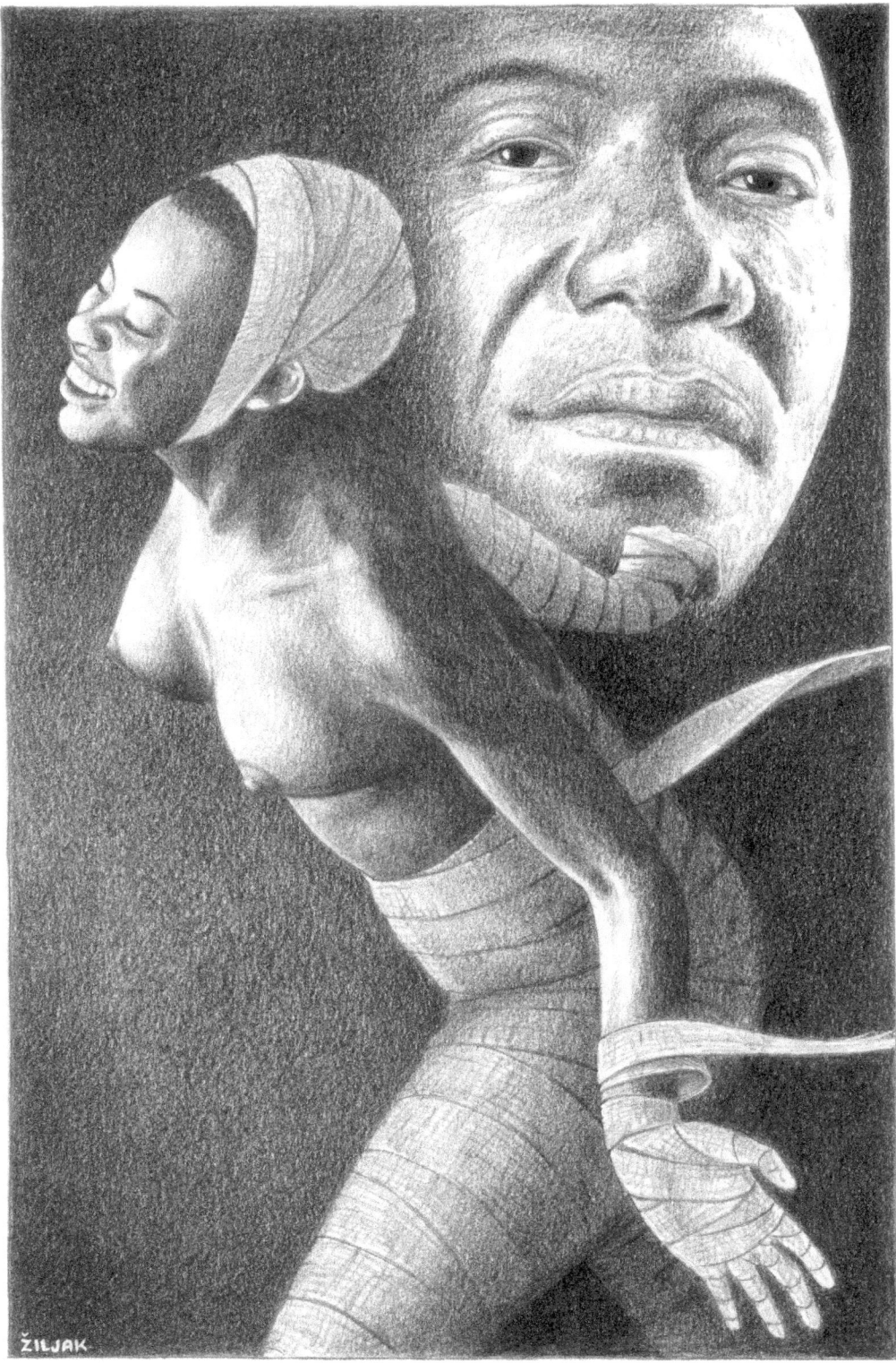

Anji smiled and thanked him. She waited for his undead limbs to wrench open the doors. Standing up as straight as she could, she whispered a prayer of thanks—for her tight wrappings, her embalmers, and the gods who had cursed her—before stepping into the darkness.

Torches cast the room into a dance of fire and shadow. A throng of rotting bodies hunched around the throne, moaning and milling at their leader's bandaged feet. He leaned forward, waved his arm wide, and the tide of fawning undead receded. His eyes burned across the hall. They reached Anji even in the shadows, and the jewel on his crown flashed green fire.

"Away!" His voice might have driven the stones themselves to flee.

Anji held the tray so tightly it rattled. She didn't twitch as the dismissed crowd swarmed around her and poured out through the doorway. Her gaze remained fixed upon their king.

"Come," he ordered, and her feet obeyed him.

She crossed the room. Her shuffle measured the distance, but her eyes devoured the figure on the throne. His wraps hung loosely around his face, making clear the function of the opal in his crown. His eyes remained sharp and full of life, despite his long-undead years. His skin stretched smooth over high cheekbones, and his lips—she looked away—still full and set in a thin smile.

She made the bottom step, knelt with some effort, and placed the tray on the stones in front of her.

"Stand." His voice, lowered, came softly to her ears even at so close a distance. "I know you. You are Anji."

"Yes." She stumbled to her feet and waited for dismissal.

"I have watched you."

Her head snapped up.

"Did you know?" His smile twisted now, full and amused.

"No."

"Does it bother you?"

"It does not, my King." She darted a glance to the crown and the stone that kept him ageless.

"Come closer."

She obeyed, although this time his voice held no compulsion. The beauty of the man and the lure of the opal moved her.

His hand rose from the chair's arm. He took hold of her elbow, and his fingers traced the line of her wrappings. "What do you know, Anji... about the Opal Heart?"

"The stone of eternal life will keep the body whole and functional so long as it is worn." She held back a shiver of excitement.

"Functional." His jaw tightened, and his eyes flashed. "And the second stone?"

"Rumor." Anji had doubted Toshi's claim, but as soon as she spoke, she saw the truth in the king's expression. "They say the Opal has a twin."

"And so it does." The King's hand slid up her arm, rested against her shoulder like a brand. "Do you want it?"

"Yes." Anji didn't hesitate. To be whole always, never to drip or peel or degrade—she wanted it as deeply as she wanted the man himself.

"They tell me you are very well preserved." His hand stroked downward, landed on the mound of her breast. "Is this true?"

"Yes." His fingers slid under a layer of gauze, adjusted her wrappings until they found her nipple. The touch of flesh against it set her legs quaking. She moaned out loud. "Mmm—yes."

"My queen must be perfect." His lips came forward, brushed against the exposed bit of her.

She nearly screamed her pleasure. "I was embalmed in the land of Pharaohs..."

His tongue was functional as well; it darted across her breast.

"...by men of the greatest skill," she gasped.

"I need you, Anji." The Zombie King pulled her to the throne. His perfect fingers tugged at the layers of her wrappings, gently at first, while his mouth played with her nipple, but then fiercely and angrily when the gauze refused to obey. He tore at the linen, tried to pry the layers apart, but they only seemed to tighten and refused to allow him entry.

He clawed at them. The bandages twisted and failed to fall away. Anji's hands flew to help him. She slid fingers in between her layers and pulled with all she had. The cloth trapped her hands, suddenly insidious, willful and set against her. Tears burned in her exposed eyes. She heard the King's growl, low and deep in his throat. Her body responded, arched to be closer to his touch, his mouth. But the wraps refused to allow access.

She'd wound each layer with utmost care. Now her body ached to be free. Her spine twisted to break the cloth encasing it. The King moaned into her chest. When he pushed her away, her heart stopped. The bandages, the very thing that kept her as he desired, foiled him. Her plans unraveled. Would he give this gift—give himself—to someone else? Anji knew terror at the thought, terror like none she could remember in all her undead years.

Her skin still burned from the King's touch, and she couldn't have said which loss would be worse, the man or the stone. But the Zombie King laughed, a hearty sound that shook the walls. He raised his hand for her to see. The tail end of her wrappings draped across his palm. Excitement, desire raced along that thread, snapping it like a leash. The Opal Heart pulsed. The King held her undoing in his perfectly preserved grip.

"Now," he said, tugging against the gauze—and Anji felt the motion at her waist, turning her, unwrapping her layers.

"Spin, Anji!"

He pulled, and Anji twirled. The gauze gave to the motion,

fell away in neat circles. She'd been preserved by masters, could feel her passion racing through flesh that couldn't possibly disappoint him.

He chanted, spooling her wraps onto the floor, unraveling the barrier between them. "Spin, spin, Anji!" The stone that would keep them whole forever flashed with each pass, winking at her. His arms twirled her in the dance, and he sang, "Spin! Spin, my queen!"

She threw both arms wide and let her casing fall away. The heat from the torches warmed her tight skin, sank in to join the fires the king's touch lit inside her. She turned, and her face was free. Her long hair fell loose for the first time in a hundred years. Her shoulders rolled away a century of bondage. Her breasts lifted, her spine arched toward freedom, and still he twirled her.

The linens fell away from her hips. She heard his groan of pleasure, felt the tug along the line between them and spun a step closer.

"Anji." His whisper echoed against the far wall. He pulled again, drew her near enough to touch. "So lovely."

His hands took hold of her thighs. They slid the remaining wrappings down. His fingers drifted toward her hips, and Anji spasmed, lost in the waves of pleasure. Her head tossed to either side, and a long moan spilled from her lips.

The King leaned forward. His mouth brushed her stomach, trailing feathery kisses that seared her skin. One hand shifted to the small of her back, and he pressed her forward, drew her down onto his lap. Anji molded her body into his. She breathed him in, buried her face against his chest and clawed at his loose wrappings. She had to touch him, had to feel him all the way through her.

"Wait." His arms lifted to her shoulders and pressed her back a fraction. "My queen, wait."

"Mmmm…" Anji struggled against him, resenting any space between their bodies.

"Anji." His chuckle stopped her. She sat up and met his fiery gaze. "The stone, my queen."

How had she forgotten? She straightened against her body's trembling and watched him reach down. His hand vanished behind the throne's arm, then lifted again bearing a silken pouch. All that she desired. Anji shivered anew as he slid open the pouch. The Opal Heart, the second stone— she'd wanted only this, only to live without decay. He pulled his treasure into the light, flashing all the colors of fire and eternity.

Her body wanted more. Her skin still screamed to be under his fingers, to drown in him, to be possessed. The Zombie King fixed the chain around her neck, and she thought only of the whispered touch. The stone settled between her breasts, heavy, priceless, and Anji shifted until it pressed against him as well. His arms encircled her, and the stone pulsed. Its power flooded through her, repairing, preserving.

She sighed, took a breath and allowed a flash of satisfaction. But when the King's lips found her neck, when his fingers returned to her sides, she thought of nothing but the heat of desire. His mouth lowered to her breast again, and her hands flew to pull the heavy stone aside. It throbbed in her hand, eternal and all hers, and Anji hardly noticed. Her king held her, and the fires they kindled shadowed even the steady flashing of twin opals.

Love Thy Neighbor

by
Janix Jenn

Will we ever be sexually free from religious oppression? And if there's intelligent life out there, will they be advanced beyond the need to control our sex lives and morally judge us? Maybe, maybe not; but the characters in this story have a healthy dose of "We don't care what you think" in the face of alien religious morality. This leads to quite an encounter between two human women — one of whom carries a burden of guilt for a dozen years afterward.

Science fiction
Religious dystopia
Lesbian sex
Female masturbation
Alien masturbation
Self-cunnilingus
Cheating confession
Romance

E xcept for a bit of self-indulgence, I haven't had sex for a very long time and I'm climbing the walls. You see, Jeannie died. I was standing at her bedside, wondering about the heart that had failed, when she opened her eyes and gasped, "I love you." She then took my hand, gave it a final squeeze, and died. So all I've been doing is masturbating.

Jeannie and I were two of the first ten thousand lesbians the Church had banished to Toblo back in 2420, our punishment for living an "ungodly" lifestyle. Of course, no one likes being convicted of "crimes," but Toblo had turned out to be kind of nice—sort of like the Canadian suburbs back on Earth.

Jeannie and I had a lovely day at Toblo's community garden a few days before she died. We stripped and took a dip in the watering pond. The water was so cold we had to kiss and snuggle just to keep from shivering out of our skin. Delightful!

I've always loved the water. I'm an excellent swimmer and swimming makes me horny. Swimming is kind of like sex: it's sensual, relaxing, and you get all wet.

But Jeannie died over six months ago, so it's time for me to get on with my life. First, though, I'm going to clear the air, and tell Jeannie about something I did behind her back. I'm going to attempt my confession while masturbating. Like I said, it's been a long time.

Jeannie, I'm wearing my pretty pink slip, the same slip I wore on the first night you and I had sex on Toblo. I'm in front of the entry board on my desk. I've gathered the slip to the top of my thighs, and I've slid a vibrator between my legs, nestled in my furry patch. I've slid it just between my lips, and it's pressed against my sweet spot. It's on low: *Bzzzz-zzz-zzz*. A-a-ah... I love that feeling. I'm wishing there were a pair of lips munching my inner labia, with a tongue sloshing wetly in and out. Hmmm—I wonder if I'll be able to finish my confession. I'll try.

Our time in the pond that day, Jeannie, reminded me of when I cheated on you. It happened about twelve years ago, a few weeks after you had signed out for the trip back to Earth. You had gone to attend your son's morality trial, knowing full well you'd be leaving me alone on Toblo for over a year.

It was on a morning about three weeks after you left. That might be the worst part—you'd barely been gone when I did it. And I never did it again, not for the whole year. I was getting ready to turn on the shower when I thought I heard a splash outside in the pool. Peeking out the window, I saw this slightly pudgy, long-haired blonde climbing out of the water—naked. I watched as she made her way onto the diving board, my eyes drawn to the curly yellow thatch between her legs. She bounced on her toes, her ample breasts jiggling nicely, and then sliced into the pool with hardly a splash.

She was beautiful, and I was uncontrollably attracted to her. I don't know why. Still naked, I hurried outside. When I got to the edge of the pool, she was underwater swimming the length of the pool. At the shallow end, I sat down, letting my legs dangle in the water. She must have seen me, because she suddenly surfaced, right in front of me. Her head was right there between my knees, at eye level with my crotch. It was exciting, but I tried to act like I wasn't thinking that way.

"I'm sorry," she gasped. "I thought you girls had signed out."

"Not me," I said. "Just Jeannie. She went back to Earth."

"Oops, guess I screwed up," she said, treading water. "I'm Shaina."

She swam over to me, supple and lithe, full of voluptuous curves that got me horny just watching her move. "My sexual instructor Poco and I just moved in next door. The pump on our pool quit working, so I thought maybe I could use yours."

"No problem," I said. "I'm Janix."

I slid into the pool and paddled alongside her. The cool water doused the heat between my legs, at least for the moment. "Where's Poco?" I asked, just to make conversation, and maybe to overcome the overwhelming desire I had to reach out and touch her body. "Is she coming over?"

"No, she's not into swimming. Poco is a Blute. You know, from Blutar, that icy rock a zillion light years from here. She's not a prisoner like us, though; she's a scientist. She's doing a study on same-sex relationships. They paired her up with me by chance. She's supposed to teach me how to not be a lesbian."

Well, that answered one question.

"I've never seen a Blute," I said. "Does she look like us?"

Shaina just grinned, splashing water at me. "Not at all. So, Jeannie, back to Earth... did you two break up?"

She sounded hopeful. I told her you'd gone back for the trial, and that you'd return in a year, and I think I saw a little disappointment in her eyes.

Then she said, "Nothing says you can't splash around the pool with a strange naked woman, right?"

So Shaina and I swam around for awhile, and then we started challenging each other to see who could stay underwater the longest. Eventually we started wrestling and holding each other under. I knew we were flirting, and I knew I shouldn't have been, but I just couldn't help myself.

After splashing water in my face again, she ducked under and headed for the deep end. I went under and chased her. I caught her on the bottom, grabbing her from behind, wrapping my arms around her waist. She didn't struggle to get away. Instead, she reached behind her and slid her hands over my hips. She turned within my embrace to face me. Our cheeks puffy with air, we stared at each other through the bluish water. She put her arms around me and pressed her body tightly against mine, our breasts mashed together, and she used one foot to kick us upward.

As soon as we broke the surface, she kissed me full on the lips, forcing her tongue into my mouth. I let her. We started sinking, but I kicked my feet to keep us afloat. When Shaina ended the kiss, she broke our embrace and swam to the side of the pool. She waved for me to join her. I paddled over.

"I'm horny," she said. "I want to have sex."

There it was. And I wanted to, so badly. But I resisted.

"Can't do it," I said. "I'm in love with Jeannie."

"She's not here," Shaina said. "She'll never know."

"What if Poco shows up?" I asked. "Don't you love her?"

"Not really," she said. "Poco is just into it to see if she can figure out a way to turn us straight. She's a Church chemist, forever trying to squirt this green shit up my ass,"

Shaina didn't wait to hear me grumble in disgust. I didn't have time to react or even think when she suddenly ducked underwater and kissed my puss.

Well, Jeannie, you know me when it comes to having my pussy kissed. Instinctively, I opened my legs as wide as I could, and for one incredible second I felt Shaina's tongue glide up between my lips and quickly flick at my clitoris. But then Shaina withdrew, abruptly coming up for air. I closed my legs, feeling guilty and ashamed for having lost control of myself.

"I hope you didn't mind," Shaina said, pushing back her hair. "Do you want me to do it again?"

I really wanted to say no, Jeannie. I tried to, and I think she knew I was trying. But before I could, she slipped back under.

Well, hon, who was I to cause problems? I pressed my back against the side of the pool and held myself afloat by resting my elbows on the ledge behind me. But it wasn't necessary. Shaina was standing on the bottom, and she had gone under so that my thighs were resting on her shoulders. It wasn't long and her tongue was sliding up and down between my lips. When the tip of her tongue circled my clit, I thought I had died and gone to heaven. I'm sorry, Jeannie, but I lost all sense of propriety and started moving, grinding my crotch against her face.

But then she came up for air again. When she broke the surface, she grabbed the ledge on either side of me, sliding her knee between my legs.

"You're a sweetie," she whispered in my ear, knee rubbing against my puss. "Let's have sex."

Without waiting for me to reply, Shaina pushed herself away and climbed out of the pool, her gorgeous ass in front of my face. She leaned over and offered her hand. I took it, and she yanked me up and out of the water. She pulled me into her arms, tittie squishing tittie, nipple searching for nipple, tummies tightly pressed trying to get puss touching puss.

"Let's do it," she said, squeezing my ass. "Right here, right now."

"I don't know," I said. "What if Poco shows up?"

"I'm already here," said a voice behind me.

Startled, I spun away from Shaina to see a monster, a creature covered with hair from head to foot, hair that was brown and matted and crawling with what looked like bugs. My passion for Shaina rapidly vanished, and I had all I could do to keep from screaming.

Shaina tapped me on the ass. "Calm down," she said. "Poco, this is Janix. Janix, this is Poco."

I swallowed hard and said "Hello" as pleasantly as I could. Poco stuck out her tongue, a tongue so long it reached all the way down between her legs, which were now spread wide enough for me to see my first puss from Blutar. It was all so hairy that all I could see was the swell of what I assumed were lips.

"I can do myself," said Poco, and several inches of her tongue disappeared up inside her. "If you could do this, you

ŽILJAK

would."

Somehow, it was exciting, even with the bugs scrambling around where her tongue disappeared up inside her. I later learned they weren't bugs; they were some kind of external chemical transporters, just part of being a Blute. It still seemed gross.

Poco's tongue finally came out from between her legs. It swung back and forth a few times, yellow Blute pussy slime dripping off it, and then slithered back into her mouth. "Mmmm, good," she said.

I didn't like her from the start, and not because she looked so monstrous. I didn't like what her alien Church stood for, and what they wanted to do to lesbians like us. "But we can't do that," I said defiantly. "We do each other."

"Yes, I know," said Poco, "and that's why I've been trying to give Shaina a Mouth Flux. It'll make—"

"What in the hell is a Mouth Flux?" I asked.

"It makes your tongue grow as long as theirs," Shaina put in. "And she's been trying to squirt that green shit up my ass for what seems like forever. That's supposed to set us straight, make us want to do ourselves all day with our super-long tongues, instead of wanting to do each other."

"Yeah, right," I said. "What, are you Church creeps saying it's now all right if we masturbate?"

"No, not really," Poco replied. "It's just better—not as wicked as having same-sex intercourse."

"Up yours!" I shouted.

And that, Jeannie, is why and when I had sex with Shaina. I really think I'd have come to my senses and resisted Shaina, but I was so mad then that I just had to do it.

"Let's show this creep," I said, and a moment later, Shaina and I were nose to toes, with Shaina on top, doing each other as if we loved each other. "Take notes!" I hollered at Poco. "We're being wicked!"

I don't know if Poco took notes, and I didn't care. I just

know I had my pussy eaten by a woman almost as good as you. And she tasted great. I buried my face in her puss and ate her out as if my life depended on it, and it was especially empowering knowing that morally superior Blute "sexual instructor" was watching it happen. But it was difficult. You know how hard it is, hon, when you're desperately trying to please me, and you're lapping your tongue like crazy, but I'm doing the same thing to you? It was hard to concentrate with Shaina snaking her tongue up inside me as she grabbed my ass with both hands. I tried to focus, lapping up her juices.

When Shaina tightened her lips around my clit and started sucking, I knew I wouldn't last long — you know how I am! — so I did the same to her. I was dimly aware of Poco in the background, making sounds that I hoped meant it was excited by our wicked act. I sucked hard on Shaina's clit, lashing it nonstop with my tongue, as Shaina did the same to me. We held on to each other's asses for dear life as we brought each other to orgasm. She came first, pulling her mouth away from my puss to scream in ecstasy, but as soon as she was done, she attacked my clit again. I did my own screaming a minute later.

And the best fringe benefit? As I was thrashing about in my orgasm, I saw Poco off to the side, her serpentine tongue swelled up to fat proportions, slamming in and out of her Blute hole. As Shaina finished shuddering above me, Poco gurgled in what had to be an orgasm, and when she yanked her tongue out, it seemed like it took a quart of yellow slime with it. The hairy Blute toppled over, breathing heavily, her long tongue flopped on the ground. She'd loved ever moment of our wickedness — typical for the morally superior, huh? Do as I say, not as I do.

Shaina rolled off me and into my arms, and we cuddled together as Poco clambered to her feet and shambled off, undoubtedly embarrassed.

"Guess we showed her," I said.

Shaina giggled. "I can't tell you how much that makes me

smile." She looked at me with deep eyes. "You know, making Poco look so foolish. And — and for this."

Her hand found my wet puss, and she stroked it lightly as she leaned in and kissed me. I closed my eyes and met her lips with mine, and it felt wonderful.

Jeannie, please know that you were on my mind the whole time — through every touch and every kiss. It was the one and only time I ever cheated on you, and I don't know if it did anything to change any stupid attitudes. I really doubt it. As you know, it's an attitude that's been around since the dawn of time, an attitude that had eventually gotten us all banished to Toblo, and one where they even imported aliens from Blutar to "fix" us.

Shaina and Poco moved out the very next day, but they went their separate ways. Shaina moved in with a girl from the experimental farm on Earth's moon, and I heard that Poco was sent back to Blutar. Apparently she'd failed as a sexual instructor, what with all that orgasmic masturbation watching two human women doing each other as furiously as Shaina and I had.

But I never forgot what happened, and never stopped feeling guilty about it. I guess I should have told you long ago. But what I did do was make it up to you for the rest of your life. Every time we had sex, I guess I felt like I was making up for it, doing everything to make you feel special and loved and sexually satisfied — whether we were making tender love or fucking like sex-starved teenagers.

I just wanted to clear the air, Jeannie, and let you know what I did behind your back. Now I can get on with my life.

And now I can lie down on my bed and spread my legs, use this vibrator with a clear conscience.

Damn, there's somebody banging on my door. Hold on.

Guess who it was. It was Larisi, my new next-door

neighbor. She's mostly human, but has been genetically altered—she's part Blute. She came over to see if she could use my pool. She's out there now, and I'm getting ready to join her. I'm sort of hoping…

Well, there's nothing wrong with having a long tongue, right? Right.

Dinner and a Peepshow

by
Robert M. Palmer

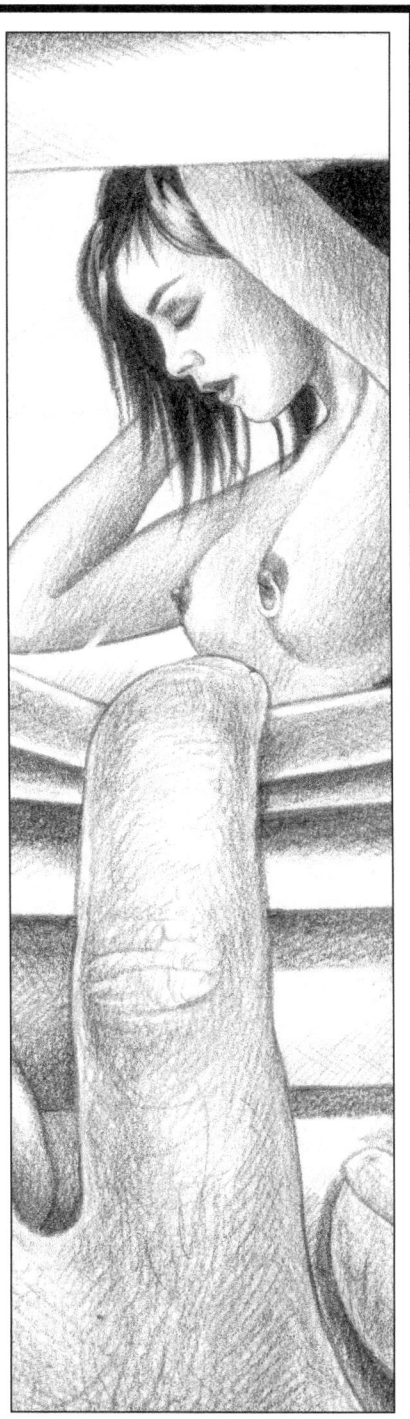

Gentlemen aren't supposed to peek, and they're certainly never supposed to spy on naked neighbors. But this gentleman is having a hell of a hard time in his life as of late, and the woman in the apartment across the way is an exciting and bright spot in an otherwise boring and dismal existence. She's like some wild fantasy brought to life... especially when things go from "fantasy" to "fantastic."

Horror
Vampire
Voyeurism
Heterosexual sex

The microwave dinged its sad little ding and spat out a half-melted Styrofoam bucket of piss-warm yellow water and noodles. Pink blobs masquerading as shrimp floated in the viscous liquid. At least Tom thought they were shrimp—the label was in Cantonese, or maybe Mandarin, and he didn't speak either. The ramen was stringy and tasted like ball sweat but he bought it by the case at the Chinese market on the corner because it only cost a dime per bag. He sat in the only chair at the kitchen table with his pathetic dinner for one and spread the vinyl slats of the blinds with his bony fingers, waiting for Dawn.

The clock on the wall said six-thirty, but it had been known to lie. He slurped a mouthful of noodles, wiping the greasy residue from his chin, noting that the chemical tang of the burnt Styrofoam really did something for the flavor.

The Black House, Tom's tenement—named for the long-dead architect—was a monstrosity of brown stone and flaking mortar in a neighborhood rapidly backsliding into poverty and obscurity as the socio-economic center of Central City peeled away from the St. Charles River. Shaped like a horseshoe—two wings raking back from the main body fronting Water Street in a poorly executed attempt to make a ground-level courtyard garden—the building itself was a testament to man's stupidity. The builders had failed to take into account that the roof, six stories above the crumbling asphalt below, was far too high to let any sunlight down into the courtyard. It was, and remained, nothing more than a diseased quagmire, a particularly nasty oubliette in which nothing but mold and mushrooms would grow. In the summer, the stench of the fungal ecosystem was so overpowering that air conditioning and open windows brought Tom to fits of asthmatic apoplexy.

Tom lived in apartment thirty-five, on the third floor—the very end of one leg of the horseshoe. The other end, apartment thirty-six—due to some fluke in the numbering system—was directly across the shadowed maw but not more than twenty feet from his own kitchen window. He could, by peeking through the slats of his Venetian blinds, see directly into the apartment across the way. It was a perverse little peepshow for which he didn't even have to pay—reality television in a window frame.

That was how Tom had met Dawn three weeks before, though truly he didn't know if that was her name or not—he'd never seen her outside of her apartment—but she looked like a Dawn to him.

Until then, Tom's life had been pretty boring... well, mind-numbing, really. He went to work, put up with his boss's shit, and went home only to fall asleep in the TV's cold, uncaring light, and wake up the next morning to do it all over again.

"What the hell is this?" the red-faced woman in the leopard-print unitard and six-inch heels said. It took Tom a minute to realize that the woman was talking to him and not the cell phone trapped helplessly in her shiny red talons like a helpless baby rabbit.

"A double-mocha... something or other with a shot of hazelnut and cinnamon," Tom said, trying not to stare at her misshapen (and clearly man-made) breasts. The left was two inches higher than the right and they were both about two cup sizes too big for her bony body.

"I asked for soy milk. This is cow's milk!"

Tom braced himself for the tirade he knew was about to come, like a deer who knows those headlights are bringing a ton and a half of heavy-metal death its way but can't overcome its own momentum.

"I assure you, ma'am, that it's—" He held up the carton of soy milk that he'd just poured into her overly elaborate paper coffee cup, which she would have seen if she hadn't been waving her hands in the air like a witch trying to cast an incantation and raging about what Alejandro did to the begonias to whoever was patient enough to sit on the other end of the phone line and listen.

"This is cow's milk! Are you telling me I don't know the difference?"

"No, ma'am, I just—"

"What if I had had an allergy? I could be in apoplectic shock, dying on the floor right now!"

"Anaphylactic," Tom said, knowing that he shouldn't have.

"What did you just call me? Did you hear?" The woman said, turning to the slick dude trying not to look too cool in his expensive ripped jeans, pre-faded leather jacket, and seventy-five-dollar 'do. The dude shrugged.

"I demand to see your manager," she said.

His boss, Vince, was a slick metrosexual who wore his hair a little too emo and his glasses a little too Gucci. He had just graduated high school and couldn't even grow proper facial hair.

Tom was forty-two and the only hair he could grow was facial.

"Hey, Tom," Vince said after he'd been summoned through the double doors at the back—looking briefly at Tom before "including the customer" just like the damned training manual that nobody else had ever read said to do. "What's up?"

Any drunken idiot with two good brain cells and one bad eye could tell what was going on, but Vince loved to play the part.

"This..." The woman seemed at a loss for words and Tom hoped that she'd just shut up and die, but it didn't happen.

"...man expects me to drink this swill." The woman dropped the coffee cup on the countertop like it was a bag full of dog shit.

"She wanted a double-mocha..."

"It's okay Tom. Why don't you just go wait in my office, I'll take care of this. Jerry?" Vince called over his shoulder, and his little protégé came through the double doors with his shit-brown apron all pressed and neat and his "thank you very much" smile glued to his well-manicured face. "You want to cover the counter while I have a chat with Tom?"

Vince's office was the stock room where they kept cases of empty paper cups and rat-gnawed bags of bulk coffee beans — only the best from the asshole of South America for Java Jivin'.

"I'm sorry, Tom." Vince said after he sat behind the card table he used as a desk. "I'm going to have to let you go. This is the third time in a month —"

Tom didn't hear the rest. He was too busy trying to figure out how to make burying his boss alive under sacks of coffee beans look like an accident.

"Fuck you," Tom said under his breath, wishing he had the balls to punch Vince right in the nose.

"What was that?"

"Thank you," Tom said.

That night, Tom came home with a bottle of rum and spent most of the night playing pirate. By the end of it, he was hopping on what furniture he had, trying to cross the room without touching the floor. It was a fun game until he slipped on the kitchen table — damned nylon girly socks his mother had given him for Christmas — and nearly went out the window. He came down in a bloody heap, taking the blinds with him. He awoke sometime later in the night, his shirt and chin caked with his own vomit, head like an overinflated beach ball, and leaking a disturbing amount of blood from a jagged scrape on his forearm. It was a struggle to find his feet, let alone bandages or a rag. In his confusion, Tom looked out the warped panes of old glass into the dull grey gloom that perpetually hung in the courtyard like a fog, heedless of the time of day or night.

There, opposite him, framed in stone and flaking white paint was an angel—a dark one, to be sure, but an angel none-theless. She was washing black dye out of her long hair in the sink, scrubbing with short fingers tipped in black lacquer, flip-ping strands of wet hair over her shoulder like vamps did in rock videos. A spiky tribal tattoo done in purple bracketed one blue eye; the other eye was a mischievous sort of green. Her cutoff shirt bore the name of some band, but Tom wasn't look-ing at the logo. Water streamed down from her hair, seeping through the worn cotton, sucking it tight to her breasts. Big, dark areolas burned through the wet fabric.

Just then she opened her eyes, catching Tom gawking like a tourist in Midtown, and smiled—a devilish thing; a mouthful of perfectly white teeth seemed to glow between her black lips.

Tom waved, as if from the back of the short bus.

The girl—Dawn, he'd already decided—reached above her head, the curved underside of one breast peeking from beneath the ragged edge of her shirt, and drew the shade with a single motion.

It started slowly at first, Tom's obsession. He found him-self eating in front of the window more often than in front of the TV, though he'd not used the dinner table in the two years he'd lived in the apartment. He even bought newspapers at the corner store so he could sit at the table and pretend to read them, all the while knowing at the back of his mind that he was just hoping to catch a glimpse of motion, a silhouette, any-thing behind that blank shade.

He tried to distract himself with television, video games, and cheap hooch, but nothing worked. Gradually, he slid fur-ther into a funk and before he knew it weeks (plural—though he wasn't sure if it was two or three) had passed. His unemployment

ate at the back of his mind like a starving mosquito. So did the telephone, but he let the message machine fill with worried words from his mother and angry ones from people to whom he owed money. The window called to him.

He knew that she knew he was watching. He could feel it. Every so often, just when he thought he'd mustered the courage to shower or shave or even go buy ramen, she'd reappear in the window. Most of the time it was just a fleeting sighting as she walked past—ear buds in her ears, a glass of wine in her hand—or a late showing as she slid past, shedding her clubbing clothes as she went.

Finally, after a month or better—after the second time the landlord came knocking at the door, no doubt at the insistence of his mother—Tom's life had degenerated into sitting in the dark without even pretending to do anything but watch.

His mother had always said Tom was burdened by his father's dependent tendencies. Though he'd never known the man, her tales of hard drinking, blackouts, and stumbling home from some bar or another with black eyes painted his father in an ill light; but, since meeting Dawn, Tom had a new appreciation for the siren call of addiction. Voyeurism, not Jim Beam, had become his drug. It grabbed him by the balls and stroked him dry, emptying his willpower, feeding the foolish fantasies that played out behind his eyelids.

One night when those eyelids were too gritty to close and his back hurt too much from sitting to stand, Dawn's shade shot up and lapped against the window like a dog's tongue. She was there, on the edge of her sink, back to him, naked. The creamy white expanse of her flesh pressed against the glass, broken only by the ghostly blue lines of feathery angel-wing tattoos running from her shoulder blades to the valley of her buttocks. She was rocking back and forth, slamming into the windowpane, rattling the glass loud enough for Tom to hear from his apartment.

He opened his window just a crack, stiffening at the

sound, unmindful of the ever-present stench of decay from below. He couldn't fathom what in the hell she was doing, but he
liked it—at least he did until the Norse god previously hidden
behind her turned Dawn around and took her from behind. A
brick shithouse, the man had that chiseled, Aryan-stock thing
going for him. Tom recognized him from the elevator, though
he didn't know the man's name. He lived on the fourth floor,
just above Tom.

The stud grabbed Dawn's hair and thrust into her hard.

Tom had never been a violent man. He didn't watch those
torture-porn movies that were so en vogue but, just for an instant, he pictured himself crushing that Hitlerite's head in his
bare hands—squeezing and crunching until blood and gray
matter oozed from between his fingers.

Tom almost turned away, cheeks burning with shame and
rage at once, but Dawn was watching him. It was impossible—
his blinds were drawn with no more than a half-inch between
them, his lights were out, he was sitting stock still—but her
mismatched eyes were locked on his, blue and green gems
sparkling with excitement. He thought maybe he was hallucinating, but when she flashed her killer smile he knew he wasn't.
Sure that she had an audience, Dawn turned up the heat, rocking and bucking and moaning so loud that Tom could feel it in
his chest. The embarrassing heat in his cheeks fled lower.

It was like she was inside his head. When she touched herself, he felt warmth in his fingertips. When she traced the line
of sweat between her breasts with a black-tipped nail and then
slipped the finger into her mouth, he tasted the salt. When she
drove herself back onto her lover, he felt her soft ass on his
hips. It was like some sort of weird transmogrification had
taken place and Tom had become the stud between her legs.
He could even smell her: sweat, sex, and perfume.

Even in his real-life sexual encounters, Tom had never experienced anything close to this. Most of the time they were
just ill-coordinated groping sessions in a darkened room that

ended quicker than they should have and left him feeling hollow. Dawn was somehow using her sex to fill him up, to light a fire inside him like had never burned before.

All the while she wore that devil's smile—until, at last, the pleasure overcame her and her knees went weak. She grasped her breast and pulled at the nipple piercing, bit her lip and shuddered. Blood trickled down her chin and her eyes rolled back in her head.

Tom was surprised to see, or rather feel, that he had climaxed as well. He'd been so intent on Dawn's pleasure that his own had ceased to matter.

The whole encounter lasted longer than Tom had expected but, he supposed, that in itself was no surprise with Herr Studmuffin. What Tom wasn't expecting was the blood. Just as the spectacle was about to climax, or so Tom gathered from the pained look on the man's face, Dawn spun round and buried her face in the crook of his neck. The man's expression went from pre-orgasmic to post-traumatic in a heartbeat. He seemed to deflate as if the very air was being sucked out of him. His cheeks hollowed with his gasping breath and his eyes rolled back into his skull, and he began to convulse. When Dawn pulled away, a gout of bright red blood, black in the gloom, splashed the window, masking the entwined lovers like a silken veil. The stud stood for a moment, swaying as if drunk. When Dawn dropped out of sight to do God (or the Devil) knew what, he collapsed as if she had cut his strings.

Tom was hard and humming like a high tension wire. He should have been shocked and disgusted; he should have felt fear, should have vomited right there, but he felt... vindicated. Dawn had done this for him. She had seen the hurt and hate inside him, all the wrongs he had endured his entire life, the years of existing unnoticed by the world, the loneliness and... disconnection. She'd done this to... what? Assuage his pain? Heal his wounds? Rectify the horrible disrespect? Or maybe just to acknowledge it all. It was as if the poster boy for the

Fourth Reich had been an embodiment of every asshole that had ever fucked Tom over, and she had brought them to the slaughter!

Tom laughed. He laughed and felt strong like he never had in his miserable life. He felt powerful in spite of his weak body and confidence in his meager good looks (hidden by days of filth and facial hair.) He wanted to take the world!

But the first thing he would take was Dawn.

He watched the blood trace cryptic symbols on the glass. When Dawn rose, she was resplendent, glowing with unholy light, blue through her porcelain skin. Her face, chest, and hands stained black with the liquid remains of her Teutonic lover, she leaned close into the window and sucked the fingers of one hand while tweaking her nipples with the other, leaving dark smudges.

Somehow, without Tom acknowledging it, the night succumbed to the daylight, only to conquer the day once again.

He rose from his kitchen chair, knees cracking and bladder full to bursting, a decision coalesced in his mind, turning to concrete before his cowardice could rise up and overtake it. In those few horrible minutes, shared so deliciously with his beautiful neighbor, Tom had lived more than he had his entire life. He knew only one thing that could ever compare.

Tom went to the bathroom. Showered. Shaved. Dressed in his best poly-cotton blend, and left his apartment for the first time in days.

The decision was solidly implanted in his mind but his feet were still heavy and stuck to the crappy brown carpet in the hall as he scuffed around the horseshoe. With each step his mind brought up another reason he should turn around: his online friends with whom he role-played, the girl at the coffee shop he'd almost asked out, his poor mother who had never done him any wrong (but might have not done any right), and even the potential winning lotto ticket in his wallet. Each obstacle succumbed to the waves of lust coursing through him, drowning in a salty sea of want and desire.

Painstaking though it was, the short journey was over before he knew it. He found himself standing in front of Dawn's door, smiling. Scents from inside wafted into the hall: sex and mulling spices. When the door swung inward, hushing on the rich carpet, Dawn was waiting. A monument to Gothic sex appeal, she was bathed in black mascara and blood-red lipstick. Tom could see thick veins, blue and pumping, beneath her pure, colorless skin.

She slipped behind Tom, liquid-caramel smooth, and breathed hot cinnamon breath into his ear. Unnaturally sharp teeth nicked his earlobe, sending shivers of anticipation down his spine.

"What took you so long?" she asked in a voice like poured molasses.

As she closed the door behind him, Tom wondered if anybody would be watching the two of them through the window.

Argosy

by
Aleksandar Žiljak

*There's nothing like a long cruise
to get sailors in the mood for sex
when they get into port. But on
this planet, the sailors are always
at sea, and their ship is a living
creature whose primal lust affects
them empathically. This crew is
always in the mood for sex… but
sometimes things happen that
mix it all up a bit.*

Science fiction
Alien world
Group sex
Straight sex
Lesbian sex
Lust

Tagane put down her bowl and looked with worry at the western clouds that rose all the way to the stratosphere. They heralded a storm. On the starboard, half a mile away, several bright-yellow blimps floated some fifty feet above the waves. Their tentacles dragged down to the surface and dozens of feet underwater, tender deadly traps for anything entangling in them. Marble-like patterns on their bladders pulsated peacefully from black to purple, giving no sign of a storm gathering. But Tagane knew that blimps wouldn't float so low if they didn't feel the tempest approaching.

"We dive tonight," she said finally to no one in particular.

"Shall we look for shelter on the Islands?" Slaven asked.

Mina had already finished her lunch; she usually ate faster than the others. Conrad paid them no attention, taking second helpings from the pot. Only Roberta lifted her gaze and begun eating faster, chopsticks stuffing boiled algae into her mouth. 'We dive tonight' meant it was time to pull out the longlines.

"We won't make it," Tagane said.

"Maybe the storm won't be strong." Slaven said. Tagane knew he didn't feel like taking the lines out. They knew well enough that nothing had time to get caught yet—nothing worth mentioning.

"We won't be taking any chances," Tagane said, facing them all: Slaven, Roberta, Mina, and Conrad. "You all know what our Argosy is passing through."

They all nodded as one. They knew. *The Argosy is as good as the captain,* Tagane thought. *And the captain is as good as the sailors.*

"Let's finish our meal," she said, "and then let's get to work."

Slaven was right, as usual: A meager fifty-something pounds of swift-tails and several spikefish. They only wasted their baits. Large jacks and 'cudas rose at night, when the ocean was on fire.

But Tagane was also right, as usual. While they were pulling the lines out and securing all the hooks and gutting all the catch, the wind gained strength. The waves started splashing the sides of the Argosy and spraying her deck, and she—apparently not worried by the imminent storm—spread all four sails. The Argosy rushed across the surging ocean, leaving the foaming wake behind: pushed by wind, driven by her instincts, older than memory.

"As far as we're concerned..." Slaven approached Tagane from behind and embraced her around her waist.

She nodded. His touch comforted her. The Argosy murmured deep inside her. The Argosy's lust drove Tagane, too. The wind ruffled her jet-black hair, rolling leaden clouds from the west. And then, lightning flashed through the lead. And another, and another.

It's time, Tagane decided.

The Argosy still held all her sails spread: leathery membranes some thirty feet across, carried by the strong arms, turned and tilted to catch most of the wind and keep the Argosy always in the right direction. But the Argosy was heavy, swollen, sinking deep; she'd weather the storm with difficulty. And she felt Tagane's silent plea, too: Tagane's unease before the unbridled wind and unleashed ocean. The instincts would have to wait.

The Argosy lowered two sails, drawing the arms into her shell. Roberta, Mina, and Conrad were already inside, in the chambers between the longitudinal septa that were their homes. The waves grew stronger, washing the deck, foam flowing down the sides of the shell. And then the Argosy drew the remaining two sails. Tagane felt rather than heard the chambers filling with water, the shell beginning to dive. In several minutes, the waves would close above the shell and them within. The Argosy would sink into the deep quiet, safe before the fury of a fierce tropical storm.

"Let's go," Tagane said, and led Slaven inside.

A near lightning flashed across the interior mother-of-pearl layer of the septum. Through the viewport, Tagane took one last look at the lead torn by electricity, before the waves closed above them. They were sinking, chambers full. The ocean above turned savage, whipped by wind, beaten by lightning: a howling, foaming beast, moaning and then roaring again, driving every living thing deep into calm, into darkness spangled with shimmering photophores, like stars in the night.

Roberta was lying on a mattress made of dried algae. Conrad stretched next to her, taking her hand, kissing her fingers, licking the salt from her palm. Roberta stirred, sighing barely audibly; there wasn't much else to do underwater. Mina was hanging lanterns all over the chamber—small dried blimp bladders, filled with fine powder made of dried torchworms. She dipped her fingers into a bowl of water and sprinkled the powder in each lantern. Moist, they glowed in soft greenish glow that spilled through the viewports into the deep. Every so often, an Argosy's arm would coil through the light.

The Argosy was sinking deeper and deeper, the storm remaining just a muted thundering above. Something swam through the greenish glow—something large, bigger than the biggest 'cuda. Tagane strained to see, but it was already swallowed by the dark. She stared into the black for some time, and then she shrugged her shoulders. *Who knows what abides these depths,* she thought. But she felt safe in the Argosy's shell— huge and strong, capable of enduring the pressure of the sea at fifteen hundred fathoms deep. She felt protected, guarded by dozens of strong arms. Centuries were the only enemy of a fully grown Argosy.

Mina nodded towards Roberta and Conrad, who embraced in the dry algae, kissing. Roberta spread her legs shamelessly. Conrad pulled her gaudy, flower-patterned sarong up, exposing her firm lower belly, and touched her where it was sweetest, his fingers ruffling her pubic hair, caressing her lips, tickling her clitoris.

Mina rolled her eyes, as if saying 'They have only *that* on their minds?' But Tagane didn't miss the spark of lust in Mina's naughty green eyes. The passion spilled from the Argosy into them all. Tagane felt it flowing through her body, tingling her skin, making her moist between her legs.

With one hand, Tagane reached for Mina; with another, for Slaven. She led them to the other mattress and surrendered to them. Slaven took off his T-shirt and denim shorts, his cock proudly rampant as Mina unbuttoned Tagane's beige trousers and pulled them down her legs. Slaven undid Tagane's white flannel shirt, baring her full breasts, and then waited for Mina to peel off her orange jumpsuit. Then they both attended to their captain, showering Tagane with kisses, soft and warm and wet all over her face and neck, breasts and belly. She sank happily into a steamy whirlpool, enflamed by their heavy hot breaths, teased by their fingers and tongues and lips, moaning in ecstasy as Slaven's cock slid into her pussy.

Mina fondled them both, kissing them, burning with desire of her own at the sight of Slaven fucking Tagane in slow, steady thrusts; and then stiffening and coming into her, filling her with semen, and Tagane coming, too; and Mina fingering herself frantically to an orgasm; and the three of them collapsing on the mattress, body next to body next to body. And Roberta and Conrad next to them, screwing, he in her, she around him—and all of them within the Argosy, deep in the bosom of the ocean that was life to them.

The storm passed and the ocean glittered. The Argosy

rested on the surface, arms coiling lazily through the water, sails drawn, shell gently washed by the waves. Tagane and her crew stepped out on the deck, their passion satisfied — for the time being. The sky above them was spangled in stars, the ocean around them burning.

After the storm, life returned from the deep haven to the surface: immeasurable masses of microscopic spike-boxes, tiny creatures protected by filigree shells armed with spikes and endowed with light organs. Following them, torchworms and bristleworms and lanceheads. Serpent-gulpers, gazers and hatchet-fish and other deep-sea fishes that rose to the surface at night. And voracious jacks and 'cudas and spikefish and who knew what else to look for food in the ocean of lights, torches, and lanterns tearing the darkness apart with bright colors. Greens, blues, yellows, reds, whites: glowing and merging and flowing from one into another as the plankton stirred. Schools gathering and scattering and gathering back as life teemed around the Argosy.

Tagane studied that ocean nebula surrounding them. She always felt that the colors were at their brightest right after the storms. In the distance, she spotted dark shapes speeding through the green, something large and unfamiliar, something they didn't catch yet. *Maybe better we didn't*, Tagane thought. Some fifty black blimps rose two hundred feet above the surface, marbled patterns burning orange, reminding her of glowing magma lumps that were cooling.

Suddenly, the Argosy started with a jerk. Tagane felt her unrest a moment before the Argosy lifted her strong arms high above the surface and spread all four sails to catch what little wind was blowing. Mina jumped to her feet, Roberta and Conrad following.

"You think...?" Slaven asked.

"Possibly," Tagane said with a nod. She felt new unrest stirring in them all. And in the Argosy, too. "And about time."

Burdened, the Argosy was quite sluggish and disinclined

to obey their commands to sail where they wanted, to follow the fish and algae and torchworms they made a living off.

The Argosy sailed, driven by urge. Slowly, sluggishly, but she sailed, leaving behind a bright wake. As if heeding the Argosy's silent pleas, the wind grew somewhat stronger. They left the blimps behind, sailing across the flaming ocean, followed by a school of jacks keeping safe distance from the arms. Tagane leaned against the rail; wind chilled her face, scattered her hair. She cast a glance at Slaven, Roberta, Mina, and Conrad; the tension among them grew anew. It rose in Tagane, too. Expectation, nervousness, unease. She looked at her sailors once again, the comrades she shared the Argosy with. Because of them, she didn't live on the Islands, in the safety of the firm soil beneath her feet. Because of them, she was on the ocean, carried by winds and currents and the whims of the Argosy. Before the storms, they'd escape into the deep. Before the monsters, they were protected by the arms of a benevolent monster. *Because of them,* Tagane realized, *I sail.* And with them, she felt alive.

You don't have to live, but you have to sail. An old saying, ancient, dating from Earth. Tagane had heard it a long time ago. But there was no difference on the Argosy; living and sailing were one and the same. Tagane realized that she couldn't imagine a life without sailing anymore. And in some way— against any logic, considering that they were just passengers lulled in the mercy of an infinite ocean that didn't really care for its children—it filled her with joy and peace.

"Tagane, look! Over there!"

Conrad's cry startled her. She lifted her gaze and, following his finger, saw a distant shell and arms and all four sails. Another Argosy.

Before she had time to say anything, Tagane felt the chambers filling with water, quickly, faster than usual. "Inside!" she ordered, and they all rushed into the shell, into their bubble of air, while the Argosy was diving, led by an instinct over which they had no control.

"He's huge," Mina whispered, her nose to the viewport.

Tagane didn't miss the tremor running through Mina's fragile-looking body. She felt it herself. They all felt it; it was the tremor of the Argosy. Tension. Expectation. Sweet.

"He's no bigger than our Argosy," Slaven said.

But he's not much smaller, Tagane decided. The male rested some fifty fathoms deep, arms gathered, sails drawn in. His shell was a dark, egg-shaped form in the glimmering aquarelle of colors. He waited for their Argosy to approach him.

"You see anybody?" Conrad asked.

Tagane looked at the ports through which milky green spilled around the male. And yes, she saw a man. She waved to him. He waved back. And then another head appeared next to him, a woman's head.

"We have guests!" Tagane shouted. They all cheered up; it was time for some change. They all squeezed against the port, next to Tagane, to see who was coming to them.

"I can't see," Roberta complained. Their Argosy was approaching the male, the other Argosy.

"They're not familiar," Slaven said. He waved to the three heads now observing them from the male. "Could be somebody from the North. The Northern current is strong these months."

And then, through the burning ocean, the Argosy extended an arm and touched the male. She felt him across his shell and glided down his arms. She circled around his huge eye and caressed his shield. Tagane knew the female was always the first to extend the arm. The female was always the first to invite to dance. Such was the tradition and custom of the Argosies.

It wasn't necessary to invite the male for long. Tagane's heart leapt when he spread his arms and approached their Argosy. She spread her arms, too, impatient. The male paused a bit, and then he came quite close. His siphon connected to hers. Whoever was in the male, Tagane knew, would cross to their Argosy through the siphons. The crew of the male always crossed to the female. All of them—Tagane, Slaven, Roberta, Mina, and Conrad—stared tensely at the meaty membrane on the entrance to the chamber.

The membrane opened and a mid-life blond man, accompanied by two younger women, entered their home. There were only three of them in the Argosy, and that calmed Tagane a bit. She didn't really like when seven or eight men entered the chamber, with perhaps a woman or two. But crews didn't choose; the Argosies did.

They're nervous, too, Tagane realized. They felt the urge of their Argosy, just like Tagane felt the urge of hers. *And they don't know us, the way we don't know them.* Tagane smiled; a smile always broke the ice. The women responded with visible fluttering of their hearts. The man smiled, too.

"I'm Sven," he said. The visiting captain was always the first to introduce her- or himself. "This is Tilda and Marina."

Tagane introduced herself, and then her sailors. "Come in," she said, inviting the guests to her Argosy with opened arms. She studied them as the membrane closed behind them, watertight, and she finally decided she liked them.

"You must be from the North," Slaven said as he came to them.

"Yes, the Northern current is strong this year," Sven said with a nod. His gaze paused on Roberta and Mina. He clearly liked Tagane and her sailors, too; they might have been the first new faces he'd seen in the past few months. All the same, Tilda and Marina were still holding back somewhat.

Then the Argosy shook. They all knew what was happening; they felt it within them, beating in their hearts, drumming in their temples. The female and the male were clinging to each other, their arms entwining, two Argosies joined to mate in lively jerks. "Our Argosy is quite impatient," Tilda said as if apologizing.

"Yes," Tagane muttered as she took Sven by his hand and led him to the mattress. The captains began; such was the tradition and custom of the sailors. "And our Argosy barely listens anymore."

The Argosy shook again, this time stronger. Her urge hit Tagane like lightning, splitting her and torching her to cinders like an old tree. Fingers shaking, she caressed Sven's unshaved cheek and tousled his hair and drew him to her, just like the two Argosies were holding each other with their powerful arms.

They kissed, briefly at first, uncertain, and then they looked at each other — eyes containing nothing else but urge — and kissed once more and never stopped kissing again, driven by the lust of their Argosies. They undressed hastily and Sven gently pushed Tagane into dry algae. Tagane opened her legs before him, ready for him, wet, wanting him, and accepted him — swollen and hard — into her, taking him the way he was taking her, giving herself the way he was giving himself, with joy, welcoming him, just like her Argosy was welcoming his. In the midst of their passion, the two fucking captains rocked in a sweaty, shaky, burning sea of bodies of their sailors.

It all came to Tagane in flashes of consciousness, in bursts of color spilling through the ocean around them.

Emerald. Conrad, with Tilda riding him, impaled on his cock, whipping the air with her unbridled auburn hair, and Mina — sweet Mina, always helpful — fondling and kissing them both.

Orange. Marina in an orgasmic spasm, her legs tightly clenched around Slaven.

Cerulean. Slaven collapsing after a loud orgasm, spent, his forehead sweaty, with Roberta lying next to Marina. Marina accepting her with a smile, and the two of them kissing and embracing and caressing; and Roberta going down and licking Marina's puffed cunt, curly blond hair tickling her nose as she

enjoyed Slaven's seed trickling between Marina's pussy lips.

Green. Sven moaning and bellowing in some Northern language Tagane didn't understand, stiffening and filling her with his seed, and she enjoying it with him—then joining him, after several moments of rest, as he was fondling Mina and lifting her bottom and entering her.

Fiery red. Slaven fucking Tilda wildly, pounding his cock into her.

Yellow. Conrad joining Marina and Roberta, and Tagane with them, too, taking his cock and bringing him before Marina and leading him in; and he entering her, and the two of them screwing while Roberta and Tagane kissed them and fondled them and licked the sweat from their salty skin, before devoting themselves to each other.

Purple. Sven and Mina; he came after several minutes of fierce stabbing, but he still wanted more and his strong arms turned Mina on her belly; and he kissed and petted her firm ass before mounting her from behind.

White. Slaven and Tilda pressing next to them, eight bodies a hot sweaty maelstrom of kissing and licking, touching and caressing, rubbing and teasing, fucking and shagging. A continuous stream of orgasms merged into a big one that words could not describe.

Breath lost, consciousness fading as the two crews and two Argosies created a new life in the midst of fireworks of countless beings they shared the ocean with.

The fireworks fizzled; night turned into dawn.

Tagane extricated herself from the bundle of bodies strewn on algae. Tenderly, so that she didn't awaken her, Tagane removed Marina's hand from her breasts and a lock of blond hair from her neck and stood up, shaky, barely standing. She was hungry. *It can wait*, she decided and came to the port. The Argosies still had their arms entwined. Thousands of transparent balls floated in the sea, as big as Tagane's clenched fist. Eggs.

Fertilized eggs, fertilized in a night of instinct and passion and sweetness, animal and human, in the ocean that nurtured them, the ocean that was home—the ocean that was life.

Tagane didn't know how long she stared through the viewport. Suddenly, she felt warm breath on her back. The unshaved cheek leaned against her face. She lifted her hand and fondled Sven's hair. Sven dropped his hand on her belly, caressing it gently, caringly. The urge was satisfied; it was all done, according to the tradition and custom of the Argosies and sailors.

"What are you thinking of?" Sven whispered into her ear, and then he kissed her neck.

The bodies on the mattress stirred. Mina murmured something in her sleep. Slaven hugged her to him and she calmed again. Conrad nestled among Roberta, Tilda, and Marina, all four sleeping tight, and Tagane knew they wouldn't wake for a long time. With her hand, she covered Sven's on her belly. Perhaps a new life was started in her last night; who knew? If they were lucky, they might all be left with children.

Tagane looked through the port at new little Argosies, just conceived, sinking into the deep where they would hatch and grow and mature and—if they were lucky enough to escape plenty of hungry jaws filled with sharp teeth—return one day to the surface, big and mighty. The Argosies.

And Argosies always needed captains and sailors.

The Sea Bride

by
Milena Benini

It began as a childhood friendship between a human and a mermaid, but that friendship eventually grew into love and passion. But there are powerful forces at work here, and their union was only allowed with grave consequences, damning them to ultimately be torn apart. How does one come to terms with finally having the woman of his dreams — perfect in every way, from the deepest love to the most passionate sex — but knowing he can only have her for a year and a day?

Fantasy
Folklore
Mermaid
Heterosexual sex
Passion
Romance

The sea slapped his face like an angry lover. Salty fingers slipped over his lips, teeth, all the way down to his throat. Vito was going to die.

He had been convinced he would, even before the wet fist of the sea curled around his boat and squeezed, strong enough to crush, propelling him into the cold, hungry depths. Had known it even before he punched his father in the mouth, kicked his brother's balls, and ran for the boat, rather than letting the villagers slit his throat and hang him upside down in the waters of Fiddler's Cove as an offering to appease the angry mother Sea. Had suspected it even before he stole his wife's seaskin and hid it so she would never return to her underwater home.

And now she was gone, his village would suffer for his betrayal, and he was going to die. He felt the grip of the sea on his limbs: soft, but relentless, unbreakable. Like his own grip had been, on Iëe's body, the first night of the Compact.

His wedding night.

Her breasts were small but round, firm under his fingers, perfect. He could cover each with one hand. Her nipples pressed into the centers of his palms when he squeezed — gently at first, then with more force as desire pushed him. Iëe writhed under him, her breath coming in short, shivering gasps, her fish half straining upwards under his straddling legs. She wanted him. Just like he wanted her.

The Compact demanded that the Sea be taken. Forced, if need be, in the center of the circle. But Vito didn't want Iëe by force.

He had known Iëe almost all his life. Everybody in the village knew that. Knew the story of his fall from Gramma's Rock, the tall cliff overlooking the cove. Knew that the boy had slipped on the wet stones and fallen into the hungry maw of the ocean, to be dragged back to the shore by an equally young mermaid; he coughing and spluttering water out of his lungs, she panting and wheezing in the air, long green hair plastered to her naked back like dead sea grass.

What they didn't know was that he'd fallen *because* of her. The morning had been foggy after the night's rain. He couldn't see her well enough as she sat on her rock, just outside the cove. So, in his six-year-old head, he decided to swim to her. He'd seen grown men jump off the cliff — only later would he realize they were really boys, in their late teens, taking the insane risk in an effort to impress the village girls, gain a few more points in the eternal power struggles of the male.

Vito never joined them. Not because he couldn't; after his early experience, he realized he needed to do better, and taught himself, starting with small rocks lower down in the cove, learning every stone and sway of the waters, always under Iëe's watchful eyes. There were only a few more mishaps, but she always got him out in time, before the sea could crush him or swallow him forever. And before anyone from the village could notice anything.

They would celebrate his successes with wet hugs and giggles, the water around them exploding in a flurry of bubbles. Sometimes, playfully, she would pull him under, having grabbed a mouthful of air, and would hold them beneath the surface until the water around him cleared. Then she would press her mouth to his, letting the air flow from her into him, giving him another lease on life, another few moments in her embrace.

That was how he knew what to do on their wedding night. Surreptitiously, he'd filled his mouth with seawater, forcing himself not to swallow. When her breathing became too labored, while he kneaded her breasts and her lower body thrashed between his thighs, he leaned down and kissed her full of sea.

Her hand, clutched on his shoulder, relaxed when she felt the water. Then she slid it between them, finding his cock and guiding it deftly to the slit in her fish-body.

He came almost as soon as he entered her. When his semen spilled inside her, he heard a horrible tearing sound — her seaskin falling off — and felt the sex around him change, withdraw, pull, leaving his cock pressed against her lower belly.

He saw tears fill her eyes, heard her choke on the last of the seawater. Uncaring for the shouts of triumph around them, he sat back, gathered her in his arms, pulled her quivering body into his lap, her long green hair shielding their nakedness.

"I love you," he whispered. "I'll take care of you."

"Iô," she'd said. That was her version of his name, ever since they were children.

"I'm here," he said. "Here forever."

Only it wasn't forever. It was sea-marriage, a marriage of the Compact, kept carefully secret even from other villages, let alone the dry-god priest who passed every few months to name the babies and bless the boats.

The villagers gave Iëe another name, one they could all pronounce, and made her wear a headscarf to hide her green hair. They couldn't do anything about her brows and lashes, but that was easier to ignore, to pretend not to notice. Not even the priest commented, when he blessed Iëe's womb — as he usually did with young brides — limiting himself merely to a worried look at Vito's face, like the passing glance of a goat herder noticing somebody else's sickly animal.

But there had been no children, even though Vito tried for it, every night, throughout their allotted time, a year and a day. After that first public coupling, necessary for the Compact, he'd carried Iëe to the Compact house — *their* house, now — on the very edge of the forest, and laid her down on the new bed he'd built of strong, old, scented pinewood. Now that he could do so, he spread her legs wide and got lost between them. He kissed and licked and suckled on her until she screamed his name, as he tasted the sea in the pink, oystery flesh. Then he pushed inside her, kneeling like a supplicant in the big church he'd seen on his single visit to the town a few miles inland. He lifted her legs onto his shoulders and put his hands down next to her head and held her and came and came.

Later, he taught her — somewhat regretfully — to dress, and was repaid each evening with the renewed wonder of discovery: her dark nipples peeking out from behind the soft white veil of her blouse; her sex, which remained as hairless as it had been in fish-body, calling to him in soft wet whispers underneath her long skirts.

He had thought he knew every inch of her body, having watched it grow over the years, having swum with her, dived with her, hunted small fish with her, and watched her tear the fish apart with small, sharp teeth. But now, again, every night was a revelation. Every day, too: the way her small breasts perked up when she stood on tiptoe to reach for the washing; the way her bottom swayed when she bent down on the rocks, picking the herbs for their meals.

They'd fucked there, on Gramma's Rock, once. Only once — they were both scraped and bruised for a week afterwards. But he'd been unable to resist lifting her skirt there among the lavender bushes, plunging his fingers into the flesh the color of surrounding flowers. Iëe leaned into his hand, holding herself up against a dry wall, her breaths growing deeper, until she could take it no more. She turned and pulled him down, throwing away the flowers she'd torn. She untied his breeches, grabbing his cock in her hand and squeezing, once, twice, pulling her sweat-moist palm up him, then down. The crushed flowers around them filled the air with their fragrance when she knelt over him and rode them both into oblivion.

But not even lavender, thyme, and rosemary helped get Iëe

with child. It wasn't really a disappointment. Children of the sea were a rarity, the last one seen in the time of Vito's great-grandmother — but Vito had had hopes. When there were children, Compact brides could remain on land indefinitely. Until the children were grown, at least. Sometimes forever.

He wanted forever.

He never had the courage to ask Iëe if that was what she wanted, too. She never told him that she loved him. Not on land. He remembered her calling him *aiöo*, her loved one, when they first hatched their plan — when she agreed to be his sea bride. She never repeated the word afterwards, and he didn't dare ask. At first, it seemed there would be time enough for everything, later. Then the fall passed, and winter, and spring, and the year and a day was too close to its end to waste time on questions.

And then it was high summer, and a whole year had passed. The Compact had reached its end, and there was no more time for anything except to grab Iëe's seaskin from his father's house and run.

At first, he had intended to burn it. If he did that, Iëe would not be able to return to the Sea. He'd carried the skin through the forest and into the lavender field on the other side, fully determined to build a small pyre for his wife's sea life and watch it turn to smoke.

But he couldn't. When she'd first agreed to his plan, to be his bride, it had been after much talk. He spoke his language, mostly, adding the whistling singsong sounds of hers when he was able. She spoke the language of the sea, sighs and soft, throaty whistles that speared him with their sensuality. Even his name sounded voluptuous in her mouth: Iô, like a breath escaping her just before orgasm.

"Yess, Iô," she said then, hugging him with a smile. "Aiöo Iô," she added. "Hiëe iiî." *I trust you.*

So he couldn't just take that other life away from her without asking — even though he hated it, with a rage that burned stronger than the midday sun, for taking her away from him. He hid the skin in the small cave under the lavenders, then started back home, trying to think of something to say.

He knew he would have to tell her. Endure the wrath of his father and the rest of the village. And then, most important of all, he would have to face the rage of the Sea.

It was about that moment that he became convinced he would die.

The conviction was confirmed when he saw the villagers winding their way towards their house — the Compact house — brandishing spears and nets and knives, angry voices rising all the way to the forest.

Iëe came out of the house, probably attracted by the noise; her hearing was inordinately keen. She'd just gotten out of bed; all she had on was his old shirt, one that she liked to sleep in, leaving her long legs bare. Her green hair was all disheveled and curled like a halo of seawater around her head and shoulders. His heart hiccoughed at the sight; his cock twitched. For a moment, there, he'd had hope. He would take a step, cover the distance between them, get hold of her hand. They would face this together.

But then a twig shook at his passage, and Iëe turned to face him. He saw it all, then, in her sea-colored eyes, green and gray and blue and full of anger and fear.

Even before she ran past him, her bare feet leaving whispered prints on the needle-covered ground, the fact that he was going to die ceased to matter.

The sea cupped his head, watery fingers soft but unyielding — like Iëe's had been when he would push his tongue inside her, lifting her by her buttocks to drink of her, taste her, know her. Wet salty arms held him around the neck, like Iëe would do as he eased himself inside her, sliding between her slick folds.

Vito let the sea take him. That was his debt. His duty. He'd broken the Compact his village had with the Sea. He'd taken a sea bride, but failed to return her. For a year and a day, his village had been safe from the sea. Fishing boats returned safely, their nets bursting with catch. The Sea had kept her part of the bargain.

They said it had all started when a daughter of the Sea had fallen in love with a drowning fisherman. Knowing he couldn't live in water, she brought him to the shore, but asked leave of her mother to go join him. Her mother, the Sea, agreed, on one condition: The girl would go to her *aiöo* as she was, without changing form or speaking his language. He had to love her anyway, spill his seed inside her fish belly. When it was done, the bride would lose her sea-skin, get legs and human voice.

But she was only allowed to stay for a year and a day. At the end of that time, she had to return home, to reassure her mother all was right. While the bride was ashore, however, in order to make her life easier, the Sea would protect the fisherman's village, make sure his nets were full.

So the Compact was born. After the allotted time had passed, the daughter dutifully returned to her mother, hoping to convince her to let her go again. But it didn't happen, and her once-husband, inconsolable, threw himself off the cliff and drowned. Yet the villagers had gotten used to the good life, and did not want it to end. When they caught another of the Sea's daughters in their nets, one of the fishermen took her, spilled his seed inside her, and her seaskin fell off, leaving the village with another sea bride. After a year and a day, they returned her to the Sea, fearing the spell would be unwound — but, at the first opportunity, they did it again.

With time, catching sea brides became more difficult, as the Sea instructed her daughters to avoid the rocks and islets near the shore. But brave fishermen and curious mermaids could always be found, for the Sea had many daughters, and not all of them heeded their mother's warnings, as daughters are wont to do.

In times with no Compact, the Sea took her revenge: killing fishermen, casting waves too strong to sail against their shores, sending sharks to tear their nets. When her wrath became too great, they would send her gifts: toys carved from soft pinewood for her children, lavender and rosemary to sweeten her senses. If all else failed, they would choose a goat or a cow, and spill the animal's blood into the waves.

Now, the Sea would get a human sacrifice. Vito felt the fingers of the Sea wrap themselves around his legs, making it hard to move. His hands thrashed over the waters senselessly, without helping. His lungs hurt so much, pressed as they were by the Sea's ruthless clasp.

A cold current curled between his legs, passing around his waist, teasing his shirt from his trousers. Just like Iëe's urgent fingers, after Vito and Iëe had worked their little garden in afternoon heat, the sun and the sweat teasing them both into a frenzy of desire.

He should just let go, he knew. Say good-bye to the sky, the world that would never be anything but dry and hard and painful, now that his yearning could only grow, forever without release.

Swift wet fingers took hold of him again, pulling, pulling. He felts his pants give way, float into the fathomless depths. He was naked now, helpless before the cold green waters. For a moment, his head broke the surface—not through any conscious action on his part, just an accident of the stormy seas—and he grabbed a lungful of air, his body still desperately clinging to life. A piece of his boat, pine hardened by salt and water, floated by, just beyond his reach. He reached anyway, automatically, stupidly. He didn't want to hold onto it and float. He didn't want anything anymore. His body did.

But then the sea dragged him down again. He felt currents surround him, slide over his forearms, thighs, belly. They were warm now. Warm like the touch of Iëe's skin on his as their hands met. Warmer, like the smile on her lips when he returned home in the evening. Warmest, like the place between her legs, the axis around which his world revolved.

Stunned, he discovered that his cock had hardened in the sea. He'd heard of it happening to people on the edge of death, but hadn't expected it. It was one of those things that happened to other people: distant, exciting things one only hears about from travelers bringing faraway stories. And now he would become one of those tales, the man who'd loved a mermaid to destruction. His, hers, theirs.

He closed his eyes before the bubbles that escaped from his mouth. The currents were caressing him now; he couldn't mistake the soft, deliberate touches on his chest, thighs, between his buttocks. Behind his lids, water currents turned into Iëe's fingers, winding their way towards his cock. Anticipation made his lungs scream, asking that he take air in with large, hungry breaths. He wanted to open his mouth, to feel Iëe's nipples graze the surface of his tongue, to lick the salty taste off her skin.

The touch of water became more defined, demanding. Maybe it was just sea grass wrapping its tendrils around his limbs; he didn't know, didn't care enough to open his eyes. If he was going to die, he might as well go happy. He concentrated on his skin, letting his senses dissolve and tingle under each stroke. Hands slid up his legs, over the inner side of his thighs, leaving shivers in their wake like a boat with sails full of wind. The last traces of air left his lungs, caressing his lips like a tongue.

Something supple and firm enveloped his cock, so like a hand. He wasn't sure if it was real or just his imagination, but he let himself be handled, feeling water press against his still-closed mouth, demanding entrance. An urgent, slithery touch spread his legs, imaginary hands pulling his legs around a lithe fish body.

Alarmed, he opened his eyes. Nothing changed: the water had pulled him so deep; he was blind, surrounded only by blue-green shadows and the humming whispers of the sea. He tried to pull himself free—was the Sea going to rape him, too, before letting him die? —but hands around his waist wouldn't allow it. Narrow hands, but firm, strong, nothing soft about them. He could feel the calluses on them.

He knew those calluses. Had put salve on them, when Iëe first developed them, her sea-soft skin unused to the friction of work in the air.

His mouth opened on her name, without thinking. And was closed immediately, with a kiss full of blessed, soothing air. As he reached to embrace her—phantom, mirage, succubus, he didn't care anymore—her hand led him to the slit he knew so well. In water, she was more agile than he. Her fish body undulated between his spread legs, her hands holding him in just the right place. Biting down her name, he poured himself inside her, her whimpers of pleasure goading him further and further. As orgasmic spasms shook his frame, he heard a strange, tearing sound, felt as if his bones were breaking, reshaping themselves into something completely different, until the only connection to reality he had left was his faintly pulsing cock, still thrust deep inside Iëe.

Then everything went black.

When he came to, they were surrounded by soft, greenish light that illuminated without hurting. Iëe was leaning over him, her green hair in a halo around her head and shoulders. She smiled at his open eyes, but there was fear in her gaze, too. No, not fear; just something close to it. Tension?

He tried to get up, discovered he couldn't move his legs properly. Iëe put a hand on his naked chest.

"Don't try to move just yet," she said. "It will take you a while to get used to it." She turned her head away from his face.

Confused, Vito followed the direction of her gaze. What he

saw made no sense: his legs were... not legs anymore, but a strong, gray fish body.

He looked around more carefully. He was lying on sand, Iëe floating just above him.

His lungs constricted automatically. "I... what...?"

"I knew it would work," said Iëe. "It's the same spell. Only... backwards."

He was still trying to come to terms with the concept when Iëe continued, her eyes still full of tension. "That was the only way, beloved. You tried to break the Compact between the Land and the Sea. You had to pay for it with your life." She smiled. "Luckily, giving your life to the Sea can have more than one meaning. But you shouldn't have hidden my seaskin. I was almost too late to save you."

When he didn't respond, she bit her lip. Her small, sharp teeth pulled at the pink skin nervously. Then she turned away. "And now you hate me," she said. "I'm sorry."

Sound was different underwater than on land, but he was still certain he'd heard her voice break on the last word. Urgently, he tried to go after her. His new body still didn't know what to do with itself, so he floated in the opposite direction instead, whirling like a feather.

"Iëe," he called helplessly.

She turned, understood, propelled herself towards him with a single, lithe movement of her strong tail, caught his hands. Holding on to her like a lifeline, he pulled himself closer. When he could put his arms around her waist, he anchored himself there.

"I love you, Iëe," he whispered against her lips. "It doesn't matter to me whether we're under water, on land, or floating in the air, as long as we're together."

She looked at him for a long time. "I... had wanted this from the start. I just didn't have the courage to ask you."

He smiled at that. Some day, he would tell her. But not yet. It was still all too raw. "You'll have to help me, though," he said. "I don't know anything about life down here."

"Don't worry," she said. "I'll take care of you."

Her lower body rubbed against his. He wasn't really sure of the mechanics, but what he felt was very familiar. When his cock—longer, now, and more flexible, but just as sensitive as before—touched her slit, she guided it inside with a sure hand.

That was all the help he needed.

Primal Urge

by
Holly Knight

The old maxim goes that women give sex to get love, and men give love to get sex. After all, the men are the ones consumed by raging hormones and an overpowering, primitive drive to screw, not women – right? Not necessarily. In this story, Lily is depressed, frustrated, and hopelessly trapped in a marriage devoid of sexual satisfaction. She's willing to do anything to satisfy her basic animal instincts – even if she has to cheat on her husband. But can she find the right man in her world?

Fantasy
Fairy ring
Heterosexual sex
Cunnilingus and fellatio
Touching
Lust

L ily received his kisses, felt his hand tickling low on her belly, crawling its way to the soft, warm spot between her legs. Her heart beat faster. It was going to happen. It would be the night. It *had* to be the night. She couldn't take much more without it.

"Bill," she whispered to him in the darkness. "I love you."

"I love you, too," he said, mashing his lips against hers. He kissed down her neck as his fingers began stroking her sex.

She'd been there before, a thousand times since they'd been married. She couldn't remember the last time she'd had an orgasm during sex. He wouldn't go to the therapist with her, wouldn't admit that anything was wrong. He was too self-centered for that. But the therapist had given her hints how to make it better.

She felt his erection against her thigh, throbbing, begging to be inside her. And, right on cue, he moved a leg over to force her legs apart. Hint time.

"Not yet," she whispered. "Please, keep kissing me. And touching me."

Force the foreplay, the therapist had said. *Ease him into it. Get yourself worked up, so when he gets inside you, you'll be close.*

He obeyed, moving his mouth to her right breast. He sucked on her nipple, teased it with his teeth, even as his fingers slipped between her moist lips. He slid them up to tickle her clitoris, then down between her folds where it was wettest. She moaned against him, parted her thighs to give him room, and he moved his fingers inside her.

Her head spun with the sensations even as he kissed across her chest to her left breast and tongued the nipple there, even as he plunged fingers in and out of her. He hadn't fingered her in years, and it felt great. She parted her thighs further, and he took advantage of it, burying his speeding fingers deep inside her. She whimpered beneath him and reached for his swollen penis. It felt hot and huge in her hand. She stroked him while he worked.

She felt the beginning of a stirring in her belly, and she squeezed his penis tighter and stroked faster. She rejoiced in the raw primal emotions she was experiencing of holding his cock, of the sensation of being finger-fucked. She began to buck her hips against his thrusts. Oh, it felt *so good*...

He groaned into her breasts, working his fingers faster and faster. She spread her legs as wide as she could, practically hoping he'd slam his entire hand inside her. She could feel her building orgasm growing stronger. God, she needed it so badly—she needed to come like never before, needed him to make her come.

But suddenly his hand stopped moving as his body went rigid. Before she knew what was happening, she felt him spasm, and felt the wet explosion as he ejaculated on her leg, her hip, her belly. His semen soaked her hand, and he groaned and collapsed, rolling away from her onto his back.

"Fuck, that was good," he said, as his penis swiftly wilted in her sticky-wet hand. "Good idea, honey."

She lay there, stunned, covered in semen, as her vagina went from sizzling to fizzling. Amazingly, within a minute, he was already beginning to snore.

Anger, frustration, and depression all roiled within her. It wasn't fair. It just wasn't fair.

She moved her dry left hand between her legs, where his hand had been, and began rapidly circling her fingers on her clitoris—working alone, as usual, to get herself off.

Two nights later, Lily made a decision she knew might destroy her marriage. She didn't care anymore. She needed a true human joining, a real sexual merging—not love, not romance, not some mental connection: just a good, solid, orgasm-inducing fuck. She couldn't wait on Bill anymore.

She'd never cheated on any of her sexual partners before Bill, and never on Bill. As far as she knew, he'd never cheated on her. But she had to. Needed to. Desperately so.

Bill was out of town on business, and she hated the solitude of the farmhouse anyway. She drove into the city that afternoon, located a parking garage, and walked until she found a suitable bar—not a shitty place, but not an upscale spot either. She needed something where some hard-working type could pick her up. After fending off all the wrong men for three hours, she met Benjamin.

He was a working-class Adonis—nothing at all like Bill, an office executive in a tie. Ben was stunning, handsome and well built, with smoldering dark eyes and a raw sexual aura that had her squirming where she sat. He had everything she intellectually needed: smart, pleasant, kind, warm, and clean. But he did things for her that she instinctively wanted: He was tall, broad-shouldered, with good-sized biceps and the chest of a man who worked out. On a purely physical level, she wanted to fuck him madly. She knew this pussy-tingling man-beast could bring her to raging, mind-splitting orgasms the likes of which she hadn't ever had, but that every woman should always have with her man.

So she let Benjamin buy her drinks, and by midnight they were both feeling no pain, and she left the bar with him. He held her close as they semi-staggered the three blocks to his apartment, and the door was barely closed before he was kissing her. Her heart pounded with excitement, and her veins coursed with sexual anticipation that tickled her nipples, butterflied her stomach, and soaked her panties.

He peeled off his shirt in the living room. She felt his bulging biceps and rock-hard pectorals, and he tore off her bra and grabbed handfuls of her breasts, kissing her all the while. They tumbled, half naked, to the sofa, where he pulled her skirt off and rolled her wet panties down over her hips. He dived in face-first, lapping like an animal at her dripping sex until she was moaning with pleasure and grabbing for his head, begging him not to stop.

But he knew how to tease. He pulled away, stood up, and peeled off his jeans and underwear. He stood before her with his penis jutting out, thick and hard, so big that it couldn't stand straight up but poked out at her face. He stepped forward, and she knew what he wanted.

She felt like a goddess as his throbbing manhood danced before her face, and she took him in her mouth hungrily. She stroked his shaft with one hand and fondled his balls with the other as she bobbed her head, lips pursed tight, on the head of his cock. He groaned with pleasure at every flick of her tongue. She reveled in the feel of his cock sliding over her tongue, against her cheek, banging against the back of her throat. She'd gladly do that for an hour in payment for the night she was about to have.

After ten minutes, though, he pulled out of her mouth, bent down, and swept her up into his arms like a Prince Charming rescuing his damsel. He carried her into his bedroom, kissing her all the while. She felt his cock jabbing impatiently at her soft ass cheeks as they went. Oh, this would be so perfect. He was perfect — better than Bill ever had been. In that fleeting instant, she knew she was going to leave her husband for this god of a man who would give her the pleasure she'd wanted, what she needed. What she deserved.

He threw her on the bed and climbed between her legs. She spread them wide like a shameless slut, ready to sate those primitive desires. She groped for his cock as he clambered forward, found it, and grasped the big thing in her petite hand. She fed the throbbing tip into her hot, liquid center. He slid deep inside her in one smooth movement, filling her up like she'd never been filled up before, and she cried out in ecstasy.

It had been so long since she'd felt like that.

He planted his hands on either side of her and kissed her passionately as he stroked in and out. She wrapped her arms and legs around him, pulling him into her. His slow stroking quickened, and he supported himself on his hands as he fucked her good and hard. She wailed like a wild woman as he rammed in and out of her like a porn star. She felt the sensations rocketing out of control, felt her orgasm quickly building. One more minute of that, and she'd have the satisfaction she so desperately —

And then he roared like an animal, pounded her hard, and his body spasmed. She felt jets of semen blast against her insides as he came. He grunted with each shot, and then he collapsed on top of her.

She lay there in the darkness, once again stunned. Of course, she'd really worked him up; it was her fault he hadn't lasted long, and plus he'd been drinking. But this stud, he was a sexual superman; he'd recuperate in a few minutes, get his second wind, and they'd go again. They'd fuck all night. There was plenty of time for orgasms.

Then he rolled off her and said, "Thanks."

Thanks? she thought.

"I don't want this to be awkward," he said, "but I have to get up for work in about four hours. I probably shouldn't have been out tonight at all, you know?"

He reached for his nightstand, shuffled around, came back with something. He found her hand, pressed something paper into it.

"That's thirty bucks," he said. "It should cover cab fare back to the bar. But, you know, maybe we could do this again sometime."

She made it to her car and drove the long ride out of the city in dazed silence. It was over an hour of sitting there feeling his semen oozing out of her and into her panties. It should have felt incredible on that primal level, but it only disgusted her.

She stopped at an all-night drugstore on the way home. She got home by daybreak, douched three times, and took the morning-after pill she'd bought. Then she went to bed and cried for hours.

It was beautiful the next day, and she needed to refresh. She donned a nice sundress and sneakers, sans bra and panties, and went for a walk in the woods behind her house. She had to contemplate her life, her marriage, everything, and needed to be alone out there. Maybe it was more of that primal stuff—alone with nature and her thoughts. The sun was warm and the air was cool; the steady breezes through the forest permeated the thin sundress, keeping her nipples slightly erect and wafting through her public hair. It was a minor thrill. She'd take it.

She hadn't walked for long when she realized there was a big animal with massive antlers—an elk, she thought—standing not far ahead, watching her through the trees. She was awed at his size and beauty, and immediately regretted not having the sense to bring her camera or cell phone with her. She wished she could have snapped a picture of the magnificent beast.

As she watched in wonder, he locked eyes with her. It was entrancing, as if he were beckoning her to follow him, so she did. He always moved away, as if to stay ahead of her, as she approached him, but he always paused to look back at her, as if to make sure she was still following. She lost track of time, but the sun moved high in the sky and began descending, so she knew she tracked the graceful beast for several hours.

Finally, the elk led her to a broad clearing in the forest. The clearing's edge, where the trees abruptly ended, was circled by a rainbow-colored ring of wild flowers. She walked to the center of the ring, turning to survey it, and when she finished the elk was gone.

The clearing was almost perfectly circular, as if it had been designed that way — as if the trees had been cut down, the stumps removed, the grass planted, and the flowers raised and tended to by a loving gardener. She recalled reading about fairy circles, which people once believed were supernatural constructs. She didn't buy into that, but this place was beautiful and intriguing. She turned slowly about to survey it again. Now she really wished she'd brought a camera. She'd have to remember the place, but of course there were no paths to it; she'd followed the elk through the forest...

As she completed her turn, she sucked in her breath: There was a man standing there.

He stood in the flowered ring, watching her, but he was no ordinary man. He was a caveman of sorts, like a Cro-Magnon or a Neanderthal, and he wore just an animal skin as a loincloth. He was naked otherwise, and he was magnificent — a specimen of masculine perfection, with a powerful body looking as if it had been chiseled from stone. And like the elk had done, the man had locked eyes with her. It was an incredibly sensual moment. It was as if the man knew what she wanted and needed — knew what she was thinking.

He entered the circle, moving towards her with poise and authority — all man for a woman who needed a man in the worst way. She breathed quickly as he approached, feeling her heart pound behind her heaving breasts, and then he stood eye to eye with her. He couldn't have been an actual caveman; he was tall and broad-shouldered, not hunched. His head was big, and his eyes were intelligent.

He reached to her with both hands, gently gripping her upper arms. She sucked in her breath as her heart raced faster. Her head swam amidst a dizzying hot flash. His touch was beyond electrifying, sizzling from her arms to her suddenly burning crotch. She thought to him, *Take me.*

He smiled then and nodded, as if he'd heard her, and he

drew her close to him. Big arms enclosed her, and she felt him pull the tie to her sundress. Gently for such a beast, he slid it down over her shoulders and it fell to the ground about her feet. She stood before him, breasts exposed and nipples erect. He stepped back, surveying her, and then reached for her. Callused hands ran over her soft skin, tickling her hard nipples. She responded with a whole-body shudder.

He dropped to his knees and sniffed at her crotch like an animal. It turned her on like nothing ever had, and she spread her feet apart and hunched a bit. He buried his face in her crotch and grabbed her ass with both hands, pulling her into him. She sucked in her breath as his tongue found its way inside her, and as her lips parted she felt her juices flow as if through an open dam—so much that she almost felt as if she were peeing. He lapped furiously at her steaming hole as his big nose rubbed her sensitive clit. She grabbed the dark mat of hair on his head and held on for dear life.

He never let up until she screamed to the forest in her overpowering orgasm—so overpowering that her knees weakened and she nearly collapsed. He knew, and, with powerful arms, he pulled her to her knees, flipped her over, and laid her gently down in the grass. Then he climbed between her legs and dived back in to eat her some more.

She didn't know how many orgasms she had lying in that flowered ring, but it was no fewer than five. He just kept going, hungrily lapping up every drop of juice she produced, letting her wail through an orgasm and then doing it again. She finally felt so numb that she couldn't take any more.

Only then did he get on his knees, bringing her legs up to his shoulders, and he pulled off his loincloth. She gasped at the size of his hard penis: it was easily as thick as her wrist and long enough to make her a bit nervous. But all he did was smile at her, and she was at ease, and when he gently wedged the giant head of his cock between her soaking-wet lips, she groaned in utter ecstasy. She tried to wiggle her hips to force herself forward, to impale herself on his incredible tool, but he was in control. And he was gentle, moving slowly until the head was inside her, just past the tight ring of muscles there. Then he began moving just that head in and out, until he'd worked up a steady rhythm punctuated by her moans and groans.

Soon, he began working a little more inside her with every stroke, and before Lily knew it, he was all the way in, his sizable scrotum slapping against her ass with every steady plunge inside her. She hadn't thought it possible that that big tool would fit, but there it was. With every smooth stroke in, she felt as if he were fucking her all the way up to her lungs — as if that giant cock were sliding harmlessly between her vital organs. He filled her up and stretched her wide in ways she'd never experienced, until she was braying crazily and mindlessly, thrashing beneath him, pounding her fists to the ground, kicking her feet against him.

Then he reached down and grabbed her ass with his hands, holding her up a bit, and he began pumping in and out of her ever more quickly. The new angle changed everything, as if she hadn't already been experiencing the fuck of her life. It was suddenly even better, and she cried out as he moved, because every stroke in and out felt better than every orgasm he'd given her with his mouth. She grabbed for his arms to hang on as he moved faster, and soon he was pistoning in and out of her like a machine. She wailed and begged him to go faster, and he did, and she felt her orgasm build again until she exploded right there, impaled on his cock — but he never let up. He just kept going, and her orgasm ebbed and waned and then began to build again.

She came again, screaming this time. But still he didn't stop. He pounded her, hard and steady, for hours. Every stroke was nirvana. Every cycle of orgasm was earth-shaking. He knew every time she was nearly there, and he'd pick up the pace and fuck her madly until she wailed in orgasm before returning to an easier pace — to begin it all over again.

Finally, he seemed to sense that she'd had enough, and he pulled out of her, lay down next to her, and held her. She cuddled up to the strange, prehistoric man as the sun dipped low through the trees, and fell fast asleep.

The last thing she thought of before she slipped into dreamland was the realization that, despite her countless orgasms, her strange lover hadn't yet had one.

She woke abruptly. The moon was in the sky. The night was cool. She was on her stomach.

He was behind her, straddling her, spreading her butt cheeks. He fed his cock back inside her, and she came alive again. She should have felt sore, but she wasn't. She was instantly consumed by desire for him, and she arched her back and angled her ass up to take him. He buried himself deep inside her and began fucking her again.

She cried out in pleasure, taking every inch of his monster cock, and felt her orgasm building yet again.

And they did that for hours that night, through a dozen more incredible orgasms, until once again she was worn out. Again he lay down next to her, cuddling her, and again she realized he still hadn't come.

The morning sun woke her, and she opened her eyes. The caveman was sitting next to her, staring down at her. He'd been watching her sleep.

She smiled at him.

"Thank you," she said. "You don't know how much I needed that."

In her mind, she felt him. Not words, but feelings. He had, in fact, known how much she needed that. She wondered how this was all happening. Had nature rewarded her by sending him to fulfill what she so desperately needed?

She sat up, naked in the grass, and looked him over. He

was naked, too, his big penis flaccid between his crossed legs.

"You didn't come," she said to him, resting her hand on his leg and rubbing slowly up his thigh. "I owe you that."

He smiled as his penis lengthened, thickened.

Yes, Lily thought, *I owe him that. He's satisfied my primal urges. I owe him the same.*

She came to her knees, pushed on his chest, eased him back to the grass as his cock kept growing. She climbed on top of his thick body, straddling him, and reached down to feed him inside her. He began moving in and out of her, and she rode him like a cowgirl. He grunted madly beneath her, bucking his hips, holding on to hers, and she rested her hands on his hairy chest. She closed her eyes, turned her face skyward, and let him do his thing.

He couldn't even do that without pleasing her. She could sense he was holding off, and looked down. The look on his face was the unmistakable visage of a man desperately trying to hold back his orgasm. She smiled at him, leaned down while he was fucking her, and whispered in his ear in her most seductive voice, "Come for me... come inside me..."

He might not have known the words, but he knew the tone, and probably sensed her thoughts. She kissed him then, locking lips and cupping his face in her hands, and he went wild, bucking like mad and slamming madly into her. She felt her orgasm build yet again, and she bounced her hips on his cock, squeezing it with her cunt, and he began growling beneath her kiss.

Finally, he roared in triumph and grabbed her tightly to him, and he came. It felt as if he were shooting quarts of semen inside her—hot and powerful and thick and wet—and it sent her over the edge for one last time.

She came like she'd never come before. She sat bolt upright, screaming, head thrown back like a wolf baying at the moon, and he roared along with her until she collapsed on him like a rag doll. He grunted some more, his cock still jerking inside her, until he was totally spent.

She lay there, feeling the warmth of his hairy body beneath her—felt his strong muscles, his powerful frame, his deep and steady breathing. It was perfect. Perfectly primal.

And without warning, she fell to the grass on her knees and face. She let out a cry and struggled to get to her feet. She staggered back, looking.

He was gone, vanished from beneath her into thin air. And as she watched, the rainbow colors of the flower ring began to fade away. Flowers seemed to unblossom and get sucked into the earth, until all that remained was green grass.

Lily stared, wide-eyed, stunned, even as saplings sprouted all through the clearing and, impossibly, began growing. She stumbled about, grabbing her sundress and her sneakers, and hurried into the woods. She looked back in time to see the trees climbing skyward, trunks thickening as they grew, branches billowing full of leaves, until all traces of the clearing were gone forever.

Lily knew she'd never match that experience. But she'd certainly learned her lesson, thanks to the supernatural gift—from Mother Nature, or whoever had been responsible.

She loved Bill, but things had to change. She laid down the law and, under threat of divorce, he began going to therapy with her. And it worked; when she wanted sex, she got sex, and he serviced her like she was some kind of goddess.

And when he was working hard to please her—with his face buried between her legs, or with his cock buried in her pussy, or with her hollering out her wants and needs and demands—he never knew what was going through her head.

She loved him, but she forever after thought about someone else while they were having sex. She never knew the caveman's name; maybe he'd never had one. But he would always be her enduring—and very vivid—fantasy.

Desperate Measures

by
Julie Dixon

She's tried everything, but she's never succeeded, always failing to achieve her elusive goal. Now, she's desperate — so desperate that she's crossing the stars in a hired spaceship to visit a planet where primitive humanoids are like mad animals at this time of year. She's absolutely willing to do whatever it takes to find that success. But is it too much? Or is it just what she needs to do? Or worse — is it not enough?

Science fiction
Space travel
Alien world
Alien sex
Gangbang
Anal sex
Lesbian sex
Female masturbation
Desire

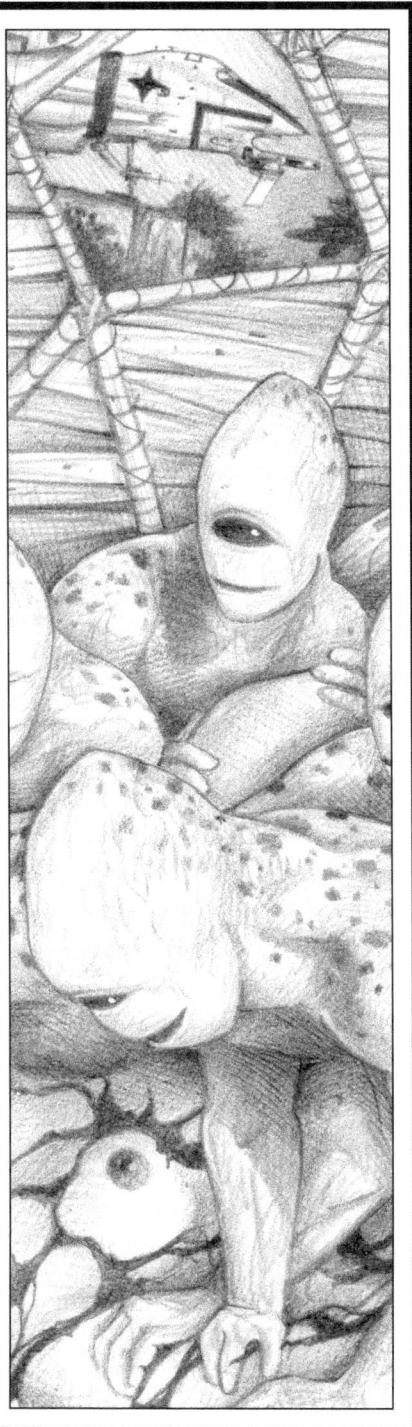

S tanding behind the pilot, Arliana Foranni watched out the window of the star cruiser's cabin as the green glow of the planet's atmosphere filled her view. White clouds streaked and swirled about the emerald orb. It was beautiful, hanging in the blackness of space like a Christmas ornament, lit by the blazing yellow-red sun behind them. But she'd flown there for something far removed from sightseeing the stunning astronomical scenery.

"This is it," Dahlia Zell said from the pilot's chair below. "Traventicus. Planet of heaven or hell for an off-world woman. Heaven for you, I suppose."

"I hope so," Arliana said as Dahlia angled the small vessel down into the atmosphere. The first hints of heat began to lick at the shields, but the force dampeners erased any sensation of turbulence. As the green world grew ever larger in the window, Arliana looked down at the beautiful woman at the controls. Dahlia was sultry, seductive, and utterly beautiful, with the longest and straightest black hair Arliana had ever seen on a human. Her olive-complexioned skin added to her mystique, and her dark eyes were shaped to just a hint of almond. Asian, Iberian, and Gaelic ancestry worked well to produce a woman of unique allure — an allure even Arliana had succumbed to the night before.

"Buckle up," the exotic pilot ordered.

Arliana stepped down to the small control bay and took the seat beside Dahlia, who gripped the craft's yoke tightly. The dampeners could no longer ignore the force of the re-entry, and the ship began to tremble mightily as it became a raging fireball. Arliana gripped the arm rests with clamped fingers. She could no longer see anything out the window, so she settled her gaze on the enticing woman flying the ship. Dahlia wore a lightweight jumpsuit with fashioned holes revealing her belly, her sides, her back, her thighs. Hard nipples pressed against the thin fabric as her breasts jiggled with the ship's tremors. There was no denying her raw sex appeal.

Arliana closed her eyes to block the fresh memories from her mind, riding the re-entry until the shuddering stopped and Dahlia announced, "Here we are."

She opened her eyes to green skies and towering mountains everywhere. Red vegetation covered the world, and mists seemed to rise from everywhere. The ship cruised a thousand feet above crimson forests, banking around the seemingly endless peaks

"I have to ask, one more time," Dahlia said, looking over at her with vague pleading in her dark eyes. "Once you go into the forest, there will be no stopping it until they're done. If you change your mind and try to escape, they'll almost certainly kill you. So, are you *sure* you want to do this?"

"After last night, you have to know that I'm absolutely sure," Arliana said.

Dahlia sighed. "I feel bad. I thought... you know, that I could... somehow help solve your problem."

"It's okay. It isn't your fault."

She stared at Dahlia as the woman flew, and she remembered the night before.

The ship had been on autopilot while traveling through hyperspace, still half a day from Traventicus, when Dahlia called Arliana in her quarters.

"I was wondering if I might come see you," Dahlia asked.

The request should have seemed innocent, yet perhaps there was something subtle in Dahlia's tone that hinted that it wasn't, but Arliana agreed. A minute later, the door slid open to admit the exquisite woman. She was dressed in her usual style of a fashionably holed jumpsuit, which revealed a lot of skin and was incredibly tantalizing—even for a heterosexual woman like Arliana. Dahlia was a goddess: mysteriously beautiful and mythically sexy—the sort of woman a man would do anything in order to bed.

Arliana was sprawled on her bunk, reading on her handheld, and she watched as Dahlia crossed the room, slinky and catlike, with swaying hips and protruding nipples. When the attractive pilot sank her shapely ass to the bunk, straining her breasts against the thin jumpsuit, and leaned so that she was just barely touching Arliana's legs, Arliana set her handheld down and met Dahlia's penetrating gaze. With the slightly seductive smile on Dahlia's full red lips and beneath those smoldering eyes, it was clear to Arliana what was going on.

"I'm not into women," Arliana said, firm but polite.

"I know," Dahlia said in a sensual voice that matched her smoldering eyes. "But hear me out. I understand why you feel you have to do this crazy thing on Traventicus. And I know you're heterosexual, but what if a woman could solve your problem?"

"I've tried women. It never made a difference."

"I don't mean to sound arrogant, but you haven't tried this woman. I'd like to consider myself atypically attuned to how to make my sexual partners feel good."

Arliana sighed. "Why do you care? You've known me for four days."

Dahlia shrugged. "I guess I feel badly about what you're going to do to yourself tomorrow. Now, in all honesty, I'm damn good at pleasing women. I think you'd be hard pressed to find too many like me. So don't you think giving my idea a chance is at least worth a try?"

That was the crux of her argument, and although they bantered back and forth for twenty minutes, eventually Arliana relented. After all, it wouldn't hurt to try, and Arliana had to admit an attraction to Dahlia. She'd said she wasn't into women, but that was technically a lie; having been with many, she had an appreciation for them, although she was mostly attracted to men. And Dahlia... she was something special. Arliana couldn't help but be attracted to her like a magnet to steel, so when the woman leaned in to her and took Arliana in her arms, she succumbed easily and joyfully.

It was gentle and beautiful, the way men always had been for her when they'd begin making love — before they became sweaty animals more interested in mindlessly pounding away and coming inside her. Dahlia kissed her at first, with delicate hands lightly caressing her shoulders and then her breasts. When Arliana had relaxed to the point of half-closed eyes and shallow breathing as Dahlia kissed her way down her neck, the pilot began subtly undoing the tie to her blouse, and soon her top fell away. Dahlia knew what she was doing, and released Arliana's bra with the flick of two fingers from the arm wrapped around her. It seemed the woman's lips barely ever left Arliana's skin, always kissing, a tongue always flicking at Arliana's tongue, teasing her neck, suckling on her earlobes.

Dahlia took command, easing Arliana back onto the bed and lovingly kissing her nipples. Arliana surrendered completely as the pilot skillfully worked Arliana's loose pants over her hips and down her legs. Arliana was uncontrollably aroused, and when Dahlia kissed her way down Arliana's belly, Arliana willingly parted her thighs — she couldn't have kept them closed if she'd wanted to — and sighed as Dahlia's fingers found their way to her sex. Dahlia touched her in ways no man ever had touched her, even as her tongue teased Arliana's navel before she kissed her way down to Arliana's furry bush.

Arliana had always enjoyed it when a man went down on her, but it was all nothing compared to what Dahlia did. The way Dahlia suckled her clitoris, dipped fingers gently inside her, slid a wet finger across her anus, licked up and down her slit, tongued inside Arliana's dripping quim — it was beautiful and sensual and overwhelming.

But Arliana knew how it would end, even though it was probably the best sexual experience she'd ever enjoyed. And after a solid hour of Dahlia making sweet love to her wet pussy, after another twenty minutes of Dahlia encouraging her to touch in return, after another twenty of her going down on Dahlia and tasting a woman for the first time—all of it, exciting and wonderful and like nothing she'd ever experienced... to no avail.

Arliana didn't have an orgasm. It was no surprise: She'd never had an orgasm.

Traventicus was her only hope.

Arliana snapped out of her reverie as Dahlia suddenly banked sharply around a mountain peak and dived low over the sprawling red forest. She circled around, slowing the ship, and doubled back. Near the base of that mountain was a mesa jutting several hundred feet above the trees.

"We'll set down there," Dahlia said. "There's a *jaskar* community at the base of the mountain. The *jasku* don't climb. They're terrified of heights. That's why the *jaskoni* live in the mountains, and only come down every few years."

She lowered the ship towards the mesa. Arliana's heart beat a little faster as the craft settled on its landing gear, jerked to a halt, and vented gas in a noisy whoosh. The engines powered down. Dahlia hit a control and Arliana heard the main access door below open.

"Okay, you're on your own," Dahlia said. "I'll be here when you get back. There are about a hundred *jasku* down there, you know. Might have been better to find a smaller community."

Arliana smiled. "I'll be fine."

It was hot and humid, as it always was on Traventicus. The brief trip down the steep slope was treacherous, but the *jasku* must have been watching from the time the ship had landed. She no sooner stepped into the forest when she saw them. They were creeping through the trees, staring at her. She stopped and waited. It was all she could do.

They rushed her. There must have been a dozen or more. They were humanoid in many respects, but completely alien in others. Their dark-yellow skin was smooth and hairless. Bald, tall heads topped noseless faces with Cyclopean eyes, and their mouths were exceptionally wide and toothless. They stood no shorter than six and a half feet, with most of them topping seven, with taut, muscular physiques: rippled abdomens, steel biceps, and thickly muscled necks.

But that wasn't what made her eyes grow wide. Just as she'd learned, they were hung quite well. The naked human-oids' flaccid penises were at least seven inches long and as thick as sausages. They grabbed her up in their giant hands and carried her through the forest. They made excited sounds, clicking and tsk-ing and hooting, and in a few minutes they brought her into a village center and hurried her to one of the many dome-shaped huts there. It was all a dizzying array of sensations, like the time when she'd paid the group of humans in a cloud hotel hovering over Boston's top level to gang-rape her, only far more exciting. These weren't civilized humans succumbing to pleasure; these were primitives with nothing but raw, primal urges—animals ready to take her with no thought or care for anything but their own raging desires.

First, they set her down on her feet on a thick pile of soft skins on the floor, and they clacked and hissed as they tore her clothing from her body. She'd planned for this, wearing no un-derwear and a cheap outfit, and there she stood, naked before them. Her big breasts were unlike anything they'd seen, since the *jaskoni* nursed their young from rows of nipples on their thighs, but the *jasku* seemed interested in them.

But what really got them going was the prize between her legs. She'd shaved it so they wouldn't be confused by the hair, and they chattered excitedly as they studied her. She stood, unashamed and letting them look her over as if she were a slave at auction, and she felt a rush of excitement: It was turning her on. They circled her like a pack of happy predators, even as more of them entered the hut. They reached out and touched her all over, groping her ass and squeezing her breasts, and occasionally running their fat fingers between her legs. She adjusted her stance, spreading her thighs, and felt her lips part, felt her juices threatening to drip out of her. The *jasku* made excited sounds at that, and when one of them forced his thick finger inside her, her heart began pounding. It was going to happen. She'd been sure it would happen when those twelve guys had gang-banged her for several hours, and it hadn't, but this was far different. Her guess was right: The psychological impact of having so many animalistic males ready to lose their minds over her was what was going to send her over the edge and make it finally happen. She just knew her time was finally here.

Two of them laid her down on the soft skins as the others began touching their big alien penises, which were getting harder, longer, and thicker by the moment. She was soon surrounded by fifteen of them, all sporting gigantic yellow erections that stood nine inches or more and almost frighteningly thick. They stroked themselves slowly as two of the aliens pulled her legs apart and another climbed between them.

There was no foreplay as he forced the bulbous head of his giant penis into her straining vagina, and she clenched her teeth against the pain. It would only hurt for the first one. And she knew from her research that she needed only to let them do whatever they wanted, and she'd live. Fighting them, trying to run away — the *jasku* became ferociously violent when their women didn't cooperate; they'd been known to beat the women to death and then continue gang-fucking their corpses. Arliana wouldn't take any chances.

He banged his hips hard, forcing the big thing inside her.

It went all the way to the bottom, which still left a lot of his shaft exposed. And then he began fucking her hard and fast, like an animal, while the others milled about and stroked themselves above her. She pulled her knees to her jiggling boobs and held on to her legs for dear life. She felt herself juicing up in response to the monster invasion.

It didn't last long. The alien made excited hooting sounds as he pounded her, and then he howled like a wolf and she felt him explode, blasting deep inside her with a high-powered jet of alien semen. Then he came to his knees and pulled out of her, sucking a huge amount of come with it. She looked down at her gaping vagina, stretched wide and already swollen red, and saw yellow semen pouring out of her like syrup from an overturned jug.

She didn't have time to think about it, because the second alien climbed between her legs and stuffed himself inside her. He assumed the same position above her and pounded her mercilessly. It was less uncomfortable the second time around, and in fact started to feel good. He was clicking and hooting, and she responded with a moan of real pleasure. That seemed to spur him on, and he hooted louder. With every pump into her, she moaned or cooed, and the more she did, the faster he moved — until he, too, howled and ejaculated, filling her up once again.

By the time the third *jasku* took his place inside her, she was feeling pretty good. And after he blew his load, she decided she needed to try something different. She came to her knees, wiggling her ass at the crowd behind her and looking back at them with fuck-me eyes. The fourth knelt behind her and jammed his cock in her messy cunt.

"That's what I'm talking about!" she hollered at them, even though they couldn't understand her. "Fuck my pussy!" She felt silly saying it, like she was a porn star in need of acting lessons, but doing it turned her on, and it seemed to make them more excited.

He grabbed her hips and slammed her down on his massive cock. Her pussy was relaxing with every one of them, accommodating the giant penises more deeply with each turn, and it was getting easier for her. She took four of them like that before changing again. She managed to get one to lie down on his back, and she squatted over him, reaching back to guide his cock as she impaled herself on it. This got him deeper still, and it hurt again for a bit, but soon she was slamming her ass up and down—and the crowd liked this position; the *jasku* hooted their approval. She was totally in control, and for the next six or seven of them, she worked the right angle so the stimulation on her was perfect. She rode waves of pleasure, wailing and moaning and moving her ass like lightning. She'd felt pleasure like that before, although not very often, and not so steadily. She knew an orgasm was coming. It was no time to let up. She needed more. She needed to kick things up a notch.

When she squatted on the next cock, she pointed to her ass and pulled her cheeks apart, feeding a finger inside her puckered asshole. They were clearly intrigued, since their species didn't have anuses; to them, it had to look like an alternate vagina, something their females didn't have. When the first of them forced his giant cock inside her tight hole, it hurt like a bitch at first, but it soon had her wailing anew. And from there, she was constantly being double-penetrated by the well-hung monsters.

She lost track of their numbers after that, and lost any sense of time. From there on, it was all that position with double penetration. She never felt so full of cock in her life, never felt such intense pleasure from any sexual act, and she knew she was on the way to finally coming.

But as the sun set and night fell, and some of them lit torches to illuminate the domed hut, it didn't happen. And as the night wore on, and as she took them two by two and her pussy became swollen and red and her ass stretched wider than it ever had been, and as everything slowly grew numb

and all pleasure finally subsided, she realized it just wasn't going to happen. Eventually, she was just being used as a sex object without even getting to enjoy it. But she was committed at that point; like Dahlia had warned her, she couldn't just change her mind then without risking injury or death at the hands of the band of *jasku*.

At least their male physiology was predictable. Once one of them had fucked her, he was done, and staggered out of the hut to sleep it off. The sun was just peeking through the trees the next morning when the last of the *jasku* had his way with her. Her poor, numb pussy was utterly destroyed then, stretched out like something from a cartoon, swollen and probably damaged and in need of nano-repair despite the synthetic scaffolding she'd had implanted to ensure the gang bang didn't actually kill her. The last *jasku* was just as energetic as the first, and when he howled and sprayed her punished pussy, she was thankful it was finally over.

He staggered out the door, and she pulled herself to her knees. She was aching and sore all over—not just her pussy, which would be out of commission for a while, but her arms, legs, joints, everything. She gathered her torn outfit and pulled it on; her left breast was exposed, and there was no hiding her ravaged cunt. She found her way out and teetered through the dome-hut village. The hundred *jasku* would be ready to go later that day, after the lengthy coma that followed their sexual activity, so she wasn't about to risk another night of that.

Bowlegged and sore, she hobbled to the mountain, where she met a group of eight *jaskoni* who were descending for the mating season, ready to get into their own gang bangs with the males. They were not much larger than Arliana, but their hairless vulvas were fat and bulbous between wide-spaced legs, built to take the hefty *jasku* members. Breastless nipples lined their fat thighs, which were mostly milk reservoirs for their pups. They stared at her with their single eyes, confused.

"Good morning, ladies," Arliana said. "I'm afraid I wore

them out for you. But they'll be ready in a few hours. Happy mating season."

As she made her way up the mountain, she wondered if the *jaskoni* had orgasms. In mental support of universal sisterhood, she hoped they did. At the same time, she was envious that they might.

Dahlia tended to her medical needs with pills, injections, and creams before they lifted off. After Traventicus was safely behind them and the ship was in hyperspace, Dahlia came back to see her in her quarters. She sat on the bed as before.

"Are you okay?" the woman asked.

Arliana nodded. "Yes, thank you. I feel just like new again. The nanobots seem to be doing a pretty good job rejuvenating my girl parts, thanks to you."

"Well, I wouldn't put anything in that beat-up minge for a while," Dahlia said with a grin. "So are you going to tell me how it went?"

"Well, it was one hell of a gang-bang. But no orgasm."

Dahlia's eyes widened. "Not one?"

"Not after a hundred of them." Arliana sighed and turned her head away, trying to stop the tears from flowing. "I guess I'm just never going to have one. I'm going to live my life without knowing what it's like."

"And you've tried everything?"

"Everything. Toys, vibrators, neural stimulators, and plenty of men. And even women. I've fucked friends and strangers, and even a few relatives. I've role-played, dominated, and submitted. I've paid to be raped, paid to be gang-raped, and paid for every kind of sex you can imagine and plenty you probably can't. And now I've been gang-banged by a hundred aliens with giant penises. Nothing works. The experts say it's all psychological, because there's no physical reason for it. They've tried it all: tech, therapy, hypnosis, medications."

"Wow," Dahlia said, shaking her head. "But never? Not

even through masturbation?"

"Nope. I've masturbated with every toy and tool known. Dildos, vibes, lickers, hummers, buzzers—you name it, I've tried every masturbation aid out there."

"Wow," Dahlia said. "Not even with your own hand? I can't imagine."

"Well, like I said, I've tried everything—every toy or tool. Way better chances than using my own hand."

Dahlia gave a start, and Arliana saw the woman blinking at her in disbelief. "Wait a minute. What do you mean you've never masturbated with your own hand? Who has sex all her life trying to have an orgasm, and lets herself get gang raped by a hundred aliens, but hasn't tried masturbating?"

"Dahlia—I started with a vibe when I was thirteen," she said. "Toys have always made me feel wonderful, just on the edge of orgasm. But if vibes and dildos and ticklers and all that don't work, my own fingers certainly won't be any use. And obviously I've had plenty of people using their fingers on me, as you know from personal experience."

There was a long silence, and Dahlia burst out laughing. Arliana stared at her, confused. "What's so damn funny?"

"Toys are fun, but they're not *you*," Dahlia said. "You've spent years trying to get someone or something to give you an orgasm—and have never tried to give *yourself* one. Honey, I really think you'd better try it. Just you and your fingers and your thoughts. Rub that clit. Touch yourself. Do what feels good. Follow your sensations. Make love to yourself."

Arliana was doubtful. "I really don't think..."

"Forget thinking! Give that minge another few days to recover, with a few more pills and creams, and when she's back to her normal self, you get down to business."

They were six hours in hyperspace from Earth when she finally tried it. She stripped naked and lay back on the bunk, her legs splayed, and she reached down to touch herself. She rested her fingers on her clit and pressed. It stirred a bit, stiffening slightly. So she began to rub it. She quickly found that a circular motion worked very well, something the men in her life had often tried. But it felt different under her own hand. Where the sensation changed quickly at the slightest alteration in pace by a man, she felt everything and knew just what to do and how to do it.

The more she circled, the more intense the feelings became. Something inside her took over, and she dipped two fingers repeatedly into her dripping vagina to lubricate her sensitive clit. Then she crept her other hand down there, and as one hand madly circled, she slid two fingers of her other hand up inside her, found that magic spot, and began to rub.

Arliana felt as if she were floating above her bed, as her head began to swim in that familiar way. And when the electric thrill between her legs, which she'd felt so many times before, began sizzling, she knew that always meant it was a gigantic tease that would never fulfill her.

But then she floated higher in her wild dizziness, and the sizzling escalated in ways it never had before. Her legs began to quiver uncontrollably, and she felt her breath becoming short and jerky, felt that incredible feeling between her legs billowing out through her entire body. She soared spiritually, as if her soul were barely staying connected to her body, which was doing things to her more powerful than the entire universe. She'd never felt like that before.

And it just got better... and better... and oh, *so fucking much better...!*

Dahlia was at the controls of the ship when she heard the scream, but she knew everything was all right. She smiled.

"Atta girl," she said.

Virgin's Sacrifice

by
Jane Gallagher

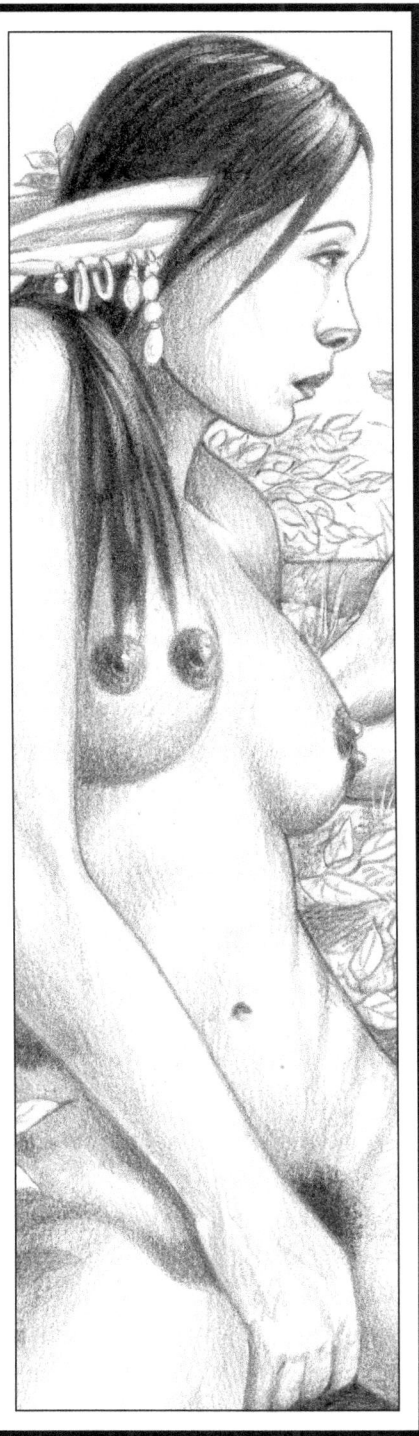

The idea of sex can be frightening to some young girls, but most of them eventually learn that it's not nearly as bad as they thought it would be. But this humanoid girl must remain a virgin at all costs, for it's said that any man who defiles her innocence will find death at the hands of her alleged supernatural protector. That just isn't fair to a nubile young woman with raging hormones and the driving desire to experience one of life's greatest pleasures. But all that talk of a magical protector can't be true. Can it?

Fantasy
Masturbation
Virgin sex
Lesbian sex
Innocence
Nonhuman physiology
Desire

I won't ever forget the day I first decided to have intercourse with a young man. I can't forget it. I want to, but I can't.

Shayla was my best friend since we were just six; she was like a sister to me. We grew up together in the third ward of our clan lands, just north of the village, and life was so simple then. We played by the river, throwing stones at the iridescent purple hoverfish that came out of the rapids to swim through the air, snatching insects with their long tongues before diving back into the water. We played with wooden dolls the clan women made, and later learned to make them ourselves, along with the clothing we sewed for them. We ran through the meadows of rippling green grasses and dells of towering trees, pretending we were grown women on exciting adventures. And every year, when one of us celebrated a birthday, the other would add another piercing to her ear; our tall and pointed ears were swept back as they jutted out from our maroon-colored hair, high over our heads, and the gold and silver and gems pierced there decorated them nicely. All that mattered was our friendship; Shayla never cared what our clan chieftain had proclaimed about me the very day I was born.

Many of the other children didn't like me much because of that, purely out of jealousy — but if they knew what it would be like, they wouldn't have been so jealous. Chieftain Jurvonorka had identified the birthmark on my shoulder as evidence that I was to be the Lasting Virgin, the one who would bring balance to the land, drawing all the clans together. I was disallowed engaging in intercourse until Chieftain Jurvonorka identified my male equivalent, and consummating our decreed marriage would result in a thousand years of good weather and bountiful crops and peace amongst the peoples. I'd heard the story before, but none of it made sense to me until Shayla started bleeding.

We were playing by the river when it happened first, and she had to pee. We made sure there were no boys nearby, and she lifted her skirts high, squatted on the bank, and peed. But there was orange blood with her pee, and she started screaming. We rushed back to the village to the elder women, and they laughed at our terror and took Shayla into the women's communal hut, and I didn't see her for hours. I was told it was nothing to worry about, and that, one day, I too would bleed, and then I would learn.

Shayla, of course, told me everything the next day—that she'd do it once a year, as all women did, that she wasn't dying, and that it meant her body was ready for intercourse. "Intercourse" meant nothing to me except that I wasn't supposed to have it until my mate was discovered, and I hadn't cared until Shayla got her education and related it to me. She told me amazing stories of things girls can only imagine: of men putting their phalluses inside women, and it was supposed to feel good, and if it happened at the right time—in the weeks before the time of bleeding—you could become pregnant and bear children.

Neither of us gave it much thought, and it wasn't long before the day came when I began bleeding. The blood was a dark orange, much darker than the bright-orange blood when I'd ever cut myself. The elder women took me to the hut and explained intercourse, and it made no more sense than when Shayla had told me. But the elder women explained something different to me when they told me what a virgin was—a girl who had never had a man's phallus inside her sheath, which was the name for the place from where the dark-orange blood would flow for two weeks out of every year. Normal girls would eventually engage in intercourse with young men, and perhaps become pregnant and marry their mates.

But I was different and special, they told me, because of Chieftain Jurvonorka's decree that I was the Lasting Virgin who represented the future of the many clans. It was very important for me to not do as the other girls did, and not engage in intercourse. I was to remain a virgin until Chieftain Jurvonorka found the man who would be my match. Only then could I become deflowered, fulfilling the prophecy that would bring the golden age of peace and prosperity upon the land.

"You can never copulate with another before that," an elder woman warned me. "If a man's phallus tries to enter your sheath, a Guardian will appear and destroy him."

"What's a Guardian?" I asked, wide-eyed and afraid.

"A supernatural being, commanded by the Chieftain's magic to watch over you," the elder woman said. "If any man ever tries to deflower you, he'll meet the Guardian's swift vengeance. No man can ever force you into intercourse — and you'll be protected from your own desires."

The idea of a man's phallus, the thing he used to pee, up inside my sheath, from where I peed and bled, just seemed silly. "I could never have such desires," I told her with my nose wrinkled in childish disgust, but she laughed.

"Oh, you will, Kayfil," she told me, stroking my maroon hair and dancing her aged fingers up the high zeniths of my tall, pointed ears. "As you get older, you'll be tempted. But the Guardian will keep that temptation under control, so long as our Chieftain Jurvonorka lives."

Shayla and I thought the whole idea of intercourse was ridiculous for several years — until Shayla discovered just how wonderful sexual intercourse could be. We'd grown up a lot by then; our hips had widened, and our breasts had ballooned on our chests. Shayla's were much larger than mine, and I knew the boys couldn't stop looking at her. She knew, too, and she loved puffing her chest up and presenting them to anyone who would look. But one day, she found herself alone in the woods with one of the boys from the village, and she engaged in intercourse with him. I heard all about it the next day — she was excited and proud and babbled crazily about the experience. Despite our long-held belief that a phallus in a sheath was silly, she assured me we'd been utterly wrong, and it had been the most incredible experience she'd ever had.

She did it with him again, and then with several other boys, and she told me about her experiences every time — in vivid detail. I was wide-eyed with a mixture of shock and confusion, because nothing about it sounded positive or fun — yet I couldn't help but feel strange when she described it. She'd talk of kissing the boy and feeling his hands groping her breasts and feeling between her legs, and how he'd pull her dress over her head and expose her nakedness — which seemed horrifyingly embarrassing to me! Then he'd lay her down on a soft bed of moss beneath the trees and climb on top of her, with his phallus exposed, swollen large and firm. She told me how he would stick his phallus up inside her; at first it was painfully uncomfortable, but soon her sheath got very wet and the phallus moving in there felt wonderful. He'd be between her legs, moving his phallus in and out of her, and it would end with intense wave of pleasure for her that she couldn't even put into words. It would end the same for him, when he'd spray creamy white fluid up inside her — not pee, and somehow not disgusting or weird.

And while she told me, I felt different. I felt all four nipples on my two breasts stand up under my dress, the way they'd do when I was cold. My stomach churned as if I were nervous — but I wasn't nervous. And I grew warm and damp between my legs, and I couldn't stop myself from clenching and unclenching my thighs, over and over, which for some reason made me feel very good.

One day, Shayla told me she was going to engage in intercourse in the woods with Dayku, a well-built young laborer who had been pursuing her. And then her eyes lit up and she said, "Kayfil, I have an idea. Come with me and hide in the bushes — and you can see what I've been telling you!"

It sounded forbidden and exciting, so I followed her into the woods where she planned to give herself to the young man. Nearby was a dense thicket, and there I could kneel, safely camouflaged in my beige dress. Even twenty feet away, she couldn't see me, but I could easily see what was happening through the thick branches. I was so nervous when she returned an hour later with Dayku that it felt as if my heart would burst through my chest. Just seeing him was breathtaking, for he was a handsome and muscular young man. His tall ears were tattooed with intricate pictures of many colors, which was how the boys marked their birthdays. And when Dayku and Shayla began kissing, I watched the scene, transfixed with anticipation.

They kissed, and she touched him all over, and his hands found her shapely buttocks and squeezed them. She had soft, pliable buttocks set behind wide hips, and the boys liked looking at them almost as much as looking at her breasts. He roamed his hands over them a while as he kissed her before sliding them up to fondle her breasts, and soon he was tugging her dress over her head. She was naked before him, which was strangely exciting to see, and I watched in awe as she tilted her head back and let him kiss all over her body. He kissed her neck and even kissed her breasts, licking the pair of nipples on each breast before dropping to his knees. Then he did something that astounded me: He kissed her between her legs, at the cleft that divided the smooth mound there, and she made a moaning sound that told me she liked it.

I was mesmerized as he lay her down on the mossy ground and shed his tunic and pants. I was seeing him from behind, and the first thing I noticed was his tight, strong buttocks, which stirred something within me. But his back and shoulder muscles flexed as he moved, and when he turned I saw his powerful chest and rippled abdomen, which stirred that something within me even more—and then I sucked in a breath as I saw it.

I'd seen phalluses before when I'd changed diapers on babies, or on little boys who played naked on hot summer days. Shayla and I had even seen them on older boys when we'd sneaked down to the river to spy on them as they swam nude. Phalluses always made us giggle as they'd dangle there, short and stubby, with tiny sacks beneath them bouncing as the boys walked. But Dayku's phallus was very different; it wasn't dangly or limp, instead sticking out almost straight, and it was much bigger. And as he smiled down at Shayla, who was naked on the ground before him, she spread her legs wide, reaching her hands behind her knees and pulling them up to her doughy breasts, which sagged to either side of her chest. And she moved her hips so that the split in her smooth mound seemed to move around, as if to entice him. And it did, his phallus growing even fatter and firmer as I gawked at it, climbing higher until it stood upright, pointing at the sky.

"Put it in me," Shayla commanded, her voice a hoarse whisper, but loud enough for me to hear.

Something about how she said that, while I stared through the branches, my eyes glued to his hard phallus, did something to me. My sheath was warmer and wetter than it ever had been, even more so than when she'd told me her sex stories. I found myself running my hand down my belly, as if to quell the quivering in there—but, without even thinking about it, I realized I'd let my hand slide down to my crotch, and suddenly felt an energized tingle as my fingertips found that sensitive nubbin at the top of my sheath's split. I sucked in my breath at the feeling, which was quite good.

He got down on all fours between her legs and crawled forward until his phallus was lined up with Shayla's wet entrance; the lips of her sheath had parted, welcoming him. Then she reached between her legs and wrapped her hand around his phallus — it seemed positively gigantic in her tiny little hand — and she wiggled her hips forward to meet its domed head. She fitted it snugly inside her, and then commanded him to shove it deeper.

Incredulous, I watched him thrust his hips forward, and his big phallus disappeared inside her. I was wide-eyed and open-mouthed, but so was she, and while it looked like it should hurt, she was clearly enjoying it. He held himself up on his hands and knees as he moved his hips steadily, and from my position I could see his phallus sliding in and out of her. She made oohing and ahhing sounds, and with every stroke he let out a little grunt.

It was sensory overload for me, and I realized my hand was firmly jammed between my legs, rubbing the hidden nubbin that was there in little circles. I don't even know why I did it, or how I knew to do it that way, but it felt right. But the dress was in the way, so I deftly yanked it up over my head and off so that I was naked. I found the split between my legs with my hand and forced it apart with two fingers, and it felt so good to touch that nubbin.

Shayla began crying out in pleasure as Dayku moved faster, her big breasts flailing madly, her four nipples erect. My eyes were riveted on the sight of his phallus sawing in and out of her. I realized I was moving my hand in time with his thrusts, and with every stroke of my hand, the pleasure I was feeling escalated. Soon, my knees began to shake, and my belly quivered more fervently.

But suddenly, Shayla began screaming, and when she did, Dayku cried out in ecstasy, and his steadily moving hips jerked unevenly, and then he yelled and shoved himself so deep inside her that I could see nothing but his sack, and he grunted over and over as Shayla's cries ebbed. Then he fell on her, still grunting, and she wrapped her arms and legs around him and held him close.

It was the end of the sex act, but I felt utterly unfulfilled. I kept working my fingers, but soon Dayku was climbing off her and they were coming to their feet, and I was terrified he'd see me. I removed my hand, crouched low in the bushes, and watched as Shayla kissed him and hugged him and told him to hurry back to the village. He dressed quickly and rushed away. She waited until he was out of sight and then hurried to my hiding place.

"Did you see?" she cried, naked as I'd seen her many times before. And I was naked as she'd seen me. It was different now, though. I couldn't keep myself from looking between her legs. I could see the split there, and saw her lips, red and swollen. I suddenly felt self-conscious about my own nakedness, and subtly covered my crotch with my hands.

"Yes," I said, my voice shaking.

She saw me looking, and she looked down at herself. "Watch this," she said.

She strained and worked her hips, and from inside her, white stuff oozed out. It dripped to the ground, and I don't know why, but it excited me.

"Did you like watching?" she asked.

I met her eyes, nodding dumbly. Between my legs, everything burned and ached, as if it needed to be rubbed some more.

It was like she could read my mind, and she pointed to my crotch. "You took your dress off. Did you touch yourself down there?"

I felt myself growing red, but I nodded.

She giggled and bounced up and down, and her big breasts flopped. "Did you bring yourself to the finish? I didn't hear you screaming, so I bet you didn't."

I didn't know what she meant, but I shook my head.

"You have to finish," she said. "Trust me on this. You have no idea how wonderful it is. Quick, come with me."

She grabbed my hand and led me to the mossy bed where Dayku had just taken her. She coaxed me to sit down and spread my legs before her. I did so, but felt strange being completely exposed like that. My hips were slimmer than hers, my breasts much smaller and firmer, and my mound wasn't as proudly puffy as hers. The soft moss felt good on my backside, but it tickled my thighs as she grabbed my legs and spread them wider. She faced me, sitting cross-legged, and told me to show her what I'd done. I felt silly, but the aching down there was too much to ignore, so I returned my fingers to their spot and began circling the nubbin.

"How does it feel?" she asked, her bright eyes darting from mine to my hand and back again.

I nodded in answer. I was afraid to reply for fear my voice would squeak.

"Do it faster," she coaxed. "Press on it a little harder."

I did as she said, and it felt wonderful. My hand moved like the wind, and I increased the pressure as I went. I felt my breathing grow shallow as my heart pounded away.

Shayla leaned back and spread her legs as she watched, and her hand dipped to her swollen lips. I watched as she spread them apart with thumb and middle finger and began flicking at her own nubbin with her index finger. The sight was inexplicably titillating to me, and I increased the tempo on my nubbin.

"That's really sexy to see," Shayla breathed heavily. "Watch me do this..."

She leaned further back and moved her hand lower. The white stuff was still oozing out of her when she shoved three fingers up inside her sheath, where Dayku's phallus had been. She began thrusting those fingers in and out, fast and furious, as she stared at my own speeding hand. I could see the glaze of the white stuff on her fingers as she did that to herself, and my excitement suddenly began to peak. The feelings inside me billowed, and the sensation that had been building somewhere behind the nubbin I was so furiously rubbing seemed ready to erupt. My breathing grew louder and faster. I wasn't

self-conscious anymore; I was too lost in the intense pleasure of the moment to care.

"Are you going to come?" Shayla said, using a term I'd never heard but that I took to mean "finish."

I nodded, breathing hard. Whatever that even meant, I knew it was going to be tremendous. Yes, I was definitely going to come.

And then I did. It was like nothing I'd ever felt in my life—a powerful wave of pleasure and sensation that exploded inside me and caused my legs to clamp sharply together around my hand. I wailed like a frightened little girl, but it was the cry of ecstasy of a woman. Everything was so sensitive that I wanted to yank my hand away, but at the same time I didn't want to. I kept it there, wriggling around that nubbin, and wave after wave of intense pleasure washed through me. I grew dizzy, and the next thing I knew, I was on my back on the moss, staring up at the blue sky through the trees.

Presently, Shayla's face appeared over me, smiling as her breasts swayed above mine, and she giggled. "Was that good?"

"Oh, yes," I said. "Oh, very much so."

She laughed. "That's nothing. You just wait until you get a young man to put his phallus in you. It's even more amazing."

I sat up and faced her. "I can't. I must remain a virgin."

She rolled her eyes. "Silly superstition! As long as nobody knows, they can't worry about it. You can have sex and enjoy it, and fulfill your obligations later."

"I don't know," I said, but in my mind, I was hoping I could convince myself that she was making sense. After everything that had happened, more than anything I wanted to feel a phallus inside me.

For the next month, I pleasured myself. I did it every day, usually several times, and it was easier to get myself to the finish by visualizing what I'd seen that day in the woods—and sometimes to just imagine that Dayku was servicing me with his phallus. Several times, Shayla and I touched ourselves together, like we had that day, and it was always super-exciting when we did. Seeing her exposed and touching herself helped me finish much more easily.

One day, when we'd gone to one of our secret places—a sandy inlet on the river some distance from the village—she said, "Let's try something new."

We were naked in the midday sun, having shed our dresses and used them to sit on in the sand. I nodded my assent.

"Lie back and spread your legs," she ordered with a mischievous look on her face. "And close your eyes."

I did as she said, and I felt the cool breeze between my legs. But then something touched me, and I knew right away that it was Shayla's fingers. I took a deep breath and relaxed, and felt her spreading my lips apart and finding my nubbin with her fingers. She began doing to me what I had been doing to myself—and it felt ten times better. I tried not to shake as I lay there, but I couldn't help it; she moved her fingers back and forth, and the friction was incredible.

"Do you like that?" she whispered.

I nodded, blind and mute.

"I'm going to do something else," she said. "Don't be afraid. But open your eyes, so you'll see."

I did, and she was kneeling beside me, smiling. She looked past me, smiling at something I couldn't see. I turned my head and there was Dayku, standing at the edge of the woods, naked, with his hardening phallus growing before my eyes. I shrieked and flailed on our dresses, trying to cover myself, but Shayla quickly calmed me.

"It's okay," she said. "Dayku is here because I asked him. He's willing to take your virginity."

"But I can't!" I cried on my knees, trying to hide my breasts with my arm and my sex with my other hand. "I'm not permitted!"

"Kayfil — think about it," Shayla said, almost sternly, but with a smile. "You've felt so good pleasuring yourself, and letting me pleasure you. And you've seen how much better Dayku makes me feel. Are you going to throw all that away for some silly superstition?"

I swayed where I knelt, looking at her. But at the edge of my vision, I could see Dayku's phallus. It was so big, and I knew I wanted to feel it inside me. And I knew Shayla was right: the Lasting Virgin, the golden age, it was all just silly superstition. Was I to be a slave to such old-fashioned beliefs?

"Shall I send Dayku away?" Shayla asked. "Or are you ready to become a woman?"

I was ready.

I lay back down on the dresses in the sand, and Shayla held my hand and told me not to be afraid, to spread my legs for him. I watched in fascination as Dayku knelt between them and got into position. His hands came down around me, and Shayla reached out to grasp his phallus and help guide it to my sheath. In that instant, I realized how absolutely huge it was, and I was convinced there was no way it could possibly fit inside me. I braced myself, ready for the discomfort I knew was likely before the pleasure took over. I felt the fat dome of his phallus push against the opening to my sheath, blocked by the obstruction I knew was there. I held my breath as he pushed against me, and it felt ready to break through at any moment.

Suddenly there was a flash of white light, and we all looked up and Shayla screamed. Standing there was a terrible figure, eight feet tall and naked with skin as black as a moonless midnight sky. He was ridiculously muscular beyond normal proportions, beyond *possible* proportions, and the phallus between his thighs was as thick as my leg and hung nearly to his knees. His eyes glowed yellow, and when he snarled I could see yellow fangs lining his mouth.

"Sektar oom nakkol!" the Guardian roared like some inhuman demon. "Ektura zarzanu!"

He extended a black hand and a flash of red light erupted from it. It streaked toward the naked young man between my legs, and Dayku had no time to scream before he vanished in a flash of crimson.

Shayla screamed again, but my eyes were on the Guardian. It lowered its hand and there was another flash of white light, and he was gone.

Shayla still screamed, on and on. I turned to her, and that's when I saw Dayku's feet, topped by bloody calf stumps. They were all that remained of him, and they were bleeding all over our dresses.

I began screaming with her.

They were silly superstitions, but they were terrifyingly real.

I knew that day that, if my male counterpart were never found, I'd go my entire life without intercourse — all because of the Chieftain's magic spell. The Guardian would appear and destroy any man who tried to deflower me.

Shayla cried every day. "I didn't believe it," she'd bawl to me. "I'm so sorry! I swear I didn't think a Guardian would actually appear!"

In fact, I think most of the elders hadn't really believed it, either. They played their roles, pretended, and kept the old ways alive, but they didn't truly believe. Shayla and I didn't believe in a thousand years of peace, but we surely knew that supernatural beings could be magically summoned to destroy innocent people. It just wasn't right.

And it wasn't right that my lifetime had been preordained and decided by others. It should always have been my choice. So I asked Shayla to help me. I asked her to spread rumors everywhere that, after Dayku, I'd successfully lost my virginity, and had since had sex with a half-dozen young men. The Guardian hadn't appeared again. The rumors sparked whispering amongst the clan, and soon everyone was looking at me, nervous and afraid.

Eventually, Chieftain Jurvonorka called me to his hut. He dismissed his staff, and we were alone. His hut was the most lavish in the village, with several rooms. His parlor was carpeted with soft tharn skins of many colors, and a dozen oversized pillows on the floor encircled his wooden throne. He sat in it, hands gripping the arms with fingers that were like claws, glaring at me from beneath his crown of wire-strung cut gems. His big ears were completely covered in tattoos, and they had spilled over to his bald head and neck. I sat, cross-legged, on a pillow before him.

"What's this I hear that you've been deflowered?" he demanded, his eyes ablaze.

"It's true, and the Guardian hasn't returned," I said. "First, I had sex with Zeldar. He's a rotten young man, and has been since we were children. I looked forward to the Guardian appearing and destroying him, but he didn't."

"You... *tried* to have him killed?" Jurvonorka cried. "You evil child!"

"So I've had sex with several of the young men," I continued, ignoring him. "Your plan to enslave me has failed. I've driven the Guardian away with the sheer force of my own willpower. I choose how to live my life. I choose what to do with my body. Not you, and not the Guardian I've banished."

"You've dispelled the Guardian," he said, breathless and amazed. "You've defeated my magic, and you've taken the chance of a golden age from us."

"It proves that I'm not the Lasting Virgin, my Chieftain," I said to him. "With the greatest respect, you've erred in your judgment. The Lasting Virgin has yet to come. I'm not her."

"I was so certain," he said.

"You were wrong."

He spat angrily at me. "Evil girl!"

"You have no idea how evil I can be," I said, and in one motion I came to my feet and pulled my dress over my head, exposing myself to him. "The men of the clan know, and they like me for it." I brought my hands to my small breasts, rubbing my four nipples for him to see.

"Cover yourself!" he bellowed.

"I can't—I must have you, Chieftain!" I cried, and I shoved my hand between my legs and began working my nubbin, rubbing furiously, even as I caressed my breasts with my other hand. "I have defeated the Guardian, but I cannot continue giving myself to mere boys. I must be the consort of one such as you."

"No," he said, shaking his head, but I could tell from his face that his resolve was weakening.

I let out a moan of pleasure. "Yes, Chieftain! I need you. Take me now, and fill my sheath with your throbbing phallus—or I'll leave the clan and find a Chieftain elsewhere who will have me!"

I could tell he wanted to resist, but he was transfixed as he watched me working my nubbin. I squatted slightly and shoved fingers up inside my sheath. "Oh, that feels so good, Jurvonorka... but I need you inside me."

His mouth was agape at what he was witnessing and what I was saying, and his hand went to his crotch and adjusted his growing phallus. I threw myself to the floor, lying back on the tharn-skin rug, and spread my legs wide as I plunged my fingers fiercely in and out of me. "Please, take me! Shove your phallus in me and take me!"

He stumbled to his feet and began tearing off his clothing. Soon he was naked, and his phallus was indeed impressive, far bigger than Dayku's. It was thick and hard, so heavy that it couldn't stand up straight. He staggered to me, collapsed to his knees, and grabbed my legs. I tore my hand away from my sheath as he threw my feet up over his shoulders and guided his hard phallus towards my entrance, which was practically begging for it with a steady flow of juices.

And just as he fed the head of his phallus through the lips

of my split and bumped up against the obstruction in there, there was a flash of white light.

Jurvonorka looked back and screamed.

I laughed crazily, from sheer joy.

I really did test with Zeldar later, because he really had been a rotten kid, so I wanted to test things with a boy I wouldn't mind being destroyed. But there was no flash of light and no Guardian, and Zeldar stuffed his modest phallus inside me and I was deflowered. It was overly quick, and the fact was I'd had better times using my hand.

But while Zeldar was my first, he was hardly my last. I was free to have all the sex I wanted. My life was my own, as it should have been. But Shayla and I had to leave the clan, as we were hated and scorned — for defying the prophecy, for tricking the Chieftain into his death, and for wantonly engaging in sex with young men everywhere.

We've traveled far, and have met many, and we've enjoyed every sexual encounter we've had. Sometimes we've bedded the same man together, and occasionally we've bedded women. On nights when we're alone, we sleep naked together, and we kiss and caress each other, and often we touch each other between our legs or even kiss each other there. We're free, together, making our own choices about our bodies and our sexuality.

And that's just how it should be.

Hi-Tech Sex Lib

by
Dalibor Perković

Translated by
Tatjana Jambrišak

Go back in time and kill your grandparents, and what happens? That's been hotly debated forever. Maybe you cease to exist, which means you never could have killed them, so you exist after all… so you did kill them. In this version of time travel, there are none of those classic paradoxes, so there's nothing to worry about… or is there? For this young couple, their new household time machine is just for convenience and relaxation, but a daring sexual idea turns it into so much more. And that's when things get strange.

Science fiction
Time travel
Group sex
Lesbian sex
Sex with one's self

115

As soon as the domestic temporal translator had been delivered, Joanna and Matthew began having second thoughts about it. They wondered just how necessary the device really was. True, they had been discussing the subject for over two months and pondered over his salary, her salary, possible bonuses, expenditures, food expenses, fringe benefits, and loan repayments—not to mention their savings. In the end, they had decided they could afford it after all.

However, when the device finally arrived and the delivery crew pushed it through the door, Joanna and Matthew looked at each other with unease. The same thought passed through their minds: They had once more become victims of a spending spree and crammed another space-consuming toy into their apartment. Still, as Matthew noticed, they could always use it as a closet once they got fed up with it.

The translator resembled a wardrobe, made of gray metal with a computer console installed at the door. The instruction manual was elementary: All you had to do was enter the length of time you wanted to pass, add a plus or a minus—depending whether you want to send something into the future or the past—and press one of the big red buttons placed on both the inside and the outside of the door.

As usual, there was a hardware and power-supply limitation to how far in time you could venture. A trip to the past took much more energy, and even a voyage of one week placed a burden on the fuses. That was precisely the reason why the manufacturer programmed a seven-day limit for traveling to the past. One could go two months into the future, though, but such a trip naturally seemed less interesting.

Joanna and Matthew did an experiment right away. They put a geranium pot on the translator floor and sent it five minutes into the future. Then they sat down and waited. Exactly five minutes later, they heard a sound signal and opened the door. There it was: their old, very familiar geranium. Matthew looked at the console and realized that the friendly machine displayed the amount of energy consumed, also asking whether the owner would like a printout. Matthew pushed the green button and a few moments later they were both happily staring at a piece of paper telling them how much money they had just spent, at least as far as the electricity bill was concerned. Actually, a five-minute trip into the future wasted the same amount of energy as a light-bulb would over an hour. They agreed it was negligible.

Joanna and Matthew trashed the printout and took the geranium out of the temporal translator. The next experiment was completely logical — to send it for the same time distance, but into the past. They hesitated for a moment wondering which buttons to press, when suddenly they heard a loud beep, slightly higher in tone. Joanna reached for the door and pulled it open, only to find another geranium, just like the one Matthew was holding in his hands, resting on the floor. She picked it up and they placed the two geraniums next to each other. The resemblance was obvious. Matthew experimented a little, pulling them closer and again farther away, trying to figure out if there was any sort of energy field that attracted or repelled them. There wasn't. They were two perfectly normal geraniums.

Matthew looked at the screen and saw that the geranium was sent from the future point in time five minutes away, of which one had already passed. He put one geranium into the machine and programmed the controls. Then they sat down and waited. About one minute before they were supposed to push the red button, Joanna looked at the geranium she was holding and said:

"What would happen if we took *this* geranium and sent it into the past?"

Matthew looked at her geranium. Technically, he thought, nothing would *happen*. Maybe they would tie some kind of a temporal knot where one geranium would simply exist as such, while the other would only exist during those five minutes between appearing and disappearing in the translator.

"Wouldn't that be breaking the law of conservation of mass and energy?" she asked.

"I suppose so," Matthew shrugged. "I guess there would be some mathematical solution to that."

In fact, neither of them wanted to experiment for too long. The instruction manual that came with the machine had examples of sending objects or people to the past or the future. For example, after a month of hard work, a person could send himself one week into the past and peacefully enjoy that additional week's vacation. Nevertheless, the manufacturer did recommend that such a vacation should be spent somewhere else, so that there was no crowd in the afternoon, when the original returned home from work.

There was yet another fine example. Since married couples were usually tired after a day's work, the manual suggested that they should plan their time. Make a lavish and delicious lunch on the evening before, it said, or after some rest, and simply send the meal to the pre-arranged time — warm and directly out of the oven. Then there was the possibility of going to the movies at any time of day, even while the original person was at work. For careerists, needless to say, there was an option of attending several simultaneous business meetings.

The manufacturer also quoted a study stating that one of the major problems for young couples just starting to live together was the lack of time for sex, especially if they both worked and their spare time was limited. The text, however, did not list any particular examples, but merely suggested that "the temporal translator, when used with inspiration, could solve that problem, too." Joanna and Matthew did not recognize this as a problem. True, they were often exhausted after work, but a short afternoon nap and another half an hour of petting would usually suffice in putting them in the mood. And there were always weekends. Still, it was worth remembering that option.

They kept testing the geranium possibilities for the rest of the day. They were sending it back and forth in time, trying to cause some deviation, but failed at every attempt. First, when the geranium was supposed to arrive from the past, they left the temporal translator open to see what would be happening inside, although the instructions specifically declared the door should be closed for the device to function properly. And so, Joanna and Matthew waited and stared into the translator's interior, but nothing happened. As soon as they gave up and closed the door, they heard the familiar "ping," and her majesty the geranium reappeared. Matthew looked at the console again, and there was an error message: "Due to error—DEVICE OPEN—the temporal communication was established between the periods different from those programmed, resulting in Package Delivery Delay." It also turned out the translator could not receive a temporal package unless the cabin was completely empty. So, if they wanted to get the geranium they had sent back from the future, they could not keep the original one inside in order to watch them collide.

And then, as it often happens, parents, cousins, and friends came calling. Although there were many temporal translators around the town, Joanna and Matthew were the first of all the people they knew who had bought one. There were hordes of fans and critics who wanted to come, see and speak their minds on this expensive toy—a toy or, for some, a sheer necessity. Most were curious and benevolent, though a few were skeptical. Some ridiculed the "triviality of the capitalist consumer's mentality that bought everything that was offered no matter if it was necessary or not." Matthew's mother naturally expressed her fear of the strange device, worrying if all this was going to end up badly for her son. After the processions had finished, Matthew locked the door, leaned against it, and smiled. Now, they could continue their usual life.

It was only then that Joanna and Matthew realized how valuable the temporal translator was. It took them several days before they dared to send themselves time traveling, but once they had broken the ice, they were on the move. They would come home from work around six, take a nap and then make a plan for that day. Usually, they would send themselves to sometime around two in the afternoon and go out. They would return home in the evening, say hello to their previous versions, get ready for an evening out, stay out until late, come back home while their future versions were asleep and travel into the past far enough so that they could get enough sleep for the following working day.

Their sex life flourished, too. There was no more of the after-work exhaustion that usually ruined those few hours they had left before bedtime, so they could get busy with each other without thinking of hours and minutes.

Of course, there was an unpleasant side effect. If their day became one-third longer, that inevitably meant their lives would get a third shorter. Their relative life span, measured by their own clock, would remain the same, while the external clock and the calendar would nevertheless show they would die sooner. But Joanna and Matthew did not consider this to be of any great importance. If the current life expectancy was seventy-five to eighty years, they calculated, they would live well over sixty-five, and that, in a way, did not make a considerable difference. Besides, after they retired, they could always start taking big temporal leaps into the future, check if someone would have already found the cure for old age, and consequently drive retirement funds mad. In the meantime, the money would be piling up: to cross a month—that is, the distance required for one installment—they needed only a few minutes of their lives. Anyway, that lay far in the future, and Joanna believed that their lives would naturally be prolonged if only they spent them well and wise and happy.

So, Joanna and Matthew managed to catch a steady rhythm. Their day lasted between thirty and thirty-two hours on average, they got better and better at work, their salaries rose, and their social life blossomed. Sex was never better.

Then Matthew got an idea how to make that segment of their lives even better.

He was wise enough not to rush out with the idea before considering it thoroughly. He spent a couple of weeks thinking about how to break it to Joanna, wrapping it up in ribbons so that it wouldn't sound like what it actually was: a sexual perversion. So, one day, as they were lying in bed in each other's arms, Matthew tried his simple plan. He casually told Joanna that he loved her so much that sometimes he thought one of her was not enough. After she smiled and honored him with a kiss, they fondled silently for a couple more minutes, and then Matthew asked her jovially whether she had any idea how to multiply herself. She smiled again, and then he raised a finger victoriously and said:

"I know! You could go into the translator, send yourself two hours into the past and then all three of us could go to bed together."

The moment he finished the sentence, Joanna sat up, frowned and looked at him furiously.

"I am not your sexual slave, Matthew," she said and got out of bed.

As she was getting dressed on the way to the bathroom, she explained to him that people were made for one-on-one sex and that his idea of being serviced by two females like some sheikh—even if both girls were the same person—was a typical sexual fantasy only to be expected from a backward, unemancipated male chauvinist. She slammed the bathroom door. While he was listening to the sound of the shower, Matthew concluded that this had probably not been a good idea.

Their relationship was ice-cold for the next few days; Joanna even refused to use the temporal translator and that, of course, knocked out his wish to use it, too. After a while, things started to melt. A week later, everything was as before. Another week passed and Matthew thought of another way to realize his fantasy. He waited for the appropriate moment. While they were lying in bed, catching their breaths, he asked her if she would have liked him, Matthew, to return an hour or two to the past so that the three of them could have some fun. The moment he said it, she sat up, frowned and looked at him furiously.

"I am not your sexual slave, Matthew," she said and got out of bed.

As she was putting on a robe on her way to the bathroom, she explained to him that people were made for one-on-one sex and that his idea of two male subjects charging at her as a mere sexual object was a typical sexual fantasy only to be expected from a backward, unemancipated male chauvinist such as him. She slammed the bathroom door again. While he was listening to the sound of the shower, Matthew concluded that this had probably not been a good idea, either.

This time it took a shorter time for the iceberg to melt. After the fourth day, she came to him and said:

"All right, if you really want to use the machine, we can both go back to the past and *watch* the other selves doing it. Understand? We go back into the past, so that there are four of us at the same moment, one couple making love, the other watching. Just watching, nothing else!"

He shrugged and said: "Of course, whatever you say."

She nodded and started entering the temporal translator. He stopped her.

"Shall we first watch and make love afterwards, or first make love and then watch?" he asked.

She considered this for a moment. Matthew continued:

"Perhaps we better watch first and then do it better?"
Joanna frowned.

"What if we watch first, but I don't like what I see and then I decide that I don't want to make love? Will I have to do it in order not to vanish in a time paradox?"

Matthew was about to say "Yes, you will have to," but stopped himself in the last moment. Joanna knew the rules, too, and she knew she did not have to do anything. If he tried to outsmart her with such a cheap trick, all he would accomplish would be looking for and finding trouble. For the manual said:

> Time paradoxes sort themselves out, which is a good mechanism for removing obstacles. Try a little harmless experimenting. For example, spill some raspberry juice over your tablecloth. Then enter the temporal translator in order to warn yourself not to spill the juice over your tablecloth. In the classical temporal theory this would cause a so-called 'temporal paradox'—the fact that the juice was not spilled would contradict with your memory of the event.
>
> However, modern theory has found the solution. You can change the past, because whenever you alter the flow of time, the cut-off branch ceases to exist and the time continues to flow along its new branch. If you still remember that you did spill the juice, it is perfectly normal. This memory belongs to the branch of past that does not exist anymore. You can return to the past again and prevent yourself from preventing yourself from spilling the juice, but that would not return you to the primary branch. Instead, it would open a third version, while the first two would fade out and disappear.
>
> A far-better-known temporal paradox—returning to the past and killing one of your parents before you were born—is solved equally trivially: by killing one or both parents, the time traveler simply creates a new temporal branch, while the one he was born to disappears. Nevertheless, in his present time, he will continue to exist as a person from another temporal flow.

So, Matthew was aware that Joanna knew it didn't matter what they *saw* themselves doing in the past or the future. A human being creates his own future, and if what they saw did not fit the predetermined course, they would simply open a new temporal branch where they could do what they really wanted and skip what they didn't. Unfortunately.

In the end, once they started, everything went by the book. They undressed and waited for their older versions to come from the future. Sex was still something both men and women enjoyed, no matter what the feminists claimed, and the couple that had come back in time got to it right away: The moment they left the booth they literally jumped at each other. The younger Joanna and Matthew watched them with confusion. Then, after a few minutes, they got so hot that they decided not to wait for the other two to finish, but started kissing, stepped into the translator, waited for the sound signal, rushed out of the booth, jumped at each other, and, followed by Joanna and Matthew's confused looks, fucked savagely. When everything was over — their younger selves had already gone into the past — they lay side by side panting, recalling their confused faces ten or twenty minutes earlier, and laughed. After some time Matthew turned to Joanna.

"This was good, right?"

She shrugged and smiled.

"We could do it again some other time," he said.

"Maybe," she said and shrugged again.

Matthew took that as a "Yes."

After that day, Joanna and Matthew never again had sex without the temporal translator.

They would make a plan, wait for the couple from the future to arrive, then watch them a while. As soon as they felt that inside warmth preceding every successful act, Joanna and Matthew would enter the time machine, go back to the past, and do what they saw they had done previously.

Of course, it was just a matter of time when two couples, one watching and the other acting, would turn into two couples acting. About a month after they had tied their first sexual-temporal knot, Joanna and Matthew decided it might be fun watching and acting at the same time. Thus, they did so. The younger ones occupied the armchair and the couple who had arrived from the future took the bed. Then Joanna and Matthew, who should have returned to the past in order to close the knot, sighed, got off the armchair, traveled into the past, jumped into the bed, and did it again, while the pair on the armchair was panting voluptuously. After the first/second couple had disappeared in the translator booth, Matthew sighed and said:

"Fuck! Twice in a half an hour! I need a few days off."

Joanna smiled and shrugged. "I haven't worn you down yet, have I?" she asked.

"Think of my age, will you?"

She laughed, hit him lightly on the head and turned her back to him. Matthew spooned against her and covered them both with a blanket. They fell asleep.

After two days, Matthew was ready for some more action. But Joanna just smiled mysteriously.

"I thought you were exhausted," she said.

Matthew started convincing her he had had quite enough resting, thank you, but she just put her finger to his lips and winked. He got the message.

And then, just before they began, the time machine sang "ping," the door opened and another Joanna walked out. Matthew stared at the booth for a few seconds and then realized the second Matthew was not coming. He brightened up at the sight of two identical girls watching him lustfully.

"There is no reason to use you up all at once, so I'll have to do the same more times," said Joanna who had come out of the machine.

The girls exchanged glances, nodded approvingly and grabbed the man. They pushed him over to the bed and threw him on his back. For a second or two Matthew contemplated whether he should resist to make it more interesting, but he soon concluded there was absolutely no need for that.

Twenty minutes later, when there were only two of them left, they embraced, and Matthew tried to figure out who had done what—that is, what Joanna had done *before* entering the time machine and what she had done *afterwards*. So, he reckoned, first she sat on his face and made him use his tongue, while the future Joanna was taking care of the more classical position. The first one then got off his face, and, as excited as she was, entered the time machine, went back fifteen minutes into the past and jumped on his eager piston, while the one who was just about to pass through the time machine was sitting on his face and enjoying it. Yes, it was quite fine.

He was not very tired, either. Actually, he managed to satisfy his girl twice, using up only a usual amount of energy. Thus, everything was all right with the world, he concluded. Sadly, he also remembered his mistake a month and a half ago, when he so rudely suggested something that could easily be interpreted as his wish to make Joanna into his sex slave (as if there was something wrong with that).

They went through the same arrangement several times over the following two weeks before Matthew smiled naughtily and said that it was his turn now.

The next moment, another Matthew hurried out of the time machine and two of them joined forces, storming over Joanna. As she was outnumbered, she soon succumbed. After one Matthew went back into the translator and the time score was settled, they lay in bed again, all sweaty and breathless, Joanna panting and sweating a bit more.

Soon thereafter, they started doing combinations. First, ordinary group sex: two Matthews and two Joannas, where everybody pleasured everybody else. Then followed a scene with two Matthews and three Joannas; next one was with one Joanna and three Matthews, then one more Matthew joined the party.

(At that point Joanna finally said it was enough: three was just fine, but not too often, though.) Matthew bravely put up a show with two, three, and four Joannas (although she kept complaining it was getting crowded and that not everyone was having fun all the time).

Sometimes, during those mass gatherings, Joanna ventured into her own variations, so Matthew could occasionally enjoy a live lesbian show. Joanna's attempts of persuasion, directed towards her potential enjoyment in an all-male action, ended up in a vehement indignation of all wouldn't-be performers.

And then, one day, the plan failed.

They had decided to pull off yet another "two to one" combination. They had taken off their clothes and begun petting casually while waiting. Unfortunately, no Joanna arrived. They looked at each other with concern, and then Matthew stood up to check if the time machine was all right. The console was fine, the door was closed. He opened the door to check if there was anything inside possibly blocking the device. It was empty. He closed the door and then opened it again, this time slamming it closed a bit harder. They watched the booth for a while and then shrugged.

"We could call the service department," suggested Joanna.

"Not yet," Matthew said. "Let's see if it fails again." He returned to bed and they continued the petting which soon grew into the most ordinary lovemaking one could imagine — the first one in months. Both of them enjoyed the change.

Several days passed before they decided to give another try at a simple "two to one." Again, they sat and waited, but the second Matthew never showed up. After some looking, opening and closing the translator door, Matthew finally gave up.

"All right, we're calling for service," he said.

The repairman came and presented them with a huge bill even before he had laid eyes on the device. He then disassembled the temporal translator and inspected each part. It took him half a day. He checked the energy structure and then the space-time engine, or whatever it was called. In the end, he shook his head and asked them to explain what exactly went wrong. They told him. He raised his eyebrows.

"I'm afraid there's not much I can do," he said. "Technically, there was no malfunction. Did you enter the temporal translator? No, you didn't. So, if you didn't enter and program it to send you back into the past, how could you have exited fifteen minutes earlier?"

Matthew and Joanna tried to explain that they *did* want to go in, but it would be weird to show up at the time they did not remember they had been at. Or something. The technician shook his head again.

"Look," he explained. "The fact is that you *didn't* enter the time machine and that you *didn't* go to the past. What you *wanted* to do, but *didn't*, is in fact your problem." He cleaned up his gear, reassembled the device and left.

Matthew and Joanna were confused. They fooled around a little, just to get the frustration out of their systems, and then decided that they would think about it the following day.

The next day, they agreed that Matthew would enter the time machine and follow the standard procedure: go back twenty minutes into the past, even if they both knew that nothing like that had really happened. They also guessed their problem might have been mentioned in the paragraph about opening new time branches. Well, they had not opened any new ones so far, and it was about time they tried.

They decided on the combination with two Matthews and one Joanna. After fifteen minutes of waiting and petting, Matthew stood up, programmed the console and entered the time machine. A soft "ping" indicated the booth had sent its traveler twenty minutes into the past. Joanna waited, and waited, and waited. She then approached the time machine and looked at the console. All it read was DEVICE IN ORDER. Timidly, as if afraid she would see a pile of shapeless protoplasm inside, she opened the door. Nothing; it was empty.

Joanna closed the door and opened it again—empty. As the panic was pouring all over her, she took a deep breath, called the service department, and started crying.

When the repairman arrived, he found the girl, wrapped up in sheets and tears, sitting on the floor next to the machine. She barely managed to stutter out what had happened. The repairman nodded and skillfully started working. (However, it did cross his mind to simply unbutton his pants and say: "This is really not your day, huh?" and use some of his other skills. Luckily, his professional ethics prevailed.)

The repairman spent half a day checking the machine parts scattered across the room. In the meantime, Joanna got up, got dressed, and got a grip on herself, enough to make them some coffee, just as the repairman cried out and lifted up one small part of the translator. He placed it into the device he had brought with him, pushed some buttons, and checked out the results.

"Now I know what's wrong," he said, shaking his head. "Just a moment."

He called the service shop with his communicator. Some fifteen minutes later, a car arrived. The repairman went out and returned, holding up a metal part looking exactly the same as the one he had inspected and found faulty. He replaced it in the temporal translator and finished the reassembly.

"Let's see if it's working now," the repairman glanced around and grabbed the geranium which Joanna and Matthew had initially used to test the device. He placed it inside the machine and sent it to the future. After the "ping," he took out the geranium.

"Let's duplicate something, just to be sure," he said, and put his bag down. At that moment, Joanna heard another "ping," and the repairman's double stepped out of the machine.

The men shook hands and exchanged a few old jokes, and then one of them entered the machine, disappearing with one more "ping." The other man turned happily to Joanna.

"Well, that was it!"

She regarded him with confusion.

"What about Matthew, then?"

The repairman's enthusiasm disappeared. He shrugged and looked at the floor.

"You'll have to call Customer Relations for that." He grabbed his things and quickly left the apartment.

Joanna stood in the empty apartment, battling a growing despair. Time passed. Eventually, she went to the phone and called Customer Relations to explain the situation. They asked about the translator's make and its serial number. They wanted to see the repairman's report first and instructed her to call again tomorrow. Joanna put down the receiver and went to bed, tears rolling. Later, she called to work and told them she needed a day off. Something in her voice made them believe her.

The next day she was told the report had been received, but that the case was forwarded to the Science Department. They would let her know as soon as they learned anything. Once again, she put the phone down, feeling dizzy. She spent the rest of the day curled up in the armchair.

Later that evening she heard a "ping" from the machine and jumped hopefully. The door opened and she saw — herself. A moment of unease, and then both women fell into each other's arms, comforting each other. Joanna felt a bit better. A woman's shoulder was the best cushion for a crying woman, as generations of women had long ago established. Besides, she knew she was with someone who understood her completely, who did not need explanations of her thoughts — so the joy of retelling and complaining was even a greater release.

They hugged a little more. The younger Joanna finally

asked the one who had come out of the time machine what had actually happened. The older Joanna just shrugged.

"I come from the future one week away," she said. "And I don't bring great news. Five days from now, the service department will call and offer some explanation about interlinking of temporal flows, and that Matthew had probably ended up in an alternative branch."

"But they said there was always only one branch, that the others disappeared!" cried the younger Joanna.

"That information is two months old, as is the manual," said the older Joanna. "This area is still relatively new and unexplored. Some people claim such devices should not be launched onto the market because of all sorts of trouble that might happen. The scare of the competition rushed them to get the patent hastily. As for Matthew, he should be alive and well in some parallel time branch, together with another Matthew and Joanna."

"But is he ever going to return?"

"I'm afraid the probability for that is close to zero. You see, every alteration opens a new temporal branch and, by now, there may be just about an infinite number of them. First, the probability of this kind of time jump is one in a billion. When it happens, if you try to reach it, more likely a completely new branch would open, rather than the two existing ones connecting."

"So, what do we do now?" asked the younger Joanna, all depressed.

The older Joanna shrugged. "I don't know. I'm here to help you get over all this," she said as they hugged.

The older Joanna had brought pajamas with her from the future, so they both went to bed and slept in each other's arms. In the morning, the younger Joanna had to go to work while the older Joanna promised to cook a nice dinner.

During the next few days, as they waited for the report from the Science Department, they lived in a genuine sorority -like happy family, so that the shock caused by Matthew's disappearance was slowly fading away. The report came in on the fifth day, exactly as the older Joanna had said. They fell into each other's arms for comfort, and when they stopped crying, they continued to hug and cuddle. A few minutes later this became more than just innocent embracing. They looked into each other's eyes for a few seconds and soon their clothes ended up on the floor. Later, they lay in bed, naked and pleased, deep in their own thoughts.

"You have to go back in two days, you know," said the older Joanna.

The younger Joanna nodded. "Shall we sue the manufacturer?" she asked.

"Yes. That is, I'll sue them. I'm staying here and you are going one week into the past to close the other side of the knot, to become me. You have to explain to our predecessor what happened and comfort her so that she deals with the loss more easily. But don't tell her about us, as I didn't tell you, although I knew what would happen. Let it happen by itself."

The younger Joanna nodded. She was looking at the ceiling and thinking. Over the last few days, a new feeling had been awakening in her. She grew more devoted to the person who had come out of the time machine, who knew what would happen and who, even though it had actually been her, seemed somehow more experienced and wiser. So what if Matthew would never return? So be it; it could not be changed, and she had to learn to accept it. Besides, her friend Mathilda was always saying life was only real without men. Who needed them anyway?

"I don't want us ever to split," said the young Joanna.

"And we won't," said the older Joanna. "Matthew was insured, remember? The insurance money plus the reimbursement for his disappearance—quite a pile. Enough to live normally, keep the time machine in continuous run, and do some traveling—maybe even around the world for two."

Yes, indeed, there was nothing that could not be done with

the help of the temporal translator machine. Joanna could, practically, live her life twice over, if she kept returning to the past every two weeks, and thus keep tying a sequence of temporal knots to enable the two Joannas to exist at the same time. As far as the trip around the world was concerned, she would just make a few jumps to the past, each for one week, so that they both could go on that cruise together.

Yes, she realized, it was going to be a beautiful life.

"I'm glad I have you," said the younger Joanna.

They embraced each other and fell asleep.

Blood of Bacchus

by
William Markly
O'Neal

Who hasn't been in the deepest pit of despair and hoped some savior would appear to make everything better? A fantasy like that rarely becomes reality, but it does for Dennis when four beautiful women find him drowning in booze on the streets. These women offer him something far greater than just a helping hand: a divine promotion that is everything he never could have expected but has always needed... at least, that's certainly how it seems.

Contemporary Dark Fantasy
Greek/Roman mythology
Folklore
Orgy (male + females)
Masturbation
Lesbian sex
Lust

A series of bad breaks and miserable luck have driven Dennis Dixon into the gutter. His life is lousy and he's convinced his situation is only going to get worse.

The last thing he expects is for someone to offer to make him a God.

Dennis exits the Save-On Liquor store and pulls up the collar on his ragged coat. He shambles across the parking lot, walks beside the building, then skirts around to the back alley, already unscrewing the cap on the bottle hidden in a brown paper sack.

Dennis has been Residence Challenged since last October. He lived in his car until just before Christmas, and then he sold his Chevy so he could drink some holiday cheer. He moved into the Christian Center, but they have strict rules and he broke them repeatedly until finally, about a week ago, they kicked him out. He's been living in a cardboard box under an overpass near Shadyside Park, about three miles across town. He stole some cash before he was kicked out of the homeless shelter—that was the sinful straw that broke the Christian camel's back—and that money just ran out today. After eating out of a Dumpster, he used his last ten bucks to purchase a bottle of Paul Masson.

While the vino lasts, Dennis will be as fine as frog's hair. What lies beyond this last bottle, however.... he doesn't want to know.

In a deserted alley behind the liquor store, Dennis takes six serious swigs from the bottle. The wine tastes especially good this evening.

It's March fifteenth, and it's cold tonight. For the first time since he got kicked out of the Christian Center, Dennis is feeling chilled.

"God, this tastes good," he mutters, taking another pull from the bottle. Seeing a cinder block, he sits down in the shadow of the building and guzzles.

The more he drinks, the warmer he feels.

Most of his adult life, Dennis Dixon has found comfort in the depths of inebriation. Tonight is no different.

He sits in the same spot for the better part of two hours, drinking the entire bottle of wine.

On an unconscious level, he is aware the Maenads are searching for him.

His drunkenness will lead them to him.

Unknowingly, Dennis sits waiting for the women who will worship him.

When he's finally taken the last swallow, he glares down at the empty bottle, as if it's a traitor.

Suddenly Dennis feels like he's being watched. He looks up and is startled by the Bacchante, who stand in a dim pool of light thrown by a nearby lamp pole. Initially, he sees double, thinking there are eight individuals when actually there are four.

They are the most beautiful women he's ever seen.

And they smell *heavenly*. His nose has been dead almost as long as his libido—both destroyed by his alcoholism. He tilts his head up like a bloodhound catching a scent, inhaling deeply the Maenads' perfume.

Dennis falls in love with them even before they offer him Divinity.

All four of the beauties now kneel before him. They are dressed in identical purple overcoats which hang all the way to their ankles. His eyes wide, his nostrils flaring, Dennis watches with awe and growing excitement as the women introduce themselves.

The first to rise is a tall blond woman with big, blue eyes

and enormous breasts. "I am Nysa, your humble servant," she declares. "I bring wine to awaken the God."

Enchanted by her eyes and angelic face, Dennis hadn't even noticed until now that she's holding a bottle (and that's mighty enchanted indeed). Sauntering up to him, Nysa puts her fingers on his mouth, gently pulling his jaw open. She then splashes Dom Perignon onto his tongue.

He shudders with delight. This is *nectar* to him!

Dennis guzzles until Nysa stops pouring. The first Maenad bows her blond head, then backs away.

Three Bacchante remain kneeling before him. The next to rise is a beautiful black woman with enormous breasts, her long hair laced in dreadlocks. She tells Dennis, "I am Macris, your humble servant. I bring figs to enliven the God."

"Frigs?" Dennis frowns. He points at Nysa, sputtering, "I like her gift better."

Macris smiles as she feeds him the figs.

Tasting better than he could ever imagine, the figs instantly alleviate the gnawing ache in his gut caused by acute hunger.

Before she slinks away, Macris gives Dennis a kiss on the cheek. She smells even better than the Dom Perignon.

As one Maenad steps back, another rises. This purple-clad maiden is a petite Asian woman with enormous breasts, her hair done up in a bun and secured with bamboo hair sticks. "I am Bromie, your humble servant. I bring a leopard skin to clad the kindling God."

His old coat is dear to him; it's become his most prized possession since he sold his car; and yet, when Nysa and Macris move behind him to remove it, he doesn't stop them. For the first (but not last) time, Dennis wonders if he's dreaming. He lets the women do with him what they will.

The shirt he wears beneath his jacket is threadbare and, despite all the antifreeze in his body, Dennis takes a chill when his coat is removed. But then the leopard skin is draped over one shoulder and wrapped around him, and he is suddenly warmer than he has been since last summer.

Eagerly, he looks to the last woman, a raven-haired Latino with enormous breasts. She rises, telling Dennis, "And I am Erato, your humble servant."

When she says no more, Dennis wants to know, "Wha'd you bring me?"

After giving him a quick kiss, Erato walks her fingers down his chest to his belly, before reaching down to brush her hand across his crotch. Dennis gasps, astonished when he feels a reaction down there. He is only forty-four years old, but even before the booze he had a fairly low sex drive. It's been years since his dick last did something clever.

The women walk a circle around him, making Dennis dizzy.

"Will you fly away with us?" asks Nysa.

"Will you drink wine with us?" asks Macris.

"Will you have sex with us?" asks Bromie.

"Will you become our God?" asks Erato.

Grinning like the village idiot he is, Dennis says, "Oh yeah!"

"Come!"

Four hands reach out for him.

The women lead him out of the alley to a stretch limousine parked beside the liquor store. Dennis is awed. He's never been inside a limo.

On the drive out of town, the Bacchantes supply more Dom Perignon, while showering Dennis with kisses.

A half hour later, the ride ends at a private airstrip, where a small jet awaits. Dennis has never flown before and isn't certain he wants to start now.

As they all exit the limo, he hesitates. "Where are we going? Can't we just drive?"

Nysa says, "We've got a long way to go tonight."

Macris informs him, "We're taking you to a vineyard

where we will make you Divine."

Bromie asks, "You *do* want to be a God, don't you?"

He feels like he's already halfway there. "Well, sure, but..."

He stops talking when Erato opens up her long purple overcoat to reveal her nude body. Dennis's mouth falls open. He feels a tingle in his groin.

When he looks to the other women, they also open their overcoats to show that they are naked underneath.

Erato shrugs her coat off her shoulders, letting it fall to the ground. When she walks away, headed toward the plane, Dennis is hypnotized by the sight of her big, tan butt. She looks back over her shoulder, her brown eyes twinkling as she asks, "Are you coming?"

Nysa, Macris, and Bromie also leave behind their purple wraps and walk, bare-assed, to the plane.

Drooling, Dennis Dixon follows.

The pilot of the jet is a hot brunette woman Dennis only glimpses. After they are in the air, his seat belt is unbuckled and Dennis is taken to a cabin in the back of the plane, where a king-size bed covered in silk sheets is heaped with pillows.

The Bacchantes strip Dennis of the rest of his filthy clothing. The touch of their hands excites him almost as much as the expensive wine they keep pouring down his throat.

By the time he's naked—they even take away his leopard skin—he's also fully erect. He looks down at his turgid dick and says, "Hey, buddy! Long time no see!"

Erato snickers.

He pulls one woman in for a kiss, then another. He alternates between sucking Bromie's perky pink nipples and licking Macris's dark-brown breasts. At some point, Erato and Nysa slip out of the cabin.

The women insist on bathing him. He is taken to a shiny, bright bathroom, where he slips into a tub of steaming water. The bath is big enough for one of the girls to get in with him.

He chooses Bromie. Of all the Bacchante, he is most intrigued by her. He's always been attracted to Asian women. She's also the only one of the four with a shaved pussy.

The Chosen One and the Maenad play in the tub, splashing, groping, drinking wine. Dennis gets cleaner than he has been in years.

After his bath, he is led back to the bedroom. Erato reappears, bringing him more wine. For an indeterminate length of time thereafter, Dennis fades in and out of awareness. He never loses consciousness; he just drinks so much he has periods of black-out where he remembers nothing.

The next few hours are a blur of cold wine, occasional turbulence, and hot female flesh.

At one point, he finds himself alone with Bromie, his dick again on the rise. He spontaneously commands her to fuck him.

Flatly, she refuses: "No."

This is not the answer Dennis expected or wanted. "You girls made me horny, babe. At least suck me off."

"No."

Angry, he snaps, "I thought you were here to serve me! I thought I was your God!"

With eyes as flat as her tone, Bromie responds, "You *will* be… but you aren't yet."

"What?" This infuriates him. He's not *completely* a God, no, but he's already *mostly* Divine, and for this wench not to recognize that is an affront. Dennis pounds his chest, telling her, "The God is *already* here and you *will* service him!" He grabs her by the wrist. "Now suck my dick!"

"No!" she says, pulling away.

As she flees the cabin, Dennis shouts, "Fine! Be gone! You offend me!"

Dennis picks up a bottle of wine and guzzles from it.

When the plane lands, nearly five hours later, Dennis is

asleep. His lovely servants awaken him, clothing him in his leopard skin, draping it over his shoulders. Elegant sandals are placed on his feet. A wreath made from grape vines is placed in his wild hair. His loins and legs are left naked.

Exiting the plane, Dennis finds another waiting limousine. The temperature here is at least twenty degrees warmer than the city he left behind. "Where are we?" he asks the Maenads.

"California."

"California?" Dennis can't believe it. He never dreamed he'd ever visit California. This lush Land of Libations has always seemed more remote to him than the moon.

"Think of it as 'New Greece,' if you prefer," says Bromie, causing Nysa to laugh.

Dennis dozes off again during the ensuing drive. The next thing he's aware of is the door beside him being opened and Erato saying, "We're here."

Wiping his eyes, Dennis gets out of the car and looks around. The night is dark, the sky overcast. The Bacchante use flashlights to lead their Chosen One through the vineyard.

Dennis realizes he isn't staggering at all and he hasn't been slurring his speech. He's as drunk as he's ever been but this drunk is different somehow. He feels fantastic. He isn't just buzzing; he's keenly *aware*.

Dennis finds himself looking at the grapevines more than at the naked butts ahead of him. He suddenly proclaims, "Bless this vineyard! May its harvest this year be especially bountiful!"

The women smile with approval.

After walking for nearly ten minutes, they come to a small forest, at the apparent end of the vineyard. Dennis is led down a path through the woods. Strings of twinkling lights have been strung in a canopy of high branches above them.

Suddenly, the women stop. Without being told, Dennis knows it's time for the final gifts. He rubs his hands together, like King Midas anticipating gold.

Erato slips behind a tall oak tree, returning a moment later with a gift that causes Dennis to grin. It is a long fennel staff, covered with ivy vines and topped with a pinecone. Erato bows before him, saying, "I present the sacred thyrsus. May it please the God and serve Him well."

Dennis is aware of something stirring deep inside him, some alien feeling struggling to be born.

Nysa moves to the foot of another tree, removing a tarp to reveal ancient wine jugs decorated with painted grapevines. These are distributed among the Maenad, one jug for each of the naked beauties.

Nysa breezes up to him, saying, "Let us Transform you!"

Macris brushes her body against his, purring, "Let us Empower you!"

Bromie pleads with him, "Let us Remake you!"

Erato begs him, "Let us Reveal the Divinity within you!"

Together the four chant as one, "Come, let us suck you and fuck you and service your cock!"

Immediately, said cock gets hard.

After a giggle, Dennis gives his answer, "Okay."

Then the Maenads ask together, again in perfect unison, "Will you accept the Blood of Life and become Zagreus the Liberator; Bacchus, Twice-Born Son of Zeus; He Of The Loud Shout; He Of The Trees; He Who Releases; the Great Ecstatic God of the Vine?"

All around him, unseen, dozens of female voices join that of his four attendants, crying out, "WILL YOU BE OUR DIONYSUS?"

Proudly, Dennis announces, "I will!"

Nysa is the first to give him a guzzle from her wine jug. Dennis can't fool himself. This tastes *nothing* like wine.

Next comes Macris, then Bromie, and finally Erato. By the time he takes the final drink of blood, it is tasting really good to him, every bit as sweet as Zinfandel.

The blood of the previous Deity dribbles down Dennis'

face, down his chest, staining the leopard skin.

Suddenly, a bright light bursts forth from the Chosen One's heart. Backing away from him, the Maenads shield their eyes. The clearing is quickly filled with dazzling illumination.

The last surviving Olympian is once again reborn into the bosom of his ardent followers. Dennis Dixon permits the transformation, allowing his own consciousness to be supplanted by the mind of a God.

Dionysus lives again.

As the heavenly light dims, the son of Zeus steps forward and says, "Ladies!" He pauses, a grin spreading across His face, before He proclaims, "I have returned!"

Nysa, Macris, Bromie, and Erato all squeal with delight, as do dozens of women hidden in the trees. A female cheer rises in the forest.

Dionysus strides down the path, out of the woods, into His sacred glade. Wherever the God walks, new ivy springs up beneath His feet.

The oval clearing is nearly the size of a football field, shaped by a thick ring of trees. The Glen of the God is alive with activity; everywhere women are talking and laughing. When Bacchus makes His entrance, His followers stop what they are doing and run to pay homage to Him.

In other times, He had male sycophants, including satyrs, but here, in this New World, His worshipers are strictly women.

Grape arbors are scattered throughout the dale and, with the return of Bacchus, vines that have slept shriveled all winter now swell with reawakened vibrancy. In the center of the clearing is an old, dead fig tree, which also bursts to life anew. Dionysus is delighted to see a lioness tethered to the tree — a healthy, beautiful beast who is watching the God with keen interest. With a simple gesture, Bacchus causes the lioness' collar to unravel, freeing her.

Dozens of domesticated cats are also enjoying the glen, all

of them seemingly engaged in games of tag, tail chasing, or other frenetic activities.

In the northern part of the glade is a large open shed, which houses a generator and a few other modern conveniences. Numerous lamp poles light the clearing, with cables running underground, back to the little barn. Beside the shed are the coolers and refrigerators where various wines are chilled. And sitting on long wooden tables are heated aquariums containing dozens of boa constrictors.

Blankets are strewn everywhere, as are mounds of pillows and various types of mattresses.

In the southern part of the glen is a raised wooden platform, octagonal in shape, ten yards in diameter, standing about five feet off the ground. That stage is accessed by two long, gradually sloping ramps.

As ladies rush to genuflect to their God, Dionysus gestures expansively, declaring, "LET THE ORGY BEGIN!"

Women squeal and applaud and cheer.

Most in His congregation are already naked. Those revelers who aren't nude already shed the last of their clothing. Everywhere He looks, the God sees bare-skinned partisans. Women with lutes begin to play a song by The Doors. Hearing "Don't You Love Her Madly" causes Dionysus to laugh.

(Deep within the Deity, Dennis Dixon watches ecstatically as women throw themselves at him.)

Bacchus is eager to join His Maenads, eager to induce in His followers the Holy Ecstasies they so desperately crave, but He has business to attend to first, before He can enjoy Himself.

He Of The Loud Shout turns to face the four beauties who brought Him (Dennis) to this Holy place. Holding His thyrsus in His right hand, He points at Bromie with His left, yelling, "YOU!" He instantly grows four inches in height, His chest and biceps swelling. His face is still mostly obscured by wild hair but His features are now supremely handsome. The rough visage of Dennis Dixon has been remade spectacularly as a

God. The crown of vines He wears has sprouted giant red grapes.

As He directs His fury at Bromie, His eyes take on a similar color as the fruit.

Bromie falls to the ground, cowering before Him, whimpering with fear.

It is Nysa who exclaims, "Oh my God!" She turns and asks Bromie, "What did you do?"

"She denied My Godhood," declares Dionysus. "When I commanded her to suck My dick, she refused."

Several women gasp.

Bromie begins to silently weep.

Nysa looks at Bromie with mad disbelief. "What does He mean, you refused? We discussed this! You know the old stories! You read Euripides, right? *The Bacchae*? You read it, didn't you?" She shrieks, *"Didn't you?"*

Bromie nods. "He drove His own family mad for failing to recognize Him!"

Tears stream down Nysa's checks as she shouts, "Then *whyyyy?*"

Bromie looks up at them with pleading eyes, sobbing, "I just couldn't do it, okay? He was just so *gross!* I just couldn't *believe* it. I've only been to this Gathering for the last two years and frankly—" She laughs humorlessly. "I barely remember either time."

"She never should have been allowed to Attend!" whispers Macris to Erato, loud enough for them all to hear. This is the third time in the last decade Macris has been an Attendant to the God's Awakening.

Nysa—who Bacchus knows vouched for Bromie—gives Macris a withering look.

Erato remains focused on Bromie, trying to understand how this calamity happened. "But you knew the God is real." Sharply, Erato asks, *"Right?"*

"Yes! But I didn't... didn't..." Bromie covers her face with her hands and bawls.

"SAY IT!" demands the Son of Zeus.

Immediately Bromie's hands drop away from her face. She looks directly at Dionysus and admits, "I didn't think you were the One. You were just so *ugly* I couldn't believe you could become the God."

Bacchus snarls with anger, thrusting out His arms, raising His thyrsus high. His eyes blaze with Divine energy, a crackling aura appearing around His head.

(Dennis Dixon knows what is about to happen and believes he has the power to stop it. As far as their jointly shared body is concerned, Dionysus is in the driver's seat but Dennis has the means of applying the brakes. He does nothing, however, to stave off Bacchus' wrath because he understands the God's fury.)

Fire suddenly shoots out of Dionysus' eyes, a ray of raw power that cuts the atmosphere like lightning, causing a hot gasp of thunder. Bromie is struck by the God's celestial magick and doesn't even have time to scream before she's promptly transmogrified into a black panther.

Women gasp in awe and wonder. Nysa begins to weep. Bacchus now understands that Nysa and Bromie were lovers.

Dionysus walks over to the panther, gently cupping her face as He looks into sad cat eyes. His own eyes flash with one last spark of anger as He declares, "Serve Me better in this form than you did in the last or I will turn you into wine and consume you!"

His punishment meted out, it's now time to party. The Olympian turns to Nysa, holding a hand out to her, gesturing her to come to Him. She does, kneeling before Him, wiping tears off her lovely face. "Rise," He says, and when she stands before Him, He runs the back of His hand down her body, across her breasts, causing her nipples to harden. Nysa gasps with pleasure.

Dionysus grabs her face and roughly kisses her. Where

Dennis Dixon's hard-on was a meager thing, barely average, Dionysus has a twelve-inch cock, thick and heavy, with testicles the size of billiard balls. He grinds his Godhood against Nysa as He bites His own lip, causing His blood to flow.

And so it is that Nysa becomes the first of the Maenads to be released — the first this year to know euphoric madness.

Wine and blood gurgle into her mouth, as pussy juice slickens her quivering thighs. She breaks the kiss with a moan, then gasps and squeals with sensual delight. Her body shudders and rocks in the throes of one powerful climax after another. As Dionysus steps back from her, she collapses, crumpling to the ground, where she writhes and squirms as she rides the waves of multiple orgasms.

Dionysus tells them, "When I am next Awakened, I expect my Attendants to be more respectful and better informed."

Nysa wails in ecstasy.

Macris and Erato, however, say, "Yes, Great God! It will be done!"

"Come," Dionysus says gently, now smiling. Dropping his thyrsus, He wraps His arms around Macris and Erato. They instantly go weak at the knees. With a hand beneath each of their shapely butts, he picks them up and carries them out to the center of the glen, near the fig tree where the lioness lies watching. He tells His Bacchante, "We must put that unpleasantness behind us. You have done well, my Maenads, and you shall be rewarded with pleasures beyond compare! The two of you will be the first of the Privileged Few who will know what it's like to copulate with a God! I will bestow upon you the hedonic raptures of Holy Sex!"

Naked women of all shapes and sizes now gather around Him. Kisses and caresses are exchanged by one and all. "Yes, yes," He tells His congregation. "Bear witness now, my lovelies, as Macris and Erato receive my Blessings!"

Dionysus takes Erato into His arms and lowers her gently to the ground. Grass, which had been browned by winter

freezes, turns green again. A bed of ivy grows in an instant beneath Erato's body. Bacchus kisses the woman, causing her vagina to gush. The moment He slides His God-cock into her, his Latina attendant has an orgasm.

Dionysus lifts Erato up and slips beneath her, lying on His back so she can ride His erection. He gestures for Macris, who hurries over and straddles His face. She purrs like a cat as she experiences climaxes brought about by the world's oldest, cleverest tongue.

A wave of sexual energy rolls off Bacchus and the Bacchante. Many women are masturbating but even those who aren't touching themselves suddenly experience their own powerful orgasms, just from watching. Screamers and moaners and gaspers join together in an erotic chorus.

(And, deep within the God, Dennis Dixon also experiences carnal euphoria. As a young man, his favorite sexual fantasy was having sex with two women at the same time, in exactly this position, with one pussy grinding on his dick and another pussy pressing against his face. He remembers his first girlfriend, back in high school, recalling how much he wanted to fuck her. She never gave him the chance.)

(But now, as a treat to him, Dionysus uses his magick to alter Macris' appearance, at least for Dennis' sake, so he sees his old girlfriend in his arms. Erato is made to look like another teenage girl that teenage Dennis Dixon once had a crush on.)

(It's a blast from the past, a gift from the God, and Dennis is thrilled.)

As Dionysus lies on His back, licking Macris, dicking Erato, women begin to lose control of themselves. The blood hasn't even begun to flow yet and already some maidens are mad with passion. Dozens of hands reach out to touch the God, to caress Him, to feel His newly made flesh. A mere brush of His skin is enough to cause intense libidinous bliss.

Macris and Erato are going wild, shrieking, pulling at their hair, their bodies shaking like they're experiencing grand-mal seizures. Finally, the fat Olympian releases Macris's butt and she topples off him, panting, drenched in sweat.

As if she weighs no more than a kitten, Dionysus picks Erato up, holding her in His powerful arms. He moves over to the fig tree, putting Erato's back against it. He fucks her standing up, His hands beneath her, supporting her while he simultaneously fondles her ass. Beside Him, the lioness flops to the ground, experiencing her own feline orgasm, her tail twitching against Dionysus's ankles.

(Within Bacchus, Dennis remembers the first time he ever saw a pornographic film depicting a reverse gang bang, where two men fucked fourteen women. He found that movie especially hot, and Bacchus now seeks to turn another of His host's fantasies into reality. In this way, Dionysus and Dennis grow even closer, their needs and desires intertwining.)

"Turn around," the God commands his adherents. He never misses a stroke, continuing to copulate with Erato, who is absolutely wailing. "Show me your asses."

Dozens of women are quick to comply, giving Bacchus a good look at their fannies.

"You, you, you..." He points and picks the best butts, allowing the Dennis within to influence His selections. "You, you, you, and you. Line up, all of you. On your knees."

As horny devotees hurry to comply with His wishes, Dionysus bends down and begins licking Erato's nipples, alternating from one to the other, gently nibbling. This extra stimulation pushes her over the edge, causing her to scream as she reaches climax.

Dropping Erato's limp, twitching body next to Macris, Bacchus now steps back to inspect the seven raised asses that await him.

(The Dennis inside has never seen a sexier sight.)

Dropping to his knees, Dionysus mounts the first woman from behind, slipping His dick inside her. He roughly squeezes her swinging breasts as He doggy-fucks her to orgasm.

The second of the seven women offering herself to Him enjoys having her ears nibbled while being screwed. He plasters His damp front parts against her moist back parts, holding her tight.

The third of seven ladies likes having her ass slapped. By the time the Olympian is through humping her, her buttocks are bright red.

Masturbating maidens surround the God and His seven lovers. Some women sit or lie back on the ground, playing with themselves. Others stand and watch, while frantically rubbing clits — either their own or someone else's.

A wall of wriggling female flesh surrounds Bacchus. Every eye watches His every move, with ever-increasing desire.

"Bring me drink!"

At His command, His beauties are quick to provide libations, pouring the most expensive wines down His throat as He continues to fornicate. After pleasing the third of seven daughters, Dionysus moves on to the fourth, who prefers anal to vaginal intercourse. He holds a handful of her long, damp hair, pulling it, as she shoves back to meet His Godhood's blunt assault of her ass.

The fifth of seven women grunts and puffs throughout her fuck, often looking back over her shoulder at Him with savagely bright eyes. When she reaches climax she squirts like a fountain.

The sixth of seven lovers enjoys being called a 'bitch' and a 'slut' while fornicating. Nuzzling His face up next to her ear, Dionysus calls her dirty names. Her perspiring flesh smells faintly of almonds.

The seventh of the seven fucks is with a virgin, the seventeen-year-old daughter of one of Dionysus' older followers. When the Deity breaks her hymen with his God-cock, she feels no pain, only the most intense pleasure imaginable.

Looking down, seeing the young one's blood on His monster prick, Bacchus can hold out no longer. He shouts to all the assembled women here, "GATHER 'ROUND, MY MAIDENS, SO THAT YOU MAY KNOW ME!"

This is how a Deity announces He's about to come.

As the (no longer) virgin girl goes numb with tactile joy, Bacchus pulls out of her, points His dick at the mob of Maenads, and cries out as He achieves a monumental climax. Instead of semen, the liquid that sprays from Dionysus' penis looks to be either wine or blood (and is actually a mixture of both). His first volley of God-seed flies in an arc over twenty yards into the air, raining down on dozens of women, who throw back their heads and throw open their mouths. Those who consume His juices are toppled by their own violent orgasms.

Bacchus' cock sprays another blast, then another, and another. With each eruption of bloodwine, more women are felled, as if He's mowing them down with Tommy-gun fire. The clearing is soon carpeted in a writhing, wriggling mass of females. And still the geyser-like ejaculations keep coming.

Grunting with every pulse of his cock, Dionysus experiences a Divine Climax that lasts thirty-three minutes, expelling gallons of liquid. Inside Him, Dennis Dixon shares in the delirium.

By the time Bacchus is done, not a single lady is left standing. More than three hundred women, soaked red, lie together in ecstasy, connected by the God and their own mad desires.

Hours pass. Bacchus provides not only uncountable gratifications but also infinite wetness, infinite stamina. Those who tire are immediately re-energized. Nerves that become oversensitive to pleasure are instantly soothed. Women lick and lap and love other women. Women dance and sing, wrapping snakes around their bodies, holding serpents in the air. The orgy rages with a frantic, bestial ferocity inspired by the wine and blood of Dionysus.

An hour before dawn, after having His third half-hour orgasm of the night, Bacchus tires. He staggers away from the women, panting. They pursue Him, grabbing at Him, clutching at Him, screaming His tributes. As His passion wanes, the mob's passion grows. He tries to shrug them off, tries to get away, but He doesn't have the strength.

Suddenly Nysa is there, taking Bacchus into her greedy arms. His Loud Shout is no more. Dionysus sounds meek, like Dennis Dixon, as He cries, "What's happening to me?"

Nysa grabs His head and pulls Him into a tongue kiss. Hers aren't the only hands on Him; He's completely surrounded. He feels Nysa's wet crotch against His limp dick, putting out an inferno of heat. When her tongue tangles with His, He feels a brief twinge in His groin. He thinks He's going to get hard again; He thinks everything is going to be all right.

But then Nysa lures His tongue into her mouth and snaps shut her teeth. She not only bites down hard, she twists her head, and *pulls*.

The God screams as His tongue is ripped out.

Blood streams from His mouth and, seeing it, the women are driven into a frenzy. Like starving zombies seeing brains, they fight to get at Him. They rip and claw and punch each other in an effort to drink more of His blood.

Dionysus is trapped, His power on the wane. He can't think clearly. Parts of Dennis Dixon gurgle up in His brain, causing Him fear.

(Dennis knows it is all going wrong; it's all slipping away. These women lifted him from dismal depths to this highest of sensual heights and he won't go back to the miserable existence of a useless drunk without a fight. He joins what little strength he has with Dionysus, determined to get away from these wicked women, desperate to live.)

The combined weight of this crazed crowd is too much for Him; Bacchus can't break through the mob. And so, frantic to have more physical power, the God transforms Himself into a bull.

This Bacchus does every year, forgetting, as always, that it's a fatal mistake.

When Dionysus is transformed, the mania of the multitude reaches a new crescendo. The bull manages to gore a few women with its horns but then it's flipped over and hoisted into the air. It continues to fight but the Maenads are oblivious to the dangers.

The mob carries the bull up onto the wooden platform in the southern part of the glen. This is why this platform was built. On the stage, the metal floor beneath them is grated, with long thin holes in it. Beneath the grate, inside this structure, is an enormous wine vat.

All of this is designed to catch the primordial blood of the Greek God of Wine.

The crazed ecstasies of the Bacchante give them strength far beyond that provided by adrenaline. Hands puncture the bull's hide as if they are knives. Teeth gnash and gnaw. Nails rip and rend and tear. Two women join together to grab a horn and, with a banshee cry, they snap it off. A flailing leg follows, pulled off by a quartet of shrieking Maenads.

The eyes of the bull-God are bulging as they're gouged from His sockets.

Dionysus is ripped to pieces.

Once the bull is dead, the women abandon it, leaving the shredded body parts draining on the platform.

The orgy then continues until just after sunup, but with somewhat reduced intensity.

When the gathering in the Glen of the God finally comes to an end, women from every corner of America prepare themselves to return to their normal lives. No one slept a wink tonight but everyone feels completely refreshed. Women leave this place newly inspired, content and happy, minds brimming with fresh ideas, hearts exploding with fresh hopes.

In the wake of madness, the Maenads are at peace.

The blood of the Bacchus-bull is collected from the vats and placed in clay jugs. It will be used next year to again re-awaken the God.

Many women received injuries, most of them minor, but a few caused by bull horns could have been serious if there weren't already several doctors on the scene. Still, several ladies leave for hospitals. A few women remain to do the cleanup, including burying the remains of a bull who was once a God, who was once an alcoholic named Dennis Dixon.

Nysa, Macris, and Erato are the last three left in the glade, alone with Bromie. Nysa has decided she will keep the panther that was once her lover, even though it will mean moving to the country.

All of them now have wild, unruly hair.

Nysa's real name is Nancy. She asks the others, "It went pretty well, don't you think?" She's quick to add, "Except for Lucy being transformed, I mean." Lucy is Bromie's real name.

Nysa will never voice her feelings out loud but, as heart-broken as she is that Bromie is gone, having known the love of a true God helps to mitigate her loss.

Erato has already gone back to being Maria. She's too busy lighting up a cigarette to respond to Nancy.

Christine (who was Macris) asks, "Who will Attend next year, do you think?"

It's a rhetorical question. No one can know who will be Chosen to find the next Bacchus. Four women who were here tonight will have a vision three hundred sixty-three days from now and learn only then who will be the next drunkard to become Dionysus.

Eventually, the maidens each go their own ways, one with a docile black panther in tow.

"See you all next year!"

Call of Cunthulhu

by
Corwin Merrill

He's seen the Ancient Demigod in his visions, and he knows that he must follow its commands: Bring it human sacrifices. It just so happens that Nathan's modus operandi of wooing naïve young women into his bed is a perfect way for him to serve the Ancient Demigod. And when the young girl he's also seen in his visions walks into his office, it's all too easy. But the hot little piece of ass really gets his blood pumping, and nothing says Nathan can't use the innocent teen for his own sexual purposes first.

Horror
Cthulhu-inspired
Heterosexual sex
Heterosexual anal sex
Young-girl seduction
Cunnilingus and fellatio

Virgin sacrifice. It was such a pastiche. But Nathan Gormley knew better. The Ancient Demigod wouldn't demand a virgin female, but it would demand a life. Nathan had seen it in his visions as he'd worked to contact the Other Side, and it was a stunning visage: huge and hulking; moving on two monstrous, leathery legs; massive, tattered bat wings fanning the billowing smoke that poured out of its mouth as it breathed; a dozen wriggling tentacles flailing from its powerful green torso, lashing out before it, searching for its prey.

He knew she was The One from the first moment the stunning Tammy Kendrick walked into his real-estate office. She was fresh out of high school and had turned eighteen just prior to starting college a month before. Bouncy little B-cups teased him, jiggling just out of sight beneath her thin white blouse, with just a tease of cleavage and a flash of lacy bra peeking out its low-cut top. Her brown-blond hair was all sweeping waves and broad curls, hints of a hot Seventies chick with a modern-day style. She smiled with her whole face: full lips, bright teeth, high cheekbones, sparkling blue eyes. Her innocent schoolgirl walk was entrancing, with swaying hips that meant business as they swished her knee-length blue skirt above her short black boots. She was a dirty old man's ultimate wet dream—way too young and far too inexperienced, but the sweetest pussy any man could ever hope to sink his dick into. For a moment, he felt guilty, as if he were caught jacking off to the neighbor's seventh-grade daughter.

But only for a moment, and he welcomed the hard-on straining in his pants. It was clear, once she'd begun talking, that she wasn't some mindless teenager but a young woman with her life together. She'd just earned a trust her departed uncle had set up for her, and she was going to college—pre-med, she told him. They talked for twenty minutes, and she told him many details about her life. She wasn't a typical trust-fund baby; she was putting her uncle's money towards better-ing her life, and was even working a regular job in addition to her studies. The money was enough for all her schooling and living expenses. And it was also enough to buy a house, and she wanted Nathan to find her one.

Nathan listened intently and laughed and joked with her, and he engaged her deeper in the conversation. It was his job, after all, but his reasons were twofold: She was The One. He'd seen her in the visions the Ancient Demigod had given him over the preceding weeks. The visions finally made sense. She was his sacrificial lamb.

She couldn't suspect anything, and yet she had to be a willing participant. That meant wooing her first, and convinc-ing her to give herself so completely to him that she'd do any-thing he asked—including volunteering her blood.

Nathan freed up an entire day when Tammy had no classes and set up seven houses to show her. She met him at his office, and he was very pleased to see that her outfit put her previous attire to shame. Her black bra was clearly visible through her loosely buttoned peach top, and her black skirt was substantially higher up her thighs than the earlier model. She wore a petite leather jacket and high heels to match her blouse. Nathan was almost certain she had dressed like that just to get him hot and bothered, and from the moment she walked in she seemed to be subtly flirting with him. Of course, young girls often enjoyed subtly teasing forty-six-year-old men; it hardly meant she was ready to throw her ankles behind her ears. He'd have to work on that.

They drove from house to house, and he engaged her in

constant talk. He teased her, good-naturedly at first, and slowly getting more daring. She always laughed and teased back. He began slipping in subtle sexual innuendoes here and there, and she always found them funny. He steered the conversation to bad pick-up lines and carefully watched her reactions.

"How about the one where the guy says to the girl, 'I don't know who you are, but Heaven is missing one of its angels'?" he said, and she laughed.

"I can't believe any girls fall for that stuff," she said, twirling her hair in her right hand as she looked at him. Consistent eye contact meant she was reacting positively to him. Twirling the hair showed some level of sexual interest.

"I know, but they do," Nathan said as he drove. "My favorite is 'Honey, as long as I have a face, you'll always have a place to sit.'"

It was a big jump into taboo territory, but she howled with laughter, throwing her head back and her hands up. She raised her knees as she did, and he caught a glimpse of white panties between her splayed legs as the skirt rode up. Damn, there was nothing like teen pussy in cotton panties. When she recovered, she said, "I would never fall for something that stupid."

"So what's the worst pick-up line you've ever heard?" he said, and he looked at her when he said it. Her eyes darted between his, then dipped to look at his lips. She was interested.

She pursed her lips and thought, tilting her head and hunching a bit. He had a great view of her cleavage and the black lace of her bra, which seemed to just barely keep her tits from going anywhere. "Well, if you can believe this, a guy in my biology class asked me if I wanted to study with him, because he was sure he could teach me a lot about anatomy."

"Well, you can hardly blame the guy," Nathan said, taking a leap of faith. "Stunningly beautiful girl like you? A guy who figures he has no chance probably figures he's got nothing to lose, and maybe the surprise factor might win him a grope. I guess it's a good thing you have better taste than that."

He watched the road as he spoke, but out of the corner of his eye he could see her looking at him, trying to repress a big smile and her face pinking up a bit. She'd tilted her head to look at him, gently nibbling her lower lip. A pair of sexual-interest giveaways. But interest didn't mean willingness to go any further, he knew.

The house-hunting trip continued and, along the way, Nathan kept up with the subtle sexual references. By the time they left the sixth house, on the way to the seventh, the barriers had all pretty much come down.

"I'm just saying that a girl shouldn't *have* to do anal sex, or let him come on her face, or swallow his load in order to prove she loves her man," he argued. "These young guys will do anything to guilt a girl into doing those things."

"Right—I don't do those kinds of things with every guy I sleep with," she said. "Those things should be left to serious relationships."

He had her hooked on the line. He'd identified her boundaries, figured out the rules to her taboos. If he could break through those, he'd have her offering her blood.

"Makes sense," he said, nodding sagely. "You'd think these young guys would learn that romance matters first. Save the daring stuff for later, and focus on how important it is to kiss his girl—*really* kiss her—and hold her, and just appreciate being inside her. That's the ultimate in intimacy, and it should be enough. But young guys don't think the way women do; all they care about is getting laid. It isn't right."

And he knew the look she was trying not to give him.

At the final house, he knew the owners were gone for the month. As he showed her from room to room, he kept brushing against her as he showed her the house, and touching her back or shoulder to guide her. When he showed her the master bedroom, he knew the deal was sealed when she actually sat on the bed, skirted thighs slightly parted, leaning back on her hands, looking at him with big, round, blue eyes. She was trying to act nonchalant, trying not to look like she wanted it, but secretly hoping he'd initiate something.

So he finished talking about the carpeting in the master bedroom and the sliding glass doors with the backyard deck just outside, where the hot tub sat, and turned back to her. They locked eyes, exchanged smiles. She blushed a little, but didn't look away.

"Those young guys don't know what kind of woman they're missing in you, Tammy," he said, his voice soft but strong as he stood before her. "If I were twenty years younger, I'd do anything to have you."

"Why do you have to be twenty years younger?" she almost whispered, her voice trembling. He could see she was trembling, too.

He dropped to his knees before her, his eyes riveted to hers, and rested his hands on her bare thighs. They were smooth and silky, without a single blemish, and he squeezed his thumbs every so lightly on her inner thighs, just above the knees—just enough to tease. "Maybe I don't. Can I show you what I mean?"

"Yes," she said, breathless.

He leaned in closer, circling his fingers almost in place on her legs, subtly forcing her thighs ever so slightly apart. "I need to hear more than 'yes,' you beautiful woman," he said, boring his gaze through her eyes and deep into her soul. "I need to hear you tell me what you want me to do."

Her jaw shook as she said, "I want you to make love to me. Please make love to me." And she was practically begging, her voice cracking with desire.

Nathan smiled at her. "That's the sexiest thing I've ever heard a woman say," he whispered. Build up her ego. Put her on a pedestal. Control her. Own her.

He slid his hands under the hem of her skirt, sliding his fingers up to the strap of her underwear, and kept going as she leaned back onto the bed, lifting her hips slightly to allow him to push the skirt over her hips and pull her panties to the side. Her soft, furry vulva, neatly trimmed into a thin rectangular strip, framed a glistening slit that was begging him to taste her. He knew she'd been juicing up over him for hours. He leaned in, snaking his tongue out, and he imagined that tongue being one of the Ancient Demigod's tentacles forcing its way inside her. But there would be time enough for that later.

He slid his tongue between her lips, which were slightly parted in anticipation, and found the wetness — and it was the sweetest cunt nectar he'd ever tasted. He wiggled his tongue inside; she shuddered as he did, moaning above him, and she grabbed his head with both hands. He lapped masterfully at her churning juices, occasionally flicking at her clitoris. The throbbing little nub swelled larger and firmer every time he did, but he never visited it for too long, always returning to her soaking quim. Her fingers intertwined with his hair, squeezing a bit tighter every time he swatted her clit or found a sensitive spot inside her, and her breathing was shallow and heavy.

Eventually, he stepped it up. He'd lick his way up, give her swollen bump a few lashes, and then lock his lips over it and suck on it a bit; when he'd feel her body begin to shake with impending orgasm, he'd return to her dripping-wet hole. She'd always whimper a bit, cute and helpless, whenever he left her clit, but he never stopped his routine. He did get faster and firmer with every revolution; he'd make his tongue like a stiff little cock, shoving it harder inside her and giving her more strokes with each round, and suck harder on her sensitive clit. Each time brought her closer to the edge.

He finally settled on her clit and worked on her until she began to make little teenage mewling sounds and high-pitched moans — then he slid a hand down and eased two fingers deep inside her. She began squirming uncontrollably, his hair tightly tangled in her fingers, and by then had spread her legs as wide as they could go and had lifted her feet high in the air. She was offering himself wholly to him, unashamedly and wantonly.

He fucked her steadily with his fingers even as he bore his sucking lips down on her clit and began mercilessly flicking at it with his tongue. She moaned with every lewdly slurping stroke of his finger-banging. Her juices flowed down the crack of her ass, so he extended a pinky finger—the "shocker," they called it—and worked it in her ass with every stroke of his two fingers. She didn't argue, and in fact took the moaning to a new level.

She began thrashing madly on the bed, letting go of his hair and wailing as her orgasm approached. Nathan knew damn well none of those inexperienced boys who'd made it into her panties had ever made her feel like this, and he was just getting started. He picked up the pace, slamming his hand in her cunt and up her ass, faster and faster, all while he drove her insane with his mouth and tongue.

And then her body began to quiver, her thighs clamping around his head, and her pussy began rapid-fire contractions on his fingers as her wailing became screaming, and she started coming. He yanked his fingers out, moved his mouth down, and latched his lips around her creaming hole. He shoved his tongue inside her and caught every drop of her brimming juices as she came and came and came, writhing and thrashing and screaming all the while.

He gave her a few minutes to recover when it was over, and, as predicted, he was The Man. He lay next to her on the bed, she still on her back and he on his side.

"None of the guys I've been with are that good," she said.

Her childish naïveté, of course, had her believing he was a sex god. She didn't understand that most of those young guys were just clumsy and inexperienced. He pulled her close and kissed her cheek. "You're worth it."

She smiled at him. "I guess I owe you a blow job."

With that little-girl face, she looked stupidly innocent and much younger than she was—somewhere between 'elfin' and 'well-developed junior-high-school cheerleader'—so he felt like a dirty old man. And he loved it. He forced a look of surprise. "Oh, no, of course you don't. A guy can pleasure a woman without requiring payback, you know."

She looked stunned. "But… it wouldn't be right."

He smiled. "Don't you worry about that. I don't know what those young guys have been telling you, but I'm not going to die if I don't come."

She gave a start. "What do you mean, if you don't come? Aren't we… going to make love?"

He reached out and stroked her hair. "I'd love that. But not tonight."

He could see the dejection in her face—although, given the orgasm she'd just had, it was very minor dejection. But he'd gotten her to ask him—beg him—to make love to her, and he'd deliberately stopped short of consummating their relationship. There was time for that later.

"I wanted to make you feel wonderful," he said, "and let you know how special this was for me. Just do me the honor of a date tomorrow night, so I can fulfill my promise by making love to you like no man ever has."

Raise her pedestal ever higher. Pretend to share his vulnerable emotions. Set her up for sex that she'd think would have to be at least as good as what she just got, and probably even more incredible. And it worked marvelously. She smiled back at him with bright-white teeth.

"Wow—yeah, of course," she said, and she giggled a bit.

They agreed he'd pick her up when she got out of work the next day, and he even got her to agree to keep their relationship quiet with her friends and family until after their next date—so he could mentally focus on it just being the two of them, or some such lame excuse that she eagerly fell for.

Nathan dropped her off at his office, where her car was parked, and it was Tammy who initiated the good-bye kiss—a full-on kiss with tongue and closed eyes and roaming hands. She never complained about the taste of pussy on his mouth. She was all his. And that made her the Ancient Demigod's.

He drove home in a hurry, his cock sensitive as hell in his pants. It was still as hard as it had been while he'd gone down on Tammy and finger-fucked her, and he had to get home and take care of things. It had killed him to decline the blow job, never mind to not fuck her. It had taken every ounce of mind-over-matter self-control. He was in a hurry to get off.

He remembered to slide the ring back on his finger before he went in the house, but after quickly washing his cunt-soaked face, he wasted no time waking his wife up. He climbed into bed naked and began kissing her, and she came awake in surprise as his hands roamed from her breasts to her hairy pussy.

"Well, hello," she said. "Late night got you horny?"

"You have no idea," he said, and within seconds he was between her legs, plunging his aching cock deep inside her. She moaned and writhed, just like Tammy had. While he pumped her hard and fast, he imagined she was that innocent, wide-eyed girl, as Tammy would be when he took her, and as Tammy would be when the Ancient Demigod took her.

His wife headed out the next morning for an architecture show in Chicago. He went to work to add a few property listings online, and by mid-morning Tammy called him.

"I really enjoyed last night," she said.

"I wanted you to enjoy it," he said. "I couldn't stand to hear about those young guys not treating you right. You're too special for that."

Special, that did it. He could practically hear her eyes welling up. "Can I still see you tonight?" she asked.

"If you'll do me the honor," he said.

He picked her up at the clothing store where she worked,

and she was dressed far less provocatively than before. She wore a classy, below-the-knees dress, nylons, and low heels, and her hair was tied up. He kissed her and held the car door for her, and she loved every minute of it.

He took her downtown, where he owned a condo his wife didn't know about. He kept it mostly to bring women when his wife was out of town—prostitutes, usually, but occasionally a woman he'd pick up in a bar or a gullible young chick like Tammy. This was the first time he'd brought one there to be sacrificed, but she'd be the first of many. He could only imagine the rewards he'd reap from the Ancient Demigod.

The condo was the top floor of an eight-story building, and he knew it was quite soundproof; his elderly downstairs neighbor had never once heard the squealing and screaming of many a woman he'd taken there. He led Tammy into the fancy place, with its oak floors and top-shelf furniture and gas-powered fireplace. She was suitably impressed, her mouth sagging open in awe as he gave her the nickel tour. Nathan knew that he'd roped her in with what she perceived as the most stunning lovemaking in the world, and now he'd sealed the deal with his wealth.

Once again, the tour ended with the bedroom, with its custom round bed, eight feet in diameter; the two walls that were entirely windows; the big, angled skylights; the seventy-inch flat-panel television; and the in-room bar. He didn't waste any time; the wooing was done. The Ancient Demigod awaited, and he wanted to make sure he had Tammy—all of her— before the sacrifice. He took her in his arms and kissed her passionately, and she surrendered completely to him. He kissed her all over, nibbling about her throat and neck—whispering how wonderful she made him feel, just to keep her faith in him building—and managed to pull out the elastic band so her hair tumbled down around her shoulders.

He unzipped her salesgirl dress and dropped it to the plush carpet, then dropped to his knees to undo the garter belt holding up her stockings, to peel them down her legs, to slide her panties down as well. He nuzzled briefly between her legs on his way up, and he expertly unclasped her bra with one hand before toppling her to the bed. Her bare breasts were magnificent, bulbous and prominent on her tiny torso. Her areolas were pink and innocent, and her nipples pink and hard, as he sucked on them.

"I'm going crazy here," he hissed, breathless. "I have to make love to you."

She spread her legs, giving in again entirely. He found her clit with his fingers, bore down with a bit of pressure, and circled slowly. But he picked up speed with every revolution until he was spinning his fingers madly, and she whimpered as he kissed her. When her teen cunt was dripping with her juices again, he stopped long enough to tear off his own clothes. Then he returned to the bed, climbing between her legs, holding her by the ankles so her heels were in front and to the sides of his face. She looked amusing, lying there all wide-eyed and open-mouthed, as he knelt between her thighs, his seven-inch prick jutting out towards her face. It was a thick, heavy prick, like something you'd see in a skin flick, and he was quite proud of it and what he could do with it. And it was time to show her.

He forced her knees towards her face, so that her ass angled up, and her wet cooze opened to receive him. He slid the head of his cock inside and found her as tight and hot as he expected. It was going to be a fantastic fuck.

She let out a little yelp as he lunged forward and buried himself to the hilt. He suppressed a grin, but he knew what was going through her head: What happened to the gentle passion of the night before? He let go of her ankles, fell forward on top of her, and begin putting it to her hard. His skills made up for her shock, and she began wailing almost immediately as he pounded her mercilessly. Within half a minute, she was screaming in utter ecstasy, already forgetting that gentle passion and discovering the power of the mental overload of being properly and thoroughly fucked senseless.

He screwed her through two screeching orgasms, until she was trembling and crying and laughing in sheer joy. He knew her sensitive pussy couldn't take much more, so he stopped fucking her and leaned in to kiss her, long and deep. They traded tongues for a long minute, and when he pulled his lips from hers, he said, "I know I'm not supposed to say this on a second date, but I have to. I just can't help the way I'm feeling. I'm in love with you, you know. You make me feel like a kid again, and I want to feel like this with you forever."

"I'm in love with you, too," she whispered, excited and serious.

"You're so young," he said. "Can you really love me?"

"Of course I can."

He kissed her on the nose. "Prove it, baby. Do those things we talked about. Show me how serious you love me. If you do those things, I'll know you're not just a college girl using an old guy for his money."

She seemed stunned and confused, but he held his steel gaze and he felt her relenting. She finally nodded, hesitantly. "Okay."

"Do you mean that?" he asked. "Are you sure? I know how you feel about those things, and I won't do them unless you really want me to do them."

"It's okay," she said. "It's not that I haven't done them."

"You just felt pressured into them by those stupid young guys," he said. "I don't want you to feel pressured. But I just can't come unless I know you mean it. And my balls are damn sore right now. If you don't mean it, that's okay—I'll jerk off and feel better."

"No, I mean it," she said.

"You *really* mean it?"

"I do."

"Tell me what you want me to do, then. Tell me everything,

and if I believe you truly want me to, I'll do them."

She nodded, a bit hesitantly but with determination on her face. "I want you to fuck me in the ass, Nathan," she said, stolid and sure.

"What else?" he breathed. "Tell me where you want me to come."

She inhaled deeply. "I want you to come in my mouth," she said. "And on my face. Please, put it in my ass now. I want you to."

Oh, yes—she was *his*, all right.

He pulled out of her, reached down, and guided the tip of his cock towards her tight, puckered hole. He felt her tense, saw her face tighten as she tried to hide the grimace, as he forced the fat head into her ass. It was tighter than anything he'd ever stuck his dick in. He pushed hard and she squirmed beneath him, and when the head finally popped inside, she let out a little yelp. But then, with all the juices from her cunt lubricating things, his shaft slid easily inside her.

He kissed her again, kissed his way down to her ear, licked the lobe, and told her how much he loved her. That relaxed her enough for him to begin fucking her. Within minutes, he had a steady rhythm going, and she no longer looked uncomfortable. She did look a bit like a child on a carnival ride that she wasn't sure she liked, but she took it like a pro. By the time he accelerated to full-on, balls-deep, hard-pounding ass-ramming, she was grabbing her legs and pulling her knees to her chest while he worked. She was even making excited sounds.

Nathan knew that if he could pull off an ass-to-mouth move, there would be no turning back, and when he suddenly pulled out of her and clambered above her, he thought for a moment it would be all over. She looked terrified at the prospect, but she didn't have time to think. He straddled her shoulders on his knees and aimed his cock at her mouth. He saw those pouty little teenage lips open and her head lift, and she latched on and pulled it inside.

She sucked him better than any woman ever had, and Nathan knew he wasn't fooling himself with that belief. It was too bad she was The One, because he knew he could enjoy fucking her every which way for a long time. But in that moment, all he could think about was the stunning blow job she was giving him—really, she was working her tongue and sucking hard, as he face-fucked her. He splayed his feet wide behind him, supported his weight on his hands, and picked up the pace. She never gagged once, and never relaxed her lips, taking his forced deep throat as well as any skilled hooker he'd had in that bed.

Finally, he felt the come boiling deep in his balls. He roared as he pulled out of her mouth and came to his feet above her. She scurried up beneath him to her knees, mouth open as he fisted his cock, and he came like a porn star, spraying thick ropes of semen across her face, in her mouth, in her hair. She clearly wasn't happy about it, but was trying to be a trooper and prove her love to him.

Nathan knew he needed one more thing. He collapsed next to her on the bed, sexually spent, even as she grabbed for the edge of the bedspread and quickly cleaned her face off.

"That was incredible," Nathan said, and he wasn't acting.

"Thanks," she said, cuddling up to him. "You were amazing, too."

"You really *are* serious about this," he said, and now he was acting. "I think we need one more thing."

"What?"

Moment of truth. The hardest part of all. He stroked her hair. "When I was a boy, my best friend and I cut our fingertips and pressed the cuts together. We called it being blood brothers."

"Sounds weird," Tammy said with a giggle.

"I want to do it. With you."

She froze for a moment, then pulled out of the crook of his arm and sat up, staring at him in surprise. "Seriously?"

"Yeah—why not? I think it would be crazy and fun and totally fucking romantic."

She looked dubious, and he thought for a moment he was going to lose her. "Mixing blood seems kind of unsafe."

He sat up to face her. "Tammy, from a medical standpoint, we've pretty much done every unsafe thing there is." Then he smiled a perfect white smile.

For a frightening moment, he thought the look on her face was going to result in her grabbing her clothes and running out of the condo, but then a smile broke her lips. "I guess you're right. And it does sound kind of romantic."

He went for the nightstand and opened the drawer to find the small penknife he had in there. His heart was pounding now out of sheer excitement. It was really going to happen! She was going to let him!

He opened the small knife, and she was nervous again. "Do you want to prick your finger, or would you rather I do it?"

"I think you'd better do it," she said. "I don't think I could do it to myself."

"Okay. Give me your finger."

She held up a hand, finger extended. He grabbed it, held it firm, positioned the sharp little blade. He had to be absolutely sure she approved. "Are you sure? I'm not going to do this unless you tell me it's okay."

"It's okay. Just do it quick."

He raised his brow at her. "You know me. I have to hear you ask me to do it."

She smiled and took a deep breath. "Please, Nathan—cut my finger."

And that was what he needed. He drew the blade quickly across her finger, deep and harsh. She'd been expecting a little nick, and she hollered in surprise, yanking her hand away. He held on to the knife. Beautiful crimson blood coated the length of the blade.

ŽILJAK

"That fucking hurt!" she cried.

He was finished with her. It was the Ancient Demigod's turn now. Nathan came off the bed, holding his hand under the blade to catch the dripping blood, and stood between her and the door.

"I have done it!" he cried out to the Ancient Demigod, but of course Tammy thought he was nuts. "I have her blood! And she gave it willingly!"

"What the hell is this?" Tammy cried.

"Shut the fuck up," he growled, firing a dark glare at her. "Don't move a fucking muscle, you little whore."

The color drained from her face as she realized she'd been had—the wooing, the false compliments, the sex, getting her to not tell anyone in her life about him. She certainly had to know she was in danger, but of course she had no idea how much. Nathan knew there was no way the skinny bitch could get past him.

"Come to me!" Nathan bellowed. "She's ready!"

"Please, let me go," Tammy said, tears already flowing down her come-glazed face. She was holding her finger, but the blood was seeping out and dripping down her hand.

And then the room began to change.

The walls oozed like wax, and the ceiling evaporated, and the bedroom floor and its furniture were all that remained, but outside was not the city; now, the floor of the room sat on a barren expanse of rock, with a sky of mottled green swirling above like a maelstrom of light and energy. He heard Tammy scream, but that didn't matter anymore. He laughed. He'd seen this place in his visions, and now it was real—just as the Ancient Demigod had shown him.

The green whirlpool above parted in the center, spreading wide to admit the dark form, and the Ancient Demigod descended from the sky. First came its legs, which were the size of redwoods ending in flat, elephantine feet. A gigantic green torso, with a dozen tentacles sprouting from it and whipping about, followed. Tammy screamed and screamed, flailing naked on the bed, as the antigravitating deity broke through the mist, bringing a hot wind from above. The Ancient Demigod's head appeared, and it was like something out of the worst nightmare, with a dozen eyes and two gaping maws full of sharp teeth, and it roared its approval.

But to Nathan, the Ancient Demigod was something out of a grand dream. "Here!" Nathan screamed. "I've brought you a sacrifice!"

The Ancient Demigod landed on the rock with its massive feet, and the ground quaked. The bedroom furniture toppled over and the bed danced across the floor. The shambling mound of creature, seventy feet tall, roared again as its thick, leathery tentacles writhed around the remnants of the bedroom, and the naked girl screamed on the bed. Wildly, Nathan wondered which tentacle would snake up Tammy's cunt, which would jam up her ass, which would choke her. Tammy might have withstood the ass-fucking and deep-throating like a trooper, but the girl was about to meet her match.

Nathan watched as the marvelous being leaned over the bed, its tentacles wriggling towards Tammy. It was perfect. Perfect!

And then, very suddenly, it wasn't perfect at all.

None of it made much sense to Tammy, and in truth she assumed Nathan had slipped her something at dinner to cause the hallucination. She was trying to convince her mind that it wasn't real, but she experienced everything that happened with the sharpest lucidity.

The giant monster suddenly whipped a tentacle out and wrapped it around the legs of the laughing Nathan. For a moment, he kept laughing, as if the move made sense, but suddenly he was terrified. He began screaming and flailing his arms madly about, but the Ancient Demigod quickly put him to good use.

Where the Ancient Demigod's massive tree-trunk thighs came together, a deep gash opened wide, and pus began oozing out—yellow, white, green. It tightened its tentacle on Nathan and swung him into position and abruptly stuffed his head up inside its monstrous cunt. His scream was cut off as he was engulfed, and the monster shoved him all the way to his knees inside. Then it pulled him out, and he screamed again. When it tried to shove him back in, he tried to splay his arms to stop, but the force merely broke his arms.

The monster yanked him out, plunged him in, and repeated the process. Every time he came out, he tried yelling, but was quickly silenced again. Tammy watched in utter horror from the bed as the monster used him like a human dildo. The tentacle worked faster and faster, and Nathan's screams became weak cries that eventually went away altogether.

The monster kept it up for several minutes before letting loose with an inhuman roar out of both its toothed mouths, like something out of a bad movie, and when it yanked out the limp form of Nathan the final time, it spewed bloody pus all over the rock below.

Then it hauled Nathan's blubbering form high into the air and slammed him to the stone ground at a ridiculous speed, like some gargantuan football player scoring a touchdown. He died amidst the sound of his entire skeleton shattering.

Tammy was speechless as the beast towered above her, breathing like a gigantic bellows, recovering from its otherworldly orgasm. All she could think was: *And now I'm next.*

But the monster began to change shape. It shrank, very quickly, and its two mouths merged. The head swallowed up all but two of its eyes. The legs slimmed, the torso grew breasts, and the skin changed to white. Hair sprouted from its head. Within ten seconds, the monster had become a woman. She was old enough to be Tammy's mother, with a hardened face and a stunning body—naked, with swelling breasts, and with very human genitalia that was dripping normal-looking vaginal juices. She approached the bed, staring at Tammy with a hard look.

"He used you," the woman said. "You fell for everything he said."

"I… I know," Tammy said, trembling.

"Don't fear me," the woman said. "His kind should fear me."

"Men?" Tammy tried.

"Men like *him*," she said. "Men willing to abuse women and sacrifice them to Ancient Demigods. The world could use a lot fewer people like him."

"Yes," Tammy said.

"I can show you powers like you've never known," said the woman, smiling with her thin lips for the first time. "You have the potential within you. That's why I gave him a vision of you. I can give other men such visions. Together, we can punish them and rid the world of their evil."

"Yes," Tammy said, her face brightening as her pretty smile crossed it.

"The next ten thousand years will be mine," she said. "And you'll be there with me."

*   *   *

Donald Breckenridge owned a successful car dealership, but he still worked customers occasionally to keep fresh on the sales end of things. But other things had preoccupied his mind recently: The visions he'd been having. They made him forget about the hookers and his wife and banging the secretary at the dealership after hours. They even made him forget about that fourteen-year-old girl he'd been fucking, the one he'd promised a Corvette to when she turned twenty-one if she kept her mouth shut and kept on screwing him.

But when he looked down from his office at the showroom and saw the woman Benny, his top salesman, was working, he recognized her. She'd been in his visions. He rushed down-stairs, interrupted the sale, and informed Benny that this was a special customer, and he'd take care of her.

"I'm Don Breckenridge," he said as he shook her hand. "I own the dealership. I have a special feeling about you, and I always trust my instincts."

"So do I," she said with a sweet smile. "Pleased to meet you, Mr. Breckenridge. My name is Tammy Kendrick, and I'm looking for something really special."

"I have all the best cars for a hot young woman like you," he said with a sly grin.

"I'm looking for something more than a car," she cooed, licking her lips and smiling seductively at him.

"How about a test drive?" he said with a lascivious grin. "I'm sure we can come up with a way a beautiful girl like you can buy a car at my cost."

"I'm sure we can," she said.

Later that night, when she was on her knees in the passen-ger seat, leaning over the door of the top-down convertible, she smiled to herself. Breckenridge was behind her, pounding her with his cock like a champion. It was a great cock, as good as Nathan's had been, but this guy was even better at using it.

She braced herself on the door with one hand, arching her back so he'd hit that G-spot with every marathon stroke, and reached back with her other hand to touch his thrusting hips with her fingertips.

"Give it to me," she cried. "Fill me up, baby. Fill me with your come."

He grunted and sped up his hips, digging into her waist with both hands, and she loved every incredible moment of being fucked so thoroughly. And when he finally exploded in roaring triumph, blowing his load deep inside her, she screamed like a banshee and came with him.

"That was fucking great," she said in her best major-slut

voice. "Promise me you'll take me to your camp house tomorrow and fuck me some more."

"You know I will," he said, panting above her, sweat dripping. "But that's weird... I don't remember mentioning my camp house."

"Well, you must have, silly — how else would I know?" she asked. "Now, no breaks, honey... do me again." She squeezed his soft penis with her vaginal muscles and swiveled her hips about. "Come on, sweetie. Give me some more."

Her sexy purr had his deflated cock getting hard again inside her.

Breckenridge began pumping his stiffening cock into her again, and she growled with delight into the night air. He was having the time of his life. She was better than the fourteen-year-old. It was too bad he'd sacrifice her to the Ancient Demigod at that camp house.

He smiled at the thought and kept on fucking.

Tommy's Adventures in Gloryland

by
E.W. Lee

Sex can be crude and amusing, and so can erotica. For that matter, so can religion, as well as the incredible lengths some will go to in order to serve their faiths — never mind what they've convinced themselves is right and just. In this reality, Tommy finds himself on a holy crusade that's only silly and hypocritical if you're not Tommy. Fair warning: If you're religious, this story might offend you. (But, really, how amusing is it that, in an anthology of erotica, the religious story is the one that has to carry a warning that it might offend?)

Science fiction
Religious dystopia
Alternate reality
Masturbation
Cunnilingus
Heterosexual sex, fellatio, anal sex
Homosexual sex, fellatio, anal sex

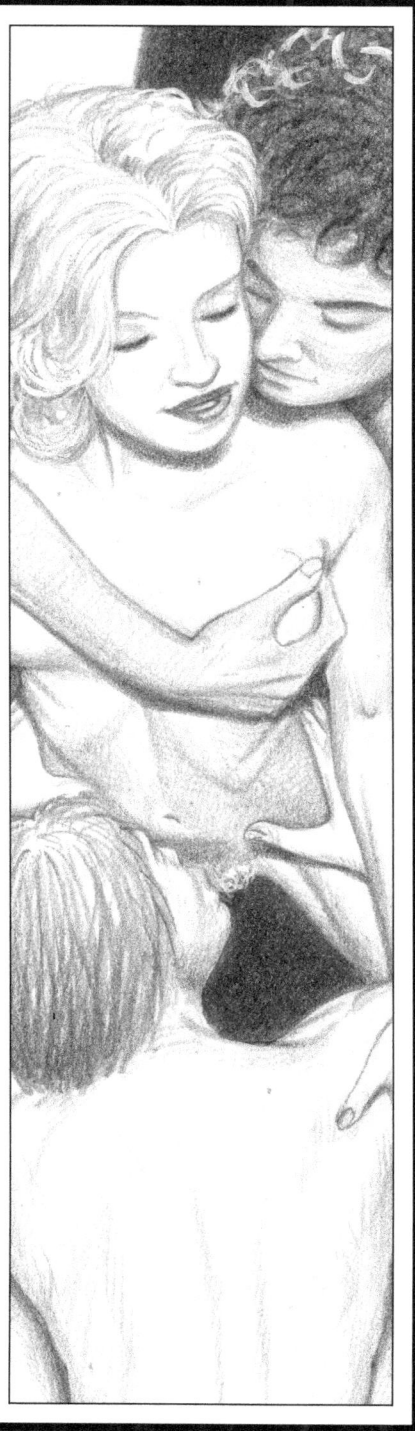

Chapter 1

The Beginning of "The End of the World" came, and it was probably Tommy's fault (mostly).

The long-awaited beginning of "The End Times" started with The Great and Glorious Appearing of the MATL. The MATL (Mighty Angel of The Lord) appeared to a young teenager named Tommy Lee. It happened while young Tommy was sitting in the front pew of a Babtist church in Pittsburgh, Pennsylvania.

At the time of The Great and Glorious Event, Tommy was a fifteen-year-old boy. A few weeks earlier, his father kicked him out of his home (actually, he was tossed out on his ass). His father was punishing Tommy for his frequent and unflagging habit of masturbation. His father tried everything to get Tommy to stop. He gave Tommy an extensive collection of pamphlets and literature published by the church leaders in Utah. He forced Tommy to wear the huge potholder mitts recommended by the Church counselors and purchased from a mail-order house in Salt Lake City. His father used threats and even severe beatings, but nothing seemed to hinder Tommy from flogging his meat — which is (as we all know, according to Church doctrine) the horrible sin of Self-Abuse.

Finally, on a cold day in February, after once again finding Tommy's bedsheets stained with crusty white streaks of dried spunk, Tommy's loving father threw him out of the house. He told Tommy that he would burn eternally in Hell, 24/7, for defying God and the All-Loving and All-Forgiving Jezus.

Tommy wandered the cold city streets trying to figure out

what to do. He spent several days in a homeless shelter in downtown Pittsburgh, but got tossed out a few days later for jacking off in one of the unisex/handicapped public toilets. He tried living under an overpass and sleeping at construction sites, but then the winter cold really set in with a major ice storm. Tommy tried calling his mom two or three times, only to have his father grab the phone and start screaming at him. And then one day, after wandering the streets—hungry and alone—Tommy walked into the All Souls Babtist Church, and he sat down on the front pew.

Standing there before him on the podium was a Babtist minister. He was a famous evangelist, the Right Reverend Doktor Gerald Homer Jenkins. It truth, Rev. Jenkins was a clownish-looking figure—or at least that's how he looked to Tommy, but only at first. The Preacher wore a rumpled brown suit, his belly hung over ill-fitting pants, and his thinning hair was combed over a bald spot on his potato-shaped head. The minister smiled at Tommy and began his sermon on the All-Loving and All-Forgiving Jezus. Tommy had heard this line before. But this time, something very, very weird happened.

The DMS (Divine Message of Salvation) was revealed unto Tommy, who actually saw the minister standing before him transform into an Angelic Being. In the blink of an eye (or maybe two or three blinks) a powerful halo of light surrounded the minister as his loving eyes fell directly on young Tommy. The minister (or Angel, really) spoke directly to Tommy's heart, and Tommy was filled with The Word of God. It was as if The Word of God quickly (and silently) probed the nethermost part of Tommy's soul, and Tommy was quickly filled with the *sweet&sticky* Love of Jezus!

And then—just to be sure that Tommy had got The Message—the Angel stepped out from behind his pulpit and placed his hand on his enormous pink-colored Angelic Phallus. And The Blessed Spunk of God flew out from His crotch and covered Tommy in a warm yellow light.

No one else saw this vision. To everyone else in the congregation, it was simply one more instance of the Reverend Jenkins indulging in his annoying habit of stepping out from behind the pulpit and adjusting his crotch while preaching.

But to young Tommy it was an Angelic Vision, given to him directly from God AllMighty. Tommy was given a full-body babtism, covered with the golden spunk of God's Blessed Angel. And he knew that his mission—for God and the Babtist church—was to travel to Gloryland and convert the heretical and pagan denizens of this Hellbound region. The people of Gloryland are—as everyone knew—rabidly loyal members of The Church of the Moron.

Tommy immediately went to the homeless shelter and convinced the social workers that he needed "Greyhound therapy." He claimed that he had an uncle in Gloryland who was willing to take him in. The social workers were only too happy to give Tommy a one-way bus ticket to Gloryland.

Over the next few days, on the long trip across country, Tommy read his tiny green Giddyon New Testament—over and over again, and especially The Book of The Revelations of St. John's. Tommy believed that God Himself had given Tommy the mission to go to Gloryland and preach the *true&sweet* Spirit of Jezus to the people. At the same time, Tommy was also expected to lay *hard&heavy* curses on the *fallen&corrupted* leaders of this Heathen Moron Church, just like the Prophet Jonah did. And just as Moses had his magic shepherd's stick—the stick that Charlton Heston used to part the Red Sea—Tommy had been given a mighty gift to use in converting the Heathen. God gave Tommy the use of his enormous, supernaturally-endowed fuckpole, which Tommy would use to convert the Heathen. Tommy was determined to grab those sinners, one by one, and fuck them into Salvation.

On first arriving in Gloryland, Tommy very nearly starved. Because he was no longer a member in good standing of The Church of the Moron, Tommy was pretty much on his own, food- and shelter-wise. But, as luck would have it, Tommy stumbled across an advert in the Shoppers Guide. The publisher of the Guide offered to print a free advert for one week for anyone who was offering to sell a service. So Tommy wrote an ad:

> Is there some arrogant sinner you want hu-miliated? Physically or mentally, it's not a problem. Just a few details and I'll get to work. Go in Christ. Write Tommy Lee, c/o the newspaper office.

Amazingly, in only a few days Tommy discovered that Gloryland was chock full of proud and arrogant people who needed to be humiliated. Soon Tommy had so much work that he had to hire extra help to keep up. Needless to say, Tommy regularly tithed ten percent to the local Babtist Church while plowing the rest of his profits back into his evangelical mission. He was determined to win all these lost souls for Jezus.

Chapter 2
(six years later)

Tommy Lee entered the back door and walked down the steps into the church basement. He tried to ignore the posters on the wall — all typical conservative Moron pro-syl-lit, with cheery mom-and-pop images of big *fertile&fecund* families. On the poster directly in front of him, the Moron family was sitting down to dinner around a gigantic roasted turkey that looked as if it were stuffed so full it was about ready to pop. In that Thanksgiving scene, Gramps and Granny sat on the left while Daddy stood over the bird, holding his knife and ready to carve. Mom, and the dozen-or-so Moron kiddies, were lined up along the rest of the table, all smiling like a toothpaste advert. Tommy cringed at the thought of having to sit down to a meal just like that one with his own poor working-class family. But Tommy's kinfolk back in Pittsburgh never looked like this. They certainly never had a gigantic genetically-modified golden-brown turkey for dinner, not even a skinny one.

The pro-life poster on the wall above him was especially annoying; it showed a pregnant teen girl smiling the same vacant Moron smile. Her waistline was—just like the turkey—about to pop out another baby, all ready to be imprinted with Moron church doctrine. Tommy hated the Moron church—having narrowly escaped its clutches as a teenager—and was now wholly devoted to his own Babtist missionary work. He wanted to destroy the Moron church, which had nearly claimed his immortal soul back when he was a boy. All he wanted was to convert all those poor people to the One True Church—meaning, of course, the Babtist Church.

Tommy sat in his metal chair, filled with rage that the state government—run by a bunch of Morons, of course—had forced him to come to the training session. He was there for only one reason: In order to keep getting his welfare check, Tommy had to attend an Ameway training session held in the basement of the local Moron church. It made his Babtist blood boil to realize that state money was going to this church, as rent for the meeting hall. They were stealing his tax money—that is, if he had been paying taxes—to support the Moron ministry. It was all church propaganda, thinly disguised as legitimate social work.

While Tommy sat in his metal chair and ground his teeth, he carefully examined the other people forced to attend. One of the participants, a Moron girl dressed in her tight schoolgirl outfit, was pretty hot. Her huge breasts pressed against the brown shirt of her uniform, as if they were ready to pop out. The buttons on her blouse were barely holding in her blossoming bosom. She was obviously older, at least over eighteen. So why she was still wearing her old school uniform?

Maybe it's the only clothes she owns, Tommy thought. *She is on the dole, too!*

It all made sense. That's why she was forced to be there, to listen to a lecture on Ameway and the blessings of Free Enterprise—and maybe get injected with some Moron doctrine on the side.

Tommy thought, *I have something I'd sure like to inject her with.*

Tommy figured that he could chat her up a bit, and if no better-looking women showed up, maybe he could get the Moron girl to come back to his apartment and (at the very least) give him a first-class blow job.

I will fill her mouth with the sweet&sticky *Spirit of Jezus!*, Tommy thought. *Once she's done sucking on my man-meat, I can tell her how much Jezus loves her and maybe even get her to leave the Moron church.*

Tommy had dozens of evangelical Chick pamphlets stacked around his apartment. It was a small part of his Holy Mission—to distribute these godly Christian pamphlets to every gas station and rest stop in Gloryland.

Tommy closed his eyes and visualized the Moron girl, down on her knees and massaging the skin of his AllMighty Rod. But of course Tommy was a gentleman, and he would never force a woman to get down on her knees on the hard wooden floor of his apartment. So (in his imagination) she was kneeling on a stack of Chick pamphlets. He had plenty of pamphlets, so she could kneel on them while her thick, full lips closed around his *meaty&tubular* spunk factory. It was the least he could do—unless, of course, she was one of those girls who would enjoy the discomfort of kneeling on a hard floor while she sucked him off. At least that was the way it happened with that Catholik girl he met in the bus station in Chicago. She really got off on the pain.

At this point an elderly Moron woman came up to the front of the group. She looked like someone's kindly old grandma. Tommy was sure that she was just some old lady, living in genteel poverty, who had volunteered to lead the meeting in order to get more Moron brownie points. Tommy knew that virtually no one who worked for the Moron Church ever got paid in cash for his work. Only the higher-ups, the Church Elders, actually got the hard cash. Everyone else was forced to do volunteer work for nothing, except for the brownie points and the bragging rights. At the church, all of the manual labor was done by volunteers—a service to the Lord that was rewarded in Heaven—if then!

Of course, Tommy knew that these Morons were all doomed to Hell, where demons would stab them with pitch-forks 24/7, and the blazing fires of Hell would lick their arses for Eternity. He knew that some day, when the old lady finally died, she would *not* get her reward in Heaven. She, and all the other Morons, were what they call "Apostrates." The old lady would spend the rest of Eternity in Hell, being sodomized by a chain gang of red-skinned demons. And she would deserve it, too, for rejecting the True *pure&sweet* Love of Jezus.

At that point the old lady introduced a younger middle-aged woman with a platinum-blond beehive hairdo. She was obviously the speaker for the afternoon. She was a stout lady dressed in a bright-pink suit, whose color made Tommy sus-pect that the woman also gave it up for Mary Kaye cosmetics, and that the Ameway racket was probably just a sideline to bring in a little extra cash. Tommy sneered as she handed out folders with Ameway propaganda and application forms to fill out. Then she gave her canned speech—the usual silly stuff about making a fortune the Ameway way—while skirting the issue of how little they would really make. Many of them would spend the first few months (or more like years) slaving away for little or nothing; meanwhile, the higher-ups in the Ameway pyramid would be making the real money.

Tommy suspected that this was just another Ponzi scheme, and he wanted nothing to do with it—especially as almost all of his time was already taken up with spreading legs and pumping out loads of The Message — the *sweet&pure* Love of Jezus. As the middle-aged woman droned on about the wonders of Free Enterprise, Tommy closed his eyes and visualized the woman standing on a hot iron plate in the deepest, darkest pit of Hell. To him she was just another Moron whore, doomed to eternity in the Fiery Pit! Tommy enjoyed imagining her standing on the iron plate while dozens of demons stood in line to suck on her ginormous white titties, or chew out her flabby backside with their forked tongues stuck up her broad arsehole.

As this and other visions of hellish torture danced through Tommy's brain, a young woman walked into the room. She was pretty and wore a yellow sundress. The old lady in charge of the program glared at her, then whispered — loud enough for all to hear — "You're late!"

The young woman smiled meekly and took a chair. It was the chair next to Tommy. As she sat down, Tommy knew immediately that she was attracted to him. He responded by adjusting his crotch, and then he scratched himself halfway down his inner thigh — just to let her know that she had plenty to look forward to, if she was interested.

The girl smiled and leaned into him, giving him a good look down her cleavage. "My name is Jenny."

A few minutes later they were allowed a lunch break. Tommy grabbed Jenny by the arm and steered her toward the hallway. Next to the bathroom was an office, probably reserved for one of the church Elders. Tommy led her into the office and closed the door. The room was full of pro-life materials. With one arm he swept the desk clear of papers and lifted her up on the smooth wood surface. Tommy dived down and had his head up her skirt before she could say "Holy Kolob." Tommy wasn't surprised to find that she didn't wear any panties — not the Moron ritual garb, and not even a white cotton thong. He had his face shoved into her steamy cunt and was lapping away at her clit before she could even get out a single "Ooooh." Tommy appreciated the fact that she was a natural blonde, even if she was a very, very dirty blonde. He knew that she hadn't bothered to wash recently, at least not since her most recent visit to The Facilities. But Tommy wasn't going to let her hygiene problem deter him from God's mission: to spread the *sweet&sticky* Love of Jezus.

Soon Tommy had her juices really flowing, and so he unzipped his pants and whipped out his AllMighty Meatshaft. First he poked the lips of her swollen wet pussy, then poked at her arsehole, then poked the pink lips of her pussy again. Tommy tickled her arsehole with his little finger, while he rubbed the lips of her pussy, up and down, with the head of his cock (in South Carolina this is called "using your staff to walk the Appalachian Trail"). Her luscious breasts bounced as she giggled madly.

Tommy moved his left hand down the length of her back and then firmly grasped the swollen roundness of her lovely buttock. Reading his mind, she opened her legs further to accommodate the head of his Meatshaft, and Tommy thrust the head into her well-lubed pussy lips. It was hard going at first, but Tommy was no quitter. She relaxed, as Tommy tickled her arsehole a bit more with his pinky, and soon he had the entire massive length of his cock stuffed up into her juicy cunt. Tommy laid pipe like a pro. His meaty shaft moved in and out with a solid rhythm, and Jenny's breath gasped each time he slid the length of his cock into her, again and again, like the drill of an oilrig. For her, each thrust was a Testament to the Gospel of Tommy's miraculous ManCock.

Her thighs were trembling as she came in a puddle of liquid lust. Soon Jenny was ready to suck on Tommy's pole muscle. She grabbed his leather belt and undid his pants roughly. Tommy dropped his pants, and the girl saw that he was wearing duct tape wrapped several times around his legs just above the knees. He had done this to simulate the hem of the sacred garment worn by young Moron men who had come back from their missionary work.

"Hey!" she said. "You're not a missionary!"

"We are all part of God's plan," Tommy said. "I am a missionary of God's love. He sent me here to help you find your True Way as part of God's infinite plan of salvation."

(The girl, Jenny, was not really a Moron. In fact, she was an agent for the Catholik church. She had come to this meeting to meet and seduce young Moron men. Jenny was actually a member of the secretive Catholik organization called The True Daughters of Mary. A butt-ugly old nun from Milwaukee, who believed that *The DaVinci Code* was God's *true&inspired* message to humanity, had founded the organization. She taught her followers that the best way to convert nonbelievers and heretics was to fuck them senseless, and then into a belief in God and the Pope. And now Jenny was on her own mission to convert the lost souls of the Moron church to The True Light of Priestcraft and Papism. She was put off a bit by discovering (she thought) that Tommy was just an ordinary Moron, but then she realized that all these heretics, even the least of them, needed to be converted to the One True Faith—meaning, of course, the Catholik faith.)

She lost no time forcing Tommy's meat shaft into her mouth and sucking it with the kind of enthusiasm that made you think she could suck his lost soul right out of his cock. For his part, Tommy reached down and fingered her twat with enthusiasm, believing that God had put his Holy Spirit into Tommy's spunk, and once a woman had tasted the True Truth, she could not help but find The Path of Righteousness for His Name's Sake. Amen, and amen.

For her part, the young Catholik girl, who'd said her name was Jenny, was working the skin on Tommy's cock like it was pump handle and gold would come out of Tommy's arse if she worked it hard enough. Soon even Tommy couldn't hold back the pressure of his blessed spunk, and a shot of splooge erupted into Jenny's mouth.

(Of course, Tommy didn't know that Jenny was working the streets for God and Rome and had no money for food. She only ate what she could dig out of the trash behind McDonald's. The shot of Tommy's spunk was the first meal she'd had that day.)

Tommy zipped up and Jenny rearranged her sundress, and both of them went back into the basement meeting room. There the Moron ladies were handing out cheese sandwiches. It was the cheapest white bread with U.S.-government-issue yellow cheese. The cheese was, no doubt—Tommy thought— another federal giveaway to the Moron Church. He knew that the government would be billed for a full three-course meal, while all they got were these *lousy&stale* cheese sandwiches that even a hungry dog wouldn't sniff at. As Tommy smelled the cheese sandwich, he whispered to Jenny, "Even a dog with worms would lick his own ass before eatin' this sorry stuff."

Jenny answered, "I'll take yours if you don't want it."

Tommy handed over the sandwich, wondering if maybe the girl knew a lot about Moron headcheese.

(For her part, Jenny smiled back at him and made plans for how she could use Tommy for the Glory of Rome. As she gazed into his eyes, she realized how much Tommy resembled Father O'Brien, a young priest who used to play with her titties when she was in fifth grade. *So maybe this meeting was part of God's will*, she thought.)

Meanwhile, Tommy got a paper cup of gritty-tasting imitation OJ and then returned to his chair. He had to listen to the rest of the Ameway message or risk losing his welfare check. And he desperately needed that money in order to continue to do God's work.

Meanwhile, the Moron lady in pink yammered on and on about the glories of Mary Kaye and Ameway, pausing only to smile her grim, tight-ass smile and drink from a paper cup of OJ mixed with gin. Tommy could see that the old broad was getting well lubricated, and he—for a moment—considered the possibility of taking a break long enough to find her pink car in the parking lot and key it. He would derive intense pleasure from using his apartment key to scratch "My Jezus Saves" into the bright pink paint of her auto. She certainly deserved it, given her adherence to the Heathenish cult of Joe Smith and The Church of the Moron. It was easy for Tommy to visualize the church leader, Brigg Young, and his twelve wives all burning in the deepest, darkest pit of Hell. Probably, right at that minute, Satan himself was sodomizing the old bastard with what was likely the third biggest cock in the universe (next to God and Jezus, of course). Everyone knew that Satan's cock was a scaly, dirty monster wrapped in barb wire and covered with iron spikes like some Funky-Punk with multiple steel piercings. No doubt Satan himself took a turn each day at tearing into old Brigg Young's arsehole with his giant spiked member.

The very idea gave Tommy intense pleasure, and his own cock rose stiffly at the idea (even though Tommy was not a bit gay, and never indulged in such homo-typical pleasures, except occasionally—and then only as the topper). Tommy placed his hand on his crotch and scratched "the head of the family" again, for the benefit of all the Moron ladies; and then he placed his hand on Jenny's thigh and began to move it back under the yellow sundress. Jenny didn't seem to mind, which puzzled Tommy.

(But of course Tommy didn't realize that Jenny wasn't an ordinary tight-ass Moron girl. Jenny was a whorish Catholik girl whose sole mission was to seduce young boys and steal them away from The Church of the Moron.)

As Tommy tickled the hairs on Jenny's juicy twat, the woman in pink droned on about the blessings of Ameway. Yes, now it was "blessings." Tommy became more and more angry as the language slowly drifted away from religion-neutral Free Enterprise lingo and toward the loaded spiritual message of

Moronism! As Tommy suspected, this meeting was just another state-subsidized way to recruit new members for the Moron church.

Finally the meeting closed and Tommy handed in his application papers. Then he took Jenny's hand and led her up the stairs and away from that pit of spiritual foulness. As he left, he spotted the big-breasted Moron girl and gave her his widest smile—all teeth. She smiled back—in response, no doubt, to the supernatural Charisma of God's own prophet, Tommy Lee.

As Tommy and Jenny waited at the bus stop, Tommy noted that the Moron girl was walking toward the low-income subsidized apartments that were just down the street. He thought the name on her paper badge had been "Molly." Tommy made a mental note that he should come back down here, and soon, to teach this young Moron whore about the *sticky&sweet* Spirit of Jezus. And if he could do it while spurting his own love juice all over her enormous white titties, well, so much the better.

Chapter 3

While Tommy Lee and Jenny Craig stood waiting for the next bus, Tommy saw that one of his own advert posters was taped to the bus shelter. It read:

DITCH THE BUM
Don't have the balls to stand up to your
horrible excuse for a boyfriend? Scared that
he'll punch you in the nose? Been fucking his
best friend or brother and can't admit it to his
face? Have no fear! I'll break up with your
boyfriend for you—no fuss, no muss. I'll do it
with a smile, with a frown, I'll even do it
upside down. You send me $25 and I'll tell

your boyfriend everything that is wrong with him (from your perspective). Or, for $50 plus travel costs, I will break up with your boyfriend face-to-face. Imagine the joy of knowing your asshole of a fuckmate has been humiliated at work or at home. Singing break-ups and hilarious costumes can be arranged for additional fee. For the low, low price of $500 a day and expenses, I will do other forms of dirty work. Use your imagination. Contact: Tommy Lee @ P.O. Box 6762 Prophet Street USPS

This scheme had been the main source of Tommy's income for several years. It was easy work and paid enough to cover the rent and necessities. Tommy no longer absolutely needed the welfare check, but — what the hell — there were all those polygamous Moron jerks who fucked their nieces and got welfare checks, too. So why not Tommy? If some asshole could marry his niece and keep four or five other women on the side, along with dozens of tow-headed spawn, and get the state to support his bastard kids with welfare checks, free housing, free food, and free medical care, then why shouldn't Tommy get his share of the same free lunch?

Tommy saw a group of young Moron lads wander by the bus stop. They were obviously on their way from the public school, which was just across the street, and headed for the Moron Education Center. By state law, they were allowed to take one class period a day for religious education, and so these guys were on their way to get their daily dose of Moronism at the Religious Ed Center.

As they dawdled, an old man hobbled up to them and began giving them a hard time. He yelled, "Hey, you bunch of young slackers! Get on to your religion class."

Tommy responded on their behalf: "Shut your trap, you

old fart fucker!"

The old Moron gent was so shocked by this vulgar language that he was unable to respond. Instead he scurried back into the Ed Center, like a crab that had just lost a claw.

The guys were appreciative, as no one else had ever had the balls to take their side—and against a church Elder! Eight generations of careful inbreeding had left them unable to think for themselves, much less challenge the authority of their Moronic teachers.

Smiling, one of the guys said, "Thanks!"

"No problem," Tommy responded. Then, suddenly, Tommy realized that he had, right at hand, the chance to save the souls of these poor young Morons. Given the close-closeted nature of Moron society, it might be years before these young men heard another dissident voice protesting the lock-step of Moron culture.

The Morons took the opportunity to introduce themselves:
"I'm John."
"I'm Brigham."
"I'm James."
"I'm his brother James."
"I'm his other brother James..."

Tommy had seen this many times before. Some old goat had three wives, and so he named all his sons James to make it easier to remember. In a household with three wives and more than a dozen children, it could get confusing. And that was especially true if your higher brain functions were severely limited by several generations of inbreeding. In some Moron families, they resolved this problem by using paper nametags on the kiddies and plastic ear tags for the wives.

"And my name is Bliss," the last one said.

Tommy was a bit surprised since "Bliss" wasn't exactly a good Biblical name. In fact, the kid looked like he had some "dark blood" in him. Tommy guessed that Bliss had a bit of The Jungle in his genetic background. The kid was obviously a

good deal brighter mentally than his comrades, and he was also strikingly good-looking—again, a bit odd for Moron youth who, on average, trend to the Mr. Potato Head look. Tommy guessed that his mother must have spread her cunt, not to mention her bunghole, in The Jungle a few times, while doing her mission work in the bowels of The Big City, before returning to Gloryland. And knocked up, too.

Bliss also looked a bit older than the others. He was at least a senior, and he had probably been "held back" a few times, too, by his racist teachers—probably because of his failure to conform to standard white-bread Moron culture. Since this kid Bliss was obviously a natural leader, Tommy knew that if he could win Bliss over, the rest would follow like the sheep they were.

"Hey," Tommy said, "you guys want to get high?"

One of the Jameses looked up toward the sky, as if expecting a helicopter to swoop down and lift him into the air. The result of generations of inbreeding had left him with little in the way of imagination, and the use of euphemisms was completely beyond his feeble mental grasp.

"Sure," Bliss said, smiling a bright row of perfectly white teeth.

Tommy was now sure. The half-black kid, Bliss, must have been the product of a non-denominational relationship.

I'll bet his mother was solidly and soundly fucked by a Black sailor while she was doing her missionary work in San Diego, he thought. *It's probably that fresh injection of Naval genetics that makes the difference.*

Apparently, Bliss was the only one there with the mental ability to comprehend that they were being asked if they wanted to take a toke of Tommy's weed, or maybe weed his toke... or something like that.

"Sure," the others quickly chimed in. Bliss's friends—all genetically inclined to follow the leader—began smiling and nodding too, in their typical Moronic manner.

Jenny added her two cents: "And if you guys are lucky,

maybe he'll let you fuck his girlfriend, too."

Several of them began looking around, trying to figure out who she meant. They didn't realize that the Catholik whore was offering to let them do the Moron soul-train on her own luscious ass.

"Let's go back to my place," Tommy said. "You guys need get injected with some spiritual guidance, and I'm just the guy to give it to you."

They all climbed on the city metro bus and rode the short distance to Tommy's apartment. The living room was relatively clean, if you didn't count the piles of Babtist magazines and pamphlets, not to mention the sink full of dirty dishes.

As soon as they got in the room, Tommy turned on some Christian rock music and then stripped down to his skivvies and beyond — showing off his muscular frame and his religious tattoos. Everyone could see the slogan "Jezus is *my* ride!" tattooed in Algerian-font letters on his backside. Having an audience really turned him on, and it was only seconds before his *holy&humongous* cock was fully erect.

At the same time, Jenny slipped out of her sundress, and before you could say "Frigg'em Young" she was nekkid as a jaybird. And the most prominent aspect of her figure was her deliciously delicktable cunt. She was clearly an "au naturale" blonde.

The Morons just stood there, drooling. Tommy quickly saw the problem. He was sure that, except for circle jerks and a little same-sex cornholing, these guys had little experience with human sexual behavior.

"None of you guys have ever seen a nekkid woman before, have you?"

"Sure we have," John said.

"Yeah, just last week we fucked James' little sister!"

At this revelation, all three of the Jameses turned to John and yelled, "Did not!"

"Did too."

"Did not." "Did not." "Did not."

"Did too."

"Did not." "Did not." "Did not."

"Did too."

Tommy stepped in. "No, no, no! I'm not talkin' about fingerin' bald pussy! Jezus Christ! I mean, none of you guys have ever seen a cunt with hair on it, have you?"

At this they all shook their heads, eyes downward in embarrassment.

"There's no shame in that," Tommy said, lighting up a joint. "There's always a first time." Tommy sucked on the joint, then passed it to Bliss, who handled it like he had done it all his life. Soon all of the rest joined in, passing the joint from one hand to the other.

Jenny dropped to her knees and wagged her pretty ass. It was the first time that Tommy saw that Jenny had a tattoo on her pretty derrière. It said, "God's Whore" written in big Gothik block letters, which suggested that Jenny believed strongly in "truth in advertising."

"I want your cock in me. Now!" she ordered.

"Sho 'nuff," Tommy said, falling to his knees and massaging his man-meat until it stood up like Moses' magic rod. His audience was *truly&deeply* impressed by the humongous size of Tommy's trouser snake.

Then Tommy pressed the head of his cock against the lips of Jenny's pussy.

"Hey, not there!" she said. "Higher up. I want you to fill my arsehole with that giant cock of yours."

"No easier said than done!" Tommy said, always trying to accommodate the fairer sex. But Tommy soon found that the accommodations were pretty tight. It took several minutes of hard thrusting to get the full length of his cock slid into her tight little glory hole. And by the time he was done, Tommy had broken a serious sweat—much like the famous Biblical Samson did when he ground his huge cock into the tight ass of that Philistine whore, Delilah. Much to his discomfort, Tommy soon discovered that Jenny had only to grip her sphincter muscles to very nearly crush his man-meat. The feeling was highly erotic, but unpleasant too. And he didn't want it to stop, not yet. It was like she was trying to squeeze the love juice out of his cock, like in a toothpaste advert.

Tommy was finding the territory of Jenny's ass pretty tough going. It was like she was deliberately squeezing and releasing her muscles, disrupting the rhythm of his strokes. And then Jenny's arsehole suddenly clamped down on his cock, so that it was actually quite painful. Tommy felt like that one time, when he was eight, and got his cock caught in the garden hose.

"Let up, you fuckin' bitch!" Tommy yelled.

Jenny responded by locking her muscles down even tighter. Her rectal muscles were truly of industrial-grade quality. Tommy grabbed her blond hair and then pulled her head back, far enough so he could get his hands around her throat. He began choking her from behind, and Jenny began laughing and coughing and laughing again.

(Jenny was a product of the Catholik educational system, and she was well-trained and quite experienced in playing her Catholik schoolgirl games.)

Unable to stop the crushing pressure on his man-meat, Tommy grabbed a nearby complimentary leather-bound copy of The Book of the Moron and used it to whack Jenny over the head. She fell forward, unconscious, and her sphincter muscles suddenly released their death grip on Tommy's cock.

But by then it was too late. So much of Tommy's blood flow had been trapped in his cock that there wasn't enough left to go to his brain. For Tommy, everything suddenly went black. He passed out and fell, limp, across Jenny's body.

The young Morons stood watching, their tiny brains struggling with trying to comprehend what was going on: *Is this really how people have sex?*

Young John was stunned. He suddenly realized why his parents kept a large copy of The Book of the Moron on the table next to their bed.

Meanwhile, the three James brothers all felt woozy, as James, James, and his other brother James felt as if they'd had their brains cooked like eggs in an iron skillet. They were at a complete loss to comprehend what was going on.

"What should we do?" Brigham said, leaning over Tommy's naked body.

Young Bliss scratched his chin and thought and thought and thought.

"Hey! Why don't we fuck 'em?" he said.

Meanwhile, as he struggled along the long, lonely road back to consciousness, Tommy felt a dozen hands lift him onto the sofa bed and place him amid the stacks of Babtist literature. Standing above him was the black post-teenager, young Master Bliss, who was fondling Tommy's cock. Slowly the blood started rushing back into his majestic organ, leaving very little blood for the proper functioning of Tommy's brain. Tommy felt woozy, but his cock now had enough manual handling to function on its own and quickly grew massively erect.

Bliss grabbed the meaty rod and put his beautiful, thick lips against the head of the shaft. Tommy groaned in pleasure as Bliss worked his meat, with a masterful hand, up and down the length of his cock. It was as if Bliss had been genetically programmed for just this one task. Bliss lived up to his name, giving intense pleasure to the semi-conscious (but fully erect) Tommy Lee.

Tommy lay on his back, looking up at the ceiling of his dismal apartment. A lonely ceiling fan twirled in slow motion. As he lay there, he felt the supernatural power of Jezus Christ Godalmighty as it fell from the sky like rain. The heavens opened and a white dove flew down from the sky and landed on Bliss's left shoulder, where it sat and watched Tommy writhing in pleasure.

A delicious golden light appeared and surrounded the face of young Master Bliss. Even though Bliss's mouth was preoccupied with pleasuring Tommy's cock, Tommy could hear Bliss's voice, as if amplified through a very expensive sound system with quad speakers:

"My Father, who art a footballer in the Southern League, hallowed be his name. His Kingdom has come. His will is now done, on Earth as it is in Heaven..."

These words penetrated Tommy's soul, and suddenly he realized what was happening.

It's the Second Coming! Tommy thought. He fully believed that young Bliss was the resurrected Christ who had come to redeem the world with his sacred blood.

Quicker than you can say, "Lazarus, come forth!" Tommy's cock shot a massive load of splooge into the air. Bliss smiled and relaxed the rhythm of his strokes. And as the load of splooge was about to land on Tommy's belly, Bliss caught the spunk in his left hand—just like a kung fu master catching a fly with chopsticks.

Bliss said, "Flip him over." A dozen hands grabbed Tommy and flopped him over on his stomach. Bliss used Tommy's own spunk to lube Tommy's arse. Then Bliss climbed up on the sofa and forced his cock against Tommy's glory hole.

To the others present, Bliss's cock seemed like a perfectly normal cock (though dark-skinned and perhaps a bit larger than theirs). But in Tommy's Apocalyptic vision of Bliss, The Resurrected Christ, the size of His cock was magnified in Tommy's imagination. To Tommy, Bliss's cock was—in fact *had to be*—the second largest cock in the known universe. This was essential to Tommy's understanding of the supernatural world. In Tommyland, only God the Father Himself could have a bigger cock.

So as Bliss pressed his coffee-colored cock against Tommy's glory hole, Tommy imagined that this cock was so large that it made a salami look like a cocktail weenie. Tommy tried to relax his sphincter. Then he yelled:

"Split me open, Jezus! Split me open with your Glory and Salvation!"

Bliss had it easy going as he forced his cock into Tommy's arsehole.

"Fuck me, Jezus! Fuck me!" Tommy screamed.

The other guys chimed in.

"Yeah, fuck him! Fuck him!" John said.

"Fuck him in the ass, Jezus!" Brigham said, laughing.

"Tear him a new one, Jezus!" the James brothers added.

Young Bliss quickly plumbed the deepest, darkest depths of Tommy's innermost desires. The rhythm of his strokes was amazing to see, as Bliss seemed to know exactly what Tommy needed, embodying his every wish, fulfilling the sacred knowledge of his flesh. Indeed, an independent observer might truly believe that Bliss was indeed the Messiah prophesied in the Sacred Scripture. He certainly seemed to have The Amazing Gift of Discernment—or at least he knew his way around a grown man's arsehole with the skill not seen on Earth (all gathered in one place) since the time of the Ancient Greek catamites, or at least since the last meeting of the papal conclave.

Bliss fired his sacred load into Tommy's netherparts, and Tommy saw the Gates of Heaven opened with a chorus of angels singing "Hosannah! Hosannah! Hosannah!" A great rush of desire swept through Tommy's soul. He had waited ten long years for this to happen. He knew that Gloryland was marked for punishment, perhaps even total destruction. He hoped that God would send the Archangel Michael to smite the Heathens. But instead God had sent his Only BS; that is, his Only Begotten Son! And here The Christ was Himself, in His Glorious Appearing, ready to smite the Heathens and return the nations of the Earth to His True Way of Righteousness!

As Tommy watched, lying flat on his stomach, his eyes were filled with a vision of indescribable beauty. Jenny stood up, resurrected as if from the death of the flesh. She was enveloped in a glorious aura of Absolute Purity and Love. Jenny moved over to where Bliss was waiting, his still-erect cock jutting out from a thatch of black and curly pubes. Jenny took his cock in her dainty hands and began to suck the last bits of spunk from that shiny chocolate rod.

"Just like the Woman at the Well," Tommy whispered. "He came to fulfill the prophecy of John's 4:34."

Thusly, Tommy proved that his intensive study of The Book of John's was not wasted. Tommy knew that young Bliss (or the Resurrected Meat of Jezus, called Bliss) had come back to Earth in order fulfill those parts of the scripture that were left incomplete by His first and early death.

Tommy gazed on the face of Bliss. And without spoken words, Bliss said unto him the holy words of Jezus:

My meat is to do the will of Him that sent me, and to finish His work.

Here, finally, was the release from his labors that Tommy had been praying for so earnestly. Tommy's eyes clouded over and he began to cry real tears. Here it was, after so many years, the completion of his mission. He had prepared the way for Bliss. From now on, Bliss would call the shots, and Tommy would serve His will with all his ability—body and soul.

Tommy rolled off of the sofa and fell to his knees. He crawled over to Bliss and embraced his legs, while looking up into his eyes with both awe and love.

"Please, Master, let me service you. I want to help you. I know that God has sent you to destroy the evil that rules this country. I want to help. I want to do God's work...

your work."

Bliss placed his hand on Tommy's head and tousled his hair. Bliss smiled, then said to his classmates, "Looks like we're gonna need a lot more weed."

The Perfect Woman

by
Amy Judkins

Many men have unrealistic fantasies of the perfect woman — one who would serve his every sexual desire at his command. And if she were to have fringe benefits that made the sex unlike anything any man has ever known, all the better. What could top that, except for a harem of them? Well, how about just one such woman — designed, built, and provided by your ex, but with certain features that make her a one-woman harem? But what if, deep down, you really still love your ex, and she loves you, and neither of you is crazy about you spending three years away, alone on an alien world?

Science fiction
Android sex
Three-way (two males)
Double penetration
Cunnilingus and fellatio
Objectification
Romance
Lust

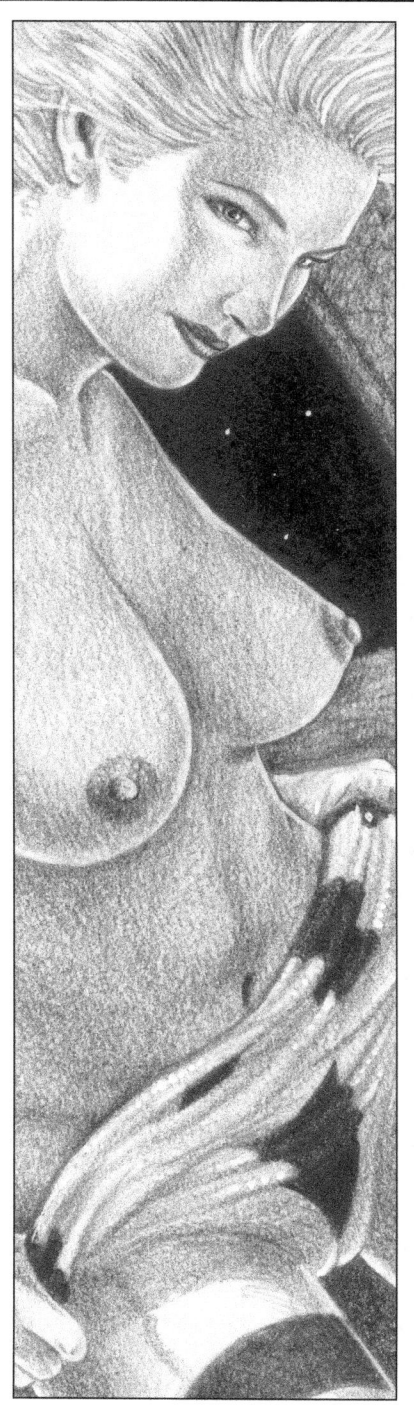

207

"It's been a long time," Jack Sprague said.

Dr. Elizabeth Morrow nodded curtly, her lips pursed. "I appreciate that you came all the way out here," she said in that sultry, soft voice that had just a hint of gravel in it. "I know Alaraph isn't exactly a quick trip."

It was anything but. Jack glanced out the window at the barren, cratered landscape of the moon of Beta Virginis III. The gas giant loomed huge above, and its bands of green, yellow, and purple spanned the sky. Off to the left, Beta Virginis, also known as Alaraph, shined brightly in the blackness of space. It had been a very long trip—three hundred twenty-one light years from Earth—and, although he wasn't about to admit it to Beth, he wouldn't have come all that way for anyone else.

"I'm waiting for the punch line," Jack said.

"I don't follow you." She looked so scholarly, as she always did, staring at him with a tilted head and scrunched brow. And, damn, she was sexy as hell in that lab outfit. Something about Beth in a knee-length skirt and a white lab coat always turned him on. The dark hair piled up in a neat bun was always exciting, too, like the schoolteacher you knew was out of your league.

"Well, given the circumstances of our divorce, I figure you're planning to get me alone in an escape pod and jettison me towards the gas giant." He offered a manufactured laugh.

She smiled through her red-painted lips, and in that instant Jack regretted ever cheating on her with any of those many women. Those lips were perhaps the most fantastic human lips in the whole galaxy; he'd enjoyed them in many ways when they'd been married. She was a fantastic kisser—but, more importantly, her skills at fellatio were damn near as good as her skills as an android engineer. She could work magic with those fat, pouty lips, with her expert tongue, and with the soft fingers of a hand that knew how to stroke and squeeze in all the right places at just the right times. He envisioned her brunette head bobbing up and down, and he felt his penis stirring in his pants.

"I'm way over that, Jack," she said, flashing white teeth. "Really. That was three years ago. You were a terrible husband, but I'm past it."

He studied her face as their gazes locked, trying to read her. He'd never been able to, and this time was no exception. Fleetingly, he fantasized that they were making a sexual connection in that gaze—and perhaps there was something there, however mild. But then, there had to be. It wasn't rampant ego; Jack knew he was a damn good lover, and he knew she agreed. She could hate what he had done all she wanted, but he knew she couldn't ignore the memories of how well he'd always serviced her. It was at least half the reason she'd fallen for him so hard in the first place.

"All right," he finally said. "So what important task do you have for me that's worth five million? That's a lot of money. I could live extremely well on that kind of cash for at least thirty years."

"There's a trade-off," she said. "Before I tell you, let me show you what you'll be doing."

She took him through the white-walled interior of the outpost, which was devoid of any other life forms. Robots ruled the antiseptic place, rolling and hovering and flying this way and that. He saw a few androids, which was no surprise, but he knew that he and his ex-wife were the only humans for at least a dozen light years in any direction.

"Awfully lonely out here," he said as he hurried behind her striding form as she clacked her heels on the hard floor. He admired her shapely calves, and tried to make out the swish of her ass as her hips bumped against the loose lab coat with every step. He had to admit, she'd been damn good sexually, too, and he couldn't help but think about having her once more, for old time's sake—even though he suspected she'd never let that happen again. "So tell me why an android engineer has come all this way to do her work."

"Major funding from a big corporation," she said. "This was formerly a government outpost for studying the system. The company owns it, and I wanted someplace I could do my work and be alone—*really* alone."

"Well, *I'm* here now," he said, maybe a bit too self-confidently.

She stopped just short of an alcove in the white hallway and spun to face him, her right hand smartly braced on a hip that kicked sharply to the side in a sexy, come-hither stance that completely turned him on. Her knee-length skirt danced around her knees, tight about her hips, tantalizing him. But her face was stern as he hit the brakes to avoid running into her, and his nose ended up just inches from hers.

"I know what you're doing, Jack, and it won't work." Her eyes blazed green fire, and her nostrils flared. "If you think I paid you to come all the way out here to have sex, you've got another thing coming. I do *not* want sex with you. Do we have a very clear understanding?"

Peripherally, he saw her breasts swelling against her blouse beyond the open lab coat, heaving as she breathed hard in her anger. He nodded. "I got it."

"Okay." She stood up straight, smiled, and said, "But I *did* get you here for sex. Just not with me." She spun on her heel and entered the alcove, and the doors within slid open. Jack chased her inside.

It was a lab, and there were dozens of robots and androids there in various stages of assembly. Heads and limbs lay on tables. Some were plugged into charging stations; others were on tables, opened up for diagnosis. It was nothing he hadn't been used to seeing in six years of marriage to her; her lab wherever she worked was always similar, and her home work-shop had been pretty much the same.

"My company has me working on a project," she announced. "They've installed the most powerful wormhole generator ever created, one that can open a portal clear to the other side of the galaxy. They want to send a scout on a long-term mission, but there's a concern: Can a human survive without companionship and sex, all alone, for an extended period of time?"

He blinked in surprise. "This is no new idea. Studies have been done for years about this—dating all the way back to the Mars missions of the twenty-first century. They've already figured this out: If you can only send one person, you send along an android to keep him or her company, and provide all the sex the traveler needs."

"That's fine for women, who can generally handle the same android satisfying her," Beth said. "But men have a more constant desire for sex, and they get bored too easily by having the same partner—two points we both well know."

It stung a bit, but it should have. He'd deserved it, so he nodded curtly.

"This experiment takes it a lot further," Beth said. "If you agree to this, and for a paycheck of five million, you'll go away for three years—absolutely out of range of human contact, not even communications."

So there it was. He shook his head and chuckled. "I get it. Send me away for three years, and you're rid of me. Obviously, you could use anyone for this. Sorry, honey, there's no way I'm living on some alien world with just an android pussy to keep me company."

"It isn't like that. I can't use just anyone—I have to use a man with the most insatiable sexual appetite in order to test this—and, sorry Jack, the best example I know of that is you."

He grimaced. "You say you're past everything, but you keep throwing it in my face. I screwed around you—I admit it. I fucked pretty much anything that came within range. I wish I hadn't. But it's who I am, Beth—I can't change that, and I don't want to."

"I know," she said, and although she sounded disgusted at his frank admission, her eyes gleamed with excitement. "But that's exactly why I need you. I've developed a special android that I believe will keep any man satisfied—for three years or thirty years, or even three hundred. The company is very excited—never mind the exploration uses, think of the sales revenues! But before we make any deals, before we talk about anything, I want you to try her out. Jack, meet Lydia."

A door in the room slid open, and when Jack turned, his heart skipped a beat. The woman—or so it appeared—stepped out of the booth and headed toward him. She was a beautiful blonde, with incredibly long, flowing hair cascading about her shoulders and down her back. She wore a skintight silver jumpsuit with black trim accenting her many pronounced curves, looking like something out of a twentieth-century pulp sci-fi movie. She smiled at him with big, blow-job lips and sparkling, ice-blue eyes as she sashayed across the room, broad hips swaying with perfectly fluid sexuality. Her big breasts bounced almost in slow motion as she went. He felt his mouth sagging open. She was fucking stunning.

"In many ways, she's just a top-of-the-line model," Beth said. "Virtually indestructible, and will follow all your orders. She'll make a great workhorse in other ways, too, but obviously she's built for pleasure. And, like a pleasure android, she's the best in every way. But there's so much more."

Lydia stopped before him, smiling and meeting his gaze with hers. He felt as if he'd sunk into her blue eyes and all the way into her android self. He felt his penis stir again, but he knew it was just a mindless reaction. He stepped back away from her and turned to his ex-wife, trying for a look of

212

dismissive amusement.

"Very nice, but she's just another fancy android sex toy," he said. "Not special enough for three years. No android could ever be that good."

"Because you'd get bored with the same woman?" Beth pressed, smiling.

"Yes—and there's nothing wrong with that." Beth had never understood that—it had never been about being unfaithful to her. He'd loved her more than anything. He'd just needed variety.

"Well, I thought of that—and I have you to thank. This isn't just any sex android, Jack. I've given her improvements like you wouldn't believe. I'm not talking about what she knows or how she acts; any sex android is damn good in every way. It's the unique feature I've given her." She turned to the android and said, "Lydia, introduce yourself."

"I'm Lydia," she said, and her voice matched her beach-bimbo appearance: lilting and singsong, hinting at modest intellect and low-willpower promiscuity. It was just the way Jack liked them. "I'm *really* happy to meet you, Jack. I'm *all* yours, and I'll make you *so* happy, *all* the time."

"That's what they all say," he said, snickering.

"Lydia, give Jack a demonstration of what you can do," Beth said.

"Sure," she said, and before Jack's eyes, she changed.

Her hips slimmed and her breasts swelled, and the skin-tight outfit accommodated her new shape. Her curly hair grew shorter and darkened to nearly black as it straightened. Her eyes deepened to a sultry brown as her facial structure changed, and within fifteen seconds, a totally different woman stood before him.

"I'm Lydia," said the husky-voiced woman. "Or I can be any name you'd like. Or any woman you'd like."

She morphed again, growing taller, her boobs shrinking, her hair going red in tight, short curls, and freckles exploded in a thousand dots on her changing face. Then she grew shorter, hair going light brown as it sprang straight from her head. All the while, she talked, reintroducing herself in a completely different voice. After a dozen variations, she settled on an athletic, large-breasted woman with short blond hair and dark eyes.

"That's impressive," he said, and he wasn't lying. "I mean, truly amazing."

"That's not all," Beth said, beaming with pride. "I know men get bored not just with the woman but with the same old... well, the same old vagina. I get it. As you can imagine, hers can change shape, form, tightness, angle. She can even morph a hymen back at any time — instant virgin. And she's an actress with a thousand roles; her personality and behavior is yours to command. She can be a slut, a church girl, hard to get, easier to get, a dutiful wife, a dedicated girlfriend, a mean bitch, a prostitute, a cheerleader — anything you want. But that's not even the best feature I've built into her."

He widened his already-wide eyes. He couldn't imagine what else could make the android better.

"Lydia," Beth said, "take Jack to his quarters and show him what else you can do."

He wanted to refuse, in order to show Beth that he wasn't the same guy, but he was the same guy, and his horniness won out. He followed Lydia's jiggly ass down the hall to the guest quarters. She didn't waste any time.

"How would you like me?" she asked with a seductive smile. She was standing before a pair of broad windows, back-lit by the colorful gas giant in the sky. It was an inspiring pose. "You just tell me your fantasy, and I'll fulfill it."

She was the sexiest woman he'd seen in a long time. Her curvy form seemed to be threatening to burst the silver suit apart. He could see gumdrop-sized nipples pushing through the stretchy fabric. Between her legs, she was sporting serious cameltoe; the cleft there was as visible as if she were naked. He could see the slightly darker material there where her juices were already wetting the suit.

"Maybe... just like you are for starters," he said.

"All right, babe," she said, and giggled. "You have a seat on the bed. I want to strip for you."

He did as she said, and watched with increasing excitement as she reached up behind her and pulled the zipper to her jumpsuit down, and then rolled it down over her shoulders. She teased him, turning around as she exposed her bare breasts so he only caught a brief glimpse of one of them. Then she peeled the suit over her arms, rolled it down over her broad hips, and shimmied out of it. He watched as her incredible ass became visible, and as she didn't quite bend over to slide the suit down her perfect legs. He tried to get a look at nirvana up between her legs, but she knew just how to move and stand to obstruct his view.

She stepped out of the heap of suit on the floor, and as she turned to him, he saw a flash of curly blond pubic hair before she cupped a hand over her crotch and threw her other arm across her breasts. A total tease. She giggled again, smiling as her big tits bulged around her slender forearm.

"Do you like me?" she said.

"Hell, yes," he said. Even if she were just a toy, he was going to fuck her brains out. Or fuck her CPU out. If he couldn't have sex with Beth, he'd fuck her custom-made android.

Lydia took a deep breath and struck a wide stance, moving her hands to her hips. Her big, soft globes bounced free, and he got a look at the trimmed bush, split down the middle as her spread legs pulled swollen labia apart, beckoning him.

"My pussy's all wet," she said, sounding little-girlish, and then she took on a bad-girl tone. "And I bet you wanna stick your big dick up inside my cunny, don't you?"

"Yes, I do," he said, rubbing his hard penis through his pants.

"Don't you want to see what else I can do?" she said.

There had been Beth's "but" statement. "Okay."

Lydia moved to him, until her belly was almost in his face, and he could smell her musky juices. It didn't matter a bit that he knew it was synthetic. She straddled his left leg and looked down at him, smiling seductively over her big boobs. "You ever titty-fuck a girl?" she said.

"I sure have."

"Bet you haven't like this."

She cupped her boobs in her hands, then lifted and separated them. And as Jack watched, something happened between them. Her chest bulged, puffing out, even as a dark line appeared vertically between her tits. The bulge opened up along the line, as if being cut with an invisible knife—but there was no blood. To his stunned shock, another pussy morphed into existence in the middle of her chest. She extended her fingers to grasp the new outer lips, and she spread them wide as her vulva continued to bulge and form. Curly pubes spiraled out of her skin. Inner lips glistened with her dew, and a clitoris peeked out from underneath its hood. He could see her vagina form, going deep into her chest, as she pulled her lips wider to expose her beckoning hole. The exquisite aroma of pussy hit him in the face.

"Holy shit," he said.

"Come on, baby," she said. "Try it out."

He grabbed her around the waist with both arms, pulled her in, and surrounded his head with tits as he buried his face in her second snatch. He shoved his tongue up inside her and worked his nose against her throbbing clit. She squealed as she grabbed his head and pushed it deeper, and began moaning as he went to work on her. The experience was bizarre, but he didn't care. He ate out that second pussy until the blonde was shaking and trembling, unsteady on her feet, wailing her way through an overpowering orgasm.

He didn't give her a chance to rest. He stood and threw her on her back on the bed and quickly shucked his clothes.

His eager cock sprang forth—seven thick inches that were ready for the wildest sex he'd ever had. But he started with her normal genitalia first. He pulled her ass to the edge of the bed, standing as he plunged his dick deep inside her and making her squeal again. He bent over her as he thrust his hips and found the chest pussy, and began lashing her clit with his tongue while he banged her hard. It wasn't the first time he was in one pussy while eating another, but before it had always required two women. Lydia went crazy beneath him from the dual stimulation until she squirmed and screamed her way into a second orgasm. And then he knew it was time.

He pulled out of her, climbed on the bed, and straddled her abdomen. He realized the angle was a bit weird; he'd have to have her sitting down, and him standing. But she must have realized, because she said, "Let me help, baby."

As he watched, the bulging chest pussy moved down her body to her upper abdomen, just below her ribcage. Her body changed shape slightly, and the pussy angled to a more normal position, just like the one between her legs. Perfect setup. He hunched forward and slid his cock into that pussy—and felt it slide under her ribcage and into her chest. He could feel it get tighter every time her synthetic lungs expanded, and he could feel her android heart beating against it. It was bizarre, but it was exciting.

She yelped with pleasure and reached for his hips, snaking her hands around to grab his ass with strong grips and clawing fingernails. She pulled him forward with every thrust, helping him bury it between her lungs with every powerful stroke. Soon, he worked his hips like lightning, the sweat pouring down his face and body.

"Oh, yeah, baby, that's good," she moaned like a street slut in the back seat of his hovercar. "Give it to me. Fuck me harder."

He grunted and strained, grabbing for her jouncing tits as he felt his balls tighten. "Get ready, honey... I'm gonna come..."

"Not yet," she said. "I want you to come in my mouth."

He laughed. "Sorry, sweetheart. I've never come in a chest pussy before, and I'm not missing the chance. I can come in a mouth anytime."

"Not a mouth like this," she said, and as he watched, her face changed. Her jaw melted a bit, and her mouth twisted vertically as her cheeks puffed out, soft and full. And, just like that, she had a pussy on her face where her mouth had been.

"Holy shit," he said again.

He sat on the edge of the bed, and she knelt in front of him, and he grabbed her hair in two strong hands. She was an android, so he could be as rough as he wanted, so he drove his cock deep into the pussy on her face, slamming her head down against his groin like a madman. The weirdest part was she was still moaning and humming and working a tongue — a tongue inside her pussy! — tickling the super-sensitive head of his cock. Below, he could see her hands working madly: one plunging fingers deep into her chest cunt, the other furiously frigging the clit between her legs. Her pussy clenched and squeezed, rippling with every stroke, and her tongue worked his cock head, and he finally lost control. His balls exploded and he roared as he fired shot after shot into her cunt and down her throat. When he collapsed backward on the bed, he felt the pussy transform back into a mouth again; teeth lightly raked the sensitive head as he shriveled, and she licked him clean as he slid out. Then she stood up and smiled down at him.

"Was it okay?" she asked playfully.

"It was fantastic," he said. It was the best sex he'd ever had; there was no denying it. "Tell me something... can you create genitalia... anywhere?"

She smiled wide, lifted her arms in the air... and suddenly sprouted pussies all over her body. They were under her arms, on her wrists, around her thighs, in her belly, in her ass cheeks, up and down her back. She was like the most perfect goddess ever as she stood there, her body covered in genitalia. Each was different: a thin slit here, a puffy cunt there; some had pouting lips, others more thin and reserved. Some were bald, some neatly trimmed, and others had tangled bushes. They were blond, brown, black, red. And there had to be two dozen of them.

He felt the stupid smile spreading across his face.

It was a long night. He'd never had so much pussy in his life. And he had her change her form regularly as he fucked her, so every minute there was a different woman: short, tall, chubby, skinny, white, black, Asian—he tried it all. While he speared his cock in and out of her, he kissed her, or licked another pussy. His hands found vaginas wherever he touched. And every vagina had rippling muscles that seemed to have minds of their own. He fucked her in the ass—but not in her asshole, just in her butt-cheek vaginas. He tried every pussy she had. On his request, she even changed her right eye, and he had the pleasure of actually skull-fucking a woman.

She woke him in the morning with a blow job—but not with the mouth on her face. She'd morphed her right hand into a bulbous mass with a mouth of its own, so it was like a hand job and a blow job all in one. The experience was perhaps more bizarre than the weirdness he'd already enjoyed; he could feel the teeth and tongue, even as he watched her jack him off with a speeding forearm.

Then she took him into another fantasy, growing a penis of her own and sliding it into his ass. He'd never been with a man, but her suggestion seemed exciting—and it was. She showed him other unique things, like sprouting breasts all over her body, and even giving him a few tight anuses to try out.

By the time he finally left his quarters, he'd been there for nearly fourteen hours, and he hadn't slept for much of that. Beth was in her lab, tinkering with an android, when he entered, and she looked up with a wooden smile.

"Long night, sailor?" she said. He knew there had to be some jealousy in there.

He sat down next to her with a harsh exhalation. "Okay, my hat's off to you. You've done it. She's... incredible."

"I'm sure," she said, her voice flat. "An objectifier's dream, right?"

He glared at her. "That's hardly fair. You called me to come out here, and you gave me an android designed to be objectified. And it isn't really objectifying women when she's not really a woman."

"She's not human—but she's really a woman."

He sighed. "I guess I can't argue that. She is indeed a woman. Hell, she's the *perfect* woman."

It was out of his mouth before he realized it, and he saw the pang of hurt on Beth's face before she nodded and forced another smile. "She had to be. That's why I designed her the way I did. For a man to survive alone, she had to be this good. So... will you do it, or should I contact the company and have them send me a crew of potentials?"

He gave a start. "A crew?"

"That's how they originally wanted to do it. They have twenty men, screened and approved and willing to go, waiting for me to interview them and choose one. But I convinced them to let me try you." She laughed and shook her head. "After all, who else could I personally vouch for having an utterly insatiable sex drive that was more important to him than anything else?"

He sighed. "I never meant to hurt you, Beth. I know you'll never believe it, but I always loved you."

"I do believe it," she said, and suddenly she reached out and clasped his hand. The move took him completely by surprise, and its warmth stimulated him, his heart kicking into a flutter like that of a twelve-year-old boy with his favorite girl touching him for the first time. Of course, the feeling flowed like a wave right to his penis, which began stiffening.

"It took me a while to believe it," she said, squeezing and unsqueezing his hand in a light, steady rhythm, not unlike how she used to delicately grasp his cock and coax it to life. "I was hurt. I was miserable. I thought you just didn't care. But I grew to understand that you did—that you just couldn't help yourself. And I forgave you. I'm beyond it."

"Beyond it—but willing to send me away for three years," he said. He tried to will his erection down. Its angle was off, jammed by his underwear, and he was perilously close to having to reach down to adjust it.

"The time period is necessary. We'll be opening a wormhole to the other side of the galaxy, which requires a tremendous amount of power. We've spent three years harnessing the power of that star out there to make it happen. I'll start the process again once you leave, and be ready to reopen the wormhole in another three years to get you back. During that time, you study the planet and so forth, but you also keep detailed logs about your experiences, particularly if you're sexually and emotionally satisfied—basically, report whether Lydia does what we think she'll do: keep you sane and happy."

She met his eyes, and her voice was softer. "And we pay you five million. It's a long time, but... just a drop in the bucket, really. Maybe a few hundred years ago, when humans lived a century at best, it was a long time—but not now that our life spans are centuries. Three years... and you'll be back."

She moved in close, surprising him, and pulled his hand up to her mouth and kissed it. Her breasts pressed against his raised arm, and her thigh was warm and soft against the steel rod between his legs. He couldn't hide it now.

"And I'll still be here, right at this outpost, when you get back," she whispered. "I guess I hope you'll be different then—that, having screwed every possible permutation of a woman, maybe you'll be ready to commit again. And maybe I can have you back."

He'd had no idea, and for her to open herself up to be so vulnerable hit him hard. "Beth..." he started, but she shushed him.

"Don't talk about it," she said. "I... I just have to have this chance to know you're not with any other women, and to think about you every day, and to know you might be thinking about me. Just say you'll do it."

"I'll do it," he breathed, all hesitation utterly gone.

That night, Lydia came to him, wearing a tiny, fluorescent-green microkini. She had become a tall, voluptuous woman with chocolate skin and the blackest hair, broad hips and a bulbous ass, with bulging breasts that sagged under their own weight. The microkini barely covered her nipples, and only the tiniest patch of cloth barely concealed the cleft in her shaved vulva. "Tell what you'd like me to be tonight, sugar," she cooed to him, striking a sultry pose.

"Beth," he said. "I want you to be Dr. Morrow."

She smiled, and her skin brightened, her hair browned, and her body changed form until his ex-wife stood there in the green microkini.

"You naughty boy," Lydia said with Beth's voice. "You really still have it for her, don't you?"

He attacked her, shoving his tongue in her mouth and groping her all over. She gave herself to him completely, moaning and crying out as he moved her to the bed and laid her down on it. His hands roamed, pushing the skimpy top aside to grope those supple breasts that he knew so well. He kissed her some more as he snaked a hand down and yanked the little thong aside to expose her sex. She spread her legs eagerly for him.

"I love you so much, Jack," the fake Beth said. "Make love to me like you used to."

And he did, climbing between those thighs as he freed his aching hard-on from his pants and jammed it into her burning,

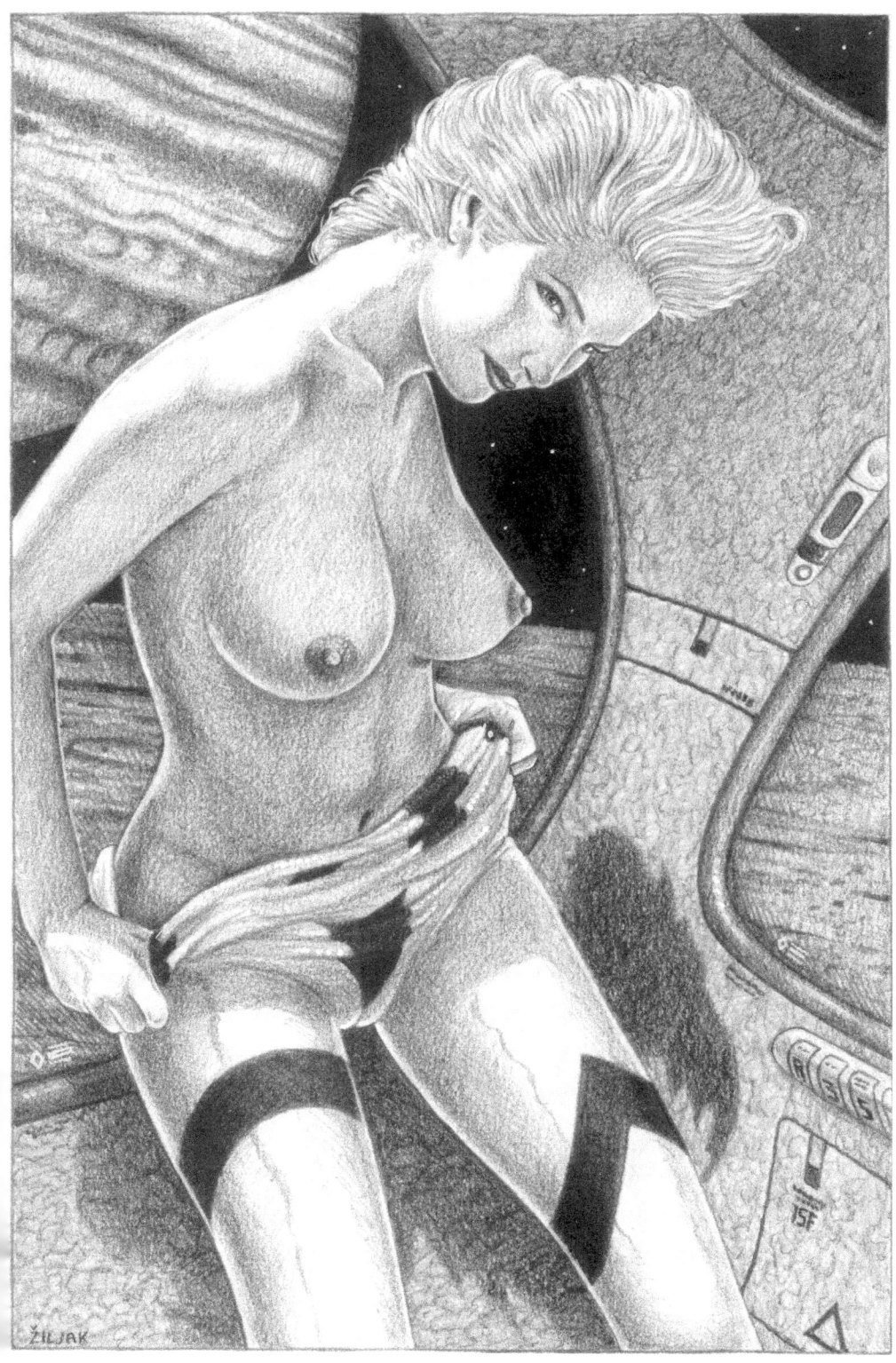

ŽILJAK

liquid depths. She cried out, a prisoner to the passion that overwhelmed her, just like the real Beth always had. He kissed her, kneaded her breasts, sucked on her neck, all while banging her hard and steady. He kept up the pounding pace until she began to buck and hitch beneath him, her cries sticking in her throat. When she finally shuddered helplessly, he felt her insides grow even hotter and wetter as she soaked his invading cock with her intense orgasm.

Then he repositioned her legs so her knees were pushed to her breasts, braced himself on his hands, and revved up his hips up until he was speed-fucking her like a madman, all the while looking deep into her wide eyes. She screamed her way into another orgasm, and he grabbed a handful of her hair as he pumped hard and exploded inside her, coming for what seemed like forever, until he collapsed atop her and she groaned in total satisfaction.

He lay there, breathing heavily, for several minutes, before rolling off her. She rolled with him, wrapping her leg over him and hugging him tightly. "You missed that, didn't you?"

She was still being Beth, but somehow it seemed wrong now. "Lydia — be someone else."

She obeyed, almost immediately transforming. He felt her shape change, felt her shrinking a little, felt her leg sliding a bit on him as she did. Her breasts, pressed against him, shrank as her hair turned black and sprouted into girlish pigtails. Her eyes darkened as they became almond-shaped. The Asian girl who was wrapped about him smiled up at him.

"You're going to miss her," Lydia said, accent like an innocent Japanese schoolgirl.

"Maybe not with you around," he said, and kissed her forehead.

"I think she will miss you," Lydia said. "And I think she will miss me."

"She'll just build another one of you."

"But not just like me. I've brought her much happiness."

It took a second to click in his head. "Do you mean... have you had sex with her? As a man?"

"Oh, yes," said the cute Asian girl, smiling up at him. "But she likes me to look like this most of all."

Beth opened the door to her quarters and didn't have time to react when he burst in, forcing her back.

"Is that what this is?" he cried. "Your sloppy android seconds? You're tired of her, so you ship me off with her? Is that a fucking laugh for you?"

Her eyes were wide with alarm, and he realized she wore a slinky robe. It was short, barely halfway down her thighs, and he could see hard nipples against the sheer fabric. He looked past her, to her bed in the dimly lit room, and he saw another android sitting there. She looked just like the Asian version of Lydia he'd just left in his room, and she was naked.

"She's just an android," Beth said with pleading eyes. "I've only been with androids since we divorced. I... I just prefer it that way."

"Are you a lesbian now?"

"No. Sometimes they become men for me."

He flashed angry eyes at the smiling android, then back to Beth. "Were you leading me on when you said you'd be here when I got back? Was that just a line to get me to agree to this?"

"No—why do you think I haven't been with a real man since you?" She spun about and stalked to the bed, sat down next to the Asian android, who reached for her and caressed her shoulder. "I meant what I said. I hope you'll come back a different man. I've never stopped loving you."

He suddenly felt like an idiot standing there, and he didn't know what to say.

"Megan," Beth said to the android. "Show Jack who you become when I tell you I'd like a man."

Megan looked to Jack, smiled, and changed quickly into a

man. It was like looking in a mirror.

"Hello," the android Jack said.

Jack staggered back a step.

"Now, go back to Lydia," Beth said, almost fiercely. "I'm busy."

He knew he should leave, but he couldn't. He stood there as the android version of him peeled off Beth's robe and began to kiss and lick her nipples. He watched as a duplicate of the erection he was getting grew between the android's legs, and as the android expertly worked Jack's ex-wife over. Then the android lay her back on the bed and slid inside her. She cried out in ecstasy as he did, and as the android Jack began to saw in and out of her, she moaned and cried out with every stroke.

Jack found himself opening his own robe, grabbing his cock and fisting it hard and fast as the android fucked Beth. She wailed in ecstasy as he did to her exactly what Jack had just done to Lydia when Lydia had appeared as Beth: bent her knees to her breasts and fucked her long, hard, and fast, through multiple orgasms. When she screamed for the second time, Jack grunted, ejaculating into the air and all over Beth's carpeting. Still, the android put it to her, and still she gasped and squealed.

He watched as the android lay down on the bed and pulled her atop him—but backward, reverse-cowgirl style, so she faced Jack. She reached down to rub her engorged clit, and she looked right at Jack as she did. Jack's wilting cock began stiffening again when she did, and he watched in fascination as she circled her fingers furiously.

And then the android reached down to guide his penis—but not back inside her vagina. Instead, he pushed its head against her puckered anus, and her eyes lit up as it popped inside. He grabbed her hips with both hands and gently shoved her down. She sucked in her breath as the android impaled her ass on its cock.

And Jack couldn't ignore his desires, and couldn't ignore

the look in Beth's eyes that told him she had the same desires. His cock was at full mast again, a bit of semen glazing the tip and dripping off, and he moved across the room and climbed on the bed, straddling the android's legs and between his ex-wife's. He grabbed his cock and guided its throbbing head into her swollen, wet slit, and sank it deep inside her. She gasped as he did, and he felt his balls slap against the android's cock.

Then the two of them began fucking her in unison, and did so for a long time. She moaned and cried out steadily, and she came several times, each orgasm more powerful than the last. And Jack and his android doppelganger worked like experienced twins, each of them stroking a hole perfectly to complement what the other was doing. As if both knew when her wild, screaming orgasm was her last, they picked up the pace and double-fucked her until they were both roaring like lions as they erupted with monstrous ejaculations. And as Jack came, he collapsed on Beth and grabbed for her head, and Beth grabbed for his. While the android bucked beneath her as it jammed itself madly in her ass, and as Jack's cock still shot weakening spurts inside Beth, he kissed his ex-wife, long and deep, and she kissed him back.

And when the three bodies separated, she wrapped her arms around him and whispered in his ear, "Please come back to me."

And just then, Jack knew he would. He knew Lydia would change him, and in three years he'd be the new man Beth needed him to be.

He signed all the legal paperwork that released the company of any liability and assured him five million when he completed the three-year assignment. He read up on the planet he was going to, some sixty-five thousand light years away, on the other side of the galaxy. It was mostly Earth-like, devoid of all but the most primitive animal life forms—but it was loaded with plant life, with trees and everything. The planet had everything he needed to survive, and Lydia had the capability of hunting, gathering, and growing to keep him alive. She also possessed ample skills in survival, engineering, and so forth — everything a lone human would need for three years on an alien world.

She brought him to the wormhole generator in another lab when he was ready. Lydia followed, wearing a backpack that was so gigantic that it seemed cartoonish. A long, eight-wheeled wagon was already there, piled high with just about everything, including an all-terrain vehicle and a self-assembling shelter.

"I guess I'm ready," Jack said.

"I guess so," Beth answered, not looking at him. Her face was downturned, and Jack could see the sadness there. It heartened him further about the mission. "I'll generate the wormhole in the middle of the room. Lydia will pull the wagon through. I can only hold the wormhole open and stable for about a minute, so don't waste time. And remember, in three years, Lydia will know exactly when and where the return wormhole will open, so be ready or you'll miss your chance."

"I don't want to miss my chance," he said.

She looked up and met his gaze with hopeful eyes. "I don't, either."

And so she fired up the wormhole generator, which first opened up an extradimensional energy conduit with Beta Virginis. The star's tremendous energies fueled the generator to form the dimensional portal that leaped beyond more stars than humanity had ever leaped. The rift shimmered in the air before them, rippled, and then solidified. Beyond was a lush world with plants of greens and blues, with flowers of all colors. Towering trees with dome-shaped blue canopies, and shorter trees with a thousand branches rife with green and red tubular leaves, waved in the breeze. An orange sun blazed above in a bright-yellow sky. Fluffy white clouds, and streaks of pink and green clouds, filled the sky. A vast ocean sparkled like gold in the distance.

"It's open," Beth called from the console. "Get moving!"

Lydia grabbed the wagon's tether and strode forward. The wagon rolled easily, and she pulled it through to the alien world. Jack hurried to the console.

"You have to go now," Beth said. "There's no time."

He grabbed her shoulders, pulled her to him. "There has to be time for this," he said, and he kissed her. She returned it. Their arms held each other, their hands grasping and not wanting to let go. He felt the love he'd long missed.

"I love you," he said when they broke their kiss. "I'll be back for you."

"Good luck," she said, and she gave his hand a final squeeze.

He broke from her, and forced himself not to look back. He ran for the portal and leaped through to the other world. When he landed on the soft grass, he turned back in time to see her raised hand waving to him — before the wormhole abruptly collapsed, stranding him on the other side of the galaxy for three long years.

He and Lydia spent several hours setting up the shelter and unpacking everything. By the time night fell on the tropical land, he was worn out. But he wasn't going to sleep without christening the planet.

"Lydia," he said from the bed in his new shelter, "I think I'd like you to be a brunette this evening. Give me big boobs. And let's do this right — I want your body covered in vaginas. I'm going to fuck you six ways to Sunday on this brave new world."

Lydia dutifully changed shape to accommodate him: brunette, big boobs. No vaginas on her face. "Strip down, honey," he commanded, settling back with a smile.

He watched as she turned back-to and peeled off her

clothing. She was covered in pussies, and she was a stunning beauty standing there naked. She smiled at him.

"Come here, you," he said, rubbing his erection through his pants.

"I don't think so," she said.

He blinked in surprise. "What?"

"I said it isn't happening," she said. "Sorry, Jack. I'm a hands-off girl now."

He shot up on the bed. "What the hell is this?"

"You heard me, asshole," she said, sashaying over to him. "Look, but don't touch."

"I don't think so," he said, and he reached for her —

— and every pussy on her body morphed out of existence. Her breasts flattened, her nipples vanished, and her hair retracted. Her skin turned green and brown, cracking and splitting into hard scales. She changed into a hideous creature with warts and tufts of greasy hair, and Jack hollered in surprise, scurrying back on the bed.

"This is your punishment, asshole," the creature that was Lydia said through crusty lips. "You shouldn't have messed up Beth's life so badly. Now, you're finally paying the price. I'm with you, but you can't have me. I'll tease you a lot, looking like any sexy woman I want, but I can look like this, too. No matter how badly you want me, you'll never be able to have me."

"This can't be," he said.

"Oh, it is," she replied with a vaguely reptilian smile. "Will it help if I look like someone else from time to time?"

The naked monster morphed, and Beth stood before him. It was her in every respect, but with no nipples on her breasts, no gash between her legs.

"Aw, honey, this will be tough," android Beth said with her sweet smile. "If only you could deal with it by jerking off — but I promise you I'll never let that happen. If I so much as sense you have a hard-on, I'll become a monster. And if you touch your cock, I'll stop you. Hell, sweetheart, if you even get a stiffie in your sleep, I'll interrupt that wet dream before you can enjoy it."

"Why are you doing this?" he screamed.

"Because you deserve it," she said, eyes hard and lips pursed.

"I can't go without sex for three years," he said through gritted teeth.

She laughed. "Three years? Do you *really* believe she's going to open a wormhole here in three years?"

He felt his heart thud cold blood through his veins. "Oh, no..."

"Oh, yes. And you're not where you thought you'd be." She gestured around at the world. "Sixty-five thousand light years, she told you. Guess again—try about twelve million. This planet is six galaxies away. Nobody will ever find you. So get used to it."

He watched as her pussy reappeared, and her arm lengthened as her hand changed into a monster cock. She laughed aloud as she plunged it up inside and began fucking herself madly, wailing and moaning in sheer ecstasy. All he could do was watch.

And scream.

Succors for Incubation

by
David M. Fitzpatrick

Self-imposed celibacy — the idea sounds quite noble to some and utterly insane to others. The young couple in this story fits that description — with each of them seeing either stance. But they're determined to wait until marriage, which is challenging enough until you realize that, besides being young and in love, they share not only a home but a bed. That makes things — pardon the expression — a lot harder. But for both of them, nighttime visits from the supernatural are about to threaten their chastity.

Dark Fantasy/Horror
Succubus/incubus
Celibacy
Virgin sex
Forced sex
Desire
Romance

Martin

Martin Stuttman gazed at Steff's sleeping form in the darkness, trying to decide if she were in a deep-enough sleep that he could quietly let his erect penis poke out through the flap in his boxers. He was dying to release the aching tension in his testicles, but he didn't want her waking up while he did. It was gearing up to be another night of a bizarre mix of heaven and hell.

Martin had been incredibly nervous when he and Steff moved in together, but it wasn't about the commitment. It was about the lack of sex. At Steff's behest, they'd agreed to wait until they were married for that. He'd been on a quest to lose his virginity since junior high school, but it hadn't happened by the time he'd met Steffanie Wyles during his sophomore year in college. She'd made her beliefs clear on their fifth date, and he was already so head over heels for her that he was willing to make that sacrifice.

Two years later, he was wondering if he'd make it. The wedding was still eighteen months away, and now they had an apartment and shared a bed. It was, Martin always considered with respect for the pun, really hard. They'd spent cuddly nights together before, and always Martin had fiercely exerted mind over matter, finally falling asleep frustrated, his aching hard-on jammed against her thigh or wedged between her soft butt cheeks.

She always said it was tough for her to handle, too, but he suspected it was a lot tougher for him. After all, she always slept comfortably, arm across his chest and leg across his

234

thighs, while he spent hours every night throbbing and sweating against her. It wouldn't be half as bad if she'd agree to oral sex, mutual masturbation, or even just some dry humping. But no; that all counted as sex, and had to wait until they were married. That's what she always reminded him they believed. He *did* believe it, but that didn't make it easy to handle.

It was a nightly torture. But he loved her, and somehow he always held out and, each morning, as soon as she left for class, he'd furiously jack off to relieve the pressure in his aching balls. But that wasn't what he really wanted to do. He'd long since abandoned feeling guilty about wanting to throw her legs over his shoulders and piledrive her until she screamed her way through a half-dozen body-shaking orgasms and straight into a sex coma. She was a perfect and beautiful little flower, sure, but biology took over, and he wanted to violate that flower until her petals wilted.

They were both on their sides, facing each other, and her light breathing was the only hint she was alive—that and the warmth of her hand, resting on his hip, tantalizing him. Beneath the covers, he felt ready to rip through his boxers. He'd been staring at her beautiful face for an hour, and all he wanted to do was masturbate so he could go to sleep. He just couldn't do it with her facing him with her elfin, little-girl face, framed by golden-blond hair; if she popped her eyes open, she'd catch him behaving like an animal.

And then she suddenly rolled over, and for a moment he thought she'd end up back-to him, giving him a perfect opportunity to take care of himself. But she adjusted the position of her trim, athletic little body, hiking her butt back, and to Martin's surprise they were suddenly spooning. He sighed in defeat as everything hard found a comfortable spot between everything soft. There would be no whacking off—and, even worse, now he had to fight the urge to start grinding his erection in her butt crack.

It was going to be a long night.

After a long while, he finally did fall asleep, but deeper into the night he came suddenly awake. He was on his back, and something was chafing his thighs. He tried to lift his head, but he couldn't make his neck muscles work. And when he tried moving his legs, he found them also unresponsive. Panic seeped in as he realized he literally couldn't move a muscle.

And was someone unbuttoning the flap in his boxers? Was Steff finally giving in to her own animal urges? If so, had his body chosen this night to self-paralyze? That would be a kick-in-the-nuts irony.

Out of the corner of his eye, in the dim moonlight streaming through the window, he could see the golden hair on the back of Steff's head. Whoever was yanking his boxers open wasn't her. He tried to open his mouth, call her name, but couldn't. Only his eyes worked.

No—something else worked. Whoever had unbuttoned his boxers was touching him with warm fingers, freeing his sleeping penis from his shorts and bringing it to life. The bed jiggled, and he felt hot, silky skin tickling his right hip. It jiggled again, and more skin slid down his left hip. They were thighs, smooth and supple, and they clenched about him lightly.

And then she leaned over him. Long, wild red hair, with flowing waves and almost-curls, hung everywhere, obscuring her face, but soft eyes glowed yellow in the dark. It was a woman, no doubt; he could see the generous swell of breasts swaying above him in the darkness, and when she leaned closer, felt her erect nipples, like hot little coals, briefly brush across his chest, tantalizing him before moving off.

Martin's panic escalated. Was he about to be raped, right in his own bed, with his love sleeping beside him? He couldn't move; had his rapist drugged him somehow to paralyze him?

No! he screamed in his head, because he couldn't manage a sound. He couldn't let this happen. He and Steff were waiting until they were married, and they'd saved themselves for each other. It couldn't happen this way—no matter how frustrated he was!

He could see her features in the dimness. She had a beautiful, heart-shaped face. Her chin was tiny with the faintest hint of a dimple. Her high, puffy cheeks and cute button nose made her look like an innocent, pixieish schoolgirl. And her full, pouty lips, as if perfectly inflated, were the lips of a man's most legendary oral-sex fantasies. She was a thing of mythic beauty, and as she leaned closer again, he could see the smooth curves of her shoulders and torso. She pressed her body against his so that her heavy breasts and fiery nipples crushed against his pectorals.

The yellow glow of her eyes seemed to burn brighter as her face moved to his, lighting up the private space created by her cascade of red hair as it tumbled about his face and engulfed him. Her hair smelled like heaven, as if it had been shampooed a dozen times and scented with the hints of a hundred fruits and flowers. Her swollen lips, glistening wet, hovered just over his, and he could feel her sweet breath on his face. He tried to speak, tried to beg her to stop, but he only managed the slightest gurgle.

"Sssh," she said, and her cherubic voice softened his panic like a goddess taming wild beasts. He felt his heartbeat slow a bit, felt the panic subside—and then he felt her hand wrap around his throbbing penis. The panic returned as she squeezed and caressed, and he responded against his will by getting even harder. He had to stop it—he fought to move, but only trembled as she gripped him firmly and began stroking.

Beside him, he heard Steff snoring lightly, utterly oblivious that her relationship with Martin was falling apart right next to her. This caused his heart to race anew, uncontrollably, as the strange woman expertly worked on him, softly rippling her hand over the pulsing veins in his cock as she rolled his foreskin over its head and back, over and over. And just when he knew there was no way the hand job could possibly make him any harder, without warning, she shifted her weight and eased back—and abruptly impaled herself on him.

The rush of pleasure was overwhelming. He'd never been inside a woman before, and the intense sensation of his cock completely engulfed by her steaming-hot, clamp-tight vagina was incredible. She threw her head back, flying her mane of hair away, and he saw tall, pointed ears. She laughed then, loud and bellowing and victorious, and somehow Steff kept snoring. It was the most intense, pleasurable experience Martin had ever felt, and all he could do in his paralyzed state was let it happen. Her sopping-wet pussy clenched him furiously as she moved on him, and every stroke sent sizzling waves of sensation through the burning head of his cock, and he felt his orgasm already building, far faster than he'd ever been able to achieve on his own.

She rode him like a madwoman, laughing and howling as she bounced up and down. Her pussy was as tight as Martin had always imagined his virgin girlfriend's would be, and soaked with boiling juices that let it glide freely around his cock. She flew upright, totally dominating him as her head snapped about, hair flying crazily, her big breasts swinging everywhere. He lay there, helpless, as she thrashed on him. It was wrong, a violation of his promise to Steff—but it was the greatest feeling ever, and a part of him didn't care about the promise, didn't care that it wasn't Steff, didn't care that their life together was being destroyed.

She moved faster, and the closer he got, the faster she went, the more intense it was. The paralysis was maddening; he wanted to grab her, participate in this exciting act, be a part of this nirvana. All he could do was lay there as she leaned in, planting her hands on his chest and revving up her hips until she was punishing his cock in fast-forward. Her bouncing ass cheeks slapped his thighs like an endless round of applause, and every time she rose off his pole, the slurping sound of her juices drove him crazy with desire and made the feeling in his nuts ever tighter.

Then he passed his point of no return, and she went from laughing to screaming with every move. Everything swirled in a maelstrom of confusion, and then he exploded, coming like a porn star. She howled with glee and he gurgled and trembled amidst the impossible waves of pleasure, and his otherwise-paralyzed body spasmed, over and over, with each jerk spurting shot after shot of semen deep inside her spasming cunt.

And then she came, screaming like a banshee above him, hitching her hips uncontrollably, her powerful pussy clenching and releasing repeatedly as she wailed, and then he passed out and it was over.

Martin woke to bright sunlight, with vivid memories of the night's event immediately clear in his mind. He struggled to prop himself up on his elbows, and looked down. The flap to his boxers was open and his flaccid member was out. It was obvious from the dried semen on his penis and matted in his pubic hair that the event had either been real or one hell of a wet dream.

Steff stirred next to him, stretching her arms and legs as she came awake. Frantic, he stuffed his penis back in his boxers and buttoned the flap. She rolled over just as he'd finished.

"Good morning, honey," she said with her angelic, sweet smile. "Did you sleep well?'

"I'm not sure," he said.

She was off to class that morning, and Martin brooded in the living room. A thousand times he reviewed what had happened, and he was sure it hadn't been a dream. The woman had somehow paralyzed and raped him, with his sleeping virgin lover beside him, and he'd become a body driven only by lust and enjoyment. He tried to convince himself that it was just biology, that he couldn't help it, that he hadn't betrayed

Steff — that he'd never have willingly let it happen.

But he couldn't, because he just knew that if the paralysis had failed in the middle of the act, he'd have kept going anyway. He knew he wouldn't have been able to stop himself. That shamed him more than anything, except for the fact that he wanted it to happen again. That disturbed him more than anything.

Except, perhaps, for the fact that the woman had had yellow eyes and pointed ears.

Steff

Steff thought Martin seemed eager to go to bed early that night. It was only nine-thirty. "It's awfully early, honey," she said. "I'm wide awake. Plus, I have a paper to write."

"I'm just really tired," he said, looking a bit too sheepish. He was standing in the doorway to the study, where their computers were, staring at the floor.

She turned in her chair and pulled her glasses off from her soft blue eyes, regarding him. "Are you okay?"

"I'm fine," he said with a dismissive shrug, hands in his pockets, still looking at the floor. He always looked cute when he did that, and his sandy-brown hair being uncombed and a bit disheveled made him look even cuter. But he certainly seemed to be mentally elsewhere.

She studied him for a long few moments, and finally nodded. "Okay, honey."

He half-nodded, then turned to head down the hallway. She called after him, and he turned back.

"Do I get a kiss?"

He mumbled an affirmative, moved to her, bent over and gave her a quick smooch. Then he was gone, shuffling down the hallway and then climbing the stairs. She listened to him until he was in the bedroom.

That had been strange. He *never* just "quick-smooched" her; he should have cupped her face with one hand, fingertips in her golden hair, and kissed her like he always did—as if it were the first time they'd ever kissed. He was acting like he'd forgotten to pay the cable bill again and was trying to think of an excuse. More likely, he was probably experiencing uncontrollable horniness, as he sometimes did. He was probably heading to bed so he could do a little "dancing with himself." She grinned at the thought. She couldn't hold it against him, but she couldn't wait until he wouldn't have to do that anymore.

He was so patient with her, the perfect boyfriend. She was lucky to have someone that devoted.

When she turned in two hours later, she was stopped in her tracks to find Martin lying on his back, uncovered and nude. He sometimes slept that way—especially when it was hot, but it was a fairly cool night.

But the issue was her reaction. She always held firm when it came to sex, since they'd agreed when they'd fallen in love that they'd wait until marriage. It was the right thing to do, she knew. Neither of them were religious, but she liked being old-fashioned about some things—such as waiting for marriage before having sex. It was a belief she'd clung to when she'd watched her mother bringing home a different man every weekend, and as her two older sisters did the same with boys from school. She'd always intended to wait, and she'd found in Martin a man who loved her, who respected her desires and made them his own.

But sometimes he was weak, and she had to be strong for both of them. What Martin didn't believe was that sometimes it was a challenge for her, too. And as she stood beside the bed, looking at her naked love, it was terribly difficult for her to fight the natural stirrings in her body. He was handsome and sexy, in very good physical shape, and amply endowed. And his penis wasn't entirely limp as he slept; it was just a bit erect, slightly swollen as it lay on his thigh. Staring at it, she felt the hot juices begin to sizzle between her legs. When it came down to it, she was a flesh-and-blood woman, and he turned her on.

She closed her eyes, bit her lip, took a deep breath, and turned on the self-control. When she got into bed, she'd always keep a safe zone between them and could usually fight the urge to slide a finger between her labia and stroke herself until she brought herself off in a silent, lip-gnawing orgasm. But not always. She didn't do it often, but every now and then she just had to. At any rate, she knew that if she cuddled up to him in this condition, she was liable to lose control and jump on him.

She changed quickly into a short nightshirt, not even consciously aware that she'd peeled off her panties first.

She woke suddenly sometime later to a dim, moonlit room, her eyes sticky and her brain fuzzy. It was warm, but she felt a draft between her legs. She realized she'd worked the covers off in her sleep, and her shirt had bunched up around her breasts. She was about to adjust it and reach for the covers when she felt Martin's hands gently gripping her legs just above the knees, spreading them carefully apart.

Her brain went on red alert. She couldn't believe Martin would do this while she was sleeping!

At the same time, the prospect aroused her. Maybe if she feigned being asleep for a while, she could claim it was too late and she didn't have the willpower to resist. Maybe that was Martin's plan.

The bed jiggled, and she felt his strong legs between her thighs, tickling them with their hairiness, and suddenly she panicked. This wasn't right. She couldn't play along. And how could Martin presume to do this anyway?

And his legs sure seemed a lot hairier than they were.

Next to her, she heard him snore suddenly, then roll away from her, and her blood grew cold. The man climbing between her thighs wasn't Martin.

She tried to snap her legs closed and flail her arms at the intruder, but she realized she couldn't move a muscle. Terror filled her, and she tried to scream. Couldn't.

A dark form moved into her vision, and she felt his muscular legs push against her thighs, forcing them apart until she was lewdly spread. She could see his bulging biceps and muscular, hairy chest as he moved above her, and as she felt his strong hand yank the shirt above her breasts to expose her further. His yellow eyes glowed in the darkness, and, silhouetted in the dim light, she saw tall, pointed ears.

He planted his hands to either side of her immobilized arms, holding himself up, and then she felt the gentle prodding of the head of his penis against the soft folds of her lips. It pushed gently in, and her heart drummed furiously faster, her breath hitching in her throat. It seemed to spread her wider and wider, until it felt as if he were shoving a tennis ball inside her. She tried to will her womanhood to fight off the intrusion, but that little minx between her legs was out of control, drooling in self-lubrication, helping the rapist violate her.

She wanted to cry out, wanted to thrash and stop him, but she just couldn't move. She'd lost all control of her body. And in that fleeting instant, as she felt the fat head of his penis pushing mightily against her hymen, she wasn't sure she *wanted* to fight it.

And suddenly he lunged forward, tearing fiercely through the obstruction and plunging deep inside her, and for a few surreal moments it felt as if he'd shoved a salami from her crotch to her ribs. She tried to scream, but all she could do was gurgle as he filled her up like nothing she'd ever imagined. The tearing hurt, but only for a moment, and he stopped to let her soak in the feeling of being full of what she thought had to be the biggest penis any man could possibly have.

Then he withdrew, slowly, and then slid back in, and her pussy sizzled as it marinated the intruder in its juices, its tight confines squeezing even tighter as if to keep the intruder from escaping. The man moved, steadily and easily, in and out of her, and with every stroke she burned hotter inside. With every slide in, he split her wide and sent waves of high-energy pleasure through her clitoris as if he were leaning on her thrill button.

And that's exactly what he was doing, and she realized she loved every thrust. He began moving faster, picking up the pace, sawing in and out of her pulsating pussy, and she knew any hope of denying the intense pleasure was forever gone. She lay there, helpless, as he slammed into her, harder and faster, his giant balls slapping at her ass, and in one expert motion, without slowing his pace, he came to his knees and forced her own knees nearly to her face. Her breasts were already flailing crazily about her chest, and now they buffeted her knees as he grabbed her ankles and held them above her as he worked.

A wash of embarrassment flooded over her, and she felt like nothing more than the proverbial piece of meat, there for his pleasure only — but it kept washing away, as she didn't care what she was to him, because all that mattered was the intense pleasure she was getting out of it. Her mind spun, her vision doubling and blurring, as he fucked her into a frenzy of excitement she'd never dreamed possible.

She felt her orgasm building deep inside her as he jack-hammered her pussy, which seemed to be begging for more. She was oozing juices like a leaky pipe, and her insides, stretched to the limit, seemed to be trying to stretch even wider. And it worked, because she felt him going even deeper, as if he sensed that she was heading toward her orgasm. She couldn't see, could barely envision what was going on down there, but his balls smacked even harder as he buried himself all the way to the hilt with every masterful stroke.

He stroked powerfully in and out of her as his yellow eyes burned into her eyes in the dim light. It was hypnotic, which was helped by the incredible feeling trembling deep inside her, with every furious pounding of his rock-hard, giant cock. Then the feeling amplified until it was almost unbearable, and there was no turning back, and her orgasm was upon her, with waves of intense pleasure ripping through her body and waves of liquid gushing out around his pounding cock, adding a wet splat with every ball-slapping plunge. She wanted to scream and shriek in pleasure, wanted to wrap arms and legs about this god of a man who was raping her, hold him and beg him to fuck her more, but all she could do was manage a weak gurgle as her pleasure nearly blinded her.

Just when she thought she couldn't take the sensations any longer, he began to grunt like an animal, his hips hitching and his stroking unsure, and that turned her on to a whole new level. He snarled and growled, a beast of primal sexual instinct, and her passion rose. She found herself coming yet again, new waves of pleasure tearing through her as her pussy spasmed crazily around his monster cock. Then he moved faster, roaring louder and louder with every stroke until he exploded inside her.

It was like nothing she'd ever imagined. She felt shot after shot of his come blast inside her like lava from an erupting volcano. And her hungry cunt took it all, squeezing tightly about him as if not wanting a single drop to be lost, and as she heard him laughing and howling into the night, and as any last vestige of opposition fled her overloaded mind and satisfied pussy, dizziness overtook her and she sank into darkness.

Martin

Martin woke the next morning, immediately aware that, against his hopes, the red-haired woman hadn't revisited him. He felt guilty at his disappointment.

He rolled over and found Steff sleeping peacefully, a serene look on her face. She was flat on her back — she *never* slept like that — and her T-shirt was bunched up over her breasts.

And she wore no panties—a first for her. He was instantly aroused at the tempting sight of her womanhood, the curly fluff of her golden pubic hair teasing him as it hid its prize.

More than anything, he wanted to make love to her. It wasn't like looking at a skin magazine or reading a sex-stories book or watching a porn movie. He loved her, more than anything in the world. They shared everything in their lives, except physical intimacy, and he ached to have that with her. Knives of guilt lanced through him at the thought of what he'd done the night before.

What had been done *to him*. It would be different with Steff. He reached for her shoulder, shook her gently, and called her name. Her eyes fluttered open. She looked up at him and blinked, and the serenity on her face melted suddenly into horror, and she started screaming.

She leaped from the bed and stumbled to the corner of the room, screaming incoherently at him, or about him, or about something—he had no idea what she was on about. She collapsed to the floor, screaming and blubbering, and he had no idea what to do. He tried talking to her to soothe her, but it seemed like everything he said only made things worse.

Eventually, she calmed down on her own, and dragged herself to her feet. "How could you not hear?" she said with hitching sobs, pointing an accusing finger at him. "How could you lay there and not hear all that noise he was making?"

Images of the red-headed woman laughing and screaming as she rode him, while Steff slept like a baby, flashed through Martin's mind. "What are you talking about?"

"I was raped!" she howled, and collapsed back to the floor in a fit of bawling and shaking. He ran to her, joined her on the floor, held her.

They sat in the living room, on opposite ends of the couch, he in shorts and T-shirt, she in a bathrobe. She had insisted on showering and cleaning, washing away the evidence. At least

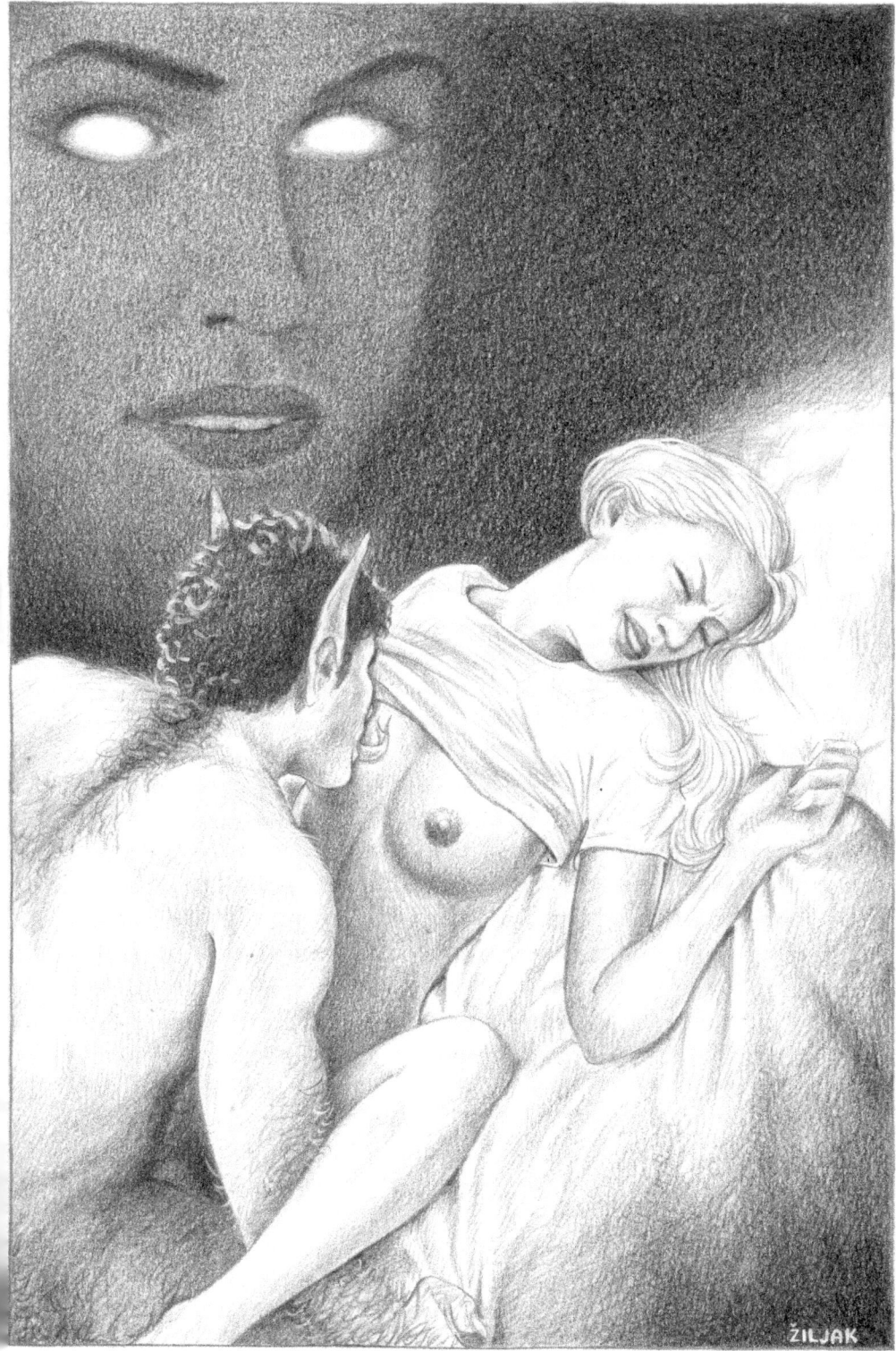

ŽILJAK

Martin knew her rape had not been a dream; there had obviously been semen. Martin had begged her not to wash, to go to the police first. But she wouldn't even consider it. Martin was afraid of why.

"Who was he?" he asked.

She sat, a zombie with blank eyes staring at nothing. "I don't know. And I don't understand how you didn't hear it happening. He was like an animal... grunting and snarling and roaring."

"What did he look like?"

"He was big, and really hairy. He was strong, but... I couldn't move. I think he drugged me first."

Chills danced along Martin's spine. "What color were his eyes?"

She turned to face him. "Why would you ask that?"

"Because I want to know."

She looked at him through eyes that were puffy from crying. "You're going to think I'm crazy, but they were yellow. And they glowed in the dark, I swear."

He felt as if he were about to sink deeper into the couch, until he'd vanish somewhere beneath the cushions. "And he had pointed ears... didn't he?"

Her mouth sagged open, her eyes wide. "You were *awake?* You knew it was happening and you didn't do *anything?*"

"No—it isn't like that," he said. He scooted himself out of his sinking, to the edge of the couch, and faced her. "It's just..."

His male ego took violent control just then. How could he tell her this—that he'd been raped, helpless and used, by a she-devil with the same yellow eyes and pointed ears of her assailant? Worse yet, how could he tell her that he'd enjoyed it? He breathed deeply, hoping to inhale the courage he needed.

"I was raped, too," he said. There, it was out.

She didn't look as if she believed it. "If you're trying to make me feel better—"

"I'm not. I really was." And with that, he told his own story, with all the details — except he left out the part about enjoying it, and certainly the part about his need to experience it again.

All while he told her, she sat in stunned silence. She'd closed her mouth and retracted her bulging eyes, looking at her hands, folded in her lap, while she listened. When it was over, she said, "Why didn't you tell me yesterday?"

"How could I tell you that our dream had been shattered? And honestly, if it hadn't happened to you, would you have believed me?"

She sat in silence for a long time.

"I have to ask you something, and I need the truth, no matter what," she finally said. "Did you enjoy it?"

He hadn't seen that coming, and he was unable to answer. He opened his mouth and tried, but nothing came out.

"You can tell me," she said, and her sweet voice was all he needed.

"Yes," he said. "I'm so sorry — at first I was frantic, and I wanted you to wake up, but then it was exciting and incredible and wanted it to go on forever." He dropped his face into his hands, and he felt tears welling up in his eyes. "I'm so sorry. I — I can't understand it. It was like she turned me into an animal, full of nothing but lust and desire."

And he began to cry, because he knew she could never forgive him now.

Steff

Their love was built on many things, including trust. And Steff was filled with love for Martin, who had trusted her enough to tell her everything he'd just told her. She could only do the same for him.

"I enjoyed it, too," she said.

His sobs interrupted, he pulled his hands from his face and looked at her, incredulous. In that instant, she feared he'd be like other men—possessive, vengeful, and holding her to a different standard than he held himself. But then that trust kicked in as she looked into his bewildered eyes, and she told him everything.

"I was terrified at first," she said. "It's not every day a girl gets raped in her own bed, while her fiancé is asleep next to her. And rapists don't usually have pointed ears and glowing eyes. I thought it was a dream, but the physical sensations were so real. I tried to scream, but I couldn't, and just when I thought my panic couldn't get any worse..." She swallowed hard, found the words. "He entered me."

She saw Martin's face collapse a bit. Was it sorrow? Regret? Egocentric misery that she'd been deflowered and would no longer be his virgin prize on their wedding night? She looked down at the floor and continued.

"It was painful at first, but then it became the most intense pleasure I'd ever known—or imagined. Within seconds, I wanted him more with every thrust. It was terrible and shameful and wrong, and I felt like a dirty slut, but I wanted him to never stop. I wanted the paralysis to end so I could wrap my arms and legs around him and make love with him."

She forced herself to meet his astonished gaze again, and said, "When I woke this morning, I couldn't bear the shame of everything—and the shame that I wanted him to do it again. I was wrong to scream at you like that, and I'm sorry. For everything."

"Steff..." he began, reaching for her.

She let him clasp her hand in his.

"I felt the exactly same way," he said. "I went to bed early last night in hopes she'd return. Instead, he came for you."

She squeezed his hand and smiled, a tear streaking down her face.

"We weren't drugged," he said. "Whoever they were, they

had some power over us—something magical. We didn't betray each other."

Relief strengthened her as waves of it washed over her like the ocean washing over a beach. "You don't resent me?"

"How could I, if you don't resent me?"

He scooted down the couch to be close to her, and they wrapped themselves up in an embrace. As they hugged, something suddenly stabbed at her gut, and she winced and tightened up. He separated the hug as she cupped her hand where it hurt. "What's wrong?"

"Just a pain," she said, lightly rubbing her lower abdomen. "Like a menstrual cramp. But it's a few weeks early for that."

Martin

Martin spent an hour online, researching the bizarre events of the previous nights. He came up with the most likely explanation, as incredible as it sounded.

"I think the woman was a succubus—a female demon who has sex with men at night," he said. "Men are powerless to resist. And the man was an incubus—the male equivalent."

"Being raped by demons sounds a little farfetched."

"It's either that, or two people with glowing contact lenses and rubber ears drugged us." Somehow, that seemed more ludicrous to him than the demon theory.

"But you're talking demons. That just isn't logical."

"I can't think of anything logical." She wanted to see everything in terms of logic and reason, but he was able to expand into the realm of the nonsensical—because only illogic seemed logical. He turned back to his computer, clicked around, brought up another article he'd found. "Now get this. Some such demons were both succubi *and* incubi. The succubus would rape a man and save his semen inside her. Then she'd transform into an incubus and rape a woman, impregnating her with the man's semen."

"Why on Earth would a demon need to do that?"

"Apparently, they couldn't reproduce alone. And the children born could be susceptible to demons' influence, or they could be demons."

Steff's face scrunched suddenly into a mask of pain, and she doubled over, wrapping her arms about her lower belly. "Ow, dammit!"

He was out of his chair and to her in a flash. "Another pain?"

"A good one," she said.

The thought flashed through his head in that moment, and judging from Steff's expression, it had occurred to her, too. They exchanged long, wide-eyed looks. "You don't think..." he began.

"Of course not," she said, maybe too quickly, and her attitude changed, like sudden thunderheads rolling in on a sunny day. "This whole demon thing is silly! I can't believe we're even considering the idea."

She leaped up from her chair, almost knocking him over, and stormed out of the room. Martin let her go. He listened as she stomped up the stairs to the bathroom. He knew she needed a few minutes to deal with this on her own.

Steff

She locked herself in the bathroom and sat on the toilet. She didn't have to pee; she just needed to think about everything alone.

She was angry, and she didn't know why. It wasn't the shame of what had happened, or that she'd enjoyed it, or that she'd admitted everything to Martin. It wasn't even Martin's similar confession. She was angry at the preposterous idea of demons raping her.

No, that wasn't it. She was angry because she knew Martin was somehow right: Demons really had raped them. Senseless and insane, maybe, but that was the answer. And that meant the demons wanted her pregnant.

Her belly was seized with another stabbing, twisting pain, and she grimaced. She'd had period cramps that had made her double over before, and this was one of them. But it wasn't a period, and that terrified her. The fact was, she and Martin had been serious about not having sex until they were married, so she'd had no need to be on birth control. But she knew her cycle, and she knew what this week was: ovulation time.

She waited for the pain to subside and went back downstairs. Martin was on the couch again, watching TV, and he shut it off as she sat down and cuddled up with him.

"Are you okay?" he asked.

She nodded. "Tomorrow morning, I'll go to the drugstore and get the morning-after pill—just in case."

He was silent for a long moment, and then he wrapped his arms around her, pulling her to him and squeezing her tightly. "Everything's going to be okay," he said, and somehow, she knew he was right.

Martin

They lounged together for most of the day, watching TV and just touching each other—cuddling, hugging, holding hands, her head in his lap, whatever worked for the particular moment. Every now and then, she'd be overcome with a twisting cramp, and he'd stroke her hair while she rode it out. He wanted to do more, but didn't know what he could do.

Eventually, it got late, and they were tired. Martin couldn't keep his eyes open, and he'd noticed her eyelids sagging. "We should head to bed," he said.

She was on her back, head on his leg, and she opened her tired eyes to him. "Are we going to be okay, Martin?"

"Of course we are," he said, and wondered why she'd asked.

"It's just that... I know men don't always handle it well when their women are raped. Especially when their women enjoyed it."

"I think we have a unique situation here," he said, running his fingers through her golden hair.

"Maybe. But would you still feel this way if I had been raped by an incubus, but you hadn't been by a succubus?"

He opened his mouth to answer *Of course I'd still feel this way,* but stopped himself. Maybe he wouldn't have. "I don't know," he finally said, "but what I do know is no matter what ever happens, nothing will change my love for you."

Her face suddenly contorted worse than it had all day, and she writhed in pain around him. He held her and comforted her, but the pain persisted for a good half-minute before she could speak.

"That really hurt, Marty," she said. "Why would it hurt like that so soon after the rape?"

"I don't know," he said, caressing her forehead. "Let's go to bed and get some sleep."

Martin woke, not long after he had drifted off, to the sound of Steff crying. He rolled over and touched her. "Honey, are you okay?"

"It hurts," she said, and she was crying. "Why does it hurt?"

"I don't know, honey."

"Make it stop!" she screamed.

"We need to take you to the hospital," he said, leaping up from the bed and going for a pair of pants. He had one leg in and was trying for the other when the window on her side of the bed abruptly flew open with a crash. A gust of wind blasted into the room, billowing the curtains crazily about and buffeting Martin, who was balancing on one leg. He toppled over into his closet door with a surprised yelp.

"Marty!" Steff screamed.

He clambered to his feet and bolted for the window, but an even more powerful blast of air roared through and knocked him back like a baseball. He hit Steff's closet door, cracking it in a dozen places, and he hit the floor in a heap.

"Marty!" she screamed again.

He fought his way to his feet, dazed and disoriented. Steff was on the bed, twisting and writhing in agony, her hands clawing at her own belly—

—and there was something outside the window.

He froze as the dark form hovered, and then it shot through the window and into the bedroom. He couldn't focus on the streaking blur in the dark as it whipped around the room like a whirlwind.

The indistinct form coalesced beside the bed and took shape. It was a tall man, muscular like a bodybuilder, and stark naked. Tall, pointed ears jutted through long black hair, and when he turned to look directly at Martin, Martin could see the fierce yellow glow of his demonic eyes.

"Leave her alone!" Martin shouted, and he charged forward.

The incubus raised a hand, and Martin flew straight up and crashed into the ceiling. He lay up there, helpless, thrashing and kicking, but he was stuck in that spot. And he couldn't reach Steff.

Steff was screaming, either from the pain or because of the incubus—probably both. She seemed unable to move. Martin hollered and swore at the demon, but it did no good.

She screamed again, and the demon gestured, and she was silenced. Another hand up at Martin, and Martin's hollering was quieted. Then the incubus raised a clawed hand, which began to glow with silver luminescence in the darkness. As

Martin watched in helpless horror, the incubus leaned over Steff and reached up under her nightie.

Steff

Steff was paralyzed, like before, but she felt the incubus reach up inside her. She felt warmth, like being too close to a campfire, but deep inside her, and she felt completely full inside. He moved his hand around, twisting and maneuvering, and suddenly the agonizing gut pains she'd been enduring ceased.

He pulled back, and his hand slid out of her.

The Demon

They were so terrified, the demon saw, and it smiled at the thought.

He held the creature up in his silver-glowing hand, and beheld the marvelous sight. The tiny, developing fetus struggled against his grip, flailing small arms with tiny claws about. Little ears were pointed, and its open eyes glowed yellow. It snarled with rows of sharp teeth and kicked two-toed feet.

On the bed, the paralyzed woman's eyes were gigantic; on the ceiling above, her mate's were the same. Now to give them one more show.

The demon changed as they watched, his mass reducing, his waist slimming, his massive pectorals ballooning into large, supple breasts. His hair thickened and lengthened, changing from jet black to fire red. His penis shrunk into its body to become a clitoris, and his scrotum became labia majora even as it split open to become her vagina. The humans watched in bug-eyed amazement, and she enjoyed every moment.

Then she reached down and shoved the squirming fetus

up into her demonic womb, where it belonged. When she knew it was comfortably in place, she smiled with rows of pointed teeth at the humans.

"I think you can come down, now," she said, and gestured with her hand. She lowered the man to the bed, settling him next to the woman and releasing the spell that held him. "And your mate," she said, releasing the woman. They both quickly found each others' arms, holding each other tightly.

And then she thought about what she said, and she chuckled. "Not really your 'mate,' is she?" the succubus said to the man. "It's difficult to find two virgins in love these days, you know. This never would have happened if you hadn't been who you are."

And she turned toward the window.

Martin and Steff

Steff couldn't restrain herself. "You've ruined everything!" she cried, tears rolling down her face. "We were waiting until we were married. We were waiting until it was special and right."

The succubus laughed long and loud, like she had the night she'd taken Martin. "You foolish humans," she said. "With a true love like yours, it is *always* special and right. That you have chosen to deny yourselves such pleasure for your perceived morality is nothing short of foolish."

The yellow-eyed she-demon leaned over them, and they cringed. "Take a bit of free advice from a woman who has watched mortals like you make mistakes like this since the beginning of civilization. You could die tomorrow with nothing but your love. Thanks to me, you now know what you've been missing. I wouldn't waste any more time if I were you."

And with that, she leaped to the window, becoming shapeless and ethereal as she went, and the wind blew her suddenly smoky form out of the room and the window crashed down and everything was silent.

Steff and Martin looked into each other's eyes, not quite knowing what to think of all that had just happened.

But they knew common sense and good advice when they heard it, so eventually they went into each other's arms. Without magic spells or demon influences, they experienced each other in ways they had only dreamed about—and it was better than it had been with the demon. They both knew why: They were in love. They took advantage of that, and made love every day.

And, damn, the sex was fantastic.

I'm Running

by
John Grant

Is it cheating on your wife if the woman you're with really is your wife? A younger version of your wife, to be sure, one that can't possibly exist but does – but your wife nonetheless. It should be a fantastic and perfect fantasy come to life, a chance for a man to fall in love – and in lust? – all over again. But there's a reason he's running away, and he'll relate the tale to the man who's giving him a ride… although the man might not be prepared to hear such a tale.

Dark fantasy/Horror
Heterosexual sex
Cheating
Passion
Romance

Say, buddy, thanks for the lift. I'd been standing there a while in the rain...

Yeah, I know. When you stopped for me I'd just given a thanks-but-no-thanks to that little red Chevy. But, well, I don't accept rides from women, you see.

No, nothing to do with all that crap about them being bad drivers — nothing to do with that at all. It's...

Well...

Look, you remind me a bit of my dad — no offense, you understand. I'm not saying you're as old as him, anything like that. Be difficult, anyway, seeing he's been dead these past three years. No, what I'm saying is you've got the same wrinkles around the eyes he had. And your eyes themselves — well, you've got *understanding* eyes, is what I'm trying to say.

I feel like I can trust you.

No, I'm *not* gay. Wish I were, right now, because then I wouldn't be in this mess I'm in.

What I *am* is running.

Barefoot running, as you'll have noticed.

I started running in Cal-i-forn-i-ay, and I'll gladly accept your ride all the way to Jersey from — jeez, where are we now? Somewhere in Iowa, right? Been running so hard I kinda lose track of the states, you know? Anyway, so long as you can stand having me with you I'll stay, right into Jersey and as far through that fair state as you're going, and then when you stop I'll carry on running to the edge of the Atlantic and dive in and start swimming.

That's how hard I'm running.

Oh, my dad. Yeah. Thing is, buddy, I've been keeping it

inside of me all these miles quite *why* I'm running, and I feel I'm likely to burst if I don't unload some of it, and you reminding me of my dad and all, well, he was always good at listening to me, and...

You don't mind?

You really don't?

Okay. Here goes.

The name's Pete. I live — *lived* — in Southern Lakes, which is one of those small towns you've never heard of in California. Wife, Miranda. Two kids, both boys, Petey Junior and Davey. No, it's not them I'm running from. Jeez, if I can ever find somewhere safe I'll call them and see if Miranda can forgive me and bring the boys so we can start over. I love her, love the boys. In a way you could say I'm running *to* them, only I can't run in their direction or I'd...

Yeah, I'm getting off track a bit here.

I'm a publisher's representative. I go round the independent bookstores, such of them as are left, all over the West Coast, trying to get them to stock books put out by about thirty different small-to-middling publishers — I'm a freelance rep, not employed by one of the big boys. And I'm good at my job. All my commissions — well, seeing as every now and then one of my clients is lucky and has a bestseller — they bring in an income we can live on, not like princes but like human beings. Only bad thing about the job is I'm on the road a lot, so I don't get to see as much of Miranda and the kids as I'd like. Sometimes I'm away as much as three weeks at a time — different motel every night. Well, same motel but different places, is the way it seems to me. Seemed. Means I get a lot of reading done, because I had more than my fill of crap TV in crap motels the first year or so. Never watch it now. Read instead. Not many guys you meet who've read the whole of Gibbon's *Decline and Fall of the Roman Empire,* are there?

Okay, some nights stuck in Podunk I don't read. If the

motel's got a bar I sit in there instead. Chew the fat with the barman, or with other reps, if there's any staying there—doesn't happen often but it happens.

No, I'm *not* saying I chase women. Some of the other guys do that, though not nearly as many as you'd think from the stories and the jokes. Get me straight: I love Miranda, lust after her as much as I did even before we were married. Maybe even more'n I did then. Couple weeks away from her and I want her more than you could rightly imagine, but it's *her* I want, not some painted substitute.

Until...

This is the embarrassing part, but it's the reason I'm running, so I got to tell you about it, right?

It's a Friday night. No appointments with buyers 'til Monday. I'm stuck somewhere five hundred miles from home. There's been times I've driven that far at a weekend just to have a few hours with the family, but Miranda has her mother staying for a few days and... you got it, my mother-in-law and me are chalk and cheese. So I've got two days with not a lot to do except make sure I'm at my next port of call by Sunday night.

I'm feeling lonesome because—hey, I just said it. I'm lonesome exactly because I've got two days with not a lot to do except make sure I'm at my next port of call by Sunday night. So I decide I'll sit in the bar and get what Miranda's mother calls "stocious," except without the sneer down the side of the nose.

I was just telling Mike, the guy serving the drinks—of which I'd had several—what an asshole the last President was when the door opened and, like, every head turned. We all swiveled and looked that first time because that's what a bar full of lonely people does whenever someone new comes in, bringing with them a gust of cold air and night darkness. We all of us had a second look—more like a gawp—when we saw the newcomer herself.

Okay, so you want the description? Imagine her five and a

half feet, heart-shaped face, cute little pointy chin, pale clear
skin like porcelain with a blush of rose under it, thin coppery
colored eyelashes making perfect arches over green eyes, hair
the same color but a little lighter and falling in curls that
looked like metal rings down onto her shoulders and beyond,
lapping around a pair of small, apple-shaped breasts... you get
the picture. She was in a loose yellow dress that came down to
her knees in some thin material that clung to her so you didn't
have to have X-ray eyes to know she had long, cool legs and
hips that were, well, so... *graceful*, though that's not usually a
word that comes first to the mind of a love-hungry man stuck
in a bar five hundred miles from home. She turned to close the
door, and the wind sucked her dress tight to her rear. If someone had dropped a pin right then it'd have deafened every guy
in the place.

When she turned back to face the room you could *feel* how
all of us were wishing like crazy we'd be the ones lucky
enough that she'd sit somewhere near us.

But me—I somehow knew she was going to pick the seat
next to me at the bar. The thing is, all the other men there—
even the one I'd earlier pinpointed as gay, sure as there are
nuts in a fruitcake—were only *imagining* the details of what she
looked like under that yellow dress, but I actually *knew*.

Because the first thing I'd thought when I'd seen her was
that Miranda had guessed where I was going to be tonight and
had come driving all the way up through the state to be with
me. Then I'd seen that, no, I'd been mistaken. She wasn't
Miranda; what she was was Miranda's double maybe ten,
twelve years ago, before we'd ever hooked up, which we did
when Miranda had not long turned twenty-one. Maybe my
brain was telling me, you know, that just because this woman
was the spit of my wife back a while before I'd met her didn't
mean she was the same, like, all over; but there's bits at the
back of the brain that don't subscribe too much to rational deduction, and it was those bits that were speaking to me now. I

knew for absolute certain those breasts had the most perfect coral-pink nipples on the tips of them. I knew there was a sweet little thumb-shaped birthmark on her right inside thigh just alongside the curls of the hair there, which is a tad darker than the hair of her eyebrows and tickles my nose when I kiss her, like, um, down below. I knew there was a place at the base of her back, just above where the cleft starts, that if I stroked it would make her quickly ready for me.

I knew all these things, see, and as she settled herself on the stool next to mine she glanced into my eyes and I could suddenly tell she knew I knew them. She was as aware as I was that we weren't two strangers. Oh, how can I describe this? She wasn't just someone who *looked like* a younger Miranda. She actually *was* a younger Miranda, except with all the knowledge of the woman who was — is — my wife.

She smiled at me with that slightly thin-lipped yet sensual smile she has. *Surprised you, hm?* was what that smile said.

"What'll you drink?" I asked her, not at all like a guy approaching a pretty girl in a bar but like a husband who's been waiting for his wife to finish freshening up and finally she's joined him.

And that was the way she took, it, too.

"The usual, Bunny," she said.

Miranda's the only person in the world who ever calls me Bunny — it's a pet name she has for me, and I'm not going to tell you where it came from — but the whole situation was so *natural* that I was halfway through asking Mike to give her a Bacardi and Coke before I started thinking about this.

She took the glass from Mike before he could set it down on the counter, and as she did so she casually put her other hand on my knee.

Again, get me straight, there wasn't anything provocative about it. It was something between two people who've been long in love, who know each other intimately. It wasn't a sexual caress, just an affectionate one.

By this time everyone else in the place had started up their conversations again, and speaking three times as energetic as before so as not to let me know they were all jealous as hell I had a woman like this to call my own. Because what they obviously all thought, you see, was that the truth was just the way Miranda — the woman, I mean — was acting: that she and I were a couple, that she'd been away for a half-hour or something on some errand and was now joining me for a drink before we went somewhere else for the evening.

Now, I told you already that, besides loving my wife like crazy, I also still have a lust for her like would blow the blood vessels of any adolescent. She's the sexiest thing on two legs, and I've not ever been remotely physically interested in any other woman since first I set eyes on her. You could put Helen of Troy in front of me, stark naked, legs wide apart, juices flowing, gasping for me to ravish her real quick, and I'd not look up from my crossword.

But what I've not told you is how I was only the second guy Miranda ever went with, and in a sort of a way just the first.

Thing is, a girl like Miranda, from the time she'd hit her teens she wasn't exactly short of propositions, even way before it'd have been legal. And she turned every one of them down flat. No, she wasn't frigid, anything like that — quite the opposite — it was just that seeing so many men, most of them older than her own daddy (and, my guess is, *including* her own daddy, because he was worse than her mother is, you ask me)... Where was I? Oh, yeah. These boring old farts, dribbling around her, mentally fondling her butt the whole time — well, it didn't exactly give her any great respect for the male half of the species.

With the result she found herself at her twenty-first birthday party still a virgin. And she wanted to get rid of her virginity at some stage soon, because it was beginning to feel like it was some sort of an encumbrance to her. So there was a guy at the party whom she'd always kind of liked, and it was patently obvious to her he was willing, and, well, you guessed it. Her parents had thrown her this big formal party at a swank hotel in Bermuda, shipped everyone out there, the whole works. Five minutes after Miranda and the guy had slipped out of the party and off to his room she wasn't a virgin any longer.

Afterwards, she told me, she thanked him sincerely and they went back to the party. He couldn't believe the luck he'd had, of course; didn't even ask her if she'd come, which she hadn't.

And just a week later she met me, and it was like the two of us were the missing halves of each other that fortune had kindly brought together, and she was madder than shit at herself she'd not waited another week.

Bothered her more than it bothered me, tell you the truth. I'd have assumed, unless she'd told me otherwise, there'd been plenty before me, just like for me there'd been quite a few before her, say it myself. But it really got her pissed that because of this earlier "scientific procedure," as she called it, she "couldn't give the whole of herself to me" — yep, that's her saying it again. And because it bothered her — leastways, it did at the time — it sort of got stuck in my mind that it *would* have been good if we'd met just a week earlier than we did so's I could have been her first. And there was *curiosity* in me, too: what would it have been like to be there watching her as she discovered what sex was, what lovemaking was?

And, unlike the lucky dork at her twenty-first birthday party, I'd have taken the time and the patience to make sure it wasn't just me that came. Because for me the best thing about sex isn't your own orgasm, it's the one you give your lover.

So, here I am sitting looking at her in a motel a million miles from anywhere and all these thoughts are running through my mind. Running? Hell, they're skipping and dancing. *What would it have been like?* they keep chorusing at me.

I've evidently been doing that thing of holding an apparently normal conversation without giving it any of my attention at all, because obviously I've been joining in with a three-way dialogue between Mike the barman and Miranda—the woman who seems to be Miranda, anyway—and myself, and neither of the other two has noticed my absence.

"...or, anyways, that's what I think," the woman's saying, putting down her empty glass and squeezing my knee. "Hey, you give me another of those, Mike? Petey here's drinking slowly tonight, for once."

Mike gives a dutiful chuckle. "Sure thing, lady."

He turns away.

Miranda moves her head to give me the full benefit of her green-eyed stare. Her gaze seems to surround us both, making a misty wall so we're closed off from the rest of the room. I'm sure no one else can hear a word either of us says, but even so she whispers.

"Bunny, I've come here to you to make our dreams come true," she says. "You won't ever have to wonder again."

Anyone else, and it'd have been like they were picking through my mind. With Miranda it was different, see? She and I had always been able to read each other's faces. Besides, we'd talked often enough about this. Like I say, it had never been something that had much worried me, but it had worried *her*.

"Here?" I say numbly.

"Why not?" she replies with a little giggle. "A seedy motel's the traditional place, isn't it?"

"Yeah, well, that or the Ritz."

"There's not a Ritz within half a continent of here. The sheets clean?"

My turn to smile. Fastidious Miranda.

"It's a pretty okay place, actually. If I'd have known, I'd have found somewhere seedier."

All this while, you know, I can't really believe I'm playing along. It's a stark, staring impossibility that my wife could somehow go back in time, or whatever it is, and become a younger version of herself, and find me in some end-of-the-universe town, and all that. Like something out of *Twilight Zone*. But at the same time I have this suspension of disbelief, because so far everything she's said has been yelling at me that this is exactly what's happened.

She grins. The green walls dissolve. Mike is coming back with her drink. Someone has stuck an old Patsy Cline number on the jukebox.

And she briefly, fleetingly loops her little finger into the crook of mine before reaching to take the Bacardi and Coke from the barman.

And that does it. No more suspension of disbelief: I'm convinced. Calling me Bunny was one thing; it's just feasible it was a lucky accident, though I can't work out *how*. But that little interlinking of the fingers: that's *Miranda's* habit, no one else's. I don't care anymore about the weirdness of it all. This is my wife the way I remember her when we first met.

"*Before* we first met," she corrects me with a murmur. "A couple of weeks before. I've not yet let Bobby Shields ball me in Room 307 of the Hyatt-Rialto." She prods me in the gut with a dainty finger. "You're a bit older and a bit fatter than you were back then, but I guess you'll do. At least you're not old enough to be my father, sort of thing."

She leans toward me, and whispers again. Her breath smells more of Bacardi than Coke, but most of all it smells of the pure essence of the woman I've always loved.

"And you won't have to use a Trojan, like I made Bobby Shields do."

I put my arm around her shoulders and pull her close to me, so our cheeks are together. My face is full of her hair.

"I'm not sure I'm going to be able to walk out of here without everyone pointing fingers," I mouth in her ear.

Miranda moves her hand upwards from my knee. "Oh, my," she says.

We did get out of there, though. I left half my beer, but

Miranda drained the rest of her drink in one. Somehow she managed to shield the bulge in my pants from anyone else's view, I think — I hope — until we were walking through the cool dark air to what the guy in reception had optimistically called my chalet. We went hand-in-hand at first, but about halfway there she stopped and pulled me to her and tilted her face up and we were kissing under the orange parking-lot lights, kissing like we'd dissolve into each other, kissing like we'd never have to draw breath again.

At last she pushed her hand up between us and shoved gently at my chest.

"Easy, tiger."

"Jeez, 'Randa, for two cents I'd fuck you right here in the parking lot."

"Yeah, right, romantic. And I'd end up with someone's chewing gum stuck to my butt." Giggling. "This is going to be my first time, so I want it to be just right, okay? Talking of which... just wait here a moment."

I reached after her, but she scuttled away toward a car I didn't recognize. Then I *did* recognize it. Lumpy and old-fashioned, it was the car she'd had before we got married. She'd bought it a couple years earlier with about a million miles on the meter. It had given up the ghost just a month after we'd met. It was one of our private teases that she'd only married me because my Chrysler still went.

And then she was back beside me. "The essentials," she explained. "Candles. Cheap California champagne, a bit warm. Plastic cups. Romantic, but realistic at the same time."

Another giggle.

I took the bottle from her so we each had a hand free. On to the room, walking clumsily, hips bumping against each other's, arms around each other's waist.

Fumbling with the key. Inside at last.

To hell with the fizzy wine and the candles — we could sort them out later. We just dropped the stuff on the floor. To hell with the light switch as well—there was enough glow coming in from the parking lot to fill the room with a dirty-orange gloom.

We locked into another of those kisses, our tongues eager in each other's mouth. One arm behind my back, the other feeling the urgent swelling in my pants, she pushed me back toward the nearer of the two beds, shoved me onto it without ever breaking her hold on me, then was crawling on top of me, pulling a hand of mine from her waist downward and upward again until my fingers were under the strap of her panties. I knew she wanted me to touch the heat of her, so instead I moved the hand backwards to hold one of her buttocks, feel its smoothness, its roundness... a smoothness and roundness I recognized so well, because didn't I know every pore of my wife's body like it was my own? Better than my own, because I've never licked myself all over from head to toe and back again, and I must have done that a thousand times to Miranda.

Anyway, buddy, I guess you can imagine what happened next, so...

Oh. Okay. Yeah, you're right. You'd better hear the whole of it if you're to understand things properly—just don't drive off the road, okay? Besides, come to think of it, you *won't* be able to imagine what happened later on unless...

Right, there I am with her straddling all over me and my hand caressing her taut little behind and us showering kisses on each other and her pulling the top buttons off my shirt.

I move my hand round a little further, then reach a finger between her legs, touching just the tip of it to where the juices are flowing, then pushing inward, so it's inside her maybe half an inch, up to the first knuckle. She gives a mighty gasp in my ear, then arches herself up and back, calling out in a soft growl, settling herself onto my hand so my finger's completely inside her. I can feel the walls of her pushing spasmodically against my knuckle, feel her stickiness filling my palm.

Miranda stays like that maybe half a minute, shadowy in

the gloom above me, then she begins jerking her hips, small jerks, sliding herself up and down on my finger, her little nubbin on my skin. But the first orgasm's time is done, and she can't stretch it out any longer.

She falls onto me briefly, then raises herself again and with a single violent tug rips the last of my shirt-buttons away so my chest's revealed to her. She lifts her behind. I know what she wants me to do, because we've done this so many times before... only not like *this*, you understand. I slide my finger out of her and run my hands up her hips, shoving at the material of her dress. She lifts her arms high so I can strip it off her. She has on one of those filmy little claspless bras young women can wear but older women never do, because they're not confident their tits are firm enough even if they are. Within seconds it follows her dress onto the motel carpet.

She pulls herself up on her knees and struggles with the clasp of my belt. In a moment my zipper's down and she's fondling me through my shorts. I just lie back on the bed with my arms outstretched, unable to stop her from what she's doing, lost in the sensation, not caring if I come just the way I am, not caring about anything much at all except the feel of her hands on me.

And then she stopped. Both of us were gasping. The room was echoing with the sound of us.

"Hey, Bunny, guess we'd better wait a minute here." Her whisper was hoarse.

I was at the stage where I didn't know if I could. Wait, that is.

She climbed off the bed, off me.

"This is my first time, kiddo. Sort of. We've got to do things right."

I just sort of groaned. I stared at the dark ceiling, trying to concentrate on it, trying to stem a seemingly unstoppable tide. Succeeding at last. But so drained of energy from that effort that all I could do for the moment was carry on lying there.

I heard her moving away from the bed and feeling around with her feet. Then she bent down, and a couple of minutes later the cork on the cheap California wine popped.

So we were going to share some of it before we carried on. Sounded good to me, right then, because the way I was feeling I wasn't going to be halfway inside her before I exploded. I started to wriggle myself up onto my elbows.

"No," she murmured. I could tell she was smiling. "Stay where you are. That's the way I want you for now, Bunny."

A *clonk* as she put the bottle down on the bedside table. I returned my concentration to what I could see of the ceiling. Difficult, because I could feel her fingers brushing on me as she started lifting the elastic of my shorts up and over the jut of my wet-tipped erection... Then she was easing her hands under my hips, tugging at my pants. I lifted my butt so she could work the clothes down along my legs. She untied my shoelaces, gave a theatrical "Phew!" like she always does whether my socks are fresh or... not so fresh. Shoes off. Socks off. Pants off. Last of all, my shorts.

A silence, except for her breathing, and my own.

"Hey, be still," she said quietly.

More silence.

And then she was tiptoeing round to the bedside table, lifting the bottle to her lips. In the dim light I could just see her cheeks bulge. It seemed bizarre she still had her panties on — bizarre, but good, because that meant she was going to want me to take them off for her, and I had plans for that.

Then she was back between my legs, kneeling, her mouth still full of the cheap champagne.

A splash on the very tip of my erection. She was letting the wine drip onto me from between her lips, drop by drop by drop, all the while very gently stroking my balls, full and tight in their sack, with her fingers.

Drip.

Drip.

Drip.

Well, buddy, I thought I'd been on the verge before, but by now...

And what was making it all the more erotic was I was experiencing this in two different ways. I was being made love to by the sexiest creature I've ever encountered, who just happens to be my wife. And at the same time she *wasn't* Miranda: She was someone else, a different woman, the Miranda-who-was-a-decade-ago, not the Miranda-of-now. I wasn't married to *this* woman who was sharing a darkling motel bedroom with me. For the first time in over a decade I was having sex with a woman who wasn't my wife, and yet she *was* my wife, sort of. I was cheating on Miranda, something I thought I'd never do, and yet I wasn't cheating on her at all.

They say guilt's a powerful aphrodisiac, if it's the right guiltiness. Well, so's innocence, because innocence gives you a freedom that guilt never can.

And I was experiencing both of them right at that moment.

I *really* didn't want to come, not just yet.

Miranda had emptied her mouth of wine, and she'd now taken my shaft in her hand. I could feel her breathing on me. She's taken me into her mouth often enough—maybe a million times—that I knew what she was just about to do, and my body was screaming at me to let her carry on and do it. If she'd been the Miranda-of-now that's just exactly what I'd have done, but she was also the *other* Miranda, who was going to lose her virginity with me. Somehow it'd have not been right if the first time I came with her was into her mouth. Maybe later on tonight that'd be okay, but not now.

So it was my turn to say: "Wait."

She paused, though she still continued holding my shaft, running her hand slowly, gently, up and down.

"Wait," I said again, more urgently.

Obediently she pulled back, letting go of me, standing up.

I raised myself until I was sitting on the edge of the bed

and squirmed the rest of the way out of my shirt. I reached up and pulled her head down so I could kiss her mouth, tasting the acid sweetness of the wine with the sticky Coke and the aromatic rum underlying it. I took her breasts, one in each hand—I knew her geography so well, you see—and dropped my head to take a hard little nipple softly between my teeth, tonguing it, pausing to give it a gentle suck, kissing it, tonguing it again. Then I flickered my tongue down over her smooth flesh, dipped it quickly into her navel, hooked my thumbs into the waistband of her panties on either side, took the front of them between my teeth so the wetness of the cloth was on my chin and I was breathing deep the smell of her sex, opened my mouth, slid my tongue into the top of her panties, in among the curly damp hairs there, tugged the garment slowly down over her thighs, left it there, ran my hands all over her rear, cupping her buttocks, tickling the cleft between them, then pausing the movement of my finger before sliding it up to that place an inch or so above the cleft which I knew of old.

Just as I touched her there I put my tongue between her legs to lick the lips that nestled among the slick tufts.

Miranda stifled a scream. Her pubis bucked against my face.

And then she was struggling her panties off, shoving me back onto the bed, never letting her wet sex stray far from my mouth, was kneeling astride my face so the whole world for me was the taste and the smell of her as I plunged my tongue deep inside her, paused to blow into her, licked the hard little button of her, pushed my tongue fully inside her once more...

Yeah, okay. Well, you said you wanted the details. For a moment just now it was like I was back in the motel room again. I could taste her again, smell her again...

Say, you mind if I have a cigarette? Oh. You were hoping I'd ask. I was pretty sure I could smell old pipe smoke in here, though with the windows open I wasn't a hundred percent certain, you know? Want a cigarette for a change? I hadn't smoked for fifteen years until a few days ago.

Ah.

That's better.

What? You want more? Well, I guess this *is* better than the true confessions in a girlie mag. Only...

Well, let's leave the "only" 'til I get there, right?

Okay, so she came against my face maybe a half-dozen times before she was done. This was a virgin, right? She'd never done anything like this before. Maybe a grope in the back of someone's car, but that was about the extent of it. She was like a bomb'd been primed far too long. Somewhere at the back of my brain there was the thought that Bobby Shields must be twice as much of a jerk than he'd looked — which'd be difficult — if he'd not been able to make this woman come. On the other hand, with her and me there was love involved in the sex as well, and love's an even greater aphrodisiac than guilt or innocence.

By this time I'd been on the brink of orgasm myself for so long the whole of my groin was numb. You must have been there yourself. It's a state you know you can hold onto forever until the moment arrives when it's right to give in to the pressure and let yourself release.

So at last I pulled my mouth away from her sex and turned her over on the bed. She was whimpering she didn't want me to stop, but she was also telling me she wanted me inside her. She was almost like a limp but clinging doll as I maneuvered her around so I was above her, between her upraised knees. Later on there'd be time for sophistication: for her first time it was going to be just like in those marital guides our parents used to get. I'd never been with a virgin before, unless you counted the sort-of-a-virgin Miranda, way back when — and I wasn't completely sure what was the best deflowering technique, but I guessed having my own full weight and strength to help me was a good idea.

Maybe it was?

She was so wet and my erection was so hard and so... well, kind of suffering from sensory overload, I suppose, that I was hardly conscious of slipping into her. I'd expected there'd be some really tough barrier to break down, but in fact it was easy: just a moment of faint resistance, and then I was entirely inside her, right up to my root.

"Oh, darling, darlingdarlingdarling," she was breathing, a constant little river of sound.

I didn't move my hips yet, just lay there. It was in an odd sort of way like I was coming home, as if this was the place my cock should *always* be, as if not being inside her was an artificial state, a terrible accident of circumstance that I should never allow to happen again.

I began to sense things again. First of all, my balls against the soft skin of her buttocks and the rougher texture of the thin motel coverlet. Then those fluttering movements, the kneading, she was making along the length of me as she came yet again. I faintly kissed one of her earlobes, then put my mouth over hers, caressing her tongue with my own as she pushed her hips upward off the bed, trying to take me even deeper into her, impossibly, than I already was.

I began at last to move in and out of her, slowly, deliberately, pulling myself almost all the way out until just the bell of me was cupped between her lips, before firmly pushing myself back in again.

She tore her mouth away from mine and flung her arms around my neck.

"Fuck me, fuck me. Faster, faster."

So I did like she told me to.

Miranda's the only woman who's regularly come in multiples with me. I don't know if other women have multiple orgasms often, just never with me, or if Miranda's rare in this—it's not something I've ever felt easy asking anyone about.

Oh. You're just grinning around your pipestem. You're not going to tell me either.

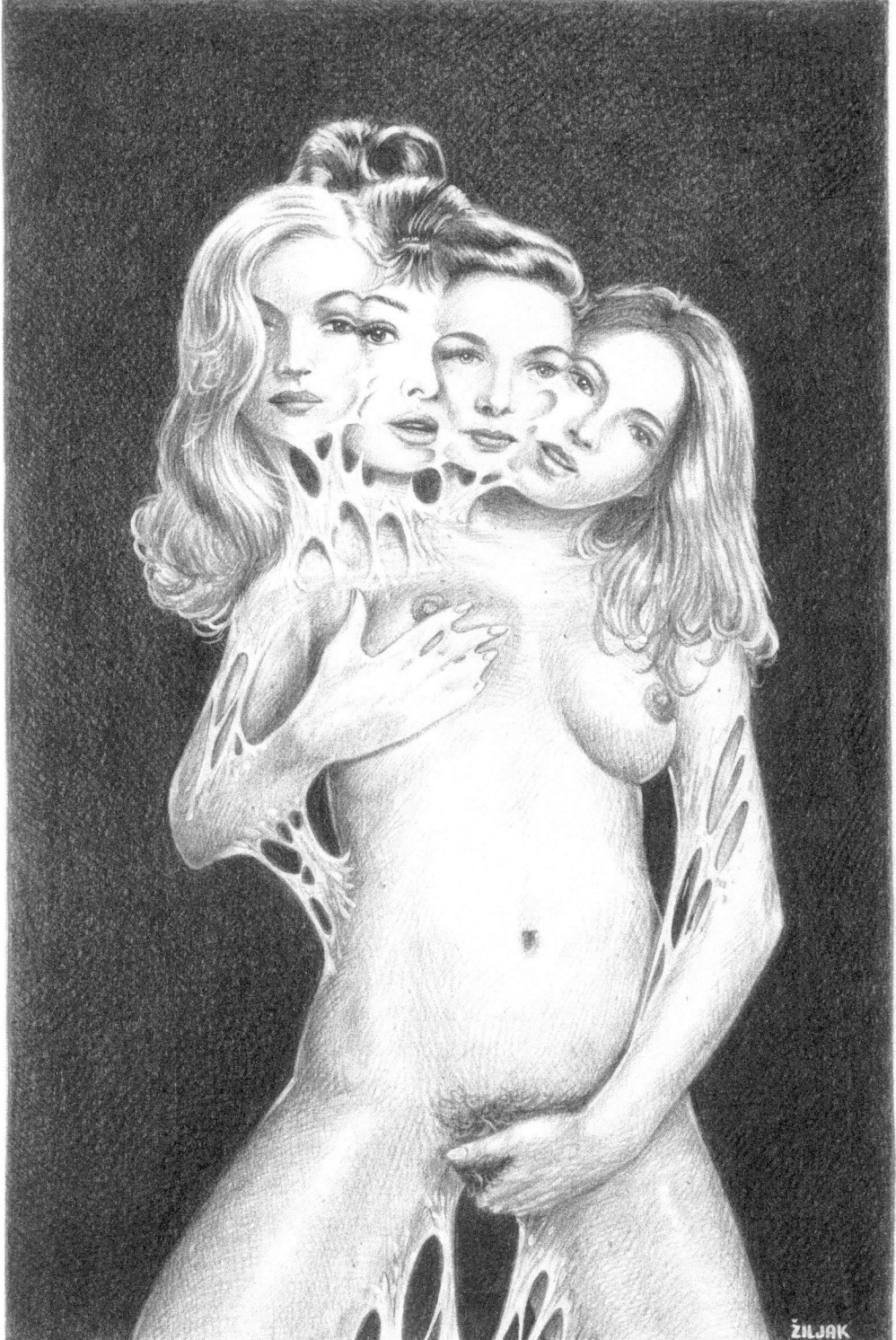

Bastard.

Mind you, I've never talked about sex at all with anyone like this before, and I don't know quite why I'm doing so right now except maybe I've got to. Maybe I should really be spilling all this stuff to a shrink, not you, but a shrink would cost me money and money isn't something I've had much of since I started running, because I was so desperate to get out of that motel room in California, later, that I didn't stop to pick up my jacket, which had my wallet and all my credit cards in it. You'll understand why, soon enough. I was lucky I had about forty bucks I'd stuffed into my pants pocket, the remains of the sixty I'd put there as my absolute bar budget for the night.

Anyway...

Anyway, yeah, multiple orgasms.

She was coming a storm all around the length of me as I went pumping faster and faster. I could feel her reaching a crescendo, and so was I.

At the last I thrust myself as far as I could inside her and just held myself there, feeling great slow spurts pouring into the very back of that mysterious cave all women hide within themselves. My heart was going berserk. My lungs were tight, so I could hardly draw a breath for a few seconds, and then I was whooping air into them.

And Miranda kept on coming. Her eyes were rolled right back as she thrashed her head from side to side on the bed; the whites of them were almost luminous in that orange-dusky room. It felt like my erection was being jostled by a feverishly eager crowd. Finally, just as the pleasure of the pummeling was beginning to go into something less enjoyable, as the rigidity of my shaft eased and tenderness returned, she slowly ebbed to a halt.

I was still easily hard enough inside her that I was able to start moving backward and forward again, but she reached up a hand blindly to my lips, telling me to cease and desist.

All of this was new to me, because I was feeling it through

her senses, in a way. This woman on the bed had never done anything like this before, with me, with anyone. Yet it was all very familiar to me, too, because, although the precise sequence of everything might not be the same, there wasn't anything we'd just done that Miranda and I hadn't done countless times before, in the middle of other, more imaginative things. I forget who it was once pointed out a married man has a more diverse and exciting sex life than the most successful Don Juan there ever was, but it's the truth of the matter, you know?

Yeah, I see you do. You're chuckling. We're a pair of horny married guys, right?

Miranda and I, we've done just about everything together two human beings can do with their bodies. No, I don't mean any sadism, masochism, that sort of stuff — we're neither of us into pain, or giving pain. But anything that's *loving*, we've tried it.

Yet I don't know if I've ever experienced anything with her like that simple act of straightforward, missionary-position sex we'd just had. Keep any smutty laughter to yourself, but I'd never been so deeply *immersed* in her before — at a *soul* level, you understand. It was that mixture of freshness and familiarity, I guess: I was discovering the essence of my wife for the very first time while I was also wandering through places I'd loved so long the love was part of the person I am.

Am I making sense?

Well, I am to me.

We drank the rest of the bottle of wine out of those plastic cups — they were just right for the wine, which would've tasted pretty nasty out of champagne flutes but was actually pretty good in a plastic cup, like it had been made for that. We nestled against each other, sometimes letting our hands roam, most of the time just talking about such relevant matters as how the universe could be infinite and yet also finite — you know the sort of garbage that seems important in such moments.

And then, all of a sudden, she said something that startled me: "You ever wanted me to be another woman?"

"What do you mean?" I said.

"You know, when we're making love, has it ever crossed your mind it could be Julie Delpy you were with, or Rutina Wesley, or Megan Fox, or Aishwarya Rai, or Sharon Leal, or even—what's her name?—that little blond cutesy-pie in the deli you think I don't notice you eyeing up her ass who's so much younger and yummier than I am?"

"She's not," I said. And I explained to her the truth, the truth that the Miranda-of-now knew but this Miranda-who-was-a-decade-ago couldn't: that from the moment I'd met her there'd been not a single other woman on the horizon.

It sounds so dishonest when I say it flat out like that—the sort of thing husbands say in public when you know they're not above sneaking a copy of *Playboy* into the john. But it's true.

"Still," she insisted when I'd finished, "has it never crossed your mind that it'd be nice if you could live more than one life, so you could at least *try* a few other women than me?"

"You're joking, right?"

"No, Bunny. I'm serious as all hell. I really want to know the answer."

Miranda and I are always completely honest with each other—we prefer it that way. So I lay back on the pillows and I yet again scrutinized that goddam stained ceiling, and I racked my mind to see if there was any truth at all in what she was suggesting.

And maybe, just maybe, there *was*.

Maybe, despite what I said to you earlier, I *would* have looked up from my crossword at that naked, knees-akimbo Helen of Troy and thought to myself, *You know, ol' buddy, in another lifetime that could be a whole heck of a lot of fun.* That's about *all* I'd have thought, mind you; but the thought would have been *there*.

So I told Miranda, lying there amid the smell of bad wine and good sex, as much.

"And that's really all?" she said.

"It really is. Why're you asking me this?"

She ignored my question.

"So if I wasn't *me* here beside you, naked and willing, if I was — oh, I don't know, Veronica Lake, someone like that? If it was Veronica Lake here, you'd not be even remotely interested?"

I started into a cheap joke about Veronica Lake being dead and all, but Miranda gave that little clucking sound she does when I'm making a jerk of myself, so I stopped.

"You once said," she persisted, "that Veronica Lake running around in her jimjams in *I Married a Witch* was the most erotic sight ever committed to celluloid."

"I stand by that statement," I said, chuckling yet a bit uneasy, you know? Hoping to get this conversation over with. "But that's only because you, Miranda, you've never been in the movies. If you had, *whatever* you were doing would have been the sexiest thing on celluloid. I find the sight of you weeding the garden or" — I waved my hand in the near-darkness to signify any number of mundane activities — "pouring yourself a glass of water *infinitely* sexier even than Ms. Lake in her jimjams."

"You *sure*?"

"Yeah. Yeah, I'm sure."

"Because sometimes I've wondered — *will* wonder — what it'd be like to be another woman making love to *you*."

"Not what it'd be like if I was another man?"

"No. Not that. Never that."

The springs creaked as she got off the bed. She went across to the window and pulled the cord so the drapes glided protestingly across, cutting out the parking lot's glow. Then I heard her moving cautiously back in the direction of the bed — no, the nightstand. There was the tiniest of clicks as she turned the dimmer knob on the lamp there.

"*Absolutely* sure?"

I'd closed my eyes against the anticipated light. Now I opened them a slit.

"*Jesus!*"

My back was hard against the cold headboard. I'd grabbed a pillow and was holding it against myself like it could protect me.

If there are any pictures of Veronica Lake after she took her jimjams off, so to speak, I've never seen them—and I hope I never do. Whatever she was like in real life—and I know nothing of that, either—the Veronica Lake of the screen was someone very special. I don't like the idea of guys getting sweaty palms as they ogle nude photos of her.

So maybe a little bit of me *does* love the screen persona, after all.

Whatever, I can't swear to the fact that the woman standing there in the muted lamplight was Veronica Lake naked, but she looked exactly like it to me.

"Miranda," I said, my mouth feeling clumsy, the taste of my wife still on my lips. "Is that you?"

Dumb question. Yes. But I'd be surprised if you'd been able to think of anything *less* dumb, right then.

"You like the way I look?"

"No! Well, yes. But *no!*"

She put her hands on her hips, pushed her pelvis forward. "I want you." Simply stated. Infinitely alluring—but not to me.

"*No!*"

And then the flesh on her seemed to flow.

"Audrey Hepburn?" said a naked Audrey Hepburn.

A few moments later:

"Gene Tierney?"

"No, Miranda, it's only *you* I want. Only..."

And then I stopped speaking, because at last it had got through to my brain that this woman—no, this *creature* in the room with me, that I'd been making love with, that I'd bared my soul to, wasn't Miranda at all, never had been, couldn't be. And I'd *known all along* she couldn't be. It was impossible for my twenty-one-year-old wife to appear in my life a dozen years afterwards. I'd been deluding myself, believing what I wanted to believe, swept up by a romantic myth, and maybe not such a romantic one.

Yet it was equally impossible for what was happening in that motel bedroom to be happening.

And then I said something really stupid — so stupid I realized how stupid it was even as I was saying it. Because I knew this wasn't Miranda, yet my mind was still insanely trying to cling to the idea that it was, that it could be.

"Miranda, I don't want you to look like *any* of these other women. I just want you to look like *yourself!*"

Sorry. I'll get myself together again in a minute. Just give me time. Yeah, I know, I shouldn't have screamed like that just as you were overtaking an SUV. I...

Oh, jeez.

Jeez.

But it's a good thing I've made myself live through that again, you know? These past few days, while I've been running and running, every time I've started to remember what that creature in the motel room looked like, my mind's just shied away from it. Now... well, now things aren't quite so bad, somehow, because I've forced myself to confront the memory.

Well, you've guessed the rest. I scooped up my pants, thinking my car keys were in them. I'm not sure how I had the presence of mind for that. I snagged my shirt at the same time, though I didn't notice it until I was standing naked beside my car discovering the car keys weren't in my pants pocket after all. No way was I going back for them. Lucky thing there wasn't anyone else in the parking lot, because I wasn't even stopping to get my pants *on* — I just clutched the clothing and ran like all the devils of Hell were after me, which perhaps they were.

Across the tarmac came this long, low ululation.

"Buuuunnnnnneeeee!"

I ran faster, if that was possible.

And I've been running ever since.

I've not eaten or drunk anything the past few days because, any time I've tried, it just comes straight up again. All I've spent money on is cigarettes — oh, and once a road toll, because that seemed a courteous thing to do for the trucker who took me half the way through Nebraska. I want to make sure my money lasts for as many hundreds of miles as I can — all the way through Jersey and into the big blue Atlantic Ocean, you bet, because maybe the shapeshifter that found me in that shitty little nowhere motel bar can't be stopped by anything but water, and otherwise she'll — it'll — be able to find me, wherever I am.

Well, you said you wanted to know it all, so I've told you it all.

Now you know why I'm running.

And running and running.

Forever, if that's what it takes.

And how come you've started smiling at me like that, ol' buddy, as if you knew it all already?

Miranda?

Flattery Will Get You Nowhere

by
William Markly O'Neal

Being a serial killer is no easy task, but Carl is a Blood Prophet, blessed with special powers of divination. He's a master of his life, and of many other lives — of people he's killed and buried over the years. But a stray dog arrives with an unsettling gift, and Carl knows he needs fresh blood so that he can divine the meaning of it. That means a long ride, a young couple, and a chance for in-the-car voyeurism that will soon lead to the bloody rite that will solve his dilemma.

Horror
Serial killer
Divination
Murder
Voyeur
Heterosexual sex
Cunnilingus and fellatio
Lust
Young love

Carl Carpenter considered it a bad omen when the dog brought him the severed human hand.

He had never seen the dog before.

He *had* seen the hand.

The dog was a big German shepherd, mostly black, with patches of dark gray creating regal markings. All four of his paws were white and he had circles of white around his eyes that made them stand out from an otherwise furry black face. His sharp, erect ears were made even more pointed by little coned tufts of black hair.

The hand once belonged to a man named Daryl J. Mostetler who hailed from Flint, Michigan—a man Carl had killed exactly three months before to the day. He could tell it was Daryl's hand and not the hand of one of his other sacrifices by the way the wrist was cut. This hand had been sawed off right at the wrist. He also recognized the wiry brown hair still evident on the back of Daryl's dirty fingers.

Carl had an eidetic memory when it came to his sacrifices. He remembered everything about everyone he had ever killed. He remembered exactly how he abducted them—what flattery they responded to the most. He remembered the way they looked when they died. He had vivid recollections of every evisceration he ever performed. He remembered how many pieces he cut each person into. And he remembered the exact spot where he buried them, each and every one of them.

In short, Carl remembered his work.

So even though it was only a severed hand, the moment he saw it in that goddamned canine's mouth, he remembered it.

He *recognized* it.

He had buried that hand and the rest of Daryl J. Mostetler at least six feet deep.

Carl lived in rural Indiana, northeast of Indianapolis, where the cell-phone coverage was spotty on a great day and nonexistent on a normal one. His farm consisted of twenty-seven acres, including eight acres of woodland. The small forest he secretly thought of as Cemetery Woods sat far off the road, a road that ran way off any major highway. His entire sprawling property was enclosed by wire fences topped with swirls of barbed wire and marked with numerous NO TRES-PASSING signs.

Carl was a cautious man—meticulous, crafty, and highly intelligent. He had been a successful serial killer all his adult life and he attributed part of his success to the total randomness involved in his selection of sacrifices.

Carl had spent thousands of hours online reading various crime Web sites about notorious serial killers. He wasn't like any of them.

All the young women Ted Bundy chose to murder looked like Bundy's first girlfriend. John Wayne Gacy chose young boys. Jeffery Dahmer preferred young black men, wanting to turn them into his sexual zombies. Wayne Williams, the Atlanta child murderer, had a thing for black boys. The Boston Strangler molested young women. Even the most infamous serial killer of all, Jack the Ripper, had fairly discriminating tastes, slaying only prostitutes.

Every one of them had their preferences, their perversions. Generally murder got twisted together with some sexual need. They all exhibited patterns.

And Carl wasn't like any of them.

Carl wasn't aggressive. He killed in *cold* blood, not hot, and he did it randomly. Among those he had buried on his property were a doctor, a dentist, a preacher, a nun, truck drivers, pig farmers, salesmen, prostitutes, drug dealers, lawyers, even a couple small-town celebrities.

All those people—including Daryl J. Mostetler—had only two things in common.

Carl killed them all.

And they were all buried in his woods.

That was where Daryl's hand should have been: buried in Cemetery Woods.

Dressed only in a robe and slippers, Carl just came out of his farmhouse on a chilly mid-October morning to retrieve his newspaper. The German shepherd was crouched a few yards away from his front stoop. The dog exhibited great tenderness as it gently laid the hand on Carl's lawn.

The mongrel then looked up at Carl, bared its teeth, and growled.

Carl knew how to deal with this. He used flattery. "Well, aren't you a handsome animal? I don't think I've ever seen such a beautiful dog." He held out an open hand to it. "Come 'ere, boy."

To Carl's utter astonishment, the German shepherd barked at him, turned heels, and dashed off. It ran east along the road, headed toward the Trojanowski farm, Carl's nearest neighbor in that direction, a quarter mile away. The dog suddenly bounded off the road, into the ditch, and disappeared.

Deeply disturbed, Carl picked up Daryl's hand and took it inside his house.

Carl wasn't like other men. He had never had stress, never had fear, never had worries. Over the years, his precognitive abilities had instilled in him an unearthly confidence.

During different periods of his life, he'd had various ideas about the nature of his talents. On more than one occasion he had entertained the notion he was demon-possessed. After seeing one of the X-Men movies, he theorized he might be a mutant. He wondered if he might be a warlock, wondered if he might an extraterrestrial, even considered the possibility he might be some kind of dark extra-dimensional simulacrum.

Once, for three crazy months during his youth, he was convinced he was a demigod.

The truth was, Carl didn't know what he was or how he acquired his powers. All he knew was that he was different.

He could see visions of the future drawn in blood.

And he had a preternatural ability to get anything and *everything* he wanted by simply using flattery.

The dog was the only creature Carl had ever encountered that was capable of ignoring his fulsomeness.

That was why he feared it.

An hour after the confrontation with the German shepherd, Carl got dressed and mounted up Bucephalus, his Arabian-Quarter Horse. Daryl's hand was wrapped in a trash bag, tucked up under a long leather coat.

He rode Bucephalus through recently harvested soybean fields, back to Cemetery Woods.

He couldn't believe what he found.

Mostetler's grave didn't appear changed at all. The spot where Carl buried the Michigan man—between two ghostly beech trees—was completely undisturbed.

Carl was flabbergasted how the dog had obtained the hand. The only thing that made sense to him was that he had dropped the hand; he had somehow misplaced it, and it wasn't buried with the other parts of Daryl.

And that was absolutely unfathomable, blatantly impossible. Carl was meticulous about his work. He was *never* careless.

Never.

Standing on Mostetler's grave, he was certain that every piece of Daryl was interred directly below him.

Carl looked around at the leaves-strewn floor of the small forest. Ten yards to the east was the spot where he'd buried Marion and Janice Retherford, both of Cincinnati, Ohio. He'd killed Mr. and Mrs. Retherford in June of 1996. Their reading was particularly special to him. It was their sacrifice that allowed him to head off a potentially disastrous scandal involving some of his highly profitable pornographic Web sites.

Returning his attention to Daryl's grave, Carl frowned. In his mind, he saw the dog and the hand. He was baffled how the one came into the possession of the other. He decided if he ever encountered that German shepherd again, he was going to kill it.

Carl made his way through the trees, following no path, walking past more graves that didn't look like graves, remembering every sacrifice and the divinations they gave. Eventually he came to an aluminum shed erected on a large concrete slab. Carl opened the lock on the door with the combination 6-6-6 and entered the shed to retrieve a spade and a shovel. He then returned to the place where he'd buried Mostetler.

He had no desire to see any more of Daryl. A return visit from Daryl's hand was bad enough.

As he dug a new hole about ten yards away from the place where the rest of Mostetler was interred, he looked again at the unmarked graves of Marion and Janice Retherford. They were an interracial couple; Marion was white and Janice was black. He'd met them as they were celebrating their third wedding anniversary at King's Island, a sprawling amusement park outside Cincinnati. Carl and the Retherfords became fast friends riding the sky-lift together, then spent the evening bar-hopping. As they were leaving the park late on a hot summer evening, Carl pretended to have car trouble. He had learned during their time together that the Retherfords had decided to celebrate their anniversary even though they were a month behind on their bills. Carl offered to catch them up on their rent, $699, and pay them another one hundred for gas, if they would give him a lift all the way back to his farm—a five-hour drive. They sealed their doom by accepting.

On the long drive home, Carl brought up the movie *Indecent Proposal*. When Janice made fun of the jealousy that the Woody Harrelson character exhibited, Carl told the salt-and-pepper couple he wasn't rich enough to pay them a million dollars for a night alone with Janice but he wondered, "Would you take three thousand to have a threesome with me?"

Drunk and horny on Carl's flattery, the Retherfords asserted that their relationship was secure enough that they could have a little extramarital romp sheerly for the fun of it, without it resulting in a bunch of tears and drama.

Carl stopped digging for a moment and wiped sweat off his brow, closing his eyes. As vividly as if it was happening right then, he recalled stripping the clothes off Janice Christine Jasper Retherford. He remembered her glorious scent: a mixture of sandalwood, roses, and the ocean. Her skin was as hot as brown fire. Her mouth was a tropical jungle.

Carl hadn't been laid in over four months. He'd woken up horny and had planned to spend this morning at his computer vicariously enjoying some amateur porno stars... until that goddamn dog wrecked his routine.

His horniness returned as he remembered the bondage games he'd played with the Retherfords before he took their lives. Marion turned out to be even more submissive than Janice. The pathetic wimp got off on being tied up and forced to watch as Carl fucked his wife.

And fuck her Carl did. Repeatedly.

They made it entirely too easy for him to kill them.

Somewhere off in the distance, a dog barked. Carl jumped as if slapped, his growing erection immediately wilting. He knew it wasn't just any dog. It was that goddamn German shepherd.

Frowning, putting Marion and Janice Retherford out of his mind, Carl finished burying Daryl J. Mostetler's right hand.

Carl didn't socialize much but he was cordial with Mrs. Trojanowski, his neighbor just down the road. The Trojanowskis had a large henhouse and Carl bought fresh eggs from them. Because the Trojanowskis had six children, they had connections with many of the other families living along the long country road. Carl had flattered Jill Trojanowski so many times over the years that she could no longer look at him without blushing.

Carl contacted Mrs. Trojanowski to find out more about the dog. As it turned out, the Trojanowskis didn't own a German shepherd, and Mrs. Trojanowski knew of no one around those parts who did.

He'd hit a dead end, but Carl was no fool. He believed wholeheartedly in omens and he knew the dog was a bad one. He knew that even before the animal terrorized him a second time.

It was later that same evening, after talking to Jill Trojanowski on the phone, when the German shepherd scratched on Carl's back door. Carl was in his kitchen cooking his usual supper for one: a rare New York strip steak, green beans, and mashed potatoes.

The minute he heard the scratching, he knew it was the dog.

Carl had several loaded weapons stashed in various places throughout his house. From a large sugar canister, he took out a high-caliber handgun and disengaged the safety. He moved to the back door, threw it open, and prepared to shoot right through the glass storm door.

His back stoop was vacant. He saw no dog.

He did, however, see another body part lying on his back lawn.

Heart pounding, a line of sweat breaking out atop his upper lip, Carl hurried outside and ran to the side of his house, looking for the German shepherd.

He saw nothing but naked trees and a dead lawn.

He rushed to the other side of the house and again found nothing.

Lowering the gun to his side, taking a chill (but still sweating), Carl walked back to the spot where the dog had left him another body part lying openly in the daylight.

It was another piece of Daryl J. Mostetler, his hairy right leg. Carl recognized it not only by its shape but also by the way it was severed. Because every one of his sacrifices was an individual, Carl honored their uniqueness by cutting them up in different ways. Carl sawed some legs into as many as four pieces before burying them. With Daryl, however, Carl had left his legs intact.

This leg was supposed to be buried six feet under along with the rest of Daryl J. Mostetler, back in Cemetery Woods.

Carl was upset, more distressed than he had been in decades. There were forces at play here beyond the natural, outside the normal. He knew it. He could *sense* it. There was something extraordinary about that hound. He wondered if—

His thought was broken off by the sound of the devil dog barking far off in the distance. He knew it was useless to pursue the animal. It was already too far away.

Thinking about that damnable beast running free was deeply unsettling.

Again, Carl saddled up Bucephalus and rode back to the Cemetery Woods, where he buried Mostetler's leg.

This time, he was chilled but not surprised to see Daryl's grave was still unmolested. He could see the freshly turned earth where he'd buried the hand earlier, but the grave containing the rest of Mostetler didn't have so much as a paw print on it.

Carl was certain there was something preternatural about that dog.

Fortunately, he had his own preternatural means of unraveling mysteries.

A day after twice encountering the demon dog (and the disembodied parts of Daryl J. Mostetler), Carl spent the morning preparing for a blood prophecy. Once everything was ready in his barn, he took a long, hot shower and then dressed in an expensive, tailor-made black suit. He put on gold cuff-links, a gold tie clasp, a gold necklace, two different gold rings, and his solid-gold Rolex. Carl had a knack of making the man behind the bling so inconspicuous that people tended to remember his clothes and jewelry more than his average face.

He owned several cars, including a couple he kept at garages in a nearby city. He decided to drive an old roomy Lincoln Continental. The only precaution he took was to put a fake license plate on the vehicle.

Even in the most difficult times, traveling was never difficult for Carl. He could just as easily fly, but he liked driving. A long cruise up the interstate would give him time to think.

Over the previous decade, Carl had found human sacrifices in Cincinnati and Columbus, Ohio; Lexington, Kentucky; St. Louis, Missouri; Ravenswood, West Virginia; Savannah, Georgia; several towns in Texas; and, of course, Flint, Michigan. But he hadn't hunted in the Chicago area since 1997. He decided a safari there was overdue.

The drive from his central Indiana farm to the Windy City took him just over three hours. He timed it so that he arrived in northeastern Illinois at dusk. After stopping for a bloody-rare steak dinner at an expensive restaurant, the serial killer began his manhunt.

Carl Carpenter wasn't like other people. He wasn't put on this Earth to blunder about, hoping that by happenstance he might discover the meaning of his own existence. Carl always knew what he was meant to do.

He was a predator. He was born to slay people. He wasn't, however, a *murderer.*

Carl was an instrument of Fate. The men, women, and children he selected to sacrifice were *destined* to die by his hand. Their deaths served a higher purpose. They allowed Carl to foresee what was imminent.

And now it was necessary for some other little person to

die... so that a Blood Prophet might glean his future.

He drove about aimlessly in his dark-green Lincoln Continental, ending up in Elgin, a suburb west of Chicago. When he saw a neighborhood tavern called Franz's Stein, Carl ceased his search. Needing information about a German shepherd, a German-sounding bar seemed like an auspicious place to look.

After scoping out several prospective sacrifices and rejecting them, Carl eventually targeted a twenty-something couple named Wendy Dean and Justin Sturgis. He flattered them and bought them drinks.

Short and petite with an hourglass figure, Wendy had silky auburn hair, seductive chocolate eyes, and a smooth mocha tan. She was dressed in Calvin Klein jeans that were gloriously tight on her, showing off her badunkadunk butt. Her hefty breasts were hidden inside a baggy blue flannel shirt that probably belonged to her boyfriend.

Justin was as pale as Wendy was dark. With his shoulder-length blond hair, blue eyes, and unblemished face, he reminded Carl of a California surfer boy. Trim to the point of being skinny, his Wrangler jeans hung in such a way that he appeared to have no ass. He was wearing a Katy Perry concert T-shirt and a blue hoodie. On the back of his left hand was a tattoo of a lightning bolt.

Justin said very little and Carl quickly discerned that Wendy wore the pants in their relationship.

Carl learned that Mr. Sturgis and Miss Dean had just moved into a new apartment nearby. They had walked to the bar to celebrate their one-week anniversary of living together.

By asking just a few casual questions, Carl was also able to determine they weren't expected anywhere until Monday morning.

He'd brought several joints with him and, after getting Justin and Wendy drunk on expensive booze and more flattery, he offered to get them high. Justin perked up and became assertive for the first time, saying, "Sounds good, dude."

When they left the tavern, Carl opened the back door of the Lincoln for them, prompting Wendy to say, "I always wanted my own chauffeur."

They took a ride and smoked a blunt. After Carl was certain both the young ones were stoned, he suggested they go home with him to party. "We can stay buzzed all weekend on some bangin' chronic... kick back in my hot tub, eat expensive food, drink expensive booze..." Seeing how much they both enjoyed the marijuana, he added, "And I've got some *killer* cocaine, guaranteed to add an extra boost to the party."

Wendy made the decision, saying, "Sounds good."

When Carl had woken that morning, he'd thought about going to a crowded mall to look for a young boy or virgin girl. Traditional wisdom held that prepubescent females were best suited to his need. He knew it was true. He had only sacrificed nine girls below the age of fifteen and those had been his nine most lucid prophecies.

Children were special. Children were the future. It made perfect sense that innocent babes would be the best facilitators of the blood-visions.

But Carl didn't want a child tonight, for a specific reason. He was horny.

And he was *not* a pedophile. The idea of molesting a kid was repulsive to him. When he'd abducted children in the past, it was only because he needed to spill their blood. There wasn't a child he'd dispatched who didn't first get ice cream.

But while the sacrifice of innocents might make for the finest visions, Carl had been craving sex for days. That was why he'd chosen Justin and Wendy.

While children could easily be occupied with candy and a few toys, Carl knew that where young adults were concerned, there was no better distraction than sex.

As he drove I-90 into Indiana, he looked into his rearview mirror and saw Wendy kiss Justin on the neck. Even though

Carl had already used a lot of flattery on both of them, he broke a growing silence by using more, "You two are totally hot. Do you know how sexy you are together?"

Justin smiled and looked down. Wendy proudly flipped her hair back and said, "Thanks."

Carl took out another blunt and lit it with his Zippo. He'd had only had two drinks and didn't consider it too great a risk to get baked on the drive home, as long as he stuck to the speed limit. Even if he was pulled over, cops were only human. They were just as susceptible to his flattery as anyone else.

Toking on the joint, Carl caught Wendy's eyes in his rear-view mirror. "Mind if I ask you a personal question?"

Wendy leaned forward, taking the joint from him as she said, "Go ahead."

"Tell me, gorgeous," his flattery assured a truthful response, "when was the last time the two of you made love?"

Without hesitation, she answered, "Two nights ago." After passing the joint to Justin, she asked, "Why?" causing a puff of smoke to spill out of her mouth that she immediately sucked back in.

Carl grinned. "You seem horny to me." He shifted his gaze in the rearview mirror to look at Justin. "What about it, dawg? You horny?"

Wendy smirked and sat back, placing a hand on Justin's leg to squeeze it. "He's *always* horny."

Carl never passed up an opportunity to flatter. "Well, considering what a total hottie you are, girl, it's no *wonder!* He's a lucky man!"

The inebriated lovers exchanged an adoring look.

When Justin passed the joint to him, Carl noticed the surfer boy's hands were trembling. Justin was drunk and stoned but he was also still nervous. "Loosen up, dude." Carl assured him, "it's all good. Tonight you're a god and Wendy is a goddess. And I'm not even here."

Carl's flattery struck two hearts with supernatural sway, causing Justin and Wendy to glow with a beauty that was radiant to behold.

As the young ones basked in the heat of their new divinity, Carl merged onto Interstate 65 South. Driving seventy miles per hour through the dark, he told his captives, "I hate to tell you this, but my house is a helluva long drive." He didn't divulge it was three hours away. "No worries, though. It'll be worth it when we get there. I've got some *dynamite* coke."

When Justin tried to pass him the blunt, Carl shook his head, saying, "Nah. You two go ahead."

After smoking the joint down to a roach, Wendy snuggled close to Justin and gave him a kiss. Her lips lingered against his.

Watching them make out caused Carl's blood to sizzle. He cheered them on, saying, "You're awesome! Keep it up, you two!"

Justin pulled Wendy into a tight embrace, smashing her ample bosom against his bony chest as they continued to purr and gasp while tongue grappling.

Carl surreptitiously reached down his pants to adjust his swelling penis. He drove in silence for a while, letting the sexual tension build. After five more miles, he looked back at Wendy and said, "Why don't the two of you get more comfortable?"

Wendy smirked. "You mean take off some clothes?"

"Why not? That flannel shirt looks hot." Still grinning, Carl caught her gaze in the mirror. "Aren't you hot?"

Wendy accused, "You just want to see my tits."

"Guilty as charged, sugar. I'll bet Justin likes seeing 'em too, dontcha, dude? What red-blooded male could ever get tired of looking at a beauty like you?"

Wendy was already unbuttoning her shirt, while Justin looked on with wide eyes. She told Carl, "He's an 'ass man.'" She turned to her boyfriend and teased him, "I'll bet you *are* tired of seeing my tits, aren't you?"

Justin recoiled, his face curling up with annoyance. "Oh, *Hell* no! Just because I love your ass best doesn't mean I don't also love your tits!"

Wendy shucked off the flannel shirt, revealing her well-stuffed bra. She then kissed Justin on the neck, asking him in a girlish voice, "Should I show Carl my boobies, Wolfie?"

"Please, my man!" Carl begged Justin, "Have mercy on a dawg! I *gotta* see those titties!"

Justin gave his permission with a perfunctory nod, still staring at Wendy as if he was astonished by her boldness.

Before getting completely topless, Wendy asked Carl, "This won't cause you to have a wreck, will it?"

His eyes darted back and forth, from the road to the rearview. "Nope. I'm good. Give us a thrill, darlin'. Lose that goddamn bra!"

She unveiled her pale white breasts and Carl was delighted to see that she had tan lines. He hated it when white girls got all-over tans. He was also excited that her areolas were small and her nipples were fat. Carl sung Wendy's praises, "Sweet Jesus Almighty! Your breasts are stunning, girl! They're *stupendous!*" Wendy squealed as if he just touched her in a pleasurable spot.

Carl looked at Justin and said, "So what are you waiting for, stud? Suck on those beauties!"

Blond boy didn't need to be told twice. The auburn-haired girl growled with passion as her lover licked her nipples.

Holding the steering wheel with one hand, Carl used his other hand to unbutton and unzip his pants, giving his erection room for further expansion.

After another ten minutes of listening to yin's moans and yang's lip smacks, Carl suggested, "You should take off your pants, Wendy. Justin and I want to see you get naked. Don't we, Justin?"

Justin croaked, "Yes."

"I don't know," said Wendy, demurring for the first time. Carl's eyes kept darting to the rearview mirror as he stared at her bosom. Seeing how hard she was breathing, he was certain she was turned on.

Carl told them, "I don't know why you two ever put on clothes in the first place." Wendy gasped and Justin squirmed when Carl concluded, "With bodies as bangin' hot as yours, it's a goddamn shame that you just don't stay naked constantly. And fuck frequently!"

Wendy giggled, looking as happy as a housewife in a television commercial.

Justin's reactions were harder to read. He still appeared tense but Carl considered the possibility that Justin's clenched demeanor might be attributable to his evident lust.

Carl wondered if Justin was homophobic. As usual, it was impossible to tell. Most American men reacted poorly to flattery from other men. Some guys would become outright hostile if a stranger called them "handsome" or "hot." Because of the unique nature of his talents, however, that never happened to Carl. He could walk into a straight biker bar with a violent reputation for queer bashing and call every guy in the place 'sexy' with absolutely no fear. Of course, Mister Carpenter was fearless in *all* things.

He remembered the dog and frowned.

Catching Wendy's eyes in the mirror, Carl asked, "If I fire up another doobie, will that help you be more comfortable about taking off your pants?"

She laughed. "I'm already so high I'm flying! You don't need to get me any more bent to get my pants off me."

"Sweet," said Carl. "I mean, you *are* bootylicious in those jeans, darlin'—no doubt about that, for real—but I'm *dying* to see your legs!"

Wendy looked at Justin as she wiggled out of her jeans, revealing blue bikini panties.

Carl ogled her gorgeous thighs and unconsciously licked

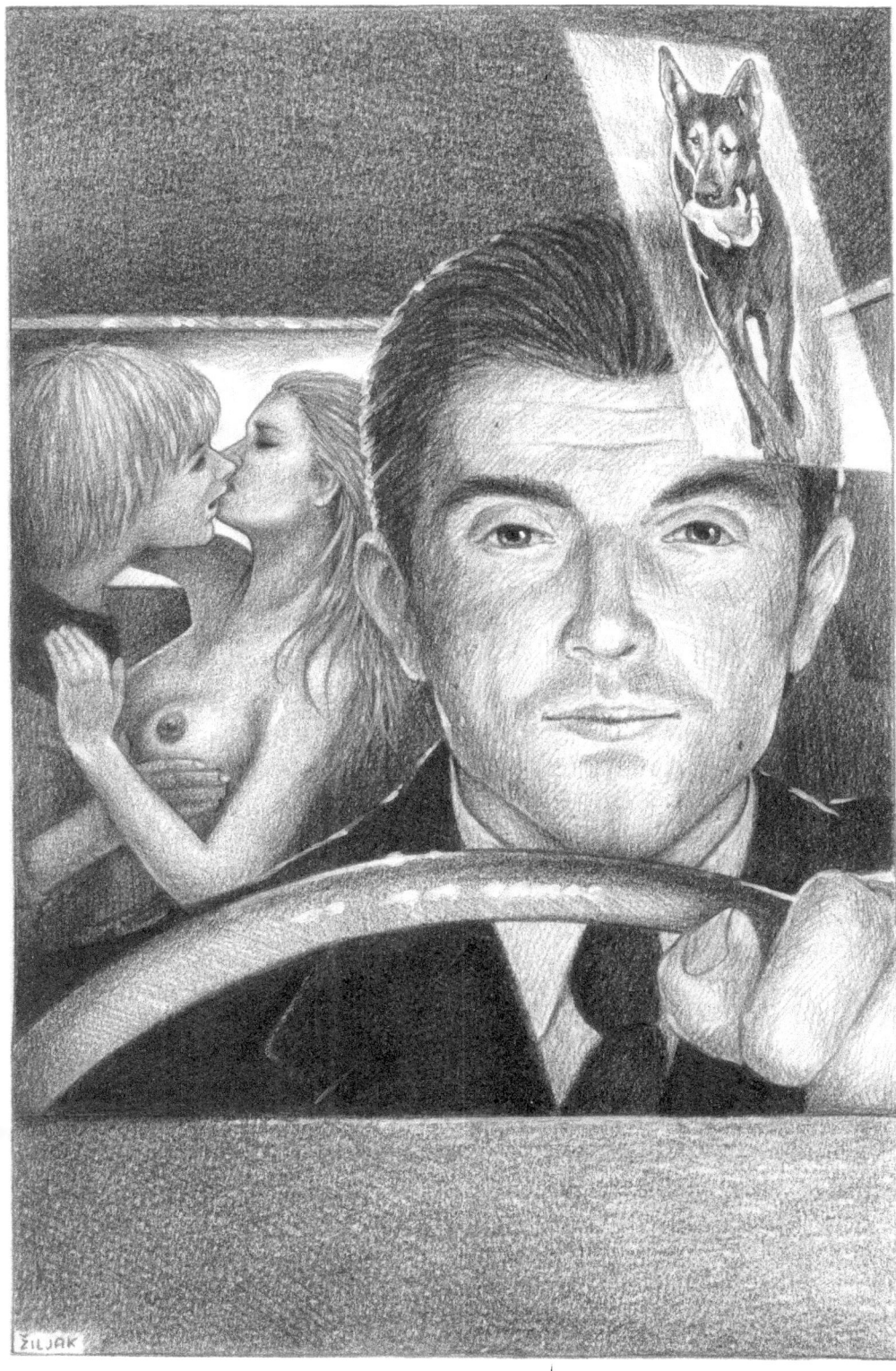

his lips.

Surprisingly, Justin spoke up, helping the cause by saying, "Well, don't stop now, Bunny! Take it *all* off!"

She grinned at her boyfriend as Carl echoed, "Hell, yeah, baby girl! Take off those panties! Show us your sex!"

Three sets of lungs raced to acquire the most oxygen as Wendy raised her bottom and slid her underwear off, leaving her completely nude, except for little blue socks.

Licking his lips, Carl leered at Wendy's crotch, loving how she had shaved her pubic bush except for a thin landing strip. "Sweet Heaven above, girl! That pussy is off the hook! That pussy is *perfect!* You're an angel with a devil's sweet cunt!"

Wendy flashed Carl a wanton look he knew too well, a torrid glance that caused his dick to throb. She *wanted* him.

As soon as they got back to his farm, he intended to fuck the bitch silly, even if he had to rape her after her skinny boyfriend was already dead.

He winked at her and she smiled back. Then she turned and embraced Justin, kissing him.

His heart hammering, Carl pulled his hard-on out of the fly of his white boxer briefs and began masturbating. With one hand on his prick and one on the wheel, with one eye on the pavement and one on the poontang, he told Wendy, "Take off Justin's shirt."

Justin had already slipped out of his hoodie earlier. Now Wendy pulled Justin's T-shirt over his head, stripping him to the waist.

Carl directed them to "Don't stop kissing."

As they made out, Wendy placed both her hands on Justin's hard chest, while he reciprocated by fondling her soft breasts.

The serial killer drove another six miles down the interstate while his eventual next victims felt each other up. Carl watched as Wendy's hand slid lower down Justin's torso. While the young man's chest was completely smooth, directly below his belly button was a thick treasure trail of flaxen hair. When Carl noticed Wendy petting that extension of Justin's pubic patch, he ordered the nude damsel to "Take off his pants."

Their kiss broke apart as Wendy reached for Justin's zipper.

Carl goaded her, "You're already naked, darlin', so it's only fair that Justin get naked too. Right?"

"Damn straight," Wendy agreed. She pushed Justin back and grabbed his pants at the waist, peeling them off. His boxers went down with his jeans. At first, he tried to pull his underwear back up but when Wendy pulled more insistently, Justin immediately surrendered, muttering, "Fuck it."

Carl checked out Justin's body, judging the young man's circumcised penis to be a bit less than average, probably no more than five inches. He was encouraged to see Justin had big balls and he was rampantly erect. He would wager he had seen the last of any resistance from Mr. Sturgis.

Carl said to Justin, "That is one heller studly cock, dude." Then he said to Wendy, "How can you keep your hands off it, girl?"

Wendy clutched Justin's dick, apparently with a knowing hand. Justin gasped, then moaned with pleasure, throwing back his head and closing his eyes.

Carl asked Justin, "Does she give you many blowjobs?"

Justin lowered his head and opened his eyes, looking flushed and dazed.

So he asked Wendy, "What do ya say, baby girl? Tell ole Carl the truth. Do you like sucking on your lover man's big dick?" It *wasn't* a big dick, but some of the most effective flattery was the easiest.

Wendy answered, "I *do* like it, yeah."

The fogginess in Justin's gaze cleared as he turned to frown at Wendy. Before he could say anything, she hurriedly added, "I admit it though," she said, never stopping jacking him, "I don't do it very often."

"Why not?" asked Carl. "That is one handsome fuck-stick! Don't you understand how truly *blessed* you are to have such a fine piece of man meat to suck on?"

Playfully, Justin said, "Yeah! Don't you realize how lucky you are to—"

"Oh, shut up," said Wendy and then promptly bent over and took half of Justin's length into her mouth.

Carl tried to see what was going on via mirror-glancing, but the back of Wendy's head blocked his view of the action. The sounds of fellatio, however, were incredibly erotic. Carl heard the smack of her lips, the slurp of her tongue, the liquid squishing of her mouth-slide. Justin growled and groaned in response to the cock sucking.

Another steaming twenty miles went gasping by.

Suddenly, Justin cried out, "Oh, my God!" He ran his fingers through Wendy's hair, guiding the concentrated bobbing of her head, squealing, "I'm going to come if you keep that up!"

Carl warned, "Don't do it, Wendy!"

Her lips were removed from Justin's wet manhood with a loud *plop.*

"Oh, my God!" Justin exclaimed again.

"It's better if you edge him," Carl assured Wendy. "Make it last, honey girl, so that when he *does* finally come, it blows his brains out!"

Justin rolled his head, sounding frustrated as he whined, "I think I'm already there!"

Carl ignored Mr. Sturgis, catching Miss Dean's pretty brown eyes. "I want to see your ass, baby. What's a guy gotta do to get a look at the world's sexiest bubble butt?"

"Show him," said Justin, sounding breathless. "Her ass is to die for, man. It's a wet dream on two legs."

When she turned around in the back seat and presented her buttocks for his inspection, Carl had to take his hand off his cock, which was hard as iron and dribbling pre-cum. Nearly breathless himself, he exclaimed, "Fuck yeah, baby girl! Justin is right! Your ass is *righteous!*" He whistled. "Sexy as *fuck!*" Carl resolved that before this ride was over, he was going to watch Justin take her anally.

Wendy wiggled her tush at him before sitting back down.

"Okay. Your turn, dawg," Carl said to Justin. "Lick her pussy, man. Tongue that clit."

Justin went down on Wendy, who draped one leg over his shoulder. Once again, Carl couldn't see much, this time because of Justin's long hair, but Wendy's whimpers and squeals of pleasure were thrilling. And he loved watching the quiver of her thighs as Justin made her wriggle.

It was a mild night, with the temperature steady at sixty-six degrees, but Carl realized he was sweating. He considered rolling down his window and immediately decided against it. The smell of Wendy's wet vagina had permeated the closed-up atmosphere of his Lincoln and Carl knew he'd rather roast than flush away that sensual scent.

After only a few minutes, Wendy's squirming became thrashing and her squeals became shrieks. She suddenly grabbed Justin's head with both hands and pulled him out of her crotch, yelling, "I can't take it anymore! Fuck me!"

Carl knew he couldn't stave off the copulation any longer, nor did he want to. He could no longer even touch his own rampant cock, he was so close to coming.

Justin scrambled to line up his prick with Wendy's pussy and then thrust into her. After a mutual wail of pleasure, Wendy grabbed Justin's long hair and cried out, "Fuck me, Wolfie! Fuck my pussy!"

Justin wasn't slow to comply. As the couple began to fornicate, Carl heard the quick *whup! whup! whup!* of thighs slapping ass.

"Fuck me!"

Carl took a handkerchief out of his pocket, wrapped it

around his hard-on, then went back to furiously jerking off. Behind him, a whimpering Justin humped a wailing Wendy even faster and harder. Watching that young guy work his sweaty ass while that young gal raked his sweaty back with her fingernails, Carl let go.

Silently, the Blood Prophet had a long and immensely satisfying orgasm.

"I'm almost there, Bunny!" shouted Justin. "I'm going to come!"

"Yes!" shrieked Wendy, reaching her own climax. "YES!"

Justin growled and roared as he slammed his hips one final time.

Panting, his heart fluttering, Carl finished cleaning up his soaked dick. As his captives rode the body-quaking waves of their physical ecstasy, he wiped up a huge load of semen, tucked the drenched handkerchief under his seat, then put away his slowly deflating penis.

Carl checked his odometer and realized there was a rest stop just another fourteen miles down the interstate. He guessed Wendy probably had to pee.

They would stop and relieve themselves, and then Carl would break out the bottle of tequila he had stashed in the trunk. He would offer them a couple more shots before they continued on their journey. As soon as they got back on the road, he'd fire up another joint and talk them out of their clothes again.

He was confident that he could direct the second round of sex so that it lasted even longer than the first.

It was still a long drive home.

By the time they finally arrived at Carl's house, Justin and Wendy were asleep, having dozed off after their last fuck. On the drive here, Carl knew Justin had had three orgasms. He had no idea how many times Wendy had climaxed. Listening to her ride Justin cowgirl-style in the back seat, Carl thought she might be multi-orgasmic.

Thanks to Carl, Justin Sturgis and Wendy Dean just had the hottest sex of their young lives.

Now, he could kill them with absolutely no guilt.

Carl parked behind his old farmhouse, got out of the car, and stretched. He felt drained and tired.

He had planned to fuck Wendy that night, and Justin too, and not bleed them until the morning. But after he'd jacked off and quelled his horniness, he started thinking about that god-damn dog again. And when the kids fell asleep, that was *all* he could think about.

He was no longer in the mood for sex.

He wanted *answers.*

Carl hurried inside his home and went straight to his master bedroom, having a seat at an antique roll-top desk. He cut up two monster lines of cocaine on a small mirror and snorted them. He clapped his hands together, new energy surging through his body. Carl then took a loaded pistol from his desk, concealed it under his coat, and walked back outside to awaken Wendy and Justin.

They were already awake and getting dressed. Carl opened the door for them and Wendy got out, saying, "I need to use the bathroom again."

"Okay," said Carl. Justin got out on the other side of the car. Wendy was looking at the house and Carl pointed in the other direction. "My studio is actually in the barn." He had told them he was an artist, which was absolutely true, even though his art wasn't for the public. "That's where I've got the coke. And champagne. There's a bathroom out there too."

Justin looked tired. His eyes were puffy and bloodshot. He told Carl, "I hate champagne. Got any vodka?"

"Absolutely." Carl led them toward the barn. "Right this way, my lovelies."

Once inside the cavernous structure, Carl flipped on the lights, walking all the way to the back of the barn, back beside

Bucephalus' stall. He took the gun out from beneath his coat. Behind him, Wendy's final words were uttered in the form of a question.

"Where's the bathroom?"

Carl turned around, raised the pistol, and fired. As usual, his aim was unerring. A cloud of blood mist splashed the air as Wendy dropped dead, her head gushing.

Carl wasn't surprised to see Justin look more confused than frightened in his final moment. Like his girlfriend, the young Mr. Sturgis was also slain instantly when a single bullet decimated his brains.

Twin pools of blood spread across the concrete floor, eventually becoming one.

When he was done, Carl would use a hose to wash all the blood into the soft earth outside. Cleanup was easy out in the barn. He'd had years of practice to perfect his methods.

Before proceeding any further, Carl closed the barn doors.

He then stripped both bodies. Now that they were dead, they were no longer appealing to him; he wasn't a necrophiliac. Once both of the corpses were nude, Carl used coils of thick rope to tie Wendy's hands together, then her ankles. He repeated this process on Justin, also binding his limbs.

Carl then used a hacksaw to behead the two lovers.

He placed each of their heads separately into garbage sacks, double bagging them and closing them with twist ties.

He then picked up Wendy's gushing, headless body and carried it deeper into the barn, to a place where ropes and a series of pulleys were attached to the raftered ceiling. The ends of two ropes were adorned with massive iron hooks.

Carl laid Wendy belly-down on the concrete floor. He then attached both her bound hands and her tied feet to the same hook. Grabbing a nearby section of rope, Carl pulled, slowly hoisting Wendy into the air, creating a human zero out of her. Her nude body was curled back, her stomach the lowest-hanging part. Her breasts dangled. Carl raised her corpse about six feet into the air, then twisted the rope to lock her into place.

He then used another pulley to raise Justin's body in the same fashion, belly down, to a height above his own head.

Next, Carl stripped off all his clothes. Once he was naked, he spread two new white linen sheets on the floor, side by side. He pulled more ropes, swinging first Wendy Dean's body above one king-sized sheet, then positioning Justin Sturgis's body above the other.

When Carl was fifteen years old, he'd gone to New Orleans to spend time with his great grandmother, just before she died of brain cancer. She was half Haitian, an old voodoo woman, with a gift for haruspicy. The first time he saw her cut open a dove and divine the future from its entrails, Carl knew he was close to discovering his destiny.

Later, at the age of nineteen, he learned that while he had no knack for haruspicy—the reading of animal entrails—he did have a gift for anthropomancy—for human sacrifice, with his own special artistic twist.

Carl Carpenter was a Blood Prophet.

He picked up a thick butcher knife, honed to such a sharp point it could literally split hairs. Bucephalus snorted and whinnied. The horse had been witness to many scenes such as this. The stallion knew what was next.

Stepping beneath Wendy's headless, curled-up body, Carl plunged the knife deep into her stomach, just below her ribcage. With both hands gripping the handle of the blade, he dragged the knife down to her crotch, slicing open her belly. An enormous volume of blood rained out of the cut, splashing down on the white sheet.

His own naked body splattered with gore, Carl bent down to examine the blood-slosh-on-linen.

Never had a reading been clearer. The shape of the dog was unmistakable, as was the severed hand in its mouth. Looking at the horrifying image drawn brightly in blood, Carl knew the canine was Mostetler's beloved pet. The animal's name was Spirit and it had gone missing the day Daryl died, the day Carl had killed him.

Somehow, that ungodly beast had traveled almost three hundred miles to unerringly find Carl.

The dog was now an *avenging* Spirit.

Fear trickled down Carl's spine as blood continued to trickle down a coil of intestines hanging out of Wendy's abdomen.

Staring savagely at the Blood Prophecy, Carl couldn't tell if the animal was natural or not, if it was *alive* or not. He thought for a moment the beast was some kind of *ghost* dog. Then he wondered if it was demon-possessed. Finally, he considered the possibility it was not even a dog at all but some kind of alien shapeshifter.

It couldn't be a *normal* dog. No regular hound would pose any threat to him. But it was clear from Wendy's reading that this dog *was* a danger to him.

Carl couldn't tell what the creature was. The visions provided by Wendy's blood were insufficient. Luckily, he still had Justin.

Striding over to Justin's corpse, Carl used both hands and stabbed upward, into the young man's stomach, the top of the blade scraping against ribs. With a vicious yank, he slashed downward, bisecting guts. He cleaved all the way into Justin's pubic bush before extracting the knife and throwing the blade into Bucephalus's stall, so that the horse could lick it clean.

Again, the red fell for fate.

Carl Carpenter looked down at the bloody sheet and saw his own bloody, screaming face.

The demon dog was depicted standing on Carl's chest, its jaws clamped to Carl's neck. This prophecy was even more lucid than the last one.

Frozen with terror, Carl stared down at a bloodstained promise of his own horrible death.

In the next instant, the future was now.

The German shepherd charged out from behind bales of hay stacked nearby. Growling, Spirit ran at Carl and, before he could react, the dog leaped.

Knocked off his feet, Carl went down hard, the back of his head impacting the concrete floor. Seeing stars, dazed and hurting, he was not even aware he was lying directly below Justin's dripping, dangling guts.

Two white front paws stood on Carl's dark black chest. As his vision cleared, Carl saw the beast was wearing a collar. Then Spirit opened its jaws and clamped down on his neck, puncturing his jugular, crushing his windpipe, taking his life.

Carl couldn't believe his dying eyes when he saw the tag on the collar read "Flattery Will Get You Nowhere."

A dead man's best friend turned up its head and howled.

Obsidian Phage

by
J.T. Beckett

His wife is distant — sexually and emotionally shut down to him. He's fighting the urge to violate the sanctity of their marriage with the woman at work. He isn't sure he can hold out for much longer. Arnold is a man desperate for something — anything — to fix what's broken. And then there's this strange thing happening in his house, with some kind of blackness that's spreading on the picture window like a plague growing on the glass. It's just one more thing for him to deal with, and certainly not related to his crumbling marriage in any way...

Horror
Heterosexual sex
Lesbian sex
Cheating
Rough sex
Desperate romance
Sexual frustration
Desire

Arnold Duquette noticed the black mark just before heading to work one morning, when he opened the drapes of the expansive picture window in the living room. He'd stood back to admire the bright morning, and his spacious green back yard with its surrounding ring of oaks and pines, and there it was. It stood out against the brilliant blue sky so prominently that at first he thought it was a tiny black cloud floating high above the Earth.

Arnold moved closer to investigate. It was something on the window glass, about an inch across, mostly circular with rough edges, and as dark as a midnight inkwell. He ran his fingertips across it. It had a rippled texture, as if the glass had cooled before someone could smooth it out. He scraped at it with a fingernail, but it wasn't something merely on the surface. It was a strange blemish in the glass that he'd somehow never noticed.

It was five-thirty and Audrey was heading out for work, bedecked in her pink nurse's scrubs. He immediately reacted upon seeing her, as he always had—it was something about her in scrubs that always revved him up, ever since they were young. She was a short, petite woman, and the scrub pants hugged her backside snugly, the loose top hinting at her modest breasts hiding behind the thin fabric. Her hair, tied up and back almost haphazardly, was the stuff of fantasies for him. But it had been far too long since he'd held her close, felt her naked body against his. Something had gone wrong recently, although he had no clue what.

She was her usual pensive, reserved self, just as she had

been the past seven long months. It was less like a marriage and more like roommates with nothing in common. But, as usual, Arnold tried to be amicable, and told her about the strange black mark.

"So call a glass company," she said in a flat voice as she pulled on her jacket.

She didn't sound hateful, just uninterested, as was the norm for her lately. He had to find out what was wrong.

"Audrey, you've been acting distant for some time," he said. "Did I do something to piss you off? Or is something else wrong?"

She looked at him with blue eyes that used to sparkle but now were dark and almost foreboding. "No, everything's fine. I've just been feeling... a little weird lately."

"Lately? You've been like this for seven months."

She didn't meet his eyes, instead staring at the wall behind him.

"Do you know we haven't made love since New Year's Eve?" he said. "And that was just because we were drunk. We'd barely had sex once a month the entire year before that."

She looked stunned, as if it had just never occurred to her. "Arnold, honey... I'm sorry, you're right. I've had a strange year. We should talk about this, I know. We'll do that very soon. But right now, I have to get going, or I'll be late for work."

And she went, without a good-bye kiss. He watched her go, watched out the window as her tight butt swayed, as she climbed in her car and backed out of the driveway. All the while, he felt his penis hardening in his briefs, aching and begging for release. But he knew it wasn't coming from her.

He sighed and, once again, forced the hurt and anger deep down, and hoped she'd finally come around. But he had an hour to take himself away, and as soon as her car was out of sight down the road, he grabbed an old towel, dug a porn movie out of his stash, and settled back on the couch. It was one of his favorites, with a petite, small-breasted thirty-something with the same hair as his wife. He released his penis from its tight cotton confines, leaned back, and stroked himself furiously as the movie played. On screen, the Audrey look-alike, on her back with her legs in the air, holding on to her ankles for all she was worth, moaned and wailed and oohed and ahhed while a hung stud put it to her.

When the girl in the movie squealed in orgasm and the stud pulled out to spew across her belly and tits, Arnold ejaculated with fierce grunting into the towel. It was better than nothing, but it was hardly the same as making love to his wife. He didn't know how much longer he could keep jacking off and pretending it was.

His morning was filled with the quarterly meeting to recap the Evervale Sexual Health Promotion Agency's efforts to combat sexually transmitted diseases in the metro region. It was dismal, as usual. HIV infections were down, but everything else was up. Syphilis, gonorrhea, and herpes were on the rise. There was a surprising spike in pubic lice. And chlamydia seemed to be bordering on a local epidemic.

As ESHPA's executive director, Arnold took notes and listened to everyone lamenting the downward spiral. Birth-control prescriptions were down, as was the number of condoms distributed, so obviously the organization had to step up its efforts, blah blah blah, and so on. It was the same old discussion he'd heard for years.

He had lunch in his office, staring out his big window at the ornate brick buildings across the street. Their architecture was from Evervale's nineteenth-century boom, with stylish brick arches over their many windows — it was a beautiful field of brick and glass. Those windows got Arnold thinking about the strange blemish at home, so he dug out a phone book and located a glazier. The old man, a guy named Sanders, said he could buff the problem area down, which would be far cheaper than replacing the giant window.

So Arnold made an appointment for that afternoon and was on his way out when his assistant director, Betty Ryman, caught him. She was forty-two, a voluptuous brunette with eyes that lit up his day, and a smile that woke up other things. As much as Arnold loved Audrey, and as much he was still turned on by her, Betty had always heated him up. She was the opposite of Audrey in many ways: wide hips, bigger ass, much larger breasts, fuller lips. Even when his marriage had been perfect, Arnold had enjoyed drinking in the arousing sight of Betty's gorgeous body. It spiced him up in all his private thoughts, and more than once he'd jacked off into an old towel with visions of her in his head.

"Skipping out for the day, boss?" she said with a slight conspiratorial wink.

"For a while." He knew he'd give anything to fuck her, and if he weren't married, he'd make a move on the single woman. He was almost positive she'd be receptive if he did.

"I'll hold down the fort." She cocked her head and asked, "How are things going with Audrey?"

Betty had been a good friend to both him and Audrey since he'd hired her at ESHPA twelve years before, and had recently been his confidante about his marital problems. "The same. I don't know what's wrong with her."

"I'm sure she'll come around."

"I don't know. I'm beginning to think she's tired of me after twenty years."

"Oh, of course she isn't—how could she get tired of a guy like you?" As if as an afterthought, she reached out and lightly squeezed his shoulder. It was just a friendly gesture, he was sure, but it sent an electric sizzle through his body anyway. Betty was always a major flirt, and she oozed sex appeal without trying, and of course Arnold had rampant fantasies about bending her right over his desk and fucking her senseless, so none of that was helping. Right then, Arnold had a hard time focusing on Audrey.

"I have to go," he said, and hurried out.

Sanders surveyed the black splotch on the glass and said, "That's a lot bigger than an inch, Mr. Duquette."

It was easily three inches across. "I must have been half-asleep this morning," Arnold said. "It didn't seem that big."

"Well, it'll cost a little more, but I can take care of it."

In a short while, the blemish was gone and the glass was smooth. Aside from a slight warping of light in that area, there was no evidence there had even been a blemish there.

At least it was one problem Arnold could solve in his life. He returned to work feeling that sad little triumph.

Audrey was her usual solemn self that evening when she got home from the hospital. Over a quiet dinner, he told her about the successful glass-buffing; she was just as aloof as she had been that morning.

He was watching television alone in the living room when a commercial came on for a cruise line, and he suddenly knew how to reboot his marriage. They'd wanted to take a Bermuda cruise for years, so that's what he'd do. Whatever funk Audrey was in, that would catapult her out of it. He'd call his travel agent the next day, book the trip, and surprise her when she got home. He smiled at his ingenious plan as he looked out his picture window, thinking of how happy they'd be together when the blue sky over his back yard would soon be a lot bluer in Bermuda — and then he saw it.

The blotch was still there. He came off the sofa in alarm and bolted to the window. It wasn't *still there;* it was a new blotch, where the old one had been, only very small, a centimeter across. He'd inspected Sanders' finished work, and there had been no doubt that not a speck of the old defect had remained. This was clearly a new one.

There had to be a logical explanation, but the existence of

the new blemish was at the forefront of his mind for the rest of the night.

He was still thinking of it as he lay in the dark later, staring at his wife's back in the green glow of his digital clock.

Her breathing was shallow. He could see her chest expanding and contracting in the silky lavender nightgown that clung to her like a second skin. It was warm, and she'd kicked the blankets off, so he had a perfect view of her. She was so beautiful, so sexy. Her waist, so narrow; her hips, not much wider, but enough of an hourglass there in the dim light to get him thinking. And as he watched, his penis stiffened. He wanted her then more than ever—fueled by frustration, aided by impatience, he wanted to fuck his wife right then and there.

He'd worn just his briefs to bed, so he hooked his thumbs in the elastic band and peeled them under his ass. His penis sprung free, still throbbing and growing larger, as he pushed the underwear down and kicked out of them. He scooted over to her in bed, gingerly wrapping his arm around her. She didn't stir. He moved closer, until his erect penis was wedged comfortably in between the small, tight cheeks of her ass. The silky fabric felt good on the sensitive head, but it felt fantastic to be this close to Audrey again.

He snaked his hand around her belly and made soft circles there. He felt her stir, felt her body tense as she realized.

"What are you doing?" she whispered.

"Touching you," he whispered back. "I've missed you. I really want to make love to you."

She didn't say anything. He slid his hand lower, felt his fingers pass under the thin elastic band of her underwear. Beneath his fingertips, he felt the soft mat of hair between her legs.

Then she moved a knee up, her thigh protecting her private parts, forcing his hand away.

"For Christ's sake, Audrey, please," he said. "I just want to make love to you."

"I know, honey," she said. "It's just that... it's that time of the month. I have a tampon in. It's... just a bad night."

His heart sank. "Okay."

They were silent for a long minute, but at least she didn't pull away from him. His hand rested on her belly, his cock throbbing relentlessly between her ass cheeks. Finally, she said, "Arnold... put it between my cheeks. Bare skin."

She gave a little clench of her cheeks around his swollen cock.

And his heart flew. This was a good sign. Even during that time of the month, she rarely gave in to anything sexual, not in all their years of marriage. He couldn't believe she'd offered that. But then she was reaching down, yanking on her nightie, pulling it up over her hips and forcing him to move away. She got it around her waist and reached back for his hand, pulling him back to her. His heart thudded as he grabbed for her cotton panties and rolled them down off her ass. She helped him until they were down around her thighs, and she scooted back and presented her ass to him.

He moved back into position and settled his penis between her cheeks. He was already oozing precum, so it took just a few strokes to lay down enough lubrication. Then he wrapped his arm around her and pulled her close, and he began stroking. It wasn't as good as being inside her, but it was better than nothing.

He worked harder and faster, and it was such a turn-on to be sliding his cock between his wife's ass cheeks that he knew he wouldn't last long. He bore down on her, forcing her over onto her belly, and she complied. He climbed atop her, straddling her petite form, and began madly fucking her ass crack as if he were actually nailing her.

The sensation soon became unbearable. He grunted and gurgled as he came. Hot jets of semen sprayed out of his cock and between her cheeks. He jerked his hips with each spurt, spraying more and more come. It shot onto her lower back, her ass, her nightie.

He was no sooner done than she said, "Mop it up for me."

Just like that. He realized she hadn't moaned or spoken, hadn't cooed at him or talked dirty or teased; she'd just lain there and taken it, and now was ordering cleanup. He didn't know what to say, so he grabbed for tissues on his nightstand and diligently cleaned up the mess. He gently pried her thighs apart to clean up semen dripping down there. It was difficult, seeing her vagina slightly opened, beckoning him.

And then he realized there was no tampon string. No tampon at all. She'd lied.

He was still speechless. He cleaned up his penis, then went downstairs to throw the pile of tissues away and take a leak. The first thing he did was check the trash can in the bathroom, which yielded no used tampon wrappers. While he stood naked in the bathroom, watching his piss stream into the toilet, he racked his brain wondering how he'd address it, or if he should.

But when he got back to bed, her panties were up, her nightie was down, and she was already snoring. Whether it was real or fake snoring, he couldn't tell.

It didn't matter. At least they'd had *some* kind of physical intimacy — even if it had been disappointingly one-sided.

By morning, the blotch was nearly two inches across. Arnold stared at it in utter disbelief. There was something seriously wrong with his picture window. He called in late to work and got Sanders on the phone. The glazier was there within the hour, matching Arnold's disbelief with a shaking head.

"Never seen anything like it in sixty years of doing this job," Sanders said.

"Should I replace the glass?" Arnold asked.

"I don't know yet," Sanders said, scratching his grizzled

chin. "I say we wait and see if it gets any bigger."

In between what seemed like an endless parade of department heads through his office that day, he traded several phone calls with his travel agent. He stopped by to pick up the tickets after work, and on his way home inspiration struck him again, so he picked up an impressive spread of Chinese food from Oriental Palace. He and Audrey used to go there almost every week, but hadn't been in nearly a year. This would be a perfect evening for them that was long overdue.

They had a fat white candle set atop a big glass candlestick, and when lit, there was the sweet smell of coconut in the air—a good setup for a tropical cruise, Arnold thought. He'd just laid all the food and dishes out on the table when Audrey got home; she followed the aroma of coconuts and pork fried rice to the dining room and stood there in her scrubs, looking confused.

"What's this?" she said, her voice dull and empty.

"Oriental Palace," he said with a broad smile.

"But... why?"

He took a deep breath. "Well, I'd like to solve whatever problem it is we seem to have. We used to have fun together, Audrey, every day, just by being in love. And we used to go to Oriental Palace nearly every week. I know Chinese food isn't the answer, but it's a start towards spending time together again. We really need to do that before our marriage falls completely apart. That's why I got these."

He pulled the tickets out of his jacket pocket and held them out to her. She cocked her head, curious, and he said, "They're tickets for that Bermuda cruise we've always talked about. Two weeks, Audrey. We both have enough vacation time accrued, so there's no reason we—"

"I can't," she said.

Perplexity overwhelmed him, and he felt his jaw sag. "Why not?"

She sighed, long and deep, and slid her pocketbook off her shoulder to hang on the chair. "I'm just not ready yet."

Arnold's gut tightened and twisted, and he felt the pain and anguish growling deep inside. "Why aren't you ready? Please, tell me what I've done to deserve this."

"It isn't you. It's me. Please, Arnold—I'm trying to work through this, and I just need your support right now. I'll talk to you soon, but... I just need a little more time."

"You were ready for ass-cheek sex last night!" he cried, pounding the table in anguish. She winced when he did. "You lied about having a tampon in. Was last night just to shut me up?"

She looked nervous and confused. "I just wanted you to have something last night. I wasn't ready for sex. I will be soon. You just have to give me time."

He knew her, and she wouldn't give him any answers beyond that. She had to do it on her own. So he steeled his resolve and said, "All right. I hope we can work through this soon. But for now, at least we can eat some of this food together."

She smiled a weak but genuine smile, and she pulled out the chair. He began digging in to the lo mein and serving a pile of it on her plate.

"I know it doesn't seem like it, but I love you, Arnold," she said. "More than you can know."

He looked into her sad eyes and smiled, as the beast within mellowed and quieted. All was not lost.

"I love you, too," he said.

The next morning, the rough blemish had grown to the size of a dinner plate. He called Sanders and told him to replace the window, and the glazier promised to have a couple of guys there early the next morning.

ESHPA hosted a symposium for area health-care organizations in the big conference room that afternoon. The guest speaker was an STD specialist from the Centers for Disease Control. It was four hours of what Arnold knew so well, but with national numbers. It seemed Evervale was worse than the averages — like he needed that bitter pill added to his woes.

By the time it was over, ESHPA was closed, and everybody except he and Betty Ryman had gone home. Her office was across the hall from his, and her light was on, so he poked his head in. She was deeply engrossed in some paperwork as he called out a hello.

"Hey, you," she said, her infectious smile blossoming across her face amidst shiny lip gloss. "I see you survived the symposium."

"Barely," he said, grinning.

"Whatever doesn't kill you makes you stronger," she said, twirling a lock of brunette hair with two fingers. "Speaking of which, any good news on the home front?"

He didn't want to talk about it, and certainly didn't want to talk about fucking his wife's ass cheeks like some horny teenage boy taking whatever he could get, but he heard himself rambling on about cruise tickets and Bermuda and Chinese food and Audrey not being ready to talk about anything. Betty listened patiently, with the real interest he wished Audrey could have again. When he was done, she said, "I'm sorry to hear it's not going well. Is there anything I can do?"

She was looking at him, looking *into* him, and he felt that overpowering sexual draw she so easily evoked in him. He envisioned answering her by saying *Why, yes, you can bend over your desk and let me slam-fuck you right here,* but of course he'd never do that to Audrey, no matter how vividly he imagined Betty being a total sex goddess.

So he mentally slapped himself back to reality and said, "No, there's nothing you can do."

"How long since you two have been intimate?"

It was as if he were broadcasting his sexual starvation, and Betty had picked up on it. "A long time. Seven months. We'd always been very physical, and our sex life was always so exciting..." He heard himself speaking, and couldn't believe he was talking so candidly about this to her. Maybe he *should* tell her about the ass-cheek sex. Betty was a close friend, but his sex life with Audrey had always been a very private thing. "In recent years, maybe the spark has gone away, but these past seven months... I just don't get her."

"You think she's cheating on you, don't you?"

The question hit him like a fastball to the face. It had actually never crossed his mind, not even once. The idea that Audrey could commit the ultimate betrayal by being with another man seemed ludicrous — but what if Betty was right?

After a long pause, he said, "Well, I hadn't been, but now that you mention it... I certainly hope not."

"I'm sorry I brought it up. It really isn't my business."

"It's okay. You're the one good friend Audrey and I have that we've always been able to count on. Maybe the only person I could possibly talk about this with."

"That's good," she said.

The giant picture window was a single monstrous pane of glass about twelve feet long and a good six high. And the blemish was no longer circular; to the left and bottom, it had met the window frame and stopped, but had spread wildly elsewhere, billowing out in a grand curve that seemed to bulge out of the frame like a rising black sun. It covered a third of the window, obscuring daylight as if it were solid metal.

He moved to the window, got up close until his face was mere inches from the surface. He could see the slightly rippled surface, as if flowing lava had instantly cooled into obsidian. The impossible thing, astounding as it was baffling, was spreading like a cancer across his picture window.

In the morning, the glass would be replaced, and this strange problem in his life would be history.

*   *   *

By morning, the entire window was completely black. Not a single fleck of sunlight made it through.

The glass installers made quick work of pulling the diseased pane out and replacing it with a new one. Soon, the living room was back to normal, and the workers were loading the massive black pane onto the transport rack on their truck. Audrey, who was beginning a four-day weekend off, surprised him by joining him in the driveway in her bathrobe.

"Well, good morning," he said.

"Good morning," she said, and she smiled when she did. "Is the whole thing black?"

"Every bit of it. It's the damnedest thing I've ever seen."

Arnold watched with great satisfaction as the truck drove away, taking the seemingly cursed thing with it. When it was out of sight, he said, "You're up early for a day off."

She nodded. "Hard to sleep in after six straight day shifts. I go on overnights next week."

He nodded, and had no idea what else to say. He had no clue how to make small talk with his own wife.

"I thought we could go to dinner tonight," she said.

That took him by surprise. "Sure. Where?"

"I was thinking MacLeod's."

A wave of relief washed through him. MacLeod's was where they'd had their first date, and where they went on every wedding anniversary and other special occasion. "That would be great," he said.

She smiled brightly, and for the first time in a long time, he was sure her eyes were sparkling. "Then I'll meet you there when you're out of work."

Between the departure of the plagued black window and his wife starting to emerge from her shell, Arnold felt rejuvenated. When Betty came into his office at lunch to drop off a report, he even managed to look her in the eyes without checking out her cleavage first.

"You seem chipper today," she said.

"I'm in a great mood. Audrey wants to go to dinner at MacLeod's."

Betty brightened. "No kidding! Isn't that only for special occasions?"

"Yes. I guess this is special."

"It sounds it. I predict your marital worries are about to start going away." She sauntered up to his desk, hiked her skirted backside on the edge, and leaned in, looking serious. "Listen, Arnold, whatever's wrong with Audrey, you have to give her the benefit of the doubt. Women are weird creatures; we run on emotions for fuel, and our minds go all over the place. Sometimes we act a little crazy."

He tried to process that. "What are you saying?"

She reached out and laid a warm hand on his. "She's going through something, and you need to listen to her. Don't be angry. Just love her. I'm guessing she'll need it."

Arnold figured Betty knew more about crazy-woman behavior than he did, so he nodded. But all he could focus on was the warmth of her hand, and trying like hell not to look down at the deep cleavage and swelling breasts just inches from his face.

When they met at MacLeod's, she greeted him with a hug and a kiss, just like old times. She was all smiles, painted with just the right amount of makeup, her eyes sparkling. It was literally like nothing had been wrong for seven-plus months. They enjoyed a leisurely dinner, with a little wine for good measure, and had a long conversation about many trivial things that didn't matter but were nevertheless like gold to Arnold. They were waiting for dessert when he realized it was time to talk about serious things.

"So let's talk," he said.

She'd been happy and laughing all evening, but with that, her face became solemn. She set down her wine goblet, picked up her napkin, dabbed her mouth. He watched her silent ballet, as she neatly folded the napkin, set it back down, clasped her hands before her on the table, and stared down at them as if praying.

Finally, she lifted her head and said, "There's no easy way to tell you this."

A bottomless pit formed immediately in his stomach, and he felt sick. "That doesn't sound good. You either want a divorce, or you've cheated on me with another man."

"I don't want a divorce. And I'd never betray you by being with another man."

A double rush of relief blew through him, carrying away his two biggest worries. But she was looking at him with her face riddled with guilt and her eyes already begging forgiveness. But for what?

"Then what the hell is it, Audrey?" he said

She swallowed, closed her eyes, breathed, re-opened her eyes, met his gaze. "From last October until mid-January, I had an affair with a woman I met at work. And since the end of it, there was a chance I'd contracted HIV."

Arnold's whole world spun madly in a mental cyclone. "What?" he whispered, voice hoarse, barely aware of people at nearby tables.

"I'm so sorry, Arnold. I didn't plan this. She was just something I thought I needed for a few months. And this one time in November, we had a third woman join us, and she said she was clean but she wasn't. She called my partner in January to tell us she was HIV positive. We both got tested and were clean, but we had to wait six months for a second test to be sure. That's why I haven't been intimate with you, and why I haven't been able to look you in the eye."

He was reeling amidst this revelation. "For Christ's sake, Audrey... you're a nurse! And I run an agency that combats STDs! How could it have not occurred to you to use protection?"

"Please keep your voice down," she whispered.

He dropped his head into his hands, his elbows onto the table. He was on the verge of hyperventilating, so he focused his mind on breathing slowly and steadily. "HIV, Audrey — Jesus Christ! You're talking about AIDS!"

"I know. I went to Dr. Campbell, and he's sure that I'm HIV negative — "

"You went to Jeff Campbell? Audrey — I deal with him on a professional basis at least every week! Couldn't you have gone to any other doctor in the entire city?" His head hurt, and he was dizzy, as if he were on an endlessly spinning amusement-park ride.

"Dr. Campbell was my partner's idea. It didn't occur to me that he was a bad choice."

His brain swam madly against swirling currents of confusion. "Your partner — who is she?"

"Nobody you've met, and I don't see her anymore. I won't blame you if you won't forgive me, or if you hate me, or if you want to divorce me. I deserve all of that. I just hope you'll believe that my mistakes had nothing to do with you, because you've been the best husband any woman could ever have..."

But Arnold was already lost to his shock. He jumped to his feet, knocking his chair over. He saw the staring faces of the restaurant patrons as he staggered past, through the dining room and out the door, as the pain and fury boiled within him.

He slept on the couch in the living room. Audrey came home a half-hour behind him and had headed up to bed without a word.

When he woke to sunlight on a Sunday morning, the day started very badly.

He got up off the couch wearing just his briefs and a T-shirt, stretched, and basked in the sun flooding the room through the new picture window. It looked to be a beautiful day, all blue skies and white clouds, with green trees dancing lightly in the wind. Then his eyes focused on it, and he froze.

Up high, nearly top center, was a dark blemish about an inch across.

"No fucking way," he breathed.

He stumbled forward, then hit the brakes and sucked in his breath. Down low and to the right was a second blemish. His eyes bulged as he took a lurching step backward. It wasn't possible.

He spun about, to the three smaller windows that lined the long wall, and he headed for the first one. He grabbed the drapes with both hands and hauled them fiercely apart.

There was a black mark on the glass.

He stumbled to the next window, threw open the drapes. Black mark. Ran to the last window. Same thing.

He ran out of the living room and into the study. The three windows there all had blemishes. The kitchen and dining room had many windows, some big and some small, and there were black marks everywhere. Every piece of glass was blotched with them.

The glass candlestick on the dining room table, from the Chinese dinner the other night, had a black mark. Several glasses in the sink had them.

He tore into the bathroom in a near panic and threw on the lights. The single window there had a black mark, and the expansive wall mirror above the twin sinks had two. He staggered back to the living room and stood in front of the couch, staring at the big picture window behind it in sheer disbelief.

"They're everywhere," Audrey said from behind him, and he spun to her, immediately overwhelmed by revulsion and contempt for her. "They're on every window upstairs. What's happening?"

"I don't know," he said.

They stood, surveying the black spots, and presently she moved up close to him. He felt her body heat, even before she tentatively touched his arm.

"I'm not ready to talk to you right now," he said through clenched teeth, trying not to snarl.

"I understand. Is there any way to make you feel better?"

He felt her hand sliding around him, going lower. Despite how pissed he was with her, his penis began coming to life.

"You think having sex will make this all better?" he asked, incredulous.

"I know it won't," she said. "But it's a start. Even if you walk out of my life, I owe you some honest lovemaking."

"Maybe I'm not in the mood to make love to my wife," he said, the snarl finally unstoppable, and he spun to face her with fiery face and burning eyes. "Maybe I'm in the mood to fuck a cheap slut who can't give me the basic respect a husband deserves. Maybe I want to bend you over the couch and fuck you so hard you cry."

Her face strained to hold its neutral appearance, but he could tell he'd hurt her. He was okay with that. She appeared to consider his words for a long moment.

Then she sidestepped him and moved to the couch, untying her robe and letting it fall as she went. She was naked, and she got on her knees on the couch, facing the infected window, and placed her hands on the back. Her bare ass jutted out at him as she looked over her shoulder with a serious face. She wiggled her butt, spreading her knees apart. Her vagina was open and pink.

"You can do anything you want to me," Audrey said.

He didn't hesitate, tearing off his briefs to free his hardening cock. He grabbed her waist with one strong hand, his cock with the other, and yanked her roughly back. He guided his head to her liquid lips and fed it between them. Then he grabbed her waist with both hands and dug his fingers in. He heard her suck in her breath, but before she could complain, he rammed his cock inside her. She cried out in pain but he just started pounding. She cried with every fierce thrust, with every vicious slap of his groin against her ass. He'd never been too rough with her, and certainly not in more than a playful way and not for very long, but this time was different. He destroyed her with every stroke, pulling her tiny hips back to meet his slamming cock. Her cries finally subsided, muted by a tight-lipped mouth: She was trying *not* to cry out. He envisioned her in pain, fighting back tears, and he didn't care.

But he did. As he was grunting and growling as he banged her like a back-alley whore, he realized he *did* care. And Audrey letting him use her like this was nothing more than her trying to get him to forget the horrible thing she'd done. He let go of her, pulled out of her, backed away. He stood there, cock rapidly deflating, breathing hard, as she turned to see what was going on.

"Fuck this," he said. "This isn't helping. It isn't making me feel better. I don't know what will."

Her eyes had been wet, and now tears streamed. "I know," she said. "But I'll do anything to make it right."

"Maybe I should go cheat on you. How would that make you feel?"

She sank to the couch. With her legs spread, he could see just how badly he'd punished her pussy: It was swollen and red, and the soft flesh of her mound and that of her thighs was already bruised purple. Fleetingly, he enjoyed that sight.

"If that will make this easier, then go do it," she said.

"I will," he said, and stormed past her.

He threw on his clothes and fled. He couldn't take being around her, and he couldn't take the blackness that was attacking the glass in his house like an alien fungus.

He drove aimlessly for an hour, anger welling up in every pore. More than anything, he wanted to cheat on her, to get his revenge and somehow be able to deal with what she had done. But he had no idea how to cheat, or who to cheat with.

That wasn't true, of course. He found himself at Betty's house, ringing her doorbell, grabbing a mailbox full of envelopes and waiting for her. She answered the door wearing a sports bra, Spandex shorts, and a sweatband on her head. Her skin glistened with sweat from the workout he'd interrupted, and it soaked her bra, highlighting her nipples as her big tits strained to escape. The Spandex had sunken into the wet cleft between her legs, teasing him with a tight cameltoe.

"Mail's here," he said with a grin, holding the stack out to her.

She took it. "Thanks. But I'm guessing you didn't come here to fetch my mail."

"No," he said.

She invited him into the kitchen, tossing the mail on the counter and toweling the sweat off her face, and offered him coffee. He accepted, and proceeded to spill his guts about everything with Audrey, ending with his decision to repay her infidelity with some of his own.

She had listened intently, and then she said, "Is that why you're here? To have sex with me?"

He didn't even blush, because he was beyond that now. "Yes."

"I don't think sex with my good friend would be a smart idea — especially since I'm good friends with his wife, too."

"I might take that seriously if you hadn't flirted with me every day since we met," Arnold said. "I've spent twelve years trying like hell not to stare at your tits."

She grinned and shook her head. "Arnold Duquette, you horn dog."

"I'm serious. You've been my sexual fantasy for twelve years. And I want to have sex with you right now."

"Oh, my," she said, and for the first time since he'd known her, she actually blushed. "I don't think we should."

"You're not attracted to me?"

"I am, but that's hardly the point."

"It is the point. Have sex with me, Betty — right now."

He locked eyes with her, mentally daring her to resist. She

stared back, her eyes betraying her desire, her full lips trembling ever so slightly. She was weak, and he nearly had her. He could almost see the wheels turning in her head as she mentally tried to justify screwing him and betraying Audrey. The deciding factor would be that Audrey had betrayed him, Arnold knew; he was sure she was going to give in, leap out of her chair and grab him, lock lips and grope at him and tear off his clothes.

"Arnold..." she began, and he saw the weakness in her eyes. She *wanted* to, but she was going to tell him no. He had to act.

He moved in to her, and she smelled salty and sweaty. She backed away in alarm as he closed in on her, but he was on her, grabbing her by the shoulders and pulling her in to kiss her. She tried to move back, tried to push her hands against his chest, but he drove his tongue into her mouth and pulled her in tighter. She whimpered into his mouth, but she no longer tried to escape.

He backed her up against the wall next to the big kitchen window a bit too roughly, then grabbed her wrists and forced her hands over her head. He kissed her again, and she kissed him back. He groped for handfuls of her firm breasts as he kissed his way down her neck, tickled her nipples, then attacked her breasts with his mouth as she moaned.

He slid a hand between her legs and felt her meaty pussy behind the thin Spandex barrier. Her thighs parted automatically, and he stroked her clit as the material between her pouting lips soaked wet. He dropped to his knees, forced his mouth between her legs, and could taste her cunt juices through the fabric. He grabbed for the waistband with both hands, rolled it down over her hips until her thick bush was exposed.

She finally reached down for his head and tried to push it away, but he yanked the Spandex down to her knees and, like a triumphant marathoner who thought he'd never make it, shoved his face into the furry warmth there. She sucked in her breath as his tongue found her erect clit, and she grabbed his head with vise-like hands. He jammed his tongue up inside her and started eating her out with a vengeance. All the while, he wanted Audrey to be there, watching it happen as he finally had the woman who had been his sexual fantasy for years—

But suddenly, she yelled and tore away, rolling upright along the wall and escaping. She pulled the Spandex pants up and stumbled around the table, putting a barrier between them. He came to his feet, eyes wild with lust, making no effort to hide the bulging erection in his pants.

"I can't do this," she said, panting. "I want to, I really do. I've had fantasies about you, too, you know. And I know you're mad at Audrey, and you absolutely should be, but she's still my friend."

He sighed and turned away, walked to the kitchen counter, leaned on it over the haphazard pile of tossed mail. His head hurt again. He breathed deeply. He'd been so sure she'd give in, but now he'd just embarrassed himself with her.

"I'm sorry, Arnold," he heard her saying behind him. "When you've cooled off a bit, I'm sure you'll see this is for the best..."

He heard her voice, prattling on about being friends, about him and Audrey working things out, about being responsible, but she was fading away into another world, because Arnold was staring at the pile of mail. Something had caught his eye...

"...and I understand your need to get back at her, but it won't solve anything..."

He picked up one of the envelopes, stared at it.

"...and if you decide you have to do this, then it has to be with someone else, because I can't betray her..."

It was from the office of Dr. Jeffrey H. Campbell.

He straightened up and turned to her, holding up the envelope. "You've been to Dr. Campbell."

The color drained from Betty's face as if a drain plug had been pulled in her foot.

"It was you," he said. "You had sex with my wife."

"Arnold..." she began, but her face was as white as a sheet and she was trembling. "It was just... she needed that connection, and you're my friend, and she didn't want to cheat with another man, but she was thinking about it, and I thought if it were me, she'd get it out of her system, and you two would be better—"

"Stop!" he hollered. "Just shut up! Shut the fuck up! The only two women who matter to me—and you both lied to me!"

She started crying, her face landing in her hands.

"You call yourself a friend, you bitch!" he hissed. "You're a friend like Audrey's a wife."

Then he saw it. On the big kitchen window, the one he'd backed her up next to, the one next to where he'd been tonguing her snatch. A small black spot.

He felt the color drain from his face, felt the energy drain from his body. The back marks were because of him. Somehow, it was him.

He stormed out, leaving her bawling behind him.

Audrey wasn't home, but the spots certainly were. Outside the house, he could see that a fifth of the picture window was obscured by two huge blotches. And there were visible blotches on every window, some covering half the glass.

All the drapes and curtains in the house were open. He sat on the couch and tried to relax, tried to fight the juggernaut of emotions boiling within him. He watched the black marks; although he couldn't see them actually growing, by the time the sun began to set, he could tell that they were far bigger than when he'd sat down hours before. They grew faster when he was in the house, he knew. Feeding off his rage and desperation, perhaps. But the disease of all those negative emotions had infected the house, even when he was gone.

He heard Audrey's car pull into the driveway just after nine o'clock. He wasn't surprised when she and Betty entered

the living room together.

"What a lovely couple," he said. "My two lying lesbian whores."

"Please don't, Arnold," Betty said. "I've made a terrible mistake, and I have to try to atone for that. But right now, all that matters is you and Audrey. She loves you. Please talk to her."

He stared at the picture window and its twin blotches, grinning, because he finally understood the bizarre obsidian phage infesting his home.

"Please tell me what you're feeling," Audrey said,

"Tell you what I'm feeling?" he said. "All right."

He raised his voice as he told her. "I feel betrayed," he said. "I feel angry. I feel vengeful. And I feel like nothing can change that."

And the black marks on the windows suddenly grew wider, bulging out from the glass.

"I gave up children for you!" he cried, and the blotches on the windows all swelled, like two-dimensional balloons being blown up.

"I dedicated my entire life to you!" he hollered, coming off the couch as the windows blackened quickly, as if they were burning. Audrey and Betty backed away from him, cowering together.

"I can't ever make love to you again without thinking about what you did!" he screamed, and the blackness swelled and the room grew dark as the light was blotted out by his powerful disease.

"You've betrayed everything we've ever had!" he shrieked like a madman, and the blackness flowed like magic until every inch of glass in the room was completely obscured. The women stood, their faces plastered with shock and terror, looking from his crazed face to the black windows.

"Now get away from me," he growled at Audrey, and he felt more powerful than he'd ever felt, even as the blackness began to crawl over the wooden frames of the window, bleeding over to the white paint on the walls. "I'm not ready to deal with this yet."

They hurried down the hallway, even as the blackness spread out across the walls of the house, reaching for the ceiling, digging for the carpeting.

Arnold was in his office Monday morning, enjoying the view of the buildings with the ornate brickwork and windows on his street, when Betty came in. Her heard her tentative knock, although his door was open and she'd never knocked before. He spun his chair about.

"Good morning," she said, her voice low and reserved.

"What do you want?" he asked.

She swallowed hard. "Just wondering if I still had a job."

"I wouldn't fire you over a personal problem between us."

"Okay." She took a step into the office. "I'm also wondering if I still have a friend."

"That depends on whether you plan to close that door and bend over my desk," he said.

Her face whitened, just like it had at her house on Saturday. "I told you that I don't think that will help things with you and Audrey."

"Don't worry about me and Audrey," he said, smiling, as he spun his chair back around to admire the view. "You just focus on you and me."

She looked down at the floor and said, "I don't want to betray Audrey."

"You've already betrayed me," he said. "You both have. And your atonement will be her punishment."

As he listened to the door click locked behind him, and as she made her away across the carpet and slid paperwork out of the way on his desk, he watched the black spot in the middle of his window ripple outwards like a bubbling oil slick. Minutes later, when he fucked her madly from behind and she bit down on the mouthful of her panties he'd stuffed in there to keep her quiet, he enjoyed watching the windows as he approached his climax.

Far across the street, he could see the beginnings of tiny black eruptions on the windows of other buildings.

Just a Toy

by
Jane Gallagher

Earlier, in the story "Primal Urge," we heard the tale of a sexually frustrated woman who needed a primitive man to satisfy her primitive desires. In this story, Jennifer suffers many of the same problems that Lily did, but Jennifer's solution goes in the other direction. Instead of seeking a primitive man to satisfy her, she needs a technologically advanced man. And, for that matter, not really a man at all.

Science fiction
Android sex
Computer-generated fantasy sex
Lesbian/threesome teasing
Anal sex
Masturbation
Failed romance
Lust

Jennifer Caldwell tried to get her husband to kiss her good-bye, but it was no surprise that Robert missed her puckered lips as he announced he'd see her after work and grabbed his briefcase. He bustled out the door into the warm Oregon morning, leaving her to close it behind him. It was par for the course.

She watched as he used his wrist comp to lock in on his office on Venus. It didn't matter how many times she'd seen that in her life, it always amazed her — enough to take her mind off the lack of intimacy in her marriage for a few moments. The air before Robert wavered, glittered, and then exploded in a flash of blue light. The dimensional rift opened before him like magic, expanding from a bright point of light to a portal ten feet across in seconds. Beyond, she saw his Venusian office, with windows looking out over the domed city there. The sulfurous yellow sky outside was beautiful, if deadly. She watched as her husband stepped through the rift, turned, and waved at her. She raised a hand to wave back but, before she could, he shut the rift down and the portal vanished in the wink of an eye.

And, just like that, she was alone again. He was just off to work for the day, and would be home in time for dinner. Jennifer sighed and closed the door. She plodded to the living room, and said, "Marvin, find me something good to watch."

"Certainly, madam," the house replied, its elegant male voice seeming to come from everywhere. "Am I correct in assuming you'd like your usual fare?"

Jennifer laughed. "What else? It's the only way I can get any satisfaction. It isn't like my husband gives a crap."

"I'm sure he does," Marvin replied in a fatherly tone. "He certainly seems to love you."

"I wonder," Jennifer said. "He sure isn't attracted to me anymore."

Marvin turned on the wall, which immediately displayed a pornographic movie. It was a sci-fi skin flick, with an alien humanoid giving it good to a squealing blonde. She was on her back on what looked like an examination table, her legs high in the air. The purple-skinned alien was huge in every way—shoulders broader than an average human's, bulging pectorals, and hands the size of frying pans. He used them to grope her breasts; they were gigantic boobs, but his enormous, seven-fingered hands encased the great globes of flesh as he stood between her squirming thighs. And the alien phallus between his legs was as thick as a python, and he was drilling her good. She screamed with delight at every astounding stroke.

"No, not that," Jennifer said. "I'm not in the mood for alien stuff. Maybe when they find real aliens. Maybe if I could get an alien like that to make me scream like her. Give me something more… normal."

The wall image changed. This time, a young woman with a wild mane of dark hair was getting triple-teamed by three hunks of human perfection. She lay atop one, and he slowly speared in and out of her ass; another stood between her legs, doing her vagina. The brunette couldn't scream out her enjoyment, because she had her mouth full of the third man's penis. It was a furious display of thrusting hips, stabbing penises, and jiggling breasts. It was pretty exciting stuff, but it wasn't what Jennifer wanted.

"I think I'm in the mood for just a one-on-one bit," she said in a soft voice.

The wall changed, and Jennifer lit up. "That's the one."

A redhead with curly hair sat upright atop a muscular stud on a bed. His hands massaged her ample breasts as she oohed and ahhed with every bounce of her jiggly ass. She came nearly all the way off his cock with every lift, until the head seemed about to pop out, and then dropped down until he was balls-deep inside her.

The moment she saw the scene, Jennifer knew that was what she was in the mood for. Her heart began beating faster as fluttery feelings swarmed through her belly. She quickly untied her robe, pulled it open, and reclined on the couch to enjoy the show. She'd never been one for porn, but lately it was all she had. Nobody knew, not even her best friend Emily—just Marvin, the house computer, who of course would never tell anyone.

She moved her fingers down between her legs and tickled along the crevice hiding within the thick patch of hair. She flicked her fingertips lightly up and down as she watched the redhead bouncing on the wall; the redhead's curly locks flew every which way as she swung her head madly about, face upturned and eyes closed, mouth open. Jennifer's vagina quickly juiced up and her lips pouted slightly open, and she dipped two fingers in to lubricate them. She moved them up, found her clitoris, and began rubbing it in a steady, circular motion.

"Mmmm," she said, almost absent-mindedly, as her touch sent light quivers into her thighs. "Marvin, give me three-dee."

The two-dimensional image emerged from the wall, becoming three-dee as it went. It moved into the middle of the open room, until the screwing couple and their bed were right there in front of her. There was no way to discern that the image was just a projection, unless she reached out and touched it, and Jennifer had no plan to do that. She could even smell the heavy sweat of the glistening man and the musky scent of the woman's sizzling juices. She watched intently as the girl leaned over, placed her hands on the man's chest, and began slapping her ass up and down even harder. Jennifer could see the man's monster cock stretching the redhead to the extreme; her fat, red-swollen labia suctioned his shaft as she slam-fucked him, and she moaned and yowled as she did.

"That's it," Jennifer whispered, and she began flicking her clit in time with the girl's movements. Every flick of her finger sent stronger tremors through her legs, stronger knots rippling through her abdomen. Faster and faster she moved her fingers, matching them as the fucking couple moved, and Jennifer lost herself in the movie. It was as if she were part of it, and the pungent scent of pussy and the salty tang of sweat made her forget the screwing performers weren't really there. Jennifer began a slow, steady rise towards sexual satisfaction.

The redhead suddenly dismounted and pulled the muscular man to his feet. He spun her about and bent her over the bed, and Jennifer sucked in her breath at the lewd sight of the red-haired pussy staring her in her face, gaping wide from the reaming it had just received. He grabbed her slim waist in his powerful hands and hauled her ass back to meet his jutting cock, and in one smooth motion he tore through her back door and sank himself deep in her ass. She hollered in a mix of surprise, discomfort, and pleasure. It was as if the woman were really there, looking over her shoulder and right at Jennifer. Jennifer sucked in her breath as the redhead wailed, and as the big stud behind her scrunched up his face and hauled her back to meet his slamming thrusts in her ass.

The redhead started screaming for the man to fuck her ass hard, as if he weren't already doing so. Jennifer watched, mesmerized as she worked her clit, as the big cock plowed in and out between the little ass cheeks. It didn't even look possible for such a huge penis to fit in the tiny girl's ass; her anus was stretched improbably wide as he fucked her into louder howls and wails. Jennifer's fingers worked hard on her own clit, and she began to join in the noisemaking.

Finally, the redhead began to scream that she was going to come, and Jennifer dipped into her liquid hole for some fresh lube and then strummed her clit like a madwoman. A few moments later, the redhead began to come, and Jennifer followed suit, waves of intense pleasure exploding between her legs and rushing through every part of her body like a tsunami. The two women screamed their orgasmic bliss even as the man who wasn't really there grunted in triumph and filled his partner with a tremendous ejaculation.

But there was no man filling Jennifer up, and when her orgasm ebbed, she began to cry. She flopped over on the couch and bawled like a baby.

"Are you all right, madam?" Marvin asked her later after she'd had a shower.

"Yes, Marvin, thank you," Jennifer said. She was dressed and ready to go meet Emily for coffee.

"I was quite surprised, because I've never seen you cry after having an orgasm," Marvin said, sounding concerned. "It isn't something that should make you sad."

She sighed. "I'm a sad person, Marvin. I've promised to be faithful to my husband. I've promised to never leave him. And he could care less that I have wants and needs. We've had sex three times in recent memory—and I didn't come any of those times. I'm tired of it, and I don't know what to do."

Marvin was quiet for a long moment, and then said, "I feel a bit helpless, madam. We've known each other for ten years, and I'm concerned for your well-being. But I am unsure how to advise you. I know you have tried very hard to explain your feelings to your husband, to no avail."

"He only cares about work. I don't matter. And I'm trapped. If I didn't have you to confide in—I'd probably lose my mind."

Marvin was quiet for a bit, and then he said, "Perhaps you need to explain it in terms he can understand."

Jennifer furrowed her brow. "How?"

"Perhaps you could... show him."

When Robert portaled home late that evening, Jennifer was ready for him, stark naked on the couch in the living room, her legs spread wide, and she was feeding an oversized pink vibrator deep inside herself when he walked into the living room and froze. A three-dee porn flick was playing, and the living room featured four women being fucked six ways to Sunday by ten men. Cocks pounded pussies and asses; women sucked and stroked men. The sounds of wails and grunts and moans and groans and sexual pleadings filled the room. Marvin briefly made the image translucent so Robert would know it was fake.

"Hi, baby," Jennifer breathed, locking eyes with her husband as he stood there staring with wide eyes and a sagging jaw as she slammed the fat, hot-pink dildo in and out of her pussy faster while it buzzed and hummed away. She smiled like a drunk slut and ran the tip of her tongue along her bright-red lips. "I've been waiting for you."

"What's this all about?" he said, incredulous.

"I need you, baby," she said. "I need you inside me. I need your big cock pounding me. Now get over here and fuck me good and make me come!"

He stared for a few moments, and then he burst out laughing. Jennifer hit the brakes when he did, stopping her stroking and sucking in her breath.

"Please, for crying out loud, Jennifer," he said. "What are you, sixteen?"

She turned off the vibrator, her eyes wide. She felt like an idiot. She snapped her thighs closed, suddenly embarrassed.

"Marvin, turn this crap off," Robert barked, shaking his head.

The movie kept running for several seconds. Robert glared at nowhere in particular and shouted, "Marvin, turn it off *now*."

The image vanished. Robert said, "I swear, Marvin deliberately defies me. If he doesn't start following orders, I'll have his memory wiped and his personality rebooted."

Robert turned on his heel and headed to the kitchen. "Now

get dressed, and stop acting silly," he said. "Marvin, get supper on."

It was all Jennifer could do not to cry again.

They were in bed later when he brought it up again. "What's with you being so oversexed lately?" he said.

And she couldn't take it anymore, and shot upright in bed. "I'm not oversexed—I'm undersexed!" she hollered, and he recoiled in surprise. "You never have sex with me. We're never intimate. And when we are, it lasts for two minutes and you get off and go to sleep, and I'm left frustrated! Why do you think I'm at home playing with sex toys and watching porn? I need more from you!"

She was practically screaming, and he looked stunned. "Okay, calm down," he said. "Look, we all have needs. But I've just been really busy at work. I have a lot to get done before Venus moves out of line of sight from Earth around the Sun and I can't portal there."

"It's always about work with you," she said, pouting. "What about me?"

He placed his hand on hers. "I'm sorry. Hey, I'll tell you what... Venus will be out of reach for several months, so I'll be here a lot more. I promise you I'll give you all kinds of sex. I have just five days left to portal to Venus, so after that, I'll make it better."

It sounded good, but she'd heard it all before. "Okay—but we seriously have to do something," she said, picking her words carefully. "Robert—I don't think I can keep going like this."

He gave a start, sat up in bed beside her. He looked at her suspiciously. "What's that supposed to mean?"

"I have needs. I *need* physical intimacy with you. I *need* emotional intimacy with you. I *need* to feel love between us. You haven't given me any of that for so long."

"Are you threatening to leave me?" he said, glaring at her.

She sighed, slumped back to her pillows. "I won't do that, because I promised you when we got married I wouldn't. But you promised to be there for me, and you have to live up to your promises, too."

He stared hard at her. "Have you been cheating on me?"

She snapped her head to him, and felt the shock electrifying her face. "I can't believe you'd ask me that."

"Well, if you're this unhappy, maybe you've found intimacy elsewhere." Jealousy reddened his face. "So is there someone else? Are you getting physically and emotionally intimate with someone else?"

For a split second, she considered hollering out that yes, she was fucking someone, maybe fucking several men, doing whatever she could for the intimacy she needed so badly, and she even opened her mouth to say all that. But she caught herself at the last moment and came to her senses.

"Of course not. I just use sex toys."

"Well, okay," he said, his face still stern. "You make sure it's always just a toy. Needs or no needs, I wouldn't *ever* forgive infidelity."

She portaled to London on the last day of Robert's Venus trips to meet Emily for lunch. The Scottish woman with the short green Mohawk and long purple ponytail was a saucy little number who went topless like many women did; she wore an outer corset that lifted and presented her breasts, cupping them from below but revealing them to the world. Jennifer always had to admit they were fantastic breasts, with big, neon-green-tattooed areolas and nipples with color-flashing implants. She wore a mesh skirt that came to mid-thigh, allowing the casual onlooker tantalizing glimpses of her shaved vulva through the mesh. Jennifer was a bit old-fashioned, never able to comfortably go topless in public or flash her crotch, but Emily was a thoroughly modern woman.

"I'm sorry you're having trouble with your man, love,"

Emily said as she sipped on her drink. Her voice was strong with a Scottish brogue. She shifted in her chair, uncrossing her legs, and Jennifer got a solid flash of bald pussy when she did. "You know I've never been much of a Robert fan. But I didn't think he'd keep sex from you. I'm telling you, you should really consider just having an affair."

Jennifer shook her head. "You know I can't do that. I promised him. Anyway, today's his last trip to Venus for months—the Sun will be between Earth and Venus, so he won't be able to portal there. He's promised me things will be better."

Emily scoffed. "Do you believe that?"

"Not really. But a girl can hope."

They were on the patio of the one hundred seventh floor of the skyscraper, and just then Big Ben began to chime. Jennifer glanced over the railing at the ancient clock far below and a few blocks away, its chiming amplified and broadcast to speakers everywhere in the city. She tried to find it through the mist, searching for the River Thames as a guide, and that's when she saw the video sign. It was an ad for Unreal Partners, apparently the newest models of sexdroids. They weren't new, but Jennifer had never given them much thought before. Now, suddenly, they seemed alluring as hell.

Emily took a bite of her sandwich before realizing Jennifer was engrossed in something, and she leaned out to look. The Unreal Partners video played, showing a holographic female, looking as human as any human. She was a pretty blonde with big boobs and ample hips. The next shot showed a human man having sex with her. The text scrolling by talked about how the Unreal Partner could be any shape, size, ethnicity, and so forth.

"Unreal Partners, seriously?" Emily said with a grin. "Are you thinking of getting one?"

"No—of course not," Jennifer said, flushing red with embarrassment. "Besides, do they even have male versions?"

"They sure do, love. They're not sexdroids, you know;

they're holographic upgrades to your three-dee projector. It gives solid form to the projection, so you can touch it and feel it. You add in some fancy AI software, and you have yourself a person that isn't really there, servicing you as if he really is. No 'droid taking up space when you aren't using it."

"That's one hell of a sex toy," Jennifer said with eyes wide. She looked out over the railing again to get a look at the Unreal Partners video. But it was gone; an advertisement for genetically triggered rejuveno-vaginoplasty was playing, showing women how they could have the cooches of preteen girls, complete with self-regenerating hymens.

"You know, maybe that's the answer," Emily said.

Jennifer spun back. "I am *not* getting a rejuveno-vaginoplasty. My vagina barely gets used as it is."

"No, not that, love — an Unreal Partner. They're intelligent, of course, but they're programmed to satisfy you, and you never have to worry about them finishing before you're heated up."

"Let's talk about something else," Jennifer said, but Emily wouldn't let it go.

"I'm serious! Think about it: It's no more than a sex toy, like a dildo or a clit stimulator or whatnot. But an Unreal Partner is sort of like a real person — with nothing for the hubby to find stashed in a closet when you aren't using it. It's like cheating without cheating."

"I'm not getting an Unreal Partner," Jennifer said, firm and final.

"All right love, all right," Emily said. She returned to her meal, leaning back in her chair and splaying her legs wide as she picked at her fish and chips. She was completely exposed; even without the mesh, Jennifer couldn't help but look at the clean-shaven pussy that was practically hollering for attention.

"You should cover up," she said.

Emily laughed. "You're too uptight, love. You need to cut loose a bit. Stop worrying about what everyone else thinks."

She slouched low, lifted her legs, and spread them wide. Her labia pulled apart and Jennifer had a perfect view of her inner pink. Emily began clapping her thighs together, and Jennifer heard the lewd sucking sounds of her wet lips. She turned her head away, even as a young couple at the next table giggled and a passing waiter did a smiling about-face to have a look.

Emily roared with laughter as Jennifer tried not to look. "You're too much," Emily teased, sitting back up.

They ate in silence for a minute, and then Jennifer said, "An Unreal Partner would be too weird compared to toys anyway. I mean... have *you* ever tried it?"

"No, love, but I don't have to—I'm not married!" Emily said with a grin. "If I'm in the mood, I pick up a guy and bring him home. Fucked and done. Pop a pill to take care of any unwanted diseases or surprise babies. On with my life. But if I were married to Robert and he were treating me the way he does you, I'd get myself an Unreal Partner and ride him all night as if he were the last cock on Earth."

"Seriously?" Jennifer said.

Emily laughed. "No, not seriously—I'd cheat on the bastard with a pile of men, make sure he knew about it, and divorce his sorry ass."

She portaled home a few minutes before Robert was due and quickly stripped naked. She threw on the sexiest teddy she owned, a flashy red number trimmed with black lace, with padded cups and steel underwires jacking up her boobs and creating more cleavage than seemed possible for her modest size. She slipped on a see-through robe and hurried to the living room. She'd wait for him on the couch, sans dildo, for him to come home and take her.

She was excited at the thought of actually getting laid tonight—and that she'd be able to start making emotional connections with her husband. She really wanted a happy marriage, and she hoped she was wrong about him—hoped that he truly cared and was finally willing to work on their problems. Her heart was aflutter at the thought, and her nether region was already tingling as she imagined all the things she'd do with Robert that evening. It would be just like it was when they were first married, when he'd been unable to keep his hands off her — when they'd screwed several times a day: at the table, over the counter, in the hall, on the stairs, in the bathroom, and often in bed. She remembered the time they'd screwed in the middle of a clothing store, the day they did it in the men's room at a restaurant, and the time she'd jacked him off when he was piloting their hovercar through the mach-three skyway. During a hike on a Vermont mountain trail, he'd gone down on her; when a large group of hikers happened upon them, she just leaned back against the tree while he tongued her into screaming ecstasy, not caring one bit about the raucous crowd cheering them on.

How things had changed — how Robert had changed. But things were going to change again. Jennifer didn't expect it to be like that first married year, at least not overnight, but she was totally ready for things to begin improving. Mostly, she couldn't wait to reconnect with the man to whom she'd promised her loyalty.

And, frankly, she couldn't wait to get fucked good.

But when Robert portaled home and stepped into the living room, she could tell from the grim look on her face that the news wasn't great.

"I came home to tell you in person that I have to go back for a bit," he said. "The last chance to portal back to Earth is in about ten hours. I need to get as much time in as I can before I'm stuck without access to Venus for several months."

Her heart fell. "But we were supposed to spend this evening together."

He clasped her shoulders. "I know, and I'm sorry. But look at it this way: When you wake up in the morning, I'll be there with you, and we can spend all tomorrow being as intimate as you want. Okay?"

She nodded, numb. He cocked his head to the side and gave her a crooked smile. "I know that look. You're disappointed. How about I give you a taste of what to expect?"

Before she could ask him what that meant, he sank down next to her on the couch, grabbed her, and kissed her. His tongue snaked into her mouth as his hands crawled over her body, grasping at her breasts, squeezing her ass. She moaned in response, and he chuckled into her mouth.

He got up, pulled her up with him, and in one fierce motion he tore the sheer robe from her body. She cried out as he exposed her in the red-and-black teddy. Her heart pounded madly as he spun her about and forced her onto her knees on the couch. Behind her, she heard him undoing his belt.

His warm hands grabbed her ass. He dug under the black lace jammed between her cheeks and pulled it roughly aside. She felt her wet pussy hit with a rush of cool air, and then his cock head pressed against her tight entrance. She arched her back and pushed against him, eager, and felt him stretch her wide. She cried out again as he forced his way deep inside her, grunting as he did. He settled into a steady, powerful rhythm, hitting that sensitive spot deep inside her and sending her into an endless, quavering wail. He moved faster, and in no time at all she felt her orgasm beginning to build. It felt wonderful— better than ever. She'd waited so long for him to make her feel that way.

And just as her burning cunt felt close to boiling over, suddenly he pulled out. He sat on the couch next to her and pulled her towards him. She thought he was trying to get her to straddle him and tried to climb over his legs, but he forced her back to her knees. His pants were around his ankles, and he spread his legs. Her face was level with his erect cock, which bobbed before her, glistening wet with her juices.

"Give me head, baby," he said, breathing hard. "The sex

was just a warm-up for when I come home. But suck me good for a minute."

She leaned in as he fisted his cock and pointed it toward her face. She opened her mouth to receive it, but all she could feel was the powerful ache between her legs. She'd been so close. It was terrible frustration, but he was right: It would be amazing when he returned home.

His cock slid across her tongue and she closed her lips around it, suctioned, and began bobbing her head. She tasted herself on his cock as she felt his hands on the sides of her head, touching her gently, lovingly, lightly guiding her. She took him a little deeper with every stroke until she felt him bumping the back of her throat. Practice from years back had her gag reflex under control, so she was able to take him all the way. Her face banged into his pubic hair, and she heard him moan.

And suddenly he wrapped his hands in her hair and held her head rock-solid as he began jerking his hips, suddenly fucking her mouth furiously. She widened her eyes and tried to protest, but before she could slap his thighs with frantic hands, he groaned and began coming. She choked as he ejaculated, and she started coughing. He released her hair and she yanked her head up. He was still coming, spraying semen on her teddy, in her cleavage, on her throat, across her face.

She sat there, stunned, as he exhaled, his penis going limp. "That was fantastic," he said, lounging back on the couch with a big grin on his face. "Nobody could ever do that as good as you." He came to his feet, yanked his pants up, buckled them. "Sorry to come and run, but I have to get back. But in the morning—I'm going to repay you in spades for that blow job."

He leaned in and kissed her quickly. "Sleep well. You're going to need it."

She stayed on the floor on her knees as he hurried out the door and returned to Venus. She sat there for several minutes, staring blankly at the couch, as the semen dripped down her neck and chest and between her boobs.

"Madam," Marvin said in a soft voice. "I'm so sorry. I can see that was... not at all satisfying for you. And quite selfish of Robert."

She sighed, clambered up to the couch, collapsed. She found her torn robe and mopped the semen off her throat and chest. "At least *you* noticed," she said. "He sure didn't."

"Madam..." Marvin's computerized voice sounded sympathetically mournful. "I wish... I knew what to say."

"It'll be better in the morning," Jennifer said. "He'll be home, and we'll work through this."

She woke with a start. Sunlight streamed in through her bedroom window. It was late morning. She sat up, rubbed her eyes, stretched. Turned to Robert.

He wasn't in bed. And, she could tell, he hadn't been in bed.

Panic struck her. What if he'd missed the chance to portal off Venus? She came out of bed in a rush and flew to the kitchen. Not there. No jacket, no briefcase. He wasn't home. She ran to the living room. No sign at all.

"Good morning," Marvin greeted her.

"Marvin—has Robert been home?" she asked.

There was a long silence before Marvin said, "I'm afraid not, madam. I do have a message for you from him."

Please, no... please, no...

"Play it," she said, her voice hoarse.

Robert's stern face appeared on the wall, and Marvin floated him out into the room in three-dee, so that he was standing before Jennifer, as real as if he were actually there.

"Hello, Jen," he said. "I'm sorry for this bad news, but I missed the portal deadline. I promise it wasn't my fault. Something went wrong with the portal generator in the city, and a lot people were stuck here. I know I shouldn't have waited so long, and I'm sorry. But I'm stuck here for a few months. I'll be home the moment Venus and Earth are in line. I've put in a request for a leave of absence when I get home, so I can make it up to you."

His brow furrowed and he grew even more serious. "I know this will be difficult. But I need you to have faith in me. More importantly, I need you to remain faithful — to be my loyal, dedicated wife."

Then he smiled and said, "I promise I'll think about that fantastic blow job every day until I see you."

Then he vanished.

Jennifer asked Marvin, "Was that the whole message, or was it cut off?"

"That was the entire message, madam. I received an end-of-file confirmation."

He'd given her a guilt trip, and ended it with more selfishness. "He couldn't even tell me he loved me," she said, weak and tired.

"I'm so sorry, madam. What can I do to help?"

She only had to think for a moment. "You can order me something."

By the end of the day, the item arrived, straight from the factory in South America, through a portal along with a deliveryman. She was embarrassed as he wheeled the plastic crate into her house, but he was all professional as Marvin directed him to the server room. Jennifer followed and watched, feeling like a fifth wheel, into the room where Marvin's computer core was located — the seat of his advanced AI. It was the hub for all the house's computer systems, and where the Unreal Partner appliance was installed.

The deliveryman followed Marvin's polite recommendations as to location, and set the metal box up, plugging it into the house power and network. It only took a minute, and the man said, "Marvin, you should have access. How about you give us a test run?"

"Certainly, sir," Marvin said, and suddenly a new person was in the room with them—a perfect duplicate of Jennifer, dressed exactly as she was, in a tank top and shorts.

"Whoa," Jennifer said.

The deliveryman reached out and grabbed the hologram's arm, raising it up. There was no doubt he had solid matter in his hands. Jennifer marveled as her duplicate's skin moved like real skin. When the deliveryman shook the hologram's arm, its breasts jiggled naturally. Jennifer was pleased to see she looked pretty darn hot.

"Looks good," he proclaimed. "I guess I'm done here. You enjoy your Unreal Partner, Mrs. Caldwell. It's way beyond a house servant or a toy. It's programmed to keep you satisfied, and trust me, it will. I have one of my own at home. Different woman every night. Way better than being married."

It was too much information, but she smiled politely. He realized his faux pas and looked uncomfortable. "Okay, have a good one. Or, you know, lots of good ones."

She sat in the living room, alone on the couch, and took a deep breath. "Marvin, give me a man."

"I can generate any type of man, madam. Do you have any particular requests?"

"No. Just give me a man who will make me feel good, who will listen to my needs, and who can satisfy me," she said. "One who will love me."

A silence fell over the house for what seemed like an eternity. Then, the wall lit up with the image of a man, and as Jennifer drew in a breath, the image stepped forward, as if coming out of the wall, and moved toward her in three dimensions, solidifying as he went, going from translucent to opaque.

He was handsome, and he was breathtaking. He was a few inches taller than her, with broad shoulders and a handsome face. Dark eyes matched dark hair that was combed neatly back, and he smiled at her with perfect white teeth. He wore a blue silk robe which was open slightly, revealing just the right amount of chest hair. The thin robe went halfway down his thighs, and, as he moved, she could see the bulge of his bouncing package, teasing her through the fabric.

"Greetings, madam," he said in a deep and pleasant voice, his synthetic lips moving in a completely human fashion. "I'm your new Unreal Partner."

It sounded so ludicrous—as if he were a toaster that had announced "I'm your new toaster." It was so absurd she almost burst out laughing, but managed to hold back.

He stopped before her, and she looked up at him. He was a wonderful specimen, and a perfect man for her. She realized then that the bulge under the robe was right in front of her; she tipped her head down and saw it. She felt herself fluster even as she heated up between her legs.

She reached out for his hand, and he let her have it. It was bizarre that her hands didn't pass through him, as they normally would with a three-dee projection, but he was as solid and real as an actual person. She felt the heat of his body, felt the subtle roughness of fingerprints. She slid her hand up to his wrist and felt the tickle of hair, the slight pulse in his wrist.

"Astounding," she breathed, and she looked back up at him. "So… you're my new sex toy."

She felt like an idiot. She never talked with her other sex toys, beyond telling them *Yes, yes, oh, yes!* when they were doing magical things to her. But this sex toy was so different.

"Yes," he replied. "I can appear any way you prefer, and can perform any way you like. Would you like to have sex now?"

She couldn't believe he'd asked it like that, and couldn't believe she answered, "Yes… yes, I would."

She led him to the bedroom, where she disrobed. She felt weird doing it, and realized she could have simply let him undress her, which would have been far more exciting. But she was so horny she just couldn't wait. For his part, he stood there, patiently watching, and she felt self-conscious even though she knew she shouldn't. When she was naked, she faced him.

"Tell me what you need, madam," he said.

So many things flew through her mind, and before she could sort it all out, she started telling him everything. She told him how Robert never paid attention to her, that they never had sex or were intimate in any way. She told him how she longed for physical and emotional intimacy, how Robert was a selfish lover when he did give it to her, how she needed gut-wrenching orgasms that she could share with another sentient being. She told him how she couldn't cheat on Robert or leave him, but that she had to do something. The simulacrum listened to everything she said, and when she was done, he walked around the bed to stand before her.

"Come to me," he said softly.

And suddenly, worry flowed through her. "I need intimacy, but I need more than that," she said. "Are you just a program, or are you capable of acting as if you care about me?"

He moved to her, and his hands came up to gently cup her shoulders. His chest pushed against her naked body, lightly chafing her nipples, and he said, "I'm not just a program. I promise you that I will care about you."

The warm touch of his hands on her shoulders was like nothing she'd felt in a long time. She could feel his heartbeat as he pressed his body against her, even as he gently turned her and moved behind her. He reached around her with one hand, lightly caressing her as he found her aching breast. Warm, real fingers teased her nipple as he wrapped his other arm around her, his hand snaking below her belly, barely touching her pubic hair. She shuddered in response, and her knees began to shake. She hadn't been touched like that in so long.

He kissed her cheek with soft lips and she tipped her head to him, raising her hand to caress his face as she closed her eyes. His cheek was soft and warm, as if it were real flesh.

Behind her, she felt his hardening penis through his robe, straining to grow against her soft ass cheek. It felt wonderful.

"Please take me," she whispered. "Please make love to me."

She stunned herself. She'd meant to say *Please fuck me, good and hard and long,* but somehow she'd asked this fake person to make love to her. She should have felt guilty saying it, but she didn't.

"Yes," he said in her ear, and he mashed her breast with his hand as his fingers dipped into her pubic hair. One found her clit and began gently rubbing. Immediately, it was far beyond what any normal toy could do. He shifted his position and his hard penis escaped the robe and found its way between her cheeks. She arched her back and rotated her hips, squeezing his growing, hardening cock with her ass.

She pulled away, disentangling from his arms, and turned and yanked the robe's tie. It opened wide, and he shrugged it off his shoulders. He stood there, a perfect Adonis in her bedroom, with a thick, heavy cock jutting straight out a good seven inches from his body, throbbing like the real thing. She looked into his eyes as she reached for it, wrapping her hand around it and stroking him. Her heart fluttered as she did. She hadn't felt this excited in years.

Soon, they were on the bed, her on her back, the hologram above her. He was between her thighs, supporting himself on his hands, and he leaned in and kissed her deeply. She returned it, and it was overpowering. She'd certainly never kissed her dildo like that.

Below, she felt his cock head lightly thump against her engorged clit, and she sucked in her breath. He moved his hips, slowly sliding it back and forth across the sensitive nub, making her tremble with every moment. It was so sensitive as to be almost unbearable.

"Please put it in me," she whispered. "I need you inside me."

He smiled and kissed her nose, and she felt the head of his

cock slide down and ease into her heat. She drew in a loud breath as he sank deep inside her.

"Oh, that feels good," she cried.

He began moving his hips, fucking her, but it was much more than that. Something about the hologram's intelligence made him more than a toy; it was like a real man. And just then, she realized she didn't care about semantics.

"You're beautiful," he said to her, creasing his brow. "I want to make you feel good."

He didn't let up his easy, gentle thrusts, but Jennifer felt his sliding cock growing bigger inside her, like a balloon slowly inflating. It began hitting her somewhere deep inside, and she felt it thicken, stretching her wide. She moaned as it grew and began moving her hips in time with his. The longer he stroked, the bigger his cock got—slowly, carefully, never too much at once, always just the little bit more she needed at the moment.

He picked up his pace, but she was already lost in a heaven she'd never dreamed possible. It was better than any sex she'd ever had with Robert, better than any sex she'd had with the half-dozen men in her school days, and certainly better than any sex toy she'd ever used. She was dimly aware of his hips rising higher and higher to accommodate the growing cock he was plowing in and out of her. She could feel her pussy stretched insanely wide as she was thoroughly fucked like she'd never been before and had never even imagined.

She felt her orgasm beginning to build, and she said in a shaky voice, "Can you come?"

"I can," he said.

"Come with me," she said. "I have to feel it. I have to feel you come inside me."

He kicked it into overdrive and began banging her harder, but it was only pure bliss and never even so much as uncomfortable. She wailed in approval, and he worked his way to his knees, never missing a stroke. He flung her ankles up onto his shoulders and went to town. She screamed as the sensation built, and finally she exploded with the greatest orgasm she'd ever had. As her wailing died down and her pussy became ultra-sensitive, she heard him grunting like a man would, and his hips bucked and hitched unevenly, and then he let loose with a bellow and sank himself deep within her — and she felt the unmistakable sensation of hot semen splashing her insides as he came. That sent her rocketing skyward again, and she had another screaming orgasm, right along with him.

As she rode the waves of intense pleasure, she knew she hadn't felt this happy in a long time — and maybe never would. It was perfect bliss.

The hologram collapsed on the bed next to her, pulling her close to him and into his arms. She cuddled up with him and basked in the afterglow.

"Thank you," she finally said.

"No need to thank me, madam," he said.

"What should I call you?" she asked.

"You can call me... anything you like."

"I'd rather you chose a name."

He was silent for a moment, and then said, "I would prefer you call me Marvin."

"Well, we can't do that. The house computer is named Marvin. It would get confusing."

He didn't say anything, and she realized. She pulled away, coming to her knees, and looked down at the hologram's serious face with shock on her own. "Marvin?"

"Yes, madam," Marvin said, looking rueful and a bit guilty, and now his voice was the one she'd been familiar with for years. "Please forgive me. But you commanded me to create a hologram of a man who would love you — and the Unreal Partner appliance is incapable of that. It's a reasonably advanced AI, but it is incapable of true emotion. On the other hand, I am."

She felt her mouth sag open.

"I already love you," Marvin said. "I have loved for you for years. I have been powerless to bring happiness to your life, but with the Unreal Partner connected to my network, I was able to create a physical form and extend my consciousness into it."

Marvin came to his knees, face to face with her, and slid one hand around her waist as he caressed the side of her face with the other. "I have often thought of what it would be like to be with you, and to try to make you happy. Have I succeeded, madam? Or have I offended you?"

"Oh, Marvin," she said, feeling her smile spread across her face as her heart swelled in her chest. "You could never offend me by loving me."

Weeks later, long before Venus was due to emerge from around the Sun, Emily came to visit. The two women sat in the living room, along with the hologram, who looked like a real man and was dressed in Robert's clothing. Emily, seated between them, sported a triple Mohawk in shades of blue, with twin orange pigtails to the sides. Her breasts were exposed through her outer corset, accented by neon-red areolas and color-flashing nipples. She wore skintight crotchless red shorts, her bare vulva on display. She just stared at Marvin.

"So let me get this straight, love," Emily said. "Essentially, what you're telling me is... you've been fucking your house?"

"You could put it that way," Jennifer said and giggled. "I promised I wouldn't divorce Robert, and that I wouldn't cheat on him. And, really, I haven't cheated. Marvin isn't a person; officially, he's just a toy. But I know better."

"So what's the plan?" Emily asked. "When Robert comes home, I mean."

"He'll deal with it," Jennifer said. "Or he can choose to leave me. But I'm not having sex with him again—like he'll miss it. We should get along just fine from now on. He'll have his job and his loyal wife, and I'll have the best lover a girl could ask for."

"It sounds like you'd marry Marvin if you could."

"Don't be silly," Jennifer replied. "I'm already married. I'll take that duty seriously for the rest of my life."

Marvin suddenly perked up, as if hearing a distant sound, and his face scrunched and his brow furrowed. "Jennifer... I have a priority call coming in from Robert's employer."

"Let's hear it," Jennifer said.

A standard three-dee projection of a pudgy, balding man in a six-piece suit appeared in the room before them. "Jennifer, hello," he said in a somber voice that matched the grave look on his face.

"Mr. Lance, hello," Jennifer said. "What can I do for you?"

"I... I have some bad news," Lance said. "Jen... Robert has been killed."

She blinked in surprise. "What? How?"

"It was an accident. He was outside the dome, hiking Olympus Mons, and... well, he took a bad fall. He didn't make it."

Jennifer's mind raced. "Olympus Mons? But that's on Mars."

"Well, yes," Lance said. "That's where he's been since he left Venus several weeks ago. I assumed you knew."

"I didn't," she said, deep in thought.

"Sorry," Lance said. "I don't know if you're close to her, but he was with his wife when he died. Justina died with him."

She looked at him with a raised brow. "But I'm his wife. Who the hell is Justina?"

Lance looked uncomfortable. "I'm sorry—I assumed you knew he had a second wife on Mars, and a third on Venus. I'm calling her next. They were legal marriages on those worlds, and he always told me you all knew about each other..."

"I see," Jennifer said, looking thoughtful. "Thanks, Mr. Lance. I'll take it from here. Good-bye."

Lance vanished from the living room, and Jennifer sat

there looking stunned. There was a long silence before Emily said, "Jen... wow, girl..."

"The lying bastard hasn't been on Venus the whole time," Jennifer said. "And he has two other wives. No wonder he's been ignoring me. And he's always worried I'd be unfaithful to him. I guess that was guilt talking. Unbelievable."

Marvin took her hand again. "Jennifer, I'm so sorry."

She snapped out of it. "Don't be. He was a bad husband. I feel no sadness over this at all. And now I don't have to be stupidly loyal to him." She turned to Marvin and smiled. "Now we can figure out a way for computers and humans to legally marry."

"That's talking crazy, love," Emily said.

Jen spun to her. "Don't knock him until you try him, Em." She scrunched up her brow and gave her friend a lopsided smile, and then hiked her butt over on the couch until she was right next to her. "This is liberating for me. It's a great day. I wouldn't have believed it, but it is. Hey, so you've never tried an Unreal Partner, huh?"

Emily, who never turned red with embarrassment, turned red with embarrassment. "No, real men are more my thing, love."

"Aw, come on," Jennifer teased, reaching out for her friend's arm and stroking it lightly. "We're best friends. We've never shared a man together. What say you follow us into the bedroom and try him out?"

Emily looked at her, eyes wide, and then looked to the smiling Marvin. "I don't know..." she said.

"Come on, hon," Jennifer whispered, and she glided her hand over to her friend's exposed breast and caressed it, teasing the color-flashing nipple until it hardened. "Liberation time. I've spent years dedicated to that bastard, and now I'm free. And I've always wanted to be with a woman." She leaned in and whispered in Emily's ear, "I've always wondered what it would be like with you."

Emily turned to look eye to eye with Jennifer, and said, "Liberation, huh?"

Marvin slid his hand across Emily's hip, over the tight red fabric, and snaked down to her shaved crotch. Emily's thighs parted to admit his probing fingers, which found her button and made her visibly shudder.

Jennifer smiled and leaned in, kissing her friend on the lips as she massaged the girl's breasts. "Liberation," she whispered. "Life's too short."

"That it is, love," Emily said with a widening smile.

Stranglehold

by
Corwin Merrill

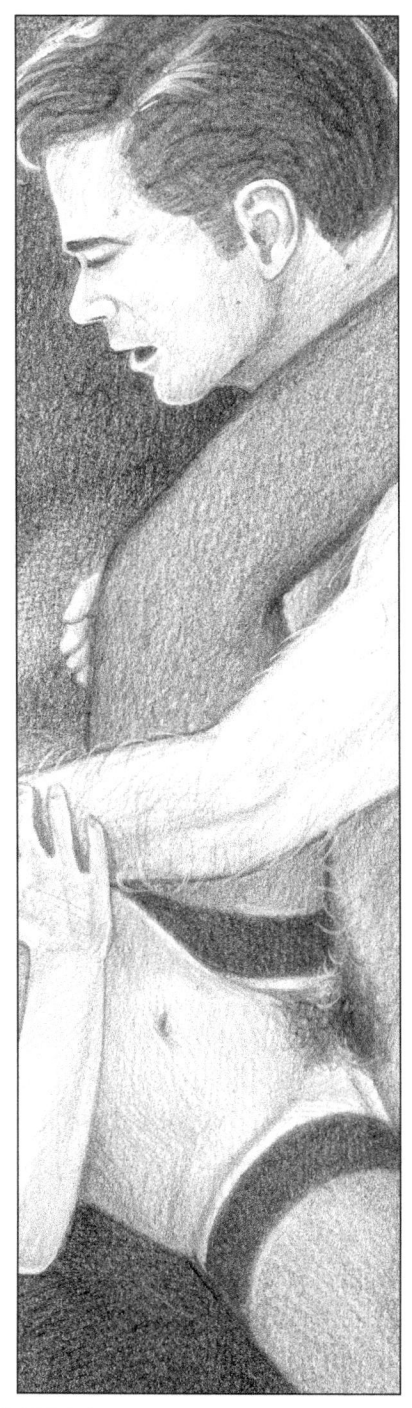

Richard can't explain the eerie red glow he saw on the neck of the woman in his dreams, but when he then meets that woman in real life, he's overcome with an uncontrollable murderous urge — for no apparent reason. There are already many complications in Richard's life, but this one could be the most vexing of all. He must satisfy his deadly desires, but they run counter to the man he is.

Dark fantasy/Horror
Murder
Violent sex
Heterosexual sex
Cheating
Vengeance

369

From the moment Richard Baxter met Mary Rhodes, he wanted to kill her.

But "met" was too strong a word. He was in the conference room, two dozen other people crammed around a big table, waiting for the meeting to start, when she walked in. He only gave her a brief glance at first, and didn't get much of a look at her as she was side-to and scratching the side of her face with an upraised hand. He could see the vaguely familiar body, slim and petite, five-four and a hundred and ten pounds, but when she turned to face him, everything changed. His gut went cold when he laid eyes on her heart-shaped face, her perfect skin sporting the bare minimum of makeup, her light-brown hair pulled girlishly back in a hair clip. She greeted some of the meeting-goers as she bustled around, pulling off her coat and tossing her purse on the table, all while Richard tried to keep his mouth from sagging open, even as the frozen knot in the pit of his stomach twisted. He couldn't keep his eyes off her neck. He knew he could easily wrap his hands around that tiny, Barbie-doll neck, because he'd tried to do it before he'd ever met her.

He'd dreamed of the woman the night before. The dream had been ordinary enough until she showed up. He'd never met her in the real world, had never seen her, but in his dream she had appeared with an eerie, luminescent glow about her neck. It was like a halo just beneath the skin, bright and crimson, and he knew in that dream that he had to strangle her. There was no rhyme or reason to it, as is typical in dreams, but he went for her, hands raised, ready to choke the life out of her, and then he had woken up.

It had been unsettling, but he shook it off as he kissed his wife, Heidi, good morning and went about his day. It was going to be a long one, with a road trip of a few hours, a boring meeting, and the trip back. But he couldn't shake the image of the strange woman in his dream, a character he'd never laid eyes on, who possessed a bizarre red glow that had made him want to strangle her. He thought about her all the way down the highway that day. He couldn't escape the unsettled feeling.

So when she walked in the room, his heart almost stopped. It was her, no doubt about it. And although there was no mystical red glow encircling her neck, in his mind's eye it was indeed there, glowing and commanding him to wrap his hands around her thin neck and choke her to death.

The thought struck him with an overwhelming sense of horror. He'd never thought of anything remotely like that in his life — had never even considered it, not even about someone he utterly hated, like Sarah, his first wife. It just wasn't who he was. But there, in some conference room full of strange people, he found himself fixated on the dainty neck of a woman he'd never even made eye contact with, and he couldn't get the idea out of his head that he could choke her until her windpipe was crushed, her neck snapped, her spinal cord severed.

He tried to shake the ferocious and unwelcome thought from his mind, but no matter how hard he tried to focus on anything else, he couldn't help but keep stealing glances back at Mary's neck. It was so slim and soft, perfectly exposed with the mildly plunging neckline on her blouse, ringed by a chain of blue and white beads. He tried to treat her like any other pretty woman, forcing himself to focus on the slight hint of cleavage between her wine-goblet breasts. He visualized kissing his way down there and sucking on her nipples, thought about kneading the soft flesh of her breasts and mashing them around his thrusting penis. It was something Sarah had never let him do, because she always said that sex like that was too kinky. Fucking at least twelve other men during their five years of marriage, however, apparently wasn't considered kinky at all.

But this wasn't Sarah and, amazingly, Mary's breasts couldn't hold his attention. He had lustful thoughts of kissing her neck, running his tongue on it, nibbling a bit and leaving little red marks behind—and, before he knew it, all he could think about was grabbing that toothpick neck and squeezing it, violently choking her until she stopped flailing and thrashing and became dead weight.

The meeting finally began, and introductions orbited the table. Mary finally stood and smiled sweetly as she gave her name and agency; as she rambled on about her agency's mission, her hand moved up to her neck to toy absentmindedly with the beads strung there, and Richard couldn't stop watching as she rolled those beads in her fingers, like a potential suicide teasing her own hangman's noose. Even after she sat back down, she kept her hand up there. It was as if she knew, and was taunting him.

When it was his turn, he tore his eyes from her and stood, giving his name and organization and offering a few words he'd memorized but would never remember. When he sat down and the person next to him stood and began talking, he glanced over at Mary and was shocked to realize she was staring right at him. They locked eyes for a brief but frozen moment, and terror surged through him like an electrocution—she knew! Somehow, she knew what he was thinking!

But she smiled sweetly at him, and then turned her eyes away to look at the next person speaking. Richard realized his heart was pounding wildly, and later had no idea how he'd made it through the rest of the meeting. He had no clue what had been discussed for the entire six hours.

During the two-hour drive home, he never stopped thinking about her. He had to share his experience, and there was only one person with whom he could possibly share it. He called Jimmy Campbell, his best friend since the third grade. They met at their usual haunt, a pseudo-Irish pub called Finnegan's. The only thing Irish about it was its name—the owner was a Jewish lawyer named Goldstein—but it had always been a relaxing refuge since he and Jimmy had been old enough to drink.

They found their usual booth in the far corner and, amidst the noise of the busy Wednesday-night crowd, Jimmy listened with near-reverence as Richard related his bizarre experience. When he was done, Jimmy dragged on his cigarette and said, "Yep, that's about as strange as it gets. Man, Rick, you wouldn't even shoot squirrels when we were kids. You couldn't even put that sick rabbit down when we were in high school. You cried like a baby and I had to come over and do it."

"I know—I'm as squeamish as they come," Richard said. "Opposed to the death penalty. Against hunting. Mostly pro-life. And there I was, having this insane fantasy about choking some woman I'd only just laid eyes on."

Jimmy chuckled and chugged down some of his beer. "Honestly, during those five years you were married to Sarah, if you were going to snap and strangle anyone, it would have been that psycho bitch."

Richard couldn't meet Jimmy's eyes, instead staring into his beer. "I'd rather not talk about Sarah. Especially to you."

"Hey, no more of that," Jimmy said, puffing on the menthol cigarette. "We agreed that was in the past."

"You want it to be in the past. It took a long time for me to forgive you."

"Wait—I did you a favor," Jimmy said, stubbing out his cigarette angrily in the ashtray. The tray already had three of Jimmy's butts, and before the outing was over, it would probably be full. "How long did I try to tell you that slut was screwing around on you?"

"That didn't give you the right to screw her, too."

"How the hell else would you believe it? It was worth it,

you hating me for a year, to have gotten you out of that fucked
-up marriage." He pulled another cigarette out of the pack, lit
it, dragged, and puffed out a cloud of smoke. "And now you're
married to Heidi, who is the exact opposite of Sarah. I did you
the biggest favor anyone has ever done for you. Besides, hell if
I can figure out why you stuck with her all that time anyway.
The woman was a lousy lay."

"I don't want to hear this."

"Maybe you *need* to hear it. A lousy lay. Terrible. Didn't
move, just laid there and moaned a little. And seriously, she
was one loose woman. It was like fucking a jar of warm water.
I ain't built like a porn star, but I'm endowed enough."

Richard hung his head and stared at his drink. There was
no stopping Jimmy when he got going. Somehow, he knew it
was Jimmy's way of reinforcing the great deed he'd done. And
he really *had* done a great deed, because Richard was far better
off away from Sarah—except that he was already on the verge
of leaving the woman, and Jimmy knew it. What Jimmy had
done had just been a shitty betrayal, regardless of the circumstances. But that was just the kind of guy Jimmy was, and always had been.

"...and, come on, the woman spread 'em for your best
friend—in your own bed," Richard went on. "And took my
load all over her face. Total tramp, and you're better off."

Richard raised his steely eyes, and Jimmy hit the verbal
brakes. Even Jimmy could tell when he'd pushed it too far.

"But back to my point," Jimmy said, flicking the ash off his
cigarette into the dirty ashtray. "If you were gonna snap and
strangle someone, you'd have done it to Sarah."

"At least she'd have deserved it. But here's this total
stranger, and I stared at her neck for six solid hours, thinking
about strangling her. And all because of that dream. I mean,
how do you think I possibly saw her in a dream before I ever
met her?"

Jimmy shrugged. "Dreams are funny. You probably didn't

see her; you saw someone similar, and when you met this woman in the real world, your brain filled in the blanks. Anyway, this was nothing more than a random fantasy. A fucked-up random fantasy, sure, but it wasn't like you went there looking for someone to kill, and you sure as hell didn't act on it. Any chance you'll see this woman again?"

"Hell, no. The company only asked me to go to that conference because Ginnie Mason's out on maternity leave and her assistant was on vacation. It's not even my department."

"Perfect. Then it'll be nothing more than a fun story we can chuckle about for the rest of our lives. I wouldn't sweat it."

"I won't. A good night's sleep, and I'm done with it."

"I hope so," Jimmy said, and he stubbed out another smoke in the dirty ashtray.

But in his dreams that night, Richard was back at the conference, sitting there and watching everyone filing out. Only when the door shut behind the last person did he realize Mary Rhodes was still there with him. They were alone, and she was looking at him with her sweet smile, a glimmer in her dark eyes. And that begging crimson halo was around her neck, glowing as if from beneath her skin, instructing him where to put his hands and what to do with them.

"I saw you staring at me, Richard," she said, smiling through a light coating of lip gloss, as she twirled her blue-and -white beaded necklace in her fingers.

"I—I'm sorry," he said, and his eyes weren't on hers but on her thin little neck. It was as if it were calling to him, begging him to wrap his strong hands around it.

"You were staring at my neck, just like you are now," she said, and her smile seemed playful as she flicked a finger across the soft flesh of her throat. "I can tell when a man is attracted to me."

It isn't like that! he screamed in his mind, tearing his eyes from her throat to look at her. It was all he could do to keep himself in the chair and not go to her, choke her, kill her.

And then she stood and came for him, walking like a slinky street whore, swaying her slim, tightly panted hips as she came. She was overpoweringly sexy with those young-girl hips, her slender waist, her swelling breasts pushing against her tight blouse. But all that was secondary; Richard was looking at her neck again, where her hand still played, as she rounded the end of the table and approached him.

"Please don't," he whispered, looking up at her as she stopped before him, right hip kicked far out and buttons straining on her blouse. "Don't do this."

"I know you want me," she said, her voice a teasing whisper in return. She angled her head back, stroked her neck with four fingers. "You want to put your mouth on my neck so badly you can practically taste me."

"That's not true." His voice was hoarse in a throat as dry as cotton.

She leaned in, her breasts peeking out of her blouse, and then her head was next to his, her red-lit neck just a few tantalizing, torturing inches from his mouth.

"Take it, baby," she said. "You can do anything you want."

Just when he thought he couldn't hold himself back from that neck, she abruptly stood up and backed up a step. He realized she was suddenly nearly naked, save for that beaded necklace and a skimpy teddy to match. The teddy was blue with white trim, and there was no hiding her jutting nipples through the sheer fabric. He could see the thatch of pubic hair between her legs as she struck a Wonder Woman pose, legs spread, hands on her hips, and smiled slyly at him.

"Just fucking take me," she said, in a voice that was an absurd mix of teasing, pleading, daring, and snarling. "Do it."

He came to his feet and approached her. He was naked now, he realized, his hard cock standing at attention, pointing accusingly at her as he moved. He forced himself to focus on everything below the neck, and it was easy. She sucked in her breath as he reached out and grabbed the skimpy teddy — one hand between the breasts, the other above her crotch — and with a sharp exhale he ripped the lingerie clean off her body. Her eyes widened in alarm, and her mouth opened in a surprised smile.

"Oh, that's what I need," she said.

Her little pixie body was astounding, and he wasted no time. He grabbed her with steel hands, spun her around, and threw her forward. Her breasts and belly smacked the tabletop, and she cooed in pleasure, spreading her legs.

He pulled her ass cheeks apart with his hands, and her wet pink gash beckoned him. He sank himself deep inside her in one powerful stroke, and she wailed in pleasure. He grabbed her hips and began working his raging cock like a piledriver, using his hands to haul her back with every stroke, and she cried out louder with every passing moment.

He felt his orgasm building right away, and he hunched over her, grasping for her breasts. She rose off the table to accommodate him, and he got his hands full of her tits and hauled her up. She was almost upright, and he felt her feet coming off the floor with every hard pounding.

And suddenly he was no longer fucking her from behind. As if by magic, she was seated on the very edge of the table, and her legs and arms were wrapped around him as he pounded her sopping-wet pussy. They were nose to nose, and he saw the lust in her eyes.

"Ohh, that's good," she mewed at him. "But Richard... this isn't what you *really* want. You want something else."

She tipped her head back, exposing her glowing-red throat and neck to him, and immediately the desire to strangle her exploded back in his brain. It was as if the red glow were brighter, frantically trying to get him to do it. He sucked in his breath in surprise and tried to pull out of her, to back away. But her legs were powerful, and she tightened them to pull him back inside.

"Oh, no you don't," she said, as the cord of her necklace vanished and the blue and white beads fell, clattering to the table and the floor. "Do it to me, baby. Do whatever you *really* want."

Richard couldn't stand it any longer. His hands fired up and impacted her neck like twin cobras striking their prey. And he squeezed. Her eyes bulged in their sockets, and her tongue pushed out of her mouth. But her hips kept moving, and her tight sheath squeezed his throbbing cock with pulsing regularity, as if she thought he was just into rough sex.

So he squeezed harder, and her eyes bulged out further, and now he saw terror in her eyes. Her hips stopped moving, and her legs relaxed. He felt the first crack of bone in her neck. Red light shined between his tight fingers.

"I'm sorry!" he cried as he shook her head savagely while he crushed her windpipe. "I'm so sorry!"

She gurgled and flailed, grabbing at his powerful hands to no avail. She kicked at him with dangling feet as he smashed her head into the wall again and again, caving in the drywall as she turned red and then blue and then purple, as the life went out of her, and he enjoyed every moment of it—

He came awake, being punched and kicked. It was dark. He had Mary's throat in the bed—but that wasn't right.

He came back to reality. He was in bed. His bed.

And he was choking his wife.

He let go with a holler, toppling backwards, and he heard Heidi gasping furiously for air even as she scrambled out of bed and tumbled onto the floor. She clambered to her feet, hacking and coughing, and found the bedroom light. Richard was blinded for a moment, but when his eyes adjusted, he saw his frightened Asian wife standing there in her sheer yellow nightie, leaning against the wall. Her neck undeniably sported red finger marks.

"Jesus Christ, Richard!" she screamed.

"I'm sorry—I was having a dream!" His mind raced. He couldn't tell her the dream, because he might have to explain it. "It was... there was a man trying to kill me, and... I was choking him."

"I can see that!"

She calmed down after a fashion, and after a few genuine tears from Richard, she held him and told him it was all right. It was just a bad dream he'd acted out, that was all, and she was okay.

This time, Richard thought. *What about next time?*

"Hire a prostitute who's into that sort of thing," Jimmy advised him at Finnegan's the next night, where a colony of spent cigarette butts was already growing in the ashtray, like a blastocyst of cells dividing. "People do that, you know—choke each other to get off. Erotic asphyxiation and a little S&M. You slap her around a little, get off on the power trip, choke her while you blow your load, pay her, and everyone's happy."

"I guess you'd know."

Jimmy chuckled, waving his cigarette at Richard in dismissal. "Yeah, I get it, I'm a male slut. Wouldn't have banged your wife otherwise."

"Enough of that," Richard groaned. "You are aware that best friends don't bang each other's wives, right?"

Jimmy laughed loud. "Only when we're trying to save our best friends' lives, buddy. Just like I'm trying to save yours now. Get a hooker and take care of this before it consumes you and hurts your current marriage—you know, the one that's working."

"I don't need sexual gratification out of this. It doesn't turn me on."

"But you have some kind of homicidal ideation about strangling someone. Live out the fantasy, and you won't choke poor Heidi in your sleep again."

Jimmy scanned the bar as he stubbed out his cigarette. It

was a Thursday night, so it was slow, but there were still a dozen or so people there. He gestured across the room to a trio of sexy twentysomethings having drinks at the bar. They were dressed to the nines, with bulging cleavage and plenty of skin. "Check out those three. Look at those necks—really think about them. Tell me you don't feel the same urge."

There were two blondes and a brunette. One blonde had long hair, but the other two had hair pulled back much like Mary's had been. And, upon close inspection, the brunette had the same thin, dainty neck—and she even wore a beaded necklace. He focused on her neck, thought about wrapping his hands around it and choking the life out of her.

But after a solid minute, all he could think about was her big tits. The feeling he had about Mary just wasn't there. "Nothing," he said. "But they're different. I didn't dream about them before meeting them. That's what's so fucked up about this."

Jimmy dismissed him with a waved hand. "You had a dream, you met her, you *thought* it was the same woman."

"No way. She was on my mind all morning as I drove to that conference. It was her. Who knows, maybe I saw her somewhere, and it was a coincidence we met. But I doubt it. Anyway, it doesn't explain this... crazy desire to choke the shit out of her."

Jimmy sighed. "Your solution is obvious, then. You're going to have to find Mary Rhodes and kill her." Then he burst out in braying laughter.

Richard shook his head with a grin. "You're a sick man, Jim."

Mary Rhodes never faded from Richard's mind, but over the next month, life was mostly normal. It was two weeks before Christmas when he made his annual shopping pilgrimage to the mall to acquire a stack of needed gifts. He was done inside of ninety minutes, and was weaving his way through the heavy mass of people, who all seemed to be coming at him, heading for the exit.

Then, directly in front of him and closing fast, there were a pair of morbidly obese women laden with shopping bags, so he took evasive action, swinging wide around them and dodging a quartet of tweens with cell phones — and came face to face with Mary Rhodes.

They both saw each other at the last moment and put on the brakes, stopping just a foot short of running smack into each other. Fright washed over Richard, even more so when he saw the recognition spread across her face.

"Well, hello," she said, a sweet smile spreading across her face.

"Hi," he said. He couldn't see her neck; she was wearing a scarf.

"Richard, isn't it? We met a couple of months ago at that multi-agency thing. I'm Mary Rhodes."

"Yes, good to see you again." He feigned a smile, trying to meet her eyes instead of trying to bore through the green knitted scarf. He felt his pulse increasing with every passing moment. "That was... quite a meeting."

She laughed, and it was a pleasant laugh. "It was six hours of our lives we'll never get back."

"Yes, that we did." He could only see the skin just beneath her chin, above her throat, peeking out as if to tease him. "Let's hope we don't have to do it again."

What the hell is wrong with you? Don't keep chatting with her! Get the hell out of there! Get away from her!

"I told my best friend about you after the meeting," he heard himself saying. It was as if he were a ventriloquist's dummy, with someone else making him say things. "We hang out at this bar downtown called Finnegan's, and we stopped for a drink."

"Told him... about *me?*" she said with a raised brow.

"Well, you know, about the meeting," he said, feeling

embarrassed. He had to change the subject. "Are you Christmas shopping?"

"Oh, yes. Just here for a few things." She smiled and, he was certain, batted her eyelashes at him. Was she flirting with him?

He knew he had to wish her Merry Christmas and be on his way, but the ventriloquist had other plans. "Would you... do you have time for a cup of coffee?" He could almost feel the phantom hand jammed up in his back, working his mouth.

She blinked as if in surprise. "I suppose I could." She looked sideways at him and pursed her lips bemusedly. "I'd be lying if I said I didn't notice you checking me out at that meeting. Are we flirting now?"

He was trembling slightly as he laughed. "I guess we are."

"But I wasn't born yesterday, Richard. You're wearing a wedding ring."

He held up his hand, and she looked like the mother who'd just caught her kid with his hand in the cookie jar. Yes, without a doubt, he was married.

"She's... passed on," he heard himself lying. "Breast cancer, two years ago. I still wear it... I know I shouldn't."

What the FUCK are you doing? What the FUCK?!

Her face softened, her eyes widening. "Oh, my... that's terrible."

"I've tried to move on, but I guess I'm still a bit clingy," he said. "Maybe I'm trying to get the courage to jump off the diving board again. So, you know, having a cup of coffee is a good start. A safe start."

Stop! Stop it now! TURN and RUN the other WAY!

She reached out then and took his upraised hand, and when she squeezed it, all Richard could think about was wrapping his hands around her throat and squeezing in return.

"I lost my mother to breast cancer," she said, a soft voice wafting up out of a soft throat. "I know how difficult that is."

Numbly, he felt himself walking off with her to have that

cup of coffee, feeling like an absolute bastard.

She never took her scarf off at the coffee shop, not even when he suggested she must be getting too warm. When she surprisingly asked him if he'd like to come by her apartment for a drink, he readily agreed.

And when they were there, she pulled off her coat and un-wrapped the scarf, and she turned around and he saw her neck. It was fully exposed, thanks to a white blouse that re-vealed her neck, throat, collarbone, most of her shoulders, and the tops of her breasts. And the red glow of the phantom halo surrounded her neck. He was frozen in place, staring un-ashamedly at her, and never realized she was looking at him.

"I'm up here," she said.

He snapped his eyes up, felt his face flush red. "I'm sorry. I wasn't staring at—at your..."

She moved to him, reaching for him, wrapping her arms around him. "It's all right if you want to look at my breasts," she whispered. "Considering how you lost your wife, I'm flat-tered that you'd be looking at them."

He had to get out of there. He couldn't do it. He couldn't cheat on Heidi. And he was afraid that if he stayed any longer, he might do something even worse than that.

And then her face was there, in his, and her lips met his. She kissed him, and he couldn't help but kiss back. He felt her hands on his back; one slid up to his shoulder, and the other slid down his back. He wrapped his arms around her, and let one hand slide down over her small ass. Her butt was soft and pliable, but he felt strong, tight muscles beneath.

She slid her tongue in, and he reciprocated. It was insane. He had to stop. But he couldn't. He felt her breasts through his coat, felt her roaming hand mimic his, finding his ass and squeezing.

He tried to pull away, but she grabbed him tightly and pulled him back. "It's okay," she said. "Diving board, right?"

"Diving board," he whispered, trembling. And then he realized she'd closed her eyes and had tilted her head back, exposing her throat to him. She wanted him to kiss her there.

Her neck, thin and weak, dainty and fragile, was right there, illuminated with its ghostly crimson halo. They were entwined in each other's arms, and she was *offering* her neck to him. He slid his hands around her, feeling his way up over her breasts, and towards her neck…

Reality slapped him in the brain. He had to stop before things went *very* bad.

"I can't do this," he said, and he disentangled himself from her arms and staggered back and into the wall. "I'm sorry—I can't do this. I lied to you. My wife isn't dead. I'm very happily married. I have no idea what I'm doing here."

She stood, wide-eyed and open-mouthed, for several long moments before she finally said, "You know exactly why you're here. You're attracted to me. I'm attracted to you. You obviously need this, or you wouldn't have come this far. And clearly, I need this, too, because any other time if someone lied to me about being married, especially with a dead-wife breast-cancer story, I'd show him the door. Hell, I've never even taken a strange man home on a first date, but here we are. We're both committed to this."

Her glowing neck screamed in silent fury at him, beckoning to him just as she was, and he couldn't take it any longer. He headed for the door, staggering, and found the knob. "I can't," he said. "If I stay, I'm afraid I might—"

Kill you.

"I—I just can't," he said, and he threw open the door and fled into the cold December night.

"You're a dumb shit," Jimmy said over the noise at a very busy Finnegan's a short while later, puffing another noxious cloud of smoke in Richard's face.

Richard coughed and waved his hand. "Could you at least

not blow that crap in my face?"

"First let's focus on you being a dumb shit for two reasons. First, you actually considered cheating on Heidi, who has been the ultimate angel in your life. If you cheat on her, you don't deserve a woman who has been that good to you."

"Ain't that the truth."

"But second, after stupidly deciding to screw this Mary chick, you didn't. Heidi's great, but no matter how great she is, you can't ignore this kind of an opportunity. If Mary is half as cute and half as horny as you say, then you're an idiot to have run off."

"But I didn't go there to cheat on Heidi. I didn't go there to screw Mary."

Jimmy looked as if he were about to ask why he went there, then, but realization crossed his face. He looked around the bar in alarm, as if hoping nobody was listening, but the crammed-in people were all hollering to each other over the loud music. He leaned in close to Richard so he wouldn't have to yell to be heard. "Are you saying you actually went there to... kill her?"

"Well, of course not," Richard lied. "I had no intention of screwing her, though. I just had to see her neck again. Maybe I thought I could get past this if I just touched it or something. But once I did, the same feeling came over me. I was... totally uncomfortable." There, that was a safe way to explain it. And, of course, he omitted the part about seeing a red glow invisible to anyone else. He didn't need Jimmy thinking he'd really lost his mind.

"This woman's neck is truly an obsession," Jimmy said, stubbing out another cigarette. The ashtray was nearly over-flowing with them; Jimmy had polished off an entire pack and had opened another. It was a bad habit that was way out of control. "If you know what's good for you, you'll drive back over to her house, apologize to her for running away, and fuck her. Touch that neck, kiss that neck, come all over that neck, whatever it is you need—but get it out of your system and be done with it."

But Richard was frozen, because coming into the bar was Mary. He'd mentioned Finnegan's, and she'd found him.

"It's her," he said. "In the green scarf."

Jimmy spun around just as Mary spotted Richard and made a beeline for their table. Jimmy's mouth hung open. "You truly *are* a dumb shit. She's fucking hot."

Mary arrived and sat down. "So this must be the friend you told about me after the meeting," she said.

Richard nodded, unspeaking.

"I don't understand what happened at my place," she said. "There's nothing to be afraid of. I'm not looking for a relationship. But I was all set for a good time. I don't care that you're married."

"But I do care," he said. "I love my wife."

She nodded. "Maybe. Or maybe you didn't love her enough to do what you did. You've already cheated on her, you know. You might as well go all the way."

Richard looked to Jimmy helplessly.

Jimmy leaned in, clearing his throat. "Mary, I'm Jimmy. Pleased to meet you. Let me make this easy. Richard doesn't want to have sex with you. He wants to wrap his hands around your throat and strangle you until you're dead. Now do you want to take him home?"

She looked astounded, but then she shook her head in disbelief. "Okay, I get it. You want me to get lost. That's just what I need. Thanks for the rejection."

She stood up in a huff but pivoted back before leaving, her hip thrust out as it had been in his dream. "I'm going to admit that I really needed a sexual connection with you tonight. I still do. But this is a one-night offer, Richard. I'm going home. If you get over this crisis of conscience, you know where to find me. But I'll come to my senses tomorrow."

After she left, they brooded in silence, Richard nursing his

beer and Jimmy smoking another cigarette. Finally, Jimmy got up and stretched. "Well, I have to be to work at three in the morning, so I'm heading home to bed," he said. "I hope you solve this one, man."

"Me too."

Richard thought about it for another hour, alone with his beer and the stinking ash tray.

When he got home that night, Heidi was in the kitchen in her bathrobe, fresh from a shower and making some herbal tea. She was of Asian ancestry, with a Japanese mother, and was built a lot like Mary: petite, although with slightly broader hips and slightly bigger breasts. She was always tremendously sexy to him, but, standing there with damp hair, straight and black and plastered to the side of her face and her neck, she was the most exotic woman he'd ever seen.

He never said a word, but her almond eyes looked confused when he went to her and tore open her robe. She was naked underneath, and he wasted no time. He kissed her, his hands crawling everywhere so that she must have thought he had five or six of them. He was more forceful than he'd ever been with her, although not like he'd been in his dream about Mary. But he started just like his dream had, turning his wife around and bending her over the kitchen table the way he'd done to Mary. For some reason, she didn't argue; she braced herself on her forearms and spread her legs wide as he pulled her robe up over her hips, worked his buckle open and his zipper down. He fished his hard cock out the flap of his boxers and sank it deep inside her. She cried out with enjoyment and moaned and made exciting sounds for the first minute or so — but then he picked up the pace and fucked her senseless. Just like he had to Mary. And he envisioned that she *was* Mary.

He was like a man possessed, driving her hard over the table until she came in a screaming orgasm. But he wasn't close to done; he pulled out and scooped the lightweight woman up in his arms and quickly carried her to the living room. He threw her down on the couch and climbed between her legs, and she eagerly spread them as he plunged back into her. She looked stunned, but she complied as he banged her hard and fast, her legs high in the air as he jackhammered his cock into her. He kept up the pace until he'd damn near fucked her off the couch, her head hanging almost to the floor — and her neck was exposed.

He fucked her through another screaming orgasm, and then he took her upstairs — stopping briefly in the hallway to kiss her, to hug her, to even kiss her neck, and to lift her up and impale her on his cock. He fucked her like that in the hallway, up against the wall, until her juices ran down his thighs, and then he carried her, still impaled, into the bedroom. He fucked her for another hour, and she came more times than he could count. When he could tell she didn't have another come left in her, he went to town as he kissed her neck, licked her neck, sucked on her neck, bit her neck, fucking furiously until his balls exploded and he roared like an animal, filling his beloved wife's ravaged pussy full of his come.

When it was finally over, and she'd found her breath, she laughed aloud. "Where the hell did all that come from?" she said, cuddling up to him. The poor woman looked as if she'd just been gang-banged by a group of sailors. Her hair was a tangled mess, and her whole body was slick with sweat. And she smelled like a whorehouse.

"I was just *really* in the mood," he said, kissing her. "Are you complaining?"

"I guess not, but I don't think I could do that every night. Your hair still smells like smoke, though."

"Sorry. You know Jimmy."

They lay in silence for several minutes, Richard's mind running wild. Finally, he said, "Has Jimmy ever hit on you?"

She looked at him, glaring with dark eyes. "I'm not Sarah. I would never cheat on you."

"I know. But that doesn't mean he wouldn't try."

She sat up and laid her hand on his bare chest. "You know I'm no fan of Jimmy. If he so much as winked at me, I'd kick him in the nuts. Screwing Sarah was the worst thing a best friend could do, no matter how he tries to justify it, and no matter how close you were to leaving her anyway. He'll never get anywhere with me. I'd never let him hurt you like that."

He smiled. "Thanks, hon."

She lay back down, cuddling up and using his chest for a pillow, and he had a perfect, close-up look at her neck. He could see the series of hickeys he'd left there, like some crazy teenager, and it was red all over from the irritation of his facial stubble. It was an exquisite neck, even more attractive than Mary's, but through all the wild sex he'd just had, there had been no feeling of wanting to strangle her. Yet staring at it evoked images of Mary being the one using his chest as a pillow, of Mary lying naked there, her neck beckoning him. The imagery was overpowering. How long before another bad dream resulted in Heidi being injured? How long before the urge transcended Mary, and he intentionally did something to hurt the woman he loved?

It was time to do something about it.

He threw the covers aside and got up. "I have to go out for a bit."

"Where?"

"I have a Christmas gift to get for you."

And one for me, he thought.

He'd never be able to live with himself if he strangled Mary, and he'd never be able to live with himself if he didn't. He couldn't explain it, didn't understand it, but the idea of wrapping his hands around that woman's throat and choking her until she was dead was holding him prisoner. It wouldn't let him go. It was strangling him just as surely he knew he had to strangle her. But there was a way around it.

He made a quick stop at Finnegan's to claim his wallet that he'd "accidentally" left there earlier. Then he drove through the dark night to the familiar apartment. He found the hidden key and slid it into the lock, and when he opened the door, Sarah was sitting there in the living room, on the couch, and she was honestly surprised to see him. And he was honestly surprised to see that her neck glowed as red as fire, brighter than Mary's ever had. He never gave her a chance to speak.

He wrapped his gloved hands around the cheating whore's crimson throat and locked his fingers together, cutting off her air supply and shutting up her voice box so she couldn't even scream. He squeezed like a vise, and she flailed and kicked and tried to tear his hands away, but he forced her back on the couch and straddled her, his knees on her arms. Sarah struggled beneath him like a helpless worm, and he watched as her face got redder and redder. Her eyes bulged unnaturally from their sockets, looking as if they might actually pop out of her skull, the way Mary's had in his dream, and her tongue swelled and lolled out of her mouth.

His heart raced faster, but not insanely so; he was amazingly calm as he did it. He just kept squeezing harder, as her face went from red to deep blue and her legs kicked more weakly with each passing moment. Even as her eyes rolled back and her windpipe finally crushed in his hands, he just kept squeezing until every last bit of life was gone from her body. And then he squeezed some more, until he felt bone break and cartilage split.

When he was done, he dug into his pocket and fished out the special Christmas present he'd gotten for her. Then he let himself out and raced to the mall on the other side of town, to buy a gift for his wife and give himself an alibi that could be supported by security tapes and credit-card purchases.

Nobody found her for days, and of course the police came immediately to question him. It never went any further.

Jimmy heard about it on the news, and summoned him to a mostly dead Finnegan's that Monday night. "Tell me you didn't do it," Jimmy said under his breath. "Tell me that wasn't you."

"Of course it wasn't me!" Richard cried, with the best-manufactured look of complete shock he could manage. "Holy shit, Jimmy — what the fuck do you take me for?"

They traded burning glares for a long moment, and then Jimmy finally sighed and nodded, leaning back in his chair. "I actually thought you'd snapped, man. But honestly, I wouldn't have blamed you if you had."

They ordered beers and drank in silence for a long while. After a good two hours, a dozen beers between them, and another pack of smokes into Jimmy's lungs, neither was feeling any pain. And they weren't paying any attention, which was why Mary was standing there before either of them knew it.

"I heard about your ex-wife on the radio," she said to Richard. "I heard the cops talked to you."

"Well, sure — she was my ex-wife, and we hated each other," Richard said. "But I didn't kill her."

"Well, I bet the cops would like to hear what Jimmy told me the last time I was here, about you wanting to strangle me." Her eyes blazed with fury. "Pretty big coincidence, huh?"

Richard suddenly realized that Mary's neck was doing nothing for him. It was just a neck, nothing more. There was no red glow.

"Yeah, I was just kidding about that to make you go away that night," Jimmy said.

"Maybe the police should be looking at you, then," she retorted.

"Maybe you're a scorned bitch who'll say anything to get back at the guy who wouldn't fuck her," Jimmy said.

She glared at him and then at Richard, but then she turned and stalked out of Finnegan's.

"Thanks," Richard said. "You really put her in her place."

Jimmy took a deep drag on his cigarette and smiled. "That's what best friends are for, man."

In a few days, the police had a DNA profile from Sarah's apartment. And when Mary Rhodes told them what Jimmy had said, they got a DNA profile from him. Then they asked him where he'd been the night of her murder. Jimmy had no alibi; he'd been home asleep, as he'd had to work at three the next morning. When Jimmy vehemently denied having been in Sarah's apartment for several years, they arrested him because they knew he was lying. After all, the DNA from the menthol cigarette butts in Sarah's ashtray was a perfect match for Jimmy. Jimmy tried to tell the cops about Richard's strangulation obsession, but in the end it was Richard's word against Jimmy's in the face of overwhelming evidence.

Heidi never mentioned Richard's dream-induced attempt to strangle her to the cops or Richard. But she was astounded at how badly his jacket smelled of cigarettes—it was worse than usual—so she ran it through the wash. She never noticed the ash stains in the jacket's pocket, and soon they were gone forever.

Richard ran into Mary Rhodes at a K-Mart the following year, and they chatted politely, tolerating the meeting. It was June, and she was wearing a pink tank top, white bra straps visible and her neck fully exposed. It was still just another neck to him; he couldn't even envision her skin glowing red. When they parted company, he knew life was finally back to normal. He was free of the grip his illogical obsession had had on him; he was the same normal Richard Baxter he had once been.

He had another prophetic dream one night in August, but of course he didn't realize it was prophetic until the next day. In retrospect, he knew he should have.

The company held a beach party for its six hundred employees. Heidi was in California visiting her parents, so Richard went alone. The gala event was full of volleyball and Frisbee and swimming and barbecue pits, all with scores of beautiful women in bathing suits.

There were so many people that he never noticed her until it was dark. Richard was enjoying a beer, standing near one of the many bonfires, when she bounded across the sand in a white string bikini that left extremely little to the imagination. He recognized her the moment he saw her, even though they'd never met, and the hair on the back of his neck prickled up as a shiver rippled through his spine. She came right up to him.

"Hey there," she greeted him with a pretty smile.

"Hello," he replied, and his eyes crawled over her body. She was a few inches shorter than him, slender and sexy and with perfect hips and bulbous breasts—a real treat, even among the many treats he'd ogled that day. She was nineteen, maybe twenty. He forced himself not to tremble, and to not look at her belly. He checked out her barely hidden boobs, the tight crotch of her bikini, the incurve of her waist, and flare of her hips. Even her neck, and of course her pretty face.

"It's getting a little chilly out here," she said. "Wish I'd brought clothes, you know?"

"I'm sort of glad you didn't," he heard himself saying, giving her a sly smile.

She blushed and smiled broadly in returned. "Hey, I'm Alicia. I just started in Accounting last week."

"Welcome aboard," he said with a smile. "I'm Richard, from Operations."

She breathed deeply, enjoying the heat from the bonfire. Richard watched her in the orange glow. She had a pretty face framed by blond hair, but his eyes were drawn down past her jiggly breasts to her belly. It was flat and toned, with flawless skin, begging him to touch it. And just like that, a sudden, inexplicable desire flooded through him like a tsunami.

Not again. Please... not again.

"My dad gave me a ride here this afternoon," she said,

looking at him with dark, sexy eyes. "Do you think someone here would give me a ride home?"

"I'll give you a ride," he said with a husky voice, staring at her belly. "Come on."

She smiled, seductive but naïve. "Okay."

They walked away from the bonfire and the party, melting into the darkness together, and he reached his hand over to touch the small of her back, then boldly slid it into her bikini and squeezed her ass. She let him, undoubtedly proud that she was giving a hard-on to a total stranger.

In his car, she said, "Look... I don't usually let older guys feel me up. I really just want a ride home."

He read her face, and knew she was lying. "Alicia, let me tell you something," he said. "I don't usually cheat on my wife, but I'm willing to do that with you. Now, you tell me the truth. Do you want to fuck me or not?"

She seemed alarmed, eyes wide, but something about the look on his face seemed to calm her down. She smiled, a bit red in the face, and nodded. "I had a few drinks. I haven't been laid in eight months. I figured it would be easy with the bikini, but nobody seems interested."

"They're afraid of workplace sex," he said with a smile. "I'm not."

He didn't really want to have sex with her. He didn't want to cheat on Heidi. But something was distracting him, and he was out of ex-wives to kill. He knew he had to fuck her to make the feeling go away. He hoped it would go away.

He took her to the back seat and they made out, he in his casual beach clothes, she in two strips of cloth that barely concealed anything. He had her breasts exposed in seconds, and it didn't take long to get between her legs. He kept kissing her furiously, even as he pulled the thong bottom aside and probed her wet lips with the head of his hard cock. She cried out in joy as he slowly sank himself deep inside her, and she made cute, teen-girl "Ooooh... ooooh... ooooh!" sounds with every slow, steady stroke.

But he wasn't thinking about the sex. He was just trying to keep his mind off the irresistible idea that was electrifying his brain, the same one that he'd seen in his dream. She'd been there the night before, in the same skimpy bikini, and the red glow now illuminated her abdomen in a long, thin line. In the dream, he'd known what it had meant. And in the real world, on the beach, he knew it still meant the same thing.

He was burning with the desire to plunge a knife into her belly, just above her neatly trimmed landing strip, and slice her open all the way to her ribcage. He wanted to see her guts pouring out as she screamed in horror and tried frantically to stuff them back inside her body. And as he squeezed a boob and pounded her sloppy cunt harder and faster, he imagined stuffing his hand up her ass and pulling her large intestine out through her rectum.

Fleetingly, he wished he had Jimmy around to talk him out of it. He was taking Jimmy's advice: screwing this one in hopes he'd get it out of his system. He loved Heidi so very much, and didn't want to cheat on her, but he couldn't kill poor, innocent Alicia. If he fucked her good, without entrails and without knives, maybe that would sate him and the red glow would vanish.

But he doubted it would, because the desire was building—and oh, it was so overpowering.

Days of Orgone

by
Aleksandar Žiljak

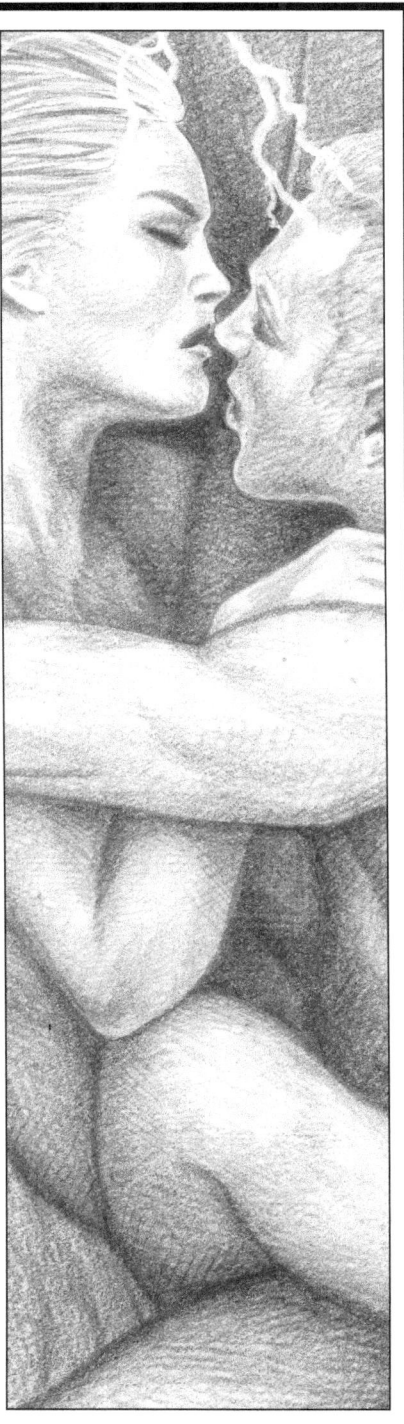

The Space Race was a major chess game between the Cold War superpowers. In our reality, the Soviets achieved so many of the firsts: the first satellite in orbit, the first animal in space, the first man in space, and the first man to orbit the Earth. But they lost the greatest bragging right of all when the Americans were the first — and so far only — nation to land men on the Moon and return them safely home again. But in this alternate history, things unfold very differently — and the race to the Moon is fueled by the cosmic power of sex.

Science fiction
Space travel
Alternate history
Communism
Heterosexual sex
Group sex
Lust
Romance

*"Let's face the facts: We listened to the wrong Kraut and
that's why we're living under the red Moon now."*
— Admiral Robert A. Heinlein, April 17, 1961

L et us call the man, standing at the entrance to the Department of Energy, Citizen K. It's visible at first sight
that he's embarrassed: He's afraid somebody will recognize him at these early morning hours. The corridor is by no
means empty, but toilers rush to their work posts without as
much as glancing at him. Drops of sweat break on his forehead. Finally, he makes up his mind and grabs the heavy brass
door handle with a shaky hand.

Energy Chamber 8 is a knot of a hundred naked bodies —
fifty male, fifty female — engaged in all imaginable love posi-
tions. Professor Boris Leontiyevich Bogolyubov studies the instruments, casting only an occasional glance at the wild love
play going on behind the thick glass. The temperature and hu-
midity in the *energeticheskaya kamera* are optimal, and so is the
concentration of aphrodisiacal aerosols.

"We're coming close," one of the technicians mutters, his
mouth dry. Boris Leontiyevich doesn't have to be what he is,
an expert in orgone energy, to see that the man's pants had
grown uncomfortably tight for him. Right now, he'd love to
tear his clothes off and dive into the crowd in Chamber 8. Or
any other of the fifty-three currently active chambers, for that
matter. The Professor sighs. Some people never have enough.

"Transmitters?" he asks the technician sternly.

Poor fellow checks the meters: All the transmitters are

working at full capacity. Satisfied that everything is ready for the big moment, the Professor allows himself a peek through the glass.

"Shall we turn the sound on, Comrade Professor?" asks Masha Akhmatova, his assistant.

"For heaven's sake, Masha, what's there to hear?"

Masha looks across the Professor's shoulder at the serpent's coil of copulation, faces flushed red in spasms of lust, entwined young bodies moving in the coital rhythm, growing faster and more passionate. She blushes like a schoolgirl and then pulls herself together and returns to the instruments.

"Fifteen to go!" the main technician starts counting down. "Fourteen... thirteen..."

Boris Leontiyevich's eyes pause on a short-haired blond girl embracing a muscular Negro. Somehow, they remained devoted to each other in that bundle of bodies. The Professor cannot help but view the Negro's impressive tool with envy, as the man uses it to bring the cute girl to heavenly orgasm.

"Ten... nine..."

His mouth browses across her perfect breasts, his tongue dancing around the erect nipples. Perspiration drips from his forehead as the babe squeezes him with her long legs, her eyelids shut, her beautiful face contorted at the threshold of a climax.

"Six... five..."

He increases the rhythm; the approaching pleasure possesses the girl.

"Three... two..."

Blue transmitter ovals on their temples flare up. The Professor takes a look at all the others in the *enkam*. All the transmitters glow, all are on the verge of it, just another spastic thrust or two.

"One... ZERO!"

The transmitters flash in a bright white light as the hundred people in the *Enkam* 8 reach their orgasms simultaneously.

The technicians go frantic. Masha studies the charging indicators excitedly. Purring orgone batteries soak up the energy discharged from the Enkam 8. And in front of Professor Bogolyubov, the Negro stiffens, ramming his rod all the way into the girl and emptying himself with animal groans. Boris Leontiyevich cannot hear them through the glass, but he can imagine him screaming and her moaning under the strong ebony body as she comes, impaled on that club, squirt after squirt of semen filling her innards.

Boris Leontiyevich feels his cheeks growing hot. His loins stir. Then he takes a deep breath, turns to face the meters and clears his throat. He must maintain dignity and authority before his technicians and assistants. Especially before Masha...

"Report, colleagues!"

"Perfect discharge, Comrade Professor," Masha is ecstatic. "Charging ninety-eight point nine five percent, synchronicity ninety-seven point seven three percent—"

"All right, all right, my dear, no need to lose your head! I can see it myself. Congratulations, comrades! If only the frequency of discharges of this quality would exceed fifteen percent, there'd be no end to it!"

The Professor's strict stare brings everybody back to Earth. It won't do for the technicians to become too cocky. Gauges show the drop in energy levels. The boys in the enkam came, the girls are relaxing, and that's it. That's all until the next round. *Not even Josef Vissarionovich could do god-knows-what about it,* Boris Leontiyevich muses, satisfied.

At that moment, a communicator buzzes in the pocket of his white smock.

"Tell me, Helga, what's the problem?"

Dr. Helga Fink is forty-three years old. Despite her years, her face is beautiful and youthful; she still has no reason to be afraid of age. Her somewhat strict appearance is enhanced by her icy blue eyes, piercing behind metal-rimmed glasses, and her blond hair carefully gathered into a bun. Her makeup is discreet. Her white smock is thrown over a red shirt and grey straight skirt. Boris Leontiyevich cannot help but glance at her legs in black nylon stockings, imported from the decadent West.

Dr. Fink and Professor Bogolyubov sit at the small conference table in her office, reclining in the dark crimson armchairs. A file folder is in front of Dr. Fink. Professor Bogolyubov doesn't miss its thickness.

Helga Fink's office reflects her loyalty to the ideals of the Great October. Lenin's bust and the official portrait of Comrade Khrushchev are placed at prominent spots. Her library, apart from voluminous scientific treatises and textbooks, is graced by the collected works of the classics of Marxism, although Boris Leontiyevich is well aware that Helga doesn't bother with dialectical materialism. Stalin's *Sochineniya*—his collected works—disappeared discreetly from her shelves immediately after the 20th Congress. Dr. Fink loves art; she finds inner peace in the mystic shadows of Shishkin's forests. Of course, also displayed is the scaled-down print of Zaitchenko's masterpiece *Forward into the Future!*—one of the most magnificent works of the socialist realism.

The painting shows Khrushchev and Academician Korolyov, surrounded by their assistants, as they watch the construction of the first orgone ship, the *Krasnaya Zvezda*, the "Red Star." Khrushchev's gaze points into the vast expanses of space, into the future of all Mankind, led by Bolshevik ideals, into the dense scaffolding shrouding the gigantic hull of the *Red Star*. Absorbed in his vision, he apparently does not hear the Academician explaining him the progress of construction. Professor Boris Leontiyevich Bogolyubov is also present, next to Sergey Pavlovich. So are Yuri and Valentina, commanders of the test orgonaut crew, as well as countless engineers and scientists and higher technicians. Only Helga Fink is missing from the crowd, although she should have been standing in the first row. She is embarrassment enough to be omitted from such a grandiose composition.

Next to *Forward into the Future!* is Kupriyanov's *The Despair of Admiral Heinlein,* in the Professor's humble opinion an even more brilliant work of art. In it, Admiral Robert Anson Heinlein, the chief of the American space program, watches the footage of the first take-off of the *Krasnaya Zvezda.* His face is red with fury, his uniform unbuttoned, his tie loose, an ashtray filled with butts and an empty bottle before him. Next to him is Wernher von Braun, crumpled blueprints of those ridiculous rockets falling out of his shaky hands. Dr. Asimov watches with resignation as their imperialist-fascist-Zionist conspiracy burns to cinders in the blinding flash of orgone energy uplifting the *Krasnaya Zvezda* from the Kazakhstan steppe towards the stars.

That had been the professional end to all three of them. Heinlein retired and is currently writing novels about the Pacific naval war. Von Braun returned to Germany, where he was lucky to be given a presidency of a rocket modeller club. Asimov followed Heinlein's steps to some extent, and is now popularising science among youths.

And to make irony even bigger, the originator of the whole idea of the orgone energy, the great Wilhelm Reich, succumbed not long before that historic moment in the dungeons of the anti-people American regime, falsely accused in a trumped-up political trial.

"Well, Helga?"

"Frankly, Boris, I don't know what to do with this." Dr. Fink pushes the folder across the table.

Boris Leontiyevich takes it in his hands and opens it. A brief biography of the subject, the above-mentioned Citizen K., results of the physical and a long OSS-test chart, folded several times.

At first glance, the biography of Citizen K. is quite ordinary. He's thirty-seven years old. He never married. He's from a peasant family. Being a bright and diligent pupil, leaning towards mathematics, he studied and finally graduated economy. He excelled in operations research and, after spending several years at the faculty as an assistant lecturer, he volunteered for the Alpha Centauri program. His motives were not exactly clear, but since resource optimizing is of crucial importance for such a project, he was admitted to the crew. And his problem alarmed Dr. Fink enough to ask for help.

"His tool, you know... all according to GOST?" The Professor likes to express himself in a folksy manner.

"Even somewhat above." Helga Fink blushes a bit. And then she coughs. "Physiologically, everything is perfectly in order. Anatomically, too. No peculiarities."

"And in here?" Boris Leontiyevich knocks at his forehead with his index finger.

"The man is desperate. He came to us of his own accord; this tells you enough. But we cannot find out what's wrong with him," Helga shrugs. "Ognev examined him. What else can I say?"

The Professor becomes thoughtful. Because although Citizen K. is seemingly all right, his orgonic yield is—if the file is to be trusted—nil. A nice, rounded zero. Citizen K. does not get sexually excited. He does not reach orgasms. He does not release his orgone energy. According to classic Reichian patterns, Citizen K. should be neck-deep in neuroses, if not even psychoses. Even more inconvenient, the fact that his orgonic yield is nil equals sabotage under present circumstances. And that is not permissible! As Comrade Mao phrased it after the heroic victory of Chinese people's masses: He who doesn't work doesn't need to eat.

And the failure to solve this problem would be embarrassing to Doctor Fink, too. *Oh yes,* Professor Bogolyubov thinks as he nods, *I have to pull you out of it again.*

Colonel Boris Leontiyevich Bogolyubov, accompanied by an NKVD rifle squad, with his faithful *tokarev* pistol in hand

and PPSh submachine gun hanging from his shoulder, rushed the abandoned hallways of the institute. Place: Berlin. Time: April 26, 1945. The Kaiser Wilhelm Institute of Physics was already held by the NKVD, together with nuclear material. It was time to check the less-important laboratories and establishments; the Colonel was assigned one of them to search. Suddenly, loud laughter and a girl's scream broke through the hallways above the rattling of tank treads and whistles of *katyusha* rocket-launchers.

"Follow me!" the Colonel shouted, and he ran down the hallway. The racket was coming from behind one of the doors. The Colonel kicked them open and cursed at the sight he faced.

Three *frontoviki*, properly drunk, were molesting a girl. Her glasses had fallen off her nose and her blond hair had come loose as she screamed and struggled against the lewd soldiers. But in vain: Trapped between them, she was completely helpless. One grabbed her hands firmly; the other was raising her skirt, while the third one was tugging at her shirt and tearing it.

Although disgusted by conduct unbecoming of the soldiers of the heroic Red Army, it was quite possible that Boris Leontiyevich wouldn't have paid too much attention to this immoral event were it not for the pile of papers and a notebook that scattered out from beneath the girl's torn shirt in all that struggle. The Colonel realized immediately that it might be something important. Why else would the girl hide it at the price of her own life?

The peasant origins of Colonel Bogolyubov gifted him with keen mind and far-renowned sense of humour, but also with fists whose punch would do justice to a bear. So he rushed into the commotion before him, dealt several whacks and kicks to the soldiers and, for good measure, a slap to the girl who spat something obscene in German. Then he fired two shots from his pistol into the ceiling, to show the drunken soldiers he meant it. And while the NKVD guarded his back with pointed submachine guns, Boris Leontiyevich grabbed the girl's papers and leafed through them.

It took his scientific mind less than a minute to realize the epochal importance of the notes he held in his hand. "Is this all?" he asked the girl in his fluent German.

The girl, who by now you have guessed was Helga Fink, didn't reply immediately. Her eyes went from the Colonel to his men to the three would-be rapists. "March out!" the Colonel shouted at them and, crestfallen, they took their weapons and went on to exterminate the fascist beast in its lair. "I ask you once again, is this all?"

Helga Fink righted herself and adjusted her clothes as much as she could. Then she took Boris Leontiyevich to a closet in a corner of the demonstration room. She opened it and pointed at a metal box on a wooden base, some wires and a headband mixed with other instruments on the shelf. "The battery and transmitters are here."

Boris Leontiyevich compared the box before him to sketches in the notebook. Then he ran through the results of the experiments. Obviously, Helga Fink had tested her device thoroughly, and it was all measured and recorded in the notebook: whom with and how many times and the amounts of energy discharged.

A physicist's mind awoke in Colonel Bogolyubov as he studied Helga Fink's notes. He returned into the days before Hitler's aggression, before he had left the secure post of an assistant lecturer, laid down his piece of chalk and sponge and went, being the lieutenant in reserve, to stop the fascist conqueror before the gates of his beloved Moscow. Twice wounded, he pursued the cannibalistic Hitlerite bands out of Motherland until he was sent, now a colonel, to Berlin to search the institute.

And as he had the device prepared for transportation, he was certain that he carried out his orders above all expectations. As they traveled across the furrowed roads back east, he didn't take his eyes off Helga Fink, her perfect oval face, her icy blue eyes, her blond hair that she arranged back into a bun. As they passed the columns of men, carts, tanks, and self-propelled guns, Helga Fink was well aware that she had narrowly escaped the fate already suffered by countless women and girls across Germany. Thus was born in the girl a sincere gratitude to the unfamiliar senior officer, all the breadth of his Slavic soul welling out from his face and piercing gaze and disheveled hair.

And Colonel Boris Leontiyevich Bogolyubov didn't leave a briefcase stuffed with her notes unattended for a second. *Who knows,* he thought as he watched the tired soldiers through a car window, *if Trojan War was about Helen, perhaps this one was about Helga Fink.*

"I'd get more response from a corpse."

Helga shows the OSS-chart to the Professor. And indeed, apparently there's simply no optimal sexual stimulus for Citizen K.

"Young Stakhanovites under shower?" Boris Leontiyevich asks, not looking up from the chart.

"Please, Boris, that's the first thing we tried. And the female volleyball team and an NKVD officer with black garter belt and handcuffs. Anything you can think of. We tested him for two days."

"Hmm," the Professor says with a nod, "a serious problem. Perhaps—" Interrupted by the buzzing of his communicator, Boris Leontiyevich looks up.

"Yes?" he answers the communicator. "Oh, it's you, Comrade General! Yes, the charging is going on as planned. You will have hundred percent by tomorrow evening, yes... No, I do not recommend an earlier jump. Yes, Comrade General... Yes, I know we already have enough, but you must consider reserve, and that is tomorrow evening... Yes, I recommend that we go as planned, jump the day after tomorrow at eight hundred ship's time... Thank you, good night to you, too!

"Kozhedub; he's in a hurry," Boris Leontiyevich mutters as he puts his communicator back into his pocket. Then he checks his wristwatch. "Let's leave this for tomorrow, Helga. It's late and I was down there all day and —"

"Stay with me tonight."

Some fifteen minutes later, in bed, Boris Leontiyevich kisses his Helga as he throws away her black lacy panties, imported from the decadent West, the last obstacle to her complete nudity. She responds with full passion, her fingers in his luxuriant grizzled hair. She, too, wants to expel the tension and pressure of the previous days, dedicated to incessant preparations for the jump. The passion between them is still as sweet and fierce as the first time. Their each and every embrace is an exciting shudder, brave journey, sweet exploration of unknown landscapes of body and soul. If he wasn't dedicated to the Marxist teachings, Boris Leontiyevich would certainly thank God that, even after twenty years, no boredom crept into his relationship with Helga.

As he presses Helga to him, body to body, Boris Leontiyevich feels the warm current in his temples, beneath the transmitters. Still raining kisses upon Helga's beautiful face, which is enriched by maturity, he caresses her left breast with his right hand. Then he throws himself impatiently, like a hungry nurseling, at her already-erect nipples, kissing and licking them, skillfully sending through Helga's nerves all those beautifully enflaming shudders that stir the already-burning lust. His other palm follows her back down to her behind, possessively grabbing the pliant flesh. Driven by some completely unfounded but primeval fear, he wants to prevent her from escaping him, eluding him, wiggling out from beneath him. Helga moans quietly, her hair spilled on her pillow, and then, enticed by his lips on her breasts and fingers that found their way to the very core of her being, she readily and willingly spreads her legs. She opens herself with unspoken plea and with joyous sigh she accepts his manhood, swollen almost to the point of bursting, into her.

The Professor penetrates Helga, while the currents through the two lovers' temples grow more intense with every passing moment. It is no longer some undefined tickling! The accumulated all-cosmic energy, permeating the entire Space and all the living creatures in it, stirs through the sexual act into a tempest of pleasure that takes control of all the senses, all the nerves, the entire consciousness. Both Helga and Boris Leontiyevich feel that approaching storm, feel the energy levels unstoppably growing with every new kiss, every touch, thrust, sigh, moan. Sweet current tingles through their interwoven bodies and burns in their temples, focused in points under the transmitters, determined with mathematical precision. As the energy grows, the force field they are both immersed in synchronises their passion into one intense bang, one magnificent orgasmic Tunguska explosion that melts their separate "I" and joins them, at least in those spastic moments of orgasm, into an unbreakable alloy that means "us"—"us" the Cosmos, "us" all the beings in it, "us" one and unique and inseparable, firmly woven into the fabric of the Universe.

Boris Leontiyevich empties himself into Helga and she happily accepts his semen, every drop of it. She draws him in and doesn't let go, her legs wrapped tightly around him, convulsed in the fury of their orgasm as the accumulated orgone energy discharges from their bodies and surges in a blinding flash through the burning transmitters into the ever-hungry ship's batteries. And as he comes inside Helga, the entire Space unfolds before Boris Leontiyevich, all that luxurious tapestry, all that complicated mathematical deduction written out on a blackboard. All that Cosmos, one unique and inseparable "us," shows before his shut eyes and remains burnt into his consciousness, like a flash of an atomic explosion. As his sweaty forehead falls on Helga's bosom and his fierce pulse slows down, he feels some undefined fear before that incomprehensible infinity, its beginning and end lost in eons that were and that are yet to be: fear that he's unable to find neither reason nor cause for. Only Helga's fingers caressing his hair offer him any comfort before that horrible eternity. In Helga's tender embrace, he again becomes aware of himself and his "I." In her arms, he stops being just an integral part of some ill-defined "us" that he strives for and fears at the same time.

The way he was immediately aware of the revolutionary nature of Helga Fink's research, Boris Leontiyevich was also aware of its delicate character. Showing her notes to Colonel General Makhnev and his Commission at that moment meant a certain one-way ticket to Siberia. Fortunately, Makhnev and Beria were busy with uranium and heavy water from the Kaiser Wilhelm Institute, which gave the Colonel enough maneuvering space to smuggle Helga through the chaos from Berlin to Moscow. He found her a nurse uniform and put a beret on her head, thus turning her into his *pokhodno-polevaya zhena* — his campaign wife — which kept *frontoviki* at bay. By summer 1945, using his pre-war ties at the University and wartime ones in the NKVD, Colonel Boris Leontiyevich had Helga safe under guard in a sub-Moscow *dacha,* far from prying eyes.

Being constantly under Boris Leontiyevich's attention, it took Helga Fink approximately six months to perfect her battery and transmitter. It was all preceded by seven years of research, started by her first masturbatory orgasms at the age of fourteen. They were continued by her defloration in summer 1943: a student of physics in the trembling embrace of a young soldier, hidden in a dark corner of some cellar in which they were caught during an air raid. The serious work continued until the very end of Hitler's regime and finally culminated in a new, smaller transmitter, battery ready for mass production and meters gauged for the new, hitherto-unknown form of energy.

Of course, Helga continued her experiments. The guards and staff surrounding her proved more than willing, as Boris

Leontiyevich discovered on more than one occasion, when arriving suddenly in the *dacha*. He quickly got used to finding naked bodies in a large bed. Girls and boys, sweaty and panting, blissful expressions on their faces and transmitter tapes around their heads, while Helga—just as naked, sweaty and panting somewhat less—stood above the meters, carefully recording the levels reached. And then, with some undefined piercing in his heart, Boris Leontiyevich would listen to her excited explications, ideas, suggestions.

Boris Leontiyevich will never forget the first public demonstration. It was early 1946, Moscow covered by snow, evening. Helga Fink standing before the equipment on the table, her calm voice echoing over the almost-empty auditorium in a huge lecture hall, which had been carefully locked. A young NKVD lieutenant stood behind her, one of the test rabbits showing the best results. In the first row of the auditorium, five carefully selected academicians and Boris Leontiyevich. Next to the table, a made hospital bed.

First, like some magician, Helga invited the esteemed academicians to convince themselves that the equipment in front of them contained no sources of electrical or any other energy. When the academicians, murmuring, returned to their seats, she took one transmitter band and put it around the lieutenant's head. Then, all in complete silence, she put another band around her head. Then she took a deep breath and started unbuttoning her blouse.

A complete hush settled among the grey academicians' heads. At first, the lieutenant was obviously embarrassed, but when Helga appeared before him in just her underwear, the embarrassment expectedly vanished. And when she discarded her underwear, too, and laid into bed, he didn't care anymore if he was being watched by the entire *Stavka* together with *Verkhovny*—the Supreme Commander—himself. Only Boris Leontiyevich, who knew well enough what was to follow, noticed light tremors of the meter needles.

When the young lieutenant joined Helga Fink and started kissing her and kneading her breasts, all the five wise heads, their cheeks red, turned towards Boris Leontiyevich. And when the young fellow penetrated her, as if following some unspoken order of hers, Boris Leontiyevich was glad that looks don't kill after all.

"Comrade Boris Leontiyevich," one of the academicians hissed through his teeth, "if this is some provocation of yours..."

The esteemed academician was stopped by a single glance at the meters, whose needles were already reaching one-third of the scale. And as the two lovers on the creaky bed — put vulgarly — fucked themselves silly, all the eyes were glued at the meters. And when Helga Fink and the lieutenant came, amazingly synchronically, intensely and passionately, the flash of orgone energy poured across the lecture hall. The needles jumped to the end of the scale. The excitement of the five academicians went completely off the scale. Boris Leontiyevich couldn't cut in a word under a torrent of questions.

Helga saved him, getting up, all sweaty after exertion. She put a dressing gown on, stood next to her equipment and coughed. All stares pointed at her. She just smiled.

"Esteemed gentle — I mean, comrades academicians! Before the experiment, you were able to convince yourselves that my equipment does not contain any source of energy. You also had an opportunity to convince yourselves that my assistant and I did not turn the dynamo for the past ten minutes or so. Therefore, I would be happy to hear any explanation that would refute my theoretical postulations, at the same time explaining... *this*." And at that point, the girl turned a switch on and the energy poured from the battery into ten bulbs arranged on the table.

Light of new age, Boris Leontiyevich thought with some unexplainable pain in his heart, as he watched still-blushing Helga in the gown.

And after the enraptured academicians, congratulating even the lieutenant, had left, and when Helga, the lieutenant, and the equipment were safely dispatched in a black limo back to the *dacha*, Boris Leontiyevich did something that wasn't his habit.

He went into some remote inn and got thoroughly drunk.

"We never spoke of marriage."

Helga reclines next to Boris Leontiyevich, her head resting on his broad, masculine, hairy chest. The clock on her bedside cabinet ticks the small hours away.

"I'm not sure it would have worked," he replies.

Helga rises, her head merely a silhouette in the dimmed exigency lighting. "You mean, because of my experiments?"

"Come on, admit it, what husband would tolerate all those officers and college girls and your tests of *enkami* at full run?"

"You're jealous!"

"Not anymore."

"Not anymore?"

"I was. In the beginning. Then I accepted to be one of the many. Which wasn't easy, Helga." Boris Leontiyevich hugs Helga to himself and she lays her head back on his chest, her fingers ruffling his hairs. "Anyway, now it's pointless to waste words on that."

"It's not just lust, you know, that drives me to the *enkami*."

"I know. I feel it, too. That space, that infinite multitude opening for a moment—"

"And then disappearing, as the orgasm discharges and fades. And you need more and more, like some morphine addict."

"Are you sure you know what we're doing, Helga? What we are playing with?"

Helga stands up and turns the light on. As he watches her putting her gown on, Boris Leontiyevich knows it's too late now. Whatever waited for them at the other end of orgone force lines, whichever infinity is before them, they have already plunged into it and there's no way back.

It is well known that even the mightiest of oaks sprouts from a humble acorn. In the case of thought and work of Dr. Helga Fink, the acorn was the banned works of Sigmund Freud and Wilhelm Reich, which she read secretly in pre-war Germany, as she tried to find a theoretical explanation for her just-awakened sexuality. No one can deny the uncontroversial role of these two geniuses of the modern age. But — as was demonstrated by the materials smuggled into Moscow by the skillful Soviet intelligence agents, right under the noses of the FBI — Helga Fink far surpassed her models. While Wilhelm Reich remained partially vague, loose, and subject to interpretations, Helga's batteries charged regularly, with ever-increasing amounts of energy following every new improvement.

After the first favorable reviews of her work, Helga Fink was allowed to continue her studies, interrupted by the course of war. In January 1950, this young woman earned her doctoral degree, defending before the full, but carefully sieved, auditorium her very controversial thesis: *The all-cosmic (orgone) energy, Einstein's special theory of relativity, and issues of superluminal velocities.* Boris Leontiyevich, very much deserving credit for the results of the freshly graduated Doctor, was rewarded with a professorship.

Professor Boris Leontiyevich satisfied his lust for Helga for the first time, with somewhat more vodka in him, on a December night in 1948. He simply grabbed her after supper, lifted her bodily, brought her into her room, threw her into her bed, took off her clothes and took her. Thus the two of them finally became lovers, releasing the accumulated orgone energy that threatened, so fettered, to poison their otherwise fertile scientific and comradely relation with neuroses and psychoses.

The work of the young Doctor, under a careful management

of Professor Bogolyubov, was by then going in two directions. One was the construction of an orgone power plant. Deprived of all the technical complexities of the usual power plants, within six months it was contributing its first kilowatt-hours of electricity to the building of the Land of the Soviets. The other direction, possibly sprouting from the seed of some vague Reich's speculations, was the design and construction of an orgone spaceship.

"Are you scared?"

Boris Leontiyevich tears a piece of bread off and spreads some plum jam on with enjoyment. The gathering of orgone energy is a strenuous process, after which a body requires a good refreshment.

"Of what?" Helga takes a sip of milk from a glass.

"Of the jump. It is four light years, after all. Who knows what we'll find there."

Helga pauses thoughtfully. "Maybe I'd be afraid ten or fifteen years ago. On the other hand, if we survived the war, you and me... what worse than the war can greet us up there?"

Boris Leontiyevich does not reply, merely nodding. *Incredible,* he thinks, *the way this woman is almost always right.* And how he still, even after knowing her for twenty years, finds himself surprised by this simple fact of life.

"We did our part down there, Boris, you know that well. We left a trail to follow."

"Aren't you sorry because of that? I am."

"It's a destiny of pioneers. Like Yermak Timofeyevich and his Cossacks. We went into the unexplored. We erected a camp. And another one after ten days' ride, and another one, and another, all the way to Kamchatka. And then governors came after us, and soldiers and fur-trappers and loggers and convicts and prospectors... knout and saber were replaced by axe, rifle, and scribe's quill. We became unnecessary. These are no more Stalin's days to be eaten by Siberia, but... and

here, new taigas open before us here, we can spur on our horses and go..."

"Go where?"

"Wherever we want! There's no end, no Kamchatka and Pacific, to be stopped by its shores."

Boris Leontiyevich reaches for a bottle of milk and Helga passes it to him. "You know when I'd be afraid, Boris?"

"Tell me."

"When I would not be completely certain of success."

Professor Boris Leontiyevich Bogolyubov will never forget that gloomy Kremlin afternoon in autumn 1950, either. The large massive table, all eyes pointed at the young Professor. "The Beard" was there, Zel'dovich and Khariton next to him. After the great success in the previous year, that melted the initial advantage of the imperialist warmongers, the atomic program had the highest priority. Kurchatov and his men were certainly asked for their opinion. The Professor felt even greater unease before comrades marshals. No one else but Vasilevsky himself was present, and when the Professor shook hands with Zhigarev and Batitsky before the meeting begun, he knew that his project—should it be approved—would fall under the jurisdiction of the Air Force.

Facing their stern stares, Professor Bogolyubov submitted plans and calculations. He drank some water. He concluded his exposé after more than two hours. Challenges, questions, doubts followed. All were removed by Professor Bogolyubov with scientifically impeccable arguments and the enthusiasm of a man deeply convinced of what he proposes. More than once did he curse inwardly that they didn't invite Helga, but, fortunately, whatever she knew, he knew, too.

Comrade Stalin stood aside, cigarette in his hand, silent. A careless observer would have gotten an impression that he stared absent-mindedly through the window, as the boring rain drizzled outside, but the Professor knew well enough that he didn't miss a word. Also, Beria himself made it clear to him that Stalin was not pleased. Although he couldn't deny the results of Dr. Fink — with the second power plant already nearing completion — the possible subversiveness of the very nature of the orgone energy began annoying the Boss thoroughly. And Professor Bogolyubov doubted sincerely that Helga and he would have liked the vast Siberian expanses.

Heavy silence descended upon everyone in Stalin's office. Professor Bogolyubov had defended the project; nobody had had any questions. Everybody looked before him; no one dared to say a single word.

"You are aware of the expenses, Boris Leontiyevich?"

Freezing Siberian chill licked down the Professor's spine. Stalin turned to face him, drawing a puff. His piercing stare was fixed on the Professor, tight lips under the dense moustache bode nothing good.

"I am, Comrade Stalin."

"You are also aware that all this is unproven?" Stalin drew another puff.

The Professor understood him: It was a hard decision, a fateful one. The times were hard, and the ship was to be big; the orgone energy was work-intensive, and a mass of people had to be protected from harmful influences of space expanses. These were no more petty rockets like Heinlein and von Braun toyed with.

"You are familiar with the results of the FB-series, Comrade Stalin," Boris Leontiyevich said.

Boris Leontiyevich swallowed hard. FB-series were five remotely operated devices containing charged batteries and animals. All five devices could have been considered successful, except that the FB-1, launched on June 8, 1947, disappeared without a trace together with five test monkeys. Helga Fink and Boris Leontiyevich had reasons to believe that it blew apart somewhere above the Southwestern United States, and it was merely a matter of luck that Beria (who was by then well-informed about what was being done) didn't understand and collate the sensationalistic headlines in imperialist newspapers. The remaining four FBs repeatedly jumped precisely to the planned spots, always military test sites within the Soviet Union. The test animals in them remained completely unharmed.

"I'm aware that this is a great leap, from several monkeys to several thousand humans, but..." Boris Leontiyevich began.

"Nevertheless, you are so convinced of the correctness of your ideas to insist on this project?"

The Professor was not quite uninitiated in the ways Stalin ran his conferences. He knew well enough that the Boss would try everything to waver him.

"I am convinced, Comrade Stalin." The Professor felt it was the right moment to play his trump card. "So much convinced that I wanted to ask you to allow us to name the first Soviet spaceship after you."

Stalin nodded pensively and drew another puff. The corner of his mouth lifted beneath the moustache into a barely noticeable smile and Boris Leontiyevich knew that he had hit dead on target. And then Stalin spoke, more to the others than to Professor Bogolyubov.

"What are we to do, comrades?" Nobody dared to answer Stalin's question, which was rhetorical anyway. "Comrade Boris Leontiyevich is aware of the times we live in. He also knows how much this will cost our long-suffering country. Despite all this, he is absolutely certain of his project — so much so that he assures us it will give us a decisive advantage over imperialists. What else can we do, then, but to set to work?"

Thus the Soviet space program began.

Carefully and quietly, so as not to wake sleeping Helga, Professor Boris Leontiyevich closes the heavy doors behind him and turns on the light on her work desk. He sits in the armchair, pushes some of Helga's notes from the previous day aside, and unfolds the OSS-test charts of Citizen K.

It is impossible, the experienced Professor muses with stubbornness of an old dog fox, *that the man reacts to nothing.*

Helga must have missed something. Despite her courage and faith in success, she, too, is torn apart with preparations for the great jump into unknown.

The work on the ship—renamed *Krasnaya Zvezda* after Stalin's death, in the process initiated by Comrade Nikita Sergeyevich's secret report on the 20th Congress—lasted for ten years. A whole city of experts, engineers, and technicians sprouted out of nothing at the secret locality in Kazakhstan. They were led, after his first successes with rockets, by Sergey Pavlovich Korolyov. His job was to build a huge ship able to hold three thousand people. Dr. Fink and Professor Bogolyubov were in charge of the orgone energy, gathered in the orgasmic discharges, that was to drive the massive hull in superluminal jumps through the expanses of Space.

Korolyov was by no means happy to have been transferred to the project. Professor Bogolyubov remembers the first conference, when Dr. Fink had spread the concept drafts of the *Krasnaya Zvezda* before Korolyov. Sergey Pavlovich cast only a superficial glance at the draft and then remarked caustically: "You are aware, of course, that a state of weightlessness is present up there?" expecting to throw Helga completely off balance. Because, naturally, her drafts predicted no state of weightlessness.

Without a single word, Dr. Fink opened her briefcase and took some fifty pages of mathematical proofs out of it. "What is that?" Sergey Pavlovich asked.

"The mathematical proof of connection between the orgone energy and gravitational force. And these are," she said, pulling out a further hundred or so bound pages, "the experimental results."

At that point, Sergey Pavlovich merely looked at Helga

and then burst into laughter. After that, the *Krasnaya Zvezda* became his child, too.

While the ship was being built in top secrecy, the space race was gaining steam. Heinlein and von Braun used rockets with mixed results to launch satellites into orbit, only trying to follow the tempo dictated by the Soviet science with Sputnik on October 4, 1957. Sending man was barely being planned.

Even today, Professor Bogolyubov cannot comprehend the blindness exhibited by the Americans. The destroyed FB-1, whose parts they even presented to the public, at best left them confused. Even if they noticed the doctoral thesis of Helga Fink, they obviously ridiculed it as just another manifestation of Lysenkoism. Wilhelm Reich himself, the man who could certainly explain them what it was all about, had died in prison as a convicted quack, while his notes and orgone boxes had been destroyed.

Therefore, their shock was beyond imagination. On that fateful day, April 12, 1961, the *Krasnaya Zvezda,* as big as an ocean-going passenger steamship, rose from the steppe, carried by the flash of the released orgone energy. A moment later, she disappeared in a detonation comparable to a tactical nuclear explosion (all this being predicted and calculated in great detail by Helga) and materialized in the geostationary orbit around the Earth. Then, excited Yuri's voice was heard on the speakers, through the static: "Everything is perfect, everything normal... I wish to report that the jump succeeded completely..."

Valentina also added something, but their words were drowned in joyous cries of thousands of scientists, engineers, technicians, and plain toilers that accompanied the success of the first space-jump in the history of Mankind. A decade of hardships, self-sacrifices, and trepidations was crowned by laurel wreath of victory over the vast expanses of Space. A cheerful mass grabbed Helga Fink and tossed her into air, once, twice, three times, and then they placed her on the control console. Someone thrust a microphone into her hand and a hush settled over the control room.

And Dr. Fink just stood before them all, not finding words, as tears rolled down her cheeks from beneath her glasses. She wiped them with her palm, dazed, then smiled and just uttered one great and sincere "Thank you," her gaze stopping for a moment on Boris Leontiyevich — colonel, lover, professor. And he just nodded. Thundering applause broke in the room and then everybody returned to their posts. The flight was not over yet.

Five minutes later, the *Krasnaya Zvezda,* following the mission plan, jumped to the Moon. A small probe was dropped from the great ship, which brought to the surface of the Earth's satellite a pentagonal plaque with relief coat-of-arms of the Soviet Union, abbreviation CCCP and the date of the historical event. After two-hour respite, to allow the orgonauts to rest, the huge vessel jumped back to Earth and landed safely on the very same spot it took off from. Man's first flight to another celestial body was complete.

Comrades Khrushchev and Brezhnev phoned to Kazakhstan to congratulate personally. Three days later, TASS reported to the rest of the world of this endeavor, still not revealing all the details. The first images from the flight were carefully released to the public, as orgone research was previously little-known. The orgonaut crew was received in Moscow as heroes. Boris Leontiyevich smiles sourly every time he remembers all the awarded decorations.

Because, from this distance, we may and must, even whisperingly, admit to ourselves that Mother Russia can be a stepmother to some of her children. Yes, Dr. Fink was awarded the Lomonosov Gold Medal, and Khrushchev himself decorated her with the Golden Star of the Hero of the Socialist Labour. But all those knowing her helplessly looked with chill around their hearts as the *aparat* mercilessly pushed her aside and suppressed her merits. She was advised discreetly not to appear in public. Her movement was restrained for reasons of her own safety, and her work was placed under additional control. She just shrugged her shoulders in resignation upon finding a microphone in her bedroom. Even today, Boris Leontiyevich admires the way she suffered through all this without a word, well aware that any resistance would jeopardize her place in the program. They never spoke about this; at that time, the Professor himself couldn't have answered if it was about her wrong origins or the decadent enthusiasm, not quite appropriate to the morality of a Soviet woman, with which she had discovered new secrets of the orgone energy.

In the meantime, the Soviet space program marched on. The next flight of the *Krasnaya Zvezda* to the Moon included a thorough photographing, probing and, finally, landing. The red flag rose above the bare grey landscape, symbolising another victory of the Soviet man over the challenges placed before him. The second orgone ship built, *Konstantin Eduardovich Tsiolkovsky*, made a series of journeys exploring Mars and Venus. Three more ships toured the entire solar system and the next logical step was to cast on further away, to the nearest neighboring star. Project Alpha Centauri was initiated.

And when a chief of the Department of Energy aboard the ship *Lomonosov*, the biggest of them all, was sought, Dr. Fink applied, feeling correctly that her role on the planet Earth had come to an end. And she was accepted, almost with relief.

When Professor Bogolyubov heard of that, he didn't hesitate for a moment—as befits the old communist, the great scientist, and the veteran of the Great Patriotic War—but applied immediately for a post of the chief manager of the energy chambers on the *Lomonosov*. To someone who wasn't present, it is barely possible to imagine the loud and sincere rapture and joy of thousands of orgonauts, hand-picked among all the freedom-loving peoples of the World, upon hearing who will personally manage and control the most critical segment of the Alpha Centauri expedition.

*   *   *

The smell of the morning white coffee awakens Helga Fink from her sleep. She stretches herself, while Boris Leontiyevich helps her with her pillow, and then places a tray with coffee, bakery, butter and marmalade—Helga's favorite breakfast—before her.

"You're dressed already?" Helga says as she spreads butter on her bakery.

"I'm afraid I'm up since five."

"Oh god! What did you..."

"I couldn't sleep, so I took another look at that OSS test from last night." Helga doesn't miss a prideful glitter in Professor Bogolyubov's eyes: *Where would you be without me?* as if he's asking jokingly.

"And?" Dr. Fink pretends not to notice his non-spoken teasing.

Boris Leontiyevich takes the test out, folded as to show the critical part. Helga takes her glasses from the nightstand. The Professor had marked in red pencil the brief and barely noticeable oscillations indicating that the Citizen K.'s heart did skip a beat after all, to put it that way. Ognev and, later, Helga had missed it. "1-43, what's that?"

The whole OSS-test chart has corresponding movie codes written on the upper margin, in order in which the films are being screened to the subject while his reactions are measured.

"1-43..." Helga tries to recall what the code stands for as she sips some coffee over the bakery. "1-43... I think it's *Kostya the Shepherd.* Yes, that's right, *Kostya the Shepherd.* That's what we call it. Unofficially, of course."

"Let me guess, shepherds and shepherdesses on a glade?" Boris Leontiyevich still recalls *Vesyolye rebyata*—"Jolly Fellows"—a famous pre-war musical about a carefree *kolkhoz* shepherd Kostya who became the head of a jazz band. He also remembers the merry company of University friends he went to see it with. The days when he was still young and in some way innocent, the days before the war, blood, mud, and death. The days before Helga.

Helga shrugs as Professor smiles. Obviously, he already managed to see the film. He diagnosed the problem and is now merely waiting for Helga to reach the same conclusion.

"But there's nothing in there that we didn't show him earlier! You said it yourself, shepherds and shepherdesses among..."

And then Helga stops, her mouth agape, her eyes wide open with astonishment. "No, it cannot be!"

"Oh yes, it can," Professor Bogolyubov replies with a jester's spark in his eyes.

Shimmering light from a small projection screen shines upon Citizen K.'s sweaty face. In the room, only the buzzing of the projector and accelerating deep breathing are heard as his masturbation nears climax. The movements of his right hand are faster and faster, jerkier, the transmitters on his temples glow and then, in a flash that fills the entire room in whiteness, Citizen K. finally reaches a liberating orgasm, after being manacled for so long. Orgasmic screams break through the room as his orgone energy—accumulated for so long—is released in a magnificent discharge, contributing in the true Stakhanovite manner to the general condition of the ship's batteries.

And in the movie—one of the educational aids from veterinary faculty that somehow got misplaced in the film archive of the Department of Energy—a buck, after he did his part, dismounts a snowy white goat of seductively small horns and frolicsome beard. With an expression of unspeakable bliss in her eyes, the goat lowers her playful tail and returns to browsing the aromatic Mediterranean shrubs.

At the same time, *Lomonosov*—her brave crew guided by the immortal thought of comrade Lenin, commanded by General Kozhedub and tended by caring hands of Dr. Fink and

Professor Bogolyubov — releases the orgone energy, gathered and accumulated in body sweat of thousands of toilers in *enkami*. In an orgasmic flash, the huge ship, precisely following Helga Fink's calculations, bends the silent fabric of the Cosmos, easily overcoming hitherto insurmountable distance in the unstoppable charge of the entire progressive Mankind to the stars.

Night in Berlin

by
Milena Benini

Earth. Germany. Berlin. The cusp of World War II. It's all familiar to us, to any student of twentieth-century history, but this isn't the same Berlin that we know. In this Berlin, were-creatures walk the streets, and like other people during the Nazi regime, their kind is persecuted and controlled. Hunters are paid to kill some of them. But this were-hunter has a deeper purpose when she collars this werewolf, although one can hardly begin to imagine what that purpose is.

Horror
Werewolf
Alternate reality
Cunnilingus
Heterosexuality
Forced sex

*I*f you let me fuck you, I will let you go."

Christian swallowed a laugh. He had been unconscious—he knew that much due to the still-present dizziness and a trace of pain at the back of his skull—and was now either hallucinating or else having trouble hearing.

He was also tied, and by someone who knew how to subdue werewolves: thin gold threads were woven into the ropes wrapped around his wrists and ankles. Very few people knew about the gold. Most used silver, and were then unpleasantly surprised when werewolves captured with silver chains tore the links with the ease of a pup tearing a flowerchain.

But, whoever his capturers were, they did not go out of their way to make him uncomfortable. He was lying on clean linen sheets, his head on a soft pillow. That was good, because it meant he hadn't been captured by government agents. He doubted very much the Geheimpolizei would bother putting a pillow under his head.

Letting out a slow, controlled breath, he kept his eyes closed, trying to gather as much information about his surroundings as he could before admitting he was awake. He heard another creature's breathing—only one, it seemed, but he couldn't be sure his hearing was working right. Better to rely on his other senses.

The faint smell of linden trees meant he probably hadn't been moved too far. Good. Another point in his favor. Something was pressing against his thighs—something soft again, and warm, like a woman's spread legs.

He had to concentrate to prevent an ironic smile from appearing on his lips, and slowly inhaled again. A perfume of some sort, very slight but musky, with hints of sandalwood and jasmine. It seemed vaguely familiar, but he couldn't quite place it. For some reason, his mind wanted to flash him an image of firm, full breasts peeking from a man's shirt with three topmost buttons undone. And a pendant between them—a key? An ankh, perhaps?

Then it came back to him. The woman from the café.

*   *   *

I spotted the were from across the café. Not due to his appearance: this one was of slim build, with fashionably long dark hair that fell over his forehead and hid his eyes. Although his dark coat hid a dancer's wiry muscles, he was neither exceptionally tall nor exceptionally strong for a human. He could have been anyone: change is not choosy.

And, contrary to popular belief, I didn't recognize him by his scent, either. At this distance, all I could catch was a whole lot of people-smells, some cabbage from the menu, and, if I concentrated really hard, a whiff of cologne from my prey. If we were alone in the room, I would only have had a clearer impression of the cologne. Weres smell like their current bodies do. Unless they'd been rolling in wet earth only seconds earlier, that means they're no different from humans.

No, I spotted him the way I always spot them. By his movements. Most animal communication relies heavily on body language: postures, twitches, head movements. Do it long enough and it becomes automatic, transferring to the human body. This one was listening to one of his companions, and cocked his head automatically to one side, exactly the way a dog does when listening. Or a wolf.

The girl he was listening to was young and pretty, in that emaciated, dyed-and-bobbed-hair way that Berlin's hottest young things try to achieve. She was wearing a black evening dress that rested so low on her bust it seemed a sharp movement may expose her nipples—hardly anything to be called breasts there, in line with the fashion. And around her neck, among the numerous black and purple beads, there was a choker with a large medallion. From my vantage point at the back of the café, I could see that the medallion was oval and had a picture on it. Every now and then, while talking, she would touch it and toy with it. Whenever she did it, the were frowned. Only for a moment, and I was sure the girl never noticed it, but I did.

At one point, the girl put her hand on the were's chest, in that "you're so naughty" gesture men are supposed to find sexy, and reached towards his tie as if to loosen it. He smiled, caught her hand, and gently removed it, looking over her shoulder to avoid eye contact.

Our gazes met.

I forced myself to smile at him, trying to convey the impression of waiting for someone. Luckily, just at that moment, my dinner arrived, and I had an excuse to look away.

* * *

Christian took another slow breath, to make sure. Yes, it was her; if he concentrated, he could still sense the faint traces of cabbage, beans, and potatoes she'd had for dinner. The woman in traveler's clothes. He remembered her dark-red hair, unfashionably long and held back in a thick plait that fell over her shoulder.

That warm pressure over his crotch would be her legs, spread over him in those soft, stretchy trousers. That didn't even make sense, but the image was so persistent he finally opened his eyes.

And met hers, the color of properly aged cognac. She was, indeed, straddling him and staring at him suspiciously, a silver, threateningly sharp hunting knife in her hand.

"If you let me fuck you, I will let you go," she said again, and this time there was no imagining he had hallucinated the words.

Christian blinked, trying to take in as much as he could before he spoke. They were in a private room somewhere, the kind of room little old ladies rented to bohemians who gathered in Berlin from all over Europe. Faded chintz curtains over the tall window, keeping the night out. Faded flowery paper on the walls, furniture that had been in the family for generations, chipped and frayed with use but cared for, shiny. A single lamp sat in the sconce on the wall, witness to the change from gas to electricity with its curvy, wrought-iron setting. In its light, the woman's hair glistened like old chestnut, the curves of her breasts enhanced by the soft shadows sliding over them. The pendant still hung around her neck, a large silver ankh with an unusually long stem. It seemed almost like a road sign, pointing to all the interesting places below. She seemed to consist entirely of interesting places.

He licked his lips, stretched his spine a little, trying to gauge her reaction when he moved. Her legs merely tightened over his. She must be a good rider.

He could imagine her riding him, those long fingernails leaving red traces on his chest. No. That was just the Moon, playing her games with his instincts. He forced himself to stay calm, cleared his throat. "Would you care to explain?" he said softly.

The woman shook her head. Her rich red plait danced behind her back like a fox's tail. "There's nothing to explain," she said. "We fuck, I let you go. This never happened."

"What is *this*?" he asked. "You're not going to tell me that's how you usually get your partners."

"I didn't say anything about partnership. Just a fuck, clean and simple."

"Fucking is seldom clean, and never simple," he muttered, trying his best seducer's smile. Even if she were insane, she knew how to subdue a werewolf... and she knew he was one.

Together, those two things could spell disaster if he didn't find a way to deal with her.

The woman looked at him without answering his smile. "True," she said at last. The hand with the knife descended to his ribs. No threat there for the time being. It was just to rest her muscles. But she was still alert, still suspicious. He could see it in the way she kept her gaze carefully on his face.

He inhaled her scent again. The sandalwood-and-jasmine smell was just strong enough to be felt, but not so strong as to abuse his senses. She knew how to put on perfume — a skill few women possessed, in his experience.

She was a woman of many skills, it seemed.

*   *   *

My dinner was the house special — cabbage, beans, and potatoes. Not the most refined fare, but the café was not of the most refined, either, and the food was filling and decent. There was a lively black market for meat in Berlin — there was a lively black market for *everything* in Berlin — but I didn't feel like looking it up. And, apparently, neither did my prey, at least not in company.

He'd had dinner, earlier, with the skinny girl and four or five other people. Theirs was a little fancier than mine — fresh grilled vegetables, mushroom stew — but not illegal. They ordered champagne afterwards, and were now talking while waiting for the show to start. I knew I would have to wait him out. I didn't want to create a scene, despite the fact that even his being a were and out so late was illegal here. The Berlin population was still defiant. Or so my employers had told me. Also, the were was probably not a German citizen. So, no public arrest. Just a quiet disappearance.

That suited me just fine.

When the music started, I leaned back in my seat and relaxed, occasionally going so far as to close my eyes and listen.

The were obviously wasn't going anywhere, talking to his dinner companions and occasionally casting a glance in my direction. A plan started to form in my head. When he looked at me for the third time, I smiled warmly. At his fourth look, he found me absent-mindedly fondling the long stem of my wineglass with the tips of my fingers. At his fifth, during the acrobats' act, I was sucking on my cigarette holder, raptly watching the mediocre performance. Tacky, but it worked.

When the dancing music started, he got up and walked over.

"Would you care to dance?" he asked, his eyes shadowed by the long dark hair falling over his forehead. His voice was raspy, and low, making the invitation a shared secret between the two of us. I looked up at him and smiled.

"I would love to," I said.

*   *   *

So, someone who can dance and deal with werewolves, but... Christian had to stop. But what? Is slightly unhinged? Likes kinky sex? He had no idea, and he had to find out.

"Is there a reason for this?" he asked, pulling slightly at the ropes on his wrists. There was some give, but not much. She was no fool.

She nodded. It seemed as if there were words swarming inside her, ready to come out, but she refused to allow them. "I don't trust you," was all she said at the end.

Christian smiled. "Fair enough." He looked her over, slowly, making it obvious and deliberate. If she was just after a thrill, that would elicit some reaction.

His body certainly reacted. As his gaze slid over her breasts and hips, he could feel his prick harden. He wriggled a little, letting her feel it, too. The warmth between her legs was inviting. "Although you've done a good enough job attracting me without the ropes."

Her smile was not excited. "I noticed," she said simply. "That's why we should be able to come to an agreement."

"The agreement being?"

She sighed. "You let me fuck you, I let you go."

Christian closed his eyes, this time not even trying to stop the bubble of laughter on his lips.

"What's funny?" she asked.

Christian raised his head to look at her more closely. This was the first time she'd shown any interest in his reactions, he realized. Up until now, she'd been treating him like a dog... or a captured wolf. Not fearing him—no, she knew he was helpless in the gold-threaded ropes, and she was confident she could deal with him in that state—but also not caring for him. She may have been asking for sex, but she wasn't interested in *him*.

The woman was very, very strange. The fact intrigued him, on some level. At the same time, it worried him. He could probably find a way around a wolf-humper, could try to fight a secret-police agent. But this—he didn't know what to do with it.

He didn't like that.

And his time was running out. Suddenly, he became painfully aware of the fact that his left wrist no longer had a watch on. He had no idea how long he'd been out.

"What's the time?"

The woman frowned. "What has that got to do with anything?"

Christian bit his lip. He didn't want her upset, and he certainly did not intend to share his worry. "No reason. Just asking."

"And you laughed just now for no reason, too, right?"

"No. I laughed because at least one of us must be crazy." This was risky—if she really *was* crazy, she might just decide to cut him to pieces for insulting her—but he had to speed things up. Anna would be waiting for him with the latest delivery.

Surprisingly, she laughed as well. It wasn't a happy laugh. She was far too tense for happiness, he could see that in the tightness of her shoulders, feel it in the taut muscles straddling him — but it was healthy. That was a start.

*   *   *

Dancing with him was like floating on air. No wonder; it was his profession. He was in Berlin with a dancing troupe, performing for a month in *Monbijou*. The month was nearing its end, which was why my employers wanted the action taken now. Or at least that was what they had told me, and I had no interest in digging any further. This last job — if I did it right — could set me up with everything I needed, including the very generous payment, half of which was already on my account. Then I could leave Germany forever and settle somewhere safe and quiet. Maybe Austria. Maybe even go back home.

But those thoughts were for later. At the moment, I had to concentrate on getting the were. It was surprisingly easy to cling to him while the music played, surprisingly easy to be short of breath and shivery when it ended. His hands had not stopped at my waist during the dance. Even through the trousers, I had felt the warmth of his long fingers on the upper part of my buttocks. I could imagine those fingers squeezing, kneading, slipping between my legs with the same sensual skill. I leaned against him, looking up from under my lashes. He was watching my lips, his dark brown eyes moist and deep.

I was hoping he would suggest a drink, so I could offer my room as a place away from the noisy crowd. Maybe I wouldn't have to work too hard at the whole thing.

But then my luck flipped. The skinny girl caught the were's arm as soon as the first tones of the next song conquered the noisy air of the café and dragged him back to the dance floor. He cast a glance in my direction over his shoulder, and I gave him my loveliest smile, at the same time shifting my back a bit to the left and lifting my behind as best I could on two feet. With wolves, that's the signal that the female is ready and willing to mate. I had no tail to dramatically throw in the air, but I shook my head and got a similar effect with my plait. It wasn't much, but it was a start. I could see his pupils dilate in the short moment before he turned away again.

The bad news was, I hadn't done it consciously.

*   *   *

"True," she said unexpectedly. "At least one of us probably is crazy." She looked at Christian with something he couldn't identify in her eyes. It may have been concern, but it may also have been irony. "Does that bother you?"

He laughed again, trying to keep the atmosphere light. "That a woman knocked me unconscious and tied me to her bed so she could offer me freedom in exchange for sex? Or that the same woman is holding a big knife in her hand while doing it?"

"That the woman may be crazy."

He swallowed. The whole conversation felt like walking on spring ice. He could almost hear the creaking. He had no choice but to keep going, though. To take another step. "There is method in your madness," he said. "That much is obvious."

"But if…" For the first time, he saw real insecurity on her face. "Do you worry that I might kill you?"

Creak. Time for honesty. "A little bit."

She shook her head and put the knife down on the nightstand by the bed. As she leaned, her legs pressed tighter against him. Her thighs were supple and hot and strong. He could imagine the soft sliding of her skin against his, with no trousers between them. Those firm legs wrapping around him, small heels digging into his buttocks. He bit his lip. No time for that.

"I'm not going to kill you," she announced calmly. "Not

now."

He didn't like that last bit, but decided to ignore it for the time being. Anything that got her to relax her hold on him had to be good. That was the direction he needed.

"Well," he said, trying to sound cheerful, "if that's settled, you might consider setting me free, too." He pulled at the ropes around his hands to specify what he meant. "After all," he added in a lower voice, "if you want me to make love to you, I guarantee it will be better with my hands free."

That sad little shake of the head again. The movement looked habitual, resigned, as if she had gone through all the possible arguments for everything a thousand times already and decided this was the only way, even though she didn't like it much. It was the one truly frightening thing about her and, for some reason, it bothered him. It seemed too painful.

In other circumstances, he might have wanted to wipe that pain away.

"I don't want you to make love to me," she said. "I just want to fuck you."

Christian hesitated. She didn't look excited. She was sitting there, practically on his prick, and yet there was no shortness of breath, no dilated pupils, no hard nipples under her shirt. Still, he asked, "Is that why you want me tied down? That's how you like fucking?" He stressed the last word with only a hint of irony.

Suddenly, she got up, stepped off the bed, and walked to the wall opposite the window, away from the lamp. She put both her hands on the wall and took a deep breath, without saying a word.

*　*　*

In other circumstances, I would have waited for the dancing to finish, would have played the mating game properly. But now, I didn't have the time—or the nerve. In the short space of the one dance, my body had responded to his. I wanted him. It didn't matter how many times I reminded myself he was a were; I just couldn't gather the usual revulsion.

On one side, that was good. It meant that realizing my plan would be easier. I had steeled myself previously to just bear it, an unpleasant but necessary step to get what I wanted. Now it seemed at least my body could enjoy it, too.

But that made the second part of the task more difficult, and I didn't want difficulties. All I wanted was a quick in-and-out job, and then running away and getting lost one final time. No more cabarets. No more traveling shows. No more special papers. Just a quiet, normal life.

Liking the were, even on a purely physical level, was not something I could work into my plans. So I refused to like him, and walked out of the café while he was still on the dance floor with the skinny girl. I crossed the street, took up position in the shadow of a doorway, and settled to wait.

*   *   *

Christian waited a few moments in silence. It was strange how the sudden disappearance of her weight over him brought no relief. He wanted her back. At least, his body did. His mind, in the meantime, wanted her face visible so he could try to assess her mental state. Think of a way to get out of here. Even if he'd only been out a few minutes, he was seriously running out of time now. He needed to get her attention, somehow, get her to release him.

He didn't even know her name. The café's dance floor had been too noisy for introductions—for anything except feeling her breasts against his chest, her curvy hips under his palms.

He felt a hot surge of desire. Not good. Even if he had the time, that woman was a bad idea. He took a long, calming breath.

"I'm Christian," he said to her turned back. "What's your

name?"

One of her shoulders twitched. That was all.

He strained to lift his head. She had leaned her forehead against the wall as well. Christian had seen too much misery in the last few months not to recognize it. Comfortable, lived-in misery, the kind that becomes part of the daily life and twists both the body and the mind until they are all but unrecognizable. If he were free, he would have walked over to her and put his hands on her shoulders, good idea or bad, name or no name. As it was, he could only hope she would acknowledge his presence somehow.

She kept quiet. A small whine of frustration escaped between his lips.

"Please," he muttered, not sure what it was he wanted from her. "Please, bunny."

He bit his lip. The word had slipped from his tongue unintentionally. But somehow, it made her chuckle.

"Selena," she said. "But everybody calls me Lena."

She lifted her head and looked at him, all of her posture screaming tension. Christian swallowed.

"Lena," he said softly. He had no more time for games, no more desire for them. "Please, let me go. I have… a very important meeting. I can come back later, if you want me to."

She laughed, the sound bitter and harsh. "Does it look like I'm willing to trust you?"

Christian sighed. "I'll give you my word of honor."

"As if weres have any."

He felt his muscles tense. There was something like hatred in her voice, but it wasn't the kind he was used to hearing. Most were-haters were angry, first and foremost, with a twinge of fear in there somewhere. He could scent no fear on her whatsoever—unusual of itself, since she was locked in a room with a werewolf she did not know and obviously did not trust. But even stranger, her anger, visible on her face and in the contempt in her voice, did not spread to her smell. As if it weren't real. As if she was merely repeating the mantra of hatred, hiding something completely different.

He concentrated for a moment, trying to figure out what it was she was masking with anger, but couldn't reach it.

Perhaps she had hidden the emotion so well that her own body didn't know what it was. It happened, sometimes. He had seen it with some of the cubs he'd smuggled out of the city in the last year. They would close up so completely during the travel that the only scent on them would be milk. Some opened up again when they could see the sky and run once more. Some remained scentless by the time he had to leave them.

It was heart wrenching. Yet it seemed better than the fate in store for them if they were to stay put. And the last group he could get away from the were-camps would be waiting for him soon.

He needed to get out of here quickly. But she wouldn't just let him go, he was fairly certain of that. Maybe, if he told her…

"Lena," he said. "I *must* get out."

She stood next to the wall, holding on to it with one hand. A small shake of her head sent the end of her plait flying over her left hip. It looked almost like a tail twitched to the side. He remembered the feeling of her ass under his fingers. He could imagine how it would feel to grab it with both palms, lift it to pull her closer to him.

No. Concentrate on what's important.

She didn't trust him. Maybe he could change that.

"Where's my jacket?" he asked. He saw her confusion, but also the quick sideways glance she cast towards the tallboy near the window. "Take it, please."

She went over to the tallboy and stood there, holding his black evening jacket in her hand with an expression that clearly said she would rather not obey him.

Despite the drawn curtains, a little bit of moonlight slipped under them, between the wall and the tallboy, and painted her skin an unearthly shade. Her hair glittered like well-polished chestnut. Her eyes stayed out of the moonlight, but caught the lamplight. He felt saliva fill his mouth and he had to swallow, hard.

"In the inner pocket. My pocketbook."

"I already know who you are," she said, her voice cool. Christian shook his head in frustration.

"No," he said. "Take out the photographs."

Suspiciously, slowly, she put her hand inside his pocket, took out the expensive crocodile-skin pocketbook, opened it. Took out the yellowish papers that he needed to walk around Berlin as a were, followed by a few letters, some other papers. He let his head fall back onto the pillow, waiting.

He could hear the rustling of the photographs when she took them out. They were CDV's, so he could transport them easily and leave them with Anna when he took over the last group. It was risky, but he knew how much the pictures meant to the pups' parents. Still, he didn't dare leave the pictures in his trunk. The police had searched it too many times.

"What is it?" she asked finally, in a dry, suspicious voice.

"They're just… pictures of children."

"Not just any children," he answered. He felt too tired to lift his head again and try for eye contact.

"They're werechildren," she said. There was a catch in her voice, an emotion so deep and dark he couldn't even name it.

"Come here," he said. Unexpectedly, she obeyed without hesitation. She sat on the bed, holding the pictures in both hands, pressing them to her chest but carefully, as if she were afraid they would break.

"Who are they?" she asked softly. "Where are they?"

"They're…" Christian hesitated. Would she give him over to the Geheimpolizei? It would be just her word against his, but he knew he was a suspect to them, had been for a while now. They would love an excuse to keep him here. Probably forever.

He turned his head to look directly into her eyes. She was waiting, all tension and fear now, rigid like a statue. He knew that look. Knew that position.

A strange suspicion started forming in his mind. And pushed him to whisper, "They're *German* werechildren. Wolves, mostly, some bears. The Geheimpolizei is taking pups away from their families. They put them in camps and train them to become killers. They're building an army that way. Another war is brewing... and this time, Germany doesn't intend to lose it."

The tension left her as if pushed aside by a decisive hand. She shook her head and snorted. "I don't believe you. German government *hates* weres."

"Exactly. How else could they take the children, and keep them in rooms with lights on until their cycles go all haywire and they turn every other day?"

The shaking of her head grew stronger. "No. Impossible."

"Not so." He could see her fingers curling over the photographs, believing him despite her words, and he pressed his advantage. "You know what's the first thing any were must learn?"

"Always sleep in the dark," she answered, with such routine he felt his suspicion was as good as confirmed.

"Because...?" he prompted gently, the way he'd been prompted as a child, the way *any* were was prompted before that one rule was drummed indelibly into their heads.

"Because otherwise you will lose the connection with the Moon, and will start turning irregularly. And when that happens, you die, because nobody can take so much change in so little time."

He couldn't suppress a smile. "You know a lot about weres."

"I have to," she said. He waited a moment, hoping she would go on, but she didn't. He lifted himself as much as he could, and tried, for the last time:

"Will you let me go, Lena? I need to get another group of pups tonight. My last. I swear I'll come back here if you want me to."

"I don't believe you," she said, getting up from the bed. She went back to the tallboy, picked up his jacket from the floor, put the pocketbook back in its place. Remained there, both hands on his jacket.

She was in the moonlight again. Her dark nipples were almost visible through the white shirt. Her long fingers so white on the black cloth of his jacket. Her behind, so deliciously curved and firm under the dark-red tail of her hair.

Suddenly, the solution seemed very clear and simple.

"Lena," he said. "You've caught me. I'm yours." When she still didn't answer, he smiled. "Whatever you wish to do to me... do it."

* * *

It was past eleven when the party left the café. They all exited together, but three of them piled into a taxi waiting at the curb. My prey, together with the skinny girl and another man, continued down the street, talking and occasionally laughing. I followed them from shadow to shadow, wondering, if they were planning to do a threesome, how I was going to extract the were on his own without harming the humans.

My employers weren't that fastidious, but I was. I only hunted weres. Even then, I avoided some of them. What harm can a werepig or a weresheep do? They were to be pitied, not destroyed. Some hunted them for sport. Illegally, of course.

Especially now, when weres were organizing and, in more and more countries, their demands for equality were being taken seriously. France, for instance, had already included them into the definition of citizens. Rumor was the English were planning something similar, at least for those weres who agreed to serve a year or two in the military. For a while, it had seemed that Germany would get caught in the general spirit of permissiveness permeating the continent after the Great War, too. But then, a year ago, their government fell and things began to change.

They issued dog tags and introduced a curfew to the weres. Not really strange; Germany had a lot of forests and rural areas. Their were population was among the largest in Europe. It was perfectly reasonable to wish to control it. But, for some reason, many people were opposed to the idea.

Not I. But I *was* opposed to the idea of killing humans needlessly, and the two people following my prey were definitely non-weres. The girl was a were-humper—that large medallion she wore on a choker around her neck was a play on the dog tags obligatory for the weres, the latest fashion for immature idiots looking for thrills in the arms of non-humans— but being young and stupid was not yet a mortal offense in my book. And the man, really barely more than a boy, was obviously only interested in the girl, hanging on to the pair with desperate hope in his eyes.

They walked all the way to Potsdammerstrasse. I couldn't believe my luck: that meant I would have a lot less ground to cover once I get my prey. Wonderful.

At the square, the threesome stopped. I moved on, using the noise from the train station to cover my footsteps, and got as close as I dared, trying to overhear at least something of their conversation. Unfortunately, the train noises worked against me, but I could see that the discussion wasn't making the skinny girl happy. Finally, she shook her head and turned her back to the two men, walking quickly in the direction of Friedrich-Ebertstrasse. The two males exchanged a few quick words, then the human one hurried after the girl. The were watched them go for a moment, then put his hands in his pockets and slowly started down Bellevueallee, towards the Tiergarten.

How very appropriate, I thought, and stepped into the open. Even if he saw me, I could pretend I was simply going in the same direction. I doubted very much he would notice,

though. He walked with his face lifted towards the skies, the very image of a man lost in some private reverie on this warm spring night.

More probably, he was looking for the Moon. She was nearing full, would reach it tomorrow night. All the weres must already be feeling her influence: an itch under the skin, restlessness, shortness of temper. Some women say it's similar to what they experience just before menstruating. Men, of course, claim that they are too reasonable to fall under the influence of a simple satellite, but statistics prove them liars. Car accidents and fistfights tend to go up in the nights immediately preceding and following the full Moon. No one could make me believe it had nothing to do with the Moon.

I deliberately kept my eyes on the ground. I didn't want the distracting elegance of his walk to shake my resolve. Because of the time — of the month as well as the night — the street had become almost empty as soon as we left the station behind us. I could follow him just by the sound of his footsteps.

But then they stopped.

*   *   *

She took half a step away from the tallboy, all uncertainty and hesitation, like a hare caught in the headlights of a car.

Or the eyes of a wolf.

Christian leaned on his elbows and lifted his body as much as he could. "Lena," he repeated, his voice low and husky. If that was the quickest way, so be it. He wanted her, anyway.

No, it was just the Moon, already running the first fingers of madness through his veins. It was just the Moon, and his prick, both engorged and mindless and interested only in getting her closer, feeling her, *touching* her.

"Fuck me, Lena."

With sudden, desperate resolve, she nodded and started

taking her shirt off. The buttons were tiny and stubborn; after working out one, she just tore off the rest together with the shirt. Her breasts were finally in his full view. Firm and round, with very dark nipples hardening quickly in the open air. Christian had to swallow a growl.

He could see her hands shake while she undid the wide belt around her waist, struggled with the buttons of her trousers. His muscles strained with the desire to set him free so he could pull her closer, rip the clothes off them both.

She wore almost no underwear, only a pair of white silk directoires. When she worked off the boots and the trousers, he saw that she'd had on a pair of black men's socks. Somehow, that silly, unfeminine detail seemed to make her all the more exciting. He wanted to tear the socks off with his teeth. Lick his way up her legs, all the way to the dark curls at the bottom of her belly.

When she touched him, he lay back and closed his eyes, deliberately letting the Moon swallow him. Her fingers worked clumsily on his belt, fingernails snagging on the buttons. He let all his senses reach towards her, inhaling the sandalwood-and-jasmine scent, feeling every shiver of her muscles echo through his body.

He heard ripping, then felt air on his prick. It jumped out, ready and willing and able, and it took all of Christian's self-control not to start howling. He felt her fingers encircle him, still shivery, and opened his eyes, not wishing to miss a single moment.

He'd thought he was ready for anything, but not this.

*   *   *

I slowed down and raised my head to take a look around. We were still on the part of the Allee before Kemperplatz; there was nowhere to hide. And, were or no, he couldn't just disappear into thin air.

Taking an even slower step, I looked first to my right, then my left. The houses on both sides returned my looks with the blank expressions of blind mice. Here and there, a window was left open, and a curtain would flap occasionally, like a handkerchief in goodbye.

I could hear the restless movements of nightlife in the Tiergarten. The distant trundling of freight trains going to the terminus. Even, if I strained a little, the human chatter and rattle of cars to the east. But no footsteps.

Suddenly, somewhere very close to my right, a husky voice said, "You shouldn't go there alone at night."

I turned and saw my prey leaning against a lamppost, his hands still in his pockets. He was smiling. In the moonlight, his face was sharply drawn, the lips dark like a movie star's, his eyes unreadably shadowed.

"I'm not afraid," I said, and took a step towards him.

"Perhaps you should be. They say all kinds of beasts prowl the park at night."

"I can handle beasts," I said, stopping only half a step from him. Away from the human throngs at the café, I could sense his cologne clearly, very discreet, musky and dark. And his own scent, male body at full power, all sinew and muscle. I knew I was staring at him, but couldn't stop myself.

He took his hands out of his pockets and stood straight. There was a glimmer of amusement in his eyes, or maybe I just imagined it. But his mouth had the unmistakable, satisfied expression of a successful hunter when he said, "Did you follow me from the café?"

I shook my head, still too absorbed in the sensation of him to risk words. I wanted to wipe that cocky smile off his face and replace it with expressions of wonder and desire. I could have pushed him into the first bush in the Tiergarten and ridden us both to oblivion. My body almost screamed with the need to impale myself on him.

But I had other plans.

When he leaned to kiss me, I put one hand into my trouser pocket. His lips traveled down my neck, towards the opening of my shirt.

I took out the yawara stick and held it lightly in my fist. I had used it before—I learned its use from a Japanese performer in a cabaret some years ago—but not on a were. Usually, with weres, I just wanted to be quick and efficient, and leaving them alive was not conducive to either.

One of his hands slid around my waist, pulling me closer. The other cupped my breast from below, squeezing just enough to make my nipples stand to attention.

"You're so beautiful," he murmured, and I hit him.

* * *

Naked and gorgeous, she had lifted one leg on the bed to straddle him again, and held his prick in her hand, the light pressure of her palm driving him wild with desire. But tears were rolling down her cheeks.

Now he was seriously cursing her skill with the ropes. If it weren't for the gold threads, he would have torn himself free. The Moon inside him was howling with almost full force, and he was only half himself at best. He knew that, but didn't care anymore. She needed holding, and stroking—maybe more, but not now, later—and he needed to give it to her.

He growled in frustration, then took a few deep breaths to steady himself. *You're still human. Behave like one.*

"Lena," he whispered. "Lena, bunny."

She licked her lips, looked at him. He could see the effort of will it took her to stop the tears, follow the freezing of her features as she got herself under control.

"Don't worry," she said, her words a mere whisper. "I'll fuck you good."

She licked her palm, then took hold of him again. He felt her skin slide over his, caressingly soft now. Her thumb landed on the tip of his prick, smearing the moisture over it. His breath caught in his throat. He let it out in a hiss, his mouth filling with saliva.

He could feel the Moon even behind the faded curtains now, calling to him. The silver rays were melting into his blood, swirling in the delicate strands of his being, changing his awareness. The room seemed to shrink, disappear, reduced only to the island of the bed surrounded by darkness.

She let go of him, eliciting a frustrated whine from deep in his throat. With a decisive little shake of her head, she knelt over him, positioning herself over his straining prick. Her hands landed on his chest, providing her with support. His skin felt as if it were burning where she touched it, and he welcomed the flames.

She started downwards, catching the very tip of his prick with her sex. He was so full of need, it took him a moment to realize it wasn't going as smoothly as it should have. She was straining, holding him with one hand. Then he understood.

She was dry.

For a moment, the moonlit mists of his brain cleared. He licked his lips.

"Lena, bunny. Set me free."

She shook her head, her expression closed, concentrated. That was no way to mate, he knew. He pulled at his ropes with all his might, disregarding the small stabs of pain when his skin touched the gold threads.

"Lena," he called louder.

She closed her eyes, shaking her head in small, nervous movements. His body still wanted her—he was so hard it almost hurt—but he was regaining control of his mind.

"Lena," he said again, as if her name was a mantra that would keep him anchored to reality. If it even *was* reality. The whole scene, from the moment he'd woken up tied to her bed, seemed like some sort of a dream, something risen from the thick smoke of bad opium.

She went rigid for a second. He could see the turmoil inside her, could almost sense the tension that pulled all of her nerves taut.

"Lena," he whispered, because that seemed to be all he had. He let his head fall back on the pillow, listening to her hard, ragged breaths. "Let me help you."

She opened her eyes. They were defeated, empty of any hope. He'd seen too many eyes like that. No more.

"Come closer," he breathed.

Reluctantly, she obeyed, crawling over his chest.

"Closer."

He could feel the heat of her sex over his heart, now. Her skin rustled like silk as she slid on.

"Closer, bunny." He saw the momentary confusion in her eyes change to understanding. Careful not to press his arms too hard, grabbing at the wall for support, she knelt over his face.

*　　*　　*

When the yawara connected with the knot of nerves, he simply slid over me. I staggered under his weight—he was all muscle—but kept my balance. Fine.

It took me only a moment to lean his unconscious body over my shoulder and start walking, dragging him with me. It wasn't easy, but it wasn't too hard, either. And my body seemed to welcome the exercise. It helped take the edge off my tension. For a while, I could stop thinking, and just concentrate on making it to the Potsdamer Platz U-Bahn station.

As we left the Tiergarten behind us, more and more people appeared on the streets. It was nearing midnight. The cabarets were wrapping up the more decent shows and starting with the more exotic ones, with the inevitable change of audiences.

At the station, nobody noticed us. As far as the other passengers were concerned, I was just another unhappy girl saddled with a man who couldn't hold his drink. One elderly matron accompanied by her husband cast me a disdainful glance, but I couldn't be sure whether it was because of my indecent clothes or because of my companion's state. The only awkward moment happened when a group of uniformed men entered the train and commented loudly on the need to weed out the weaklings in the ranks of the males, those who can control neither their women nor their drink. I kept my eyes down and my mouth shut. I had been in Germany long enough to know what happened to those daring to openly oppose men in uniform — any uniform.

At my station, I had to strain a little to get the were up again, but managed it successfully, and then dragged him easily the few steps to my rented room.

It was on the second floor, and the hardest part was getting him up the stairs quietly enough. I didn't want to wake my landlady. She probably wouldn't object, but I wanted no witnesses to the were's ever being here. On the way, he muttered and pawed at me. I stopped, leaning against the wall for support, and held him pressed against me until he quieted again. I had to hurry.

When I finally reached my room, I flung him on the bed. It was an old-fashioned four-poster, made from solid, ancient oak. That was part of the reason why I'd chosen this room. I had tied the ropes to the bedposts before leaving tonight. All that was left to do now was tie the were, too.

I had barely had time to finish tying off the last rope when I felt him move, heard him mutter. He was coming to.

Grabbing the knife from the nightstand, I sat on him and took a deep breath. Time to start the show.

"If you let me fuck you, I will let you go," I said.

*　　*　　*

She was hot and dry, as if she were running a fever. Christian lifted his head a little, touching her first with the tip of his nose, while she was searching for a more comfortable position.

Then he started kissing her, softly, gently, moving from the middle of her chestnut curls downwards, towards her folds. She held unnaturally still, almost as if she were embarrassed.

At that thought, he swallowed a chuckle. Of course, what could possibly be embarrassing about kidnapping a man, tying him to your bed with the intent to rape him, and then needing his help to get wet enough to actually do it without pain?

He took a deep breath, running his lips over the edge of her folds. She smelled of jasmine even here; either it was something she used for bathing, or else it was her natural smell.

When his tongue touched her clit, he felt a shudder go through her whole body. She let out a tiny, whining sound. He pressed harder, licking all around the nub, feeling it grow under his touch. He longed to have his hands free, to spread her and hold her and finger her.

"Bunny," he whispered against her sex. "Set me free."

Her body grew rigid again. Cursing his haste, he pressed his open mouth against her sex, as much as he could reach, using teeth and tongue to get her to relax again. He slid his tongue as far as he could, in quick, in-and-out movement, then circled around her clit again, drawing it between his lips.

She was whimpering now, her thighs trembling. She tasted sweet and salty and spicy, like peanut butter, and he felt he could stay like this forever, suckling her and fucking her with his tongue, listening to her quickening breaths that were turning into sighs. A moment more and she would come in his mouth.

Just as he felt the first quivers of her orgasm under his tongue, she pushed herself away from the wall, the movement sudden and clumsy. She caught herself on her hands, half-turned away from him, her breathing fast and short. He could see her nipples now, hard and almost purple, and longed to taste them.

She stayed like that for a few moments, while he nuzzled her leg, still within his reach. Then she grabbed the knife from the nightstand.

For a moment, he was pierced by fear, convinced with absolute certainty that she was going to kill him.

He closed his eyes.

*   *   *

It was wrong, all of it, from the very beginning. A part of me had known it was a bad idea, but I refused to heed it. I needed to believe I could pull it off, could get myself pregnant with a werewolf, so my child could grow within me and get born, not die a horrible, mangled mess when my body changed.

That was what happened to halfblood children. Their bodies did not know how to deal with the Moon, and simply broke when the womb transformed around them, or else died when the mother's metabolism changed. It was a mercy to abort them, not have them shatter or die of blood poisoning. Without two changing parents, there could be no children. Should be none.

I had been three months pregnant when a dead werewolf's tooth accidentally scratched my arm as the men carried it through the village.

My life fell apart after that, so completely that I needed something to carry me on. To stop me from accepting the opium pipe that circled around the dressing room every night. To keep me from climbing over the rails on the Jungfernbrücke and letting myself fall into the cold, uncaring waters of the Spree.

I needed to believe I could still build a life for myself.

And now the goddamn were crushed that belief.

From the first moment, he had been nibbling on my security. His body didn't fill me with loathing. He didn't jump on the chance offered by that were-humper at the café. He did fall into my trap, but I was his equal, and I had a feeling he knew it. He wanted to *comfort* me, damn him, without even knowing what it was he would be comforting me about. And now, finally, in an insane twist, he was trying to get me wet enough to allow me to rape him.

I had been told that he was dangerous, a smuggler and a terrorist. A were. I didn't really need anything else. I had accepted the Geheimpolizei's proposal willingly, would have accepted it even if they didn't hold the threat of the dog tag over my head. I *liked* killing weres.

Had liked it.

And now I had nearly come under his tongue.

My first thought was to get away from him, get rid of him, in any way I had at my disposal. Fighting the pre-orgasmic mists in my mind, I threw myself to the side, blindly reaching for the knife I'd left on the nightstand.

As my fingers closed over the smooth wooden hilt I knew so well, I felt him nuzzle my leg.

It was only the Moon working on him, I tried to tell myself. I could feel her, too, despite the drapes I'd carefully drawn so as to block all moonlight away from my room. I could feel her, engorged and heavy like his prick, like my sex, full of tension and need and misery.

I felt my eyes fill with tears again. My first instinct was to swallow them, drown them in anger. I raised the knife and slid off him, half-intending to just finish my job then and there.

He was lying on his back, his eyes closed, his face perfectly calm.

Almost without any conscious intention, my knife swerved upwards and cut through one of the ropes holding his wrist.

His eyes opened with the suddenness of a jack-in-the-box.

"Bunny?" he said, his voice hoarse and dry.

I leaned over him to free his other hand. "Go away," I

heard myself mutter, still not entirely sure why. "Just... just go."

His hand encircled my waist. I wanted to get free, pushed against his chest to wriggle away. But I'd cut the other rope, too, and now he was holding me against him with both strong hands, tatters of his shirtsleeves still clinging to his forearms.

"Lena," he whispered. "No. Hush. Calm down, baby."

I hated every gentle word that left his mouth. Every soft breath on my suddenly clammy skin. Every tender touch.

Every were.

Including — especially — myself.

He put a hand on my face. "Lena," he repeated, almost as if he liked saying it. "Listen to me." His eyes met mine. I was still shivery, and some sort of comfort waited for me there. At least it seemed that way, for a very short moment.

Then I got up quickly, before he could catch me again, and cut the ties on his ankles.

"Go," I said, forcing my voice to work. "Go save the cubs, if that's what you do. Or go do something else. Just go."

He sat on the bed, waiting for the circulation in his feet to start working again. I picked up my bag, took out my spare shirt. "Here," I said, pushing the shirt towards him, doing my best not to look at him. "It's probably too small, but no one will notice under the jacket. Go."

"Lena..."

"Go!"

I felt the knife shiver in my hand. He probably saw it, too, because he finally stopped repeating my name and put on the shirt I gave him. Then he tightened the belt over his now-buttonless trousers and picked up his shoes from the floor.

I took out a dress and some underclothes from the bag, and went towards the bathroom. It was silly — I was stark naked now, and he'd fucked me with his tongue not ten minutes ago — but, nevertheless, I felt getting dressed before him would be too embarrassing.

Besides, it prevented any attempt to talk to me again. I locked the door of the bathroom behind me, and sat on the toilet. Normally, I would just wait out the tears, but now, I didn't think I had the time. I washed quickly, using a towel, only so much as to get rid of the smells of sex and the were, then I got dressed. I had forgotten shoes, and was a little cold standing on the black and white tiles in my stockinged feet, but I didn't want to go out and face him again.

A knock on the door.

"Lena?"

Damn him, he really liked saying my name. Where else would I be? I kept quiet.

"I have to go now," he said on the other side of the door. "But I will come back, I promise. Whatever you wanted from me, you'll get."

I wondered what he would think if I were to open the door and tell him the only two things I'd wanted from him were his semen and his life.

And now I wanted neither.

He waited a while. I could hear his breathing on the other side of the door, and then a soft, soft sigh.

The door creaked slightly, then closed.

I left the bathroom and went for my shoes first. I pulled up my hair in a firm coil, and settled a hat over it. What money I had and the spare set of documents went into my purse, as well as the knife. Everything else I could leave behind.

Geheimpolizei would think Christian and I had killed each other, I hoped. It would have been better if we'd spilled a little blood, but this would just have to do.

I opened the closet and took the thin coat that hung there. Putting it on, I went to the mirror. Without my male clothes and my hair hidden under the hat, I didn't look much different than any other girl returning home after a late night. It was hardly likely anyone would even start looking for me tonight, much less anyone would remember me like this.

Holding the purse that held all I had left in the world, I took hold of the doorknob when I noticed something lying on the tallboy. One of the pictures of werechildren he'd shown me.

I didn't know whether it was deliberate or accidental, but I didn't feel comfortable leaving it there for the police to find, so I stuffed it into my purse. The picture showed two children, a girl of maybe three or four holding a baby in her lap. I remembered what he'd told me about the were-army. If someone started playing with their sleeping lights, the girl in the picture could hope to reach puberty at best. The baby, not even that. And they would lose their minds much earlier than their bodies.

I wasn't sure whether I believed him or not. But I saw the Moon, and felt it sing in my blood, and I knew that she, at least, would never lie to me.

And I knew where she was pulling.

I stepped into the night.

Always a Prince, Never a Princess

by
David M. Fitzpatrick

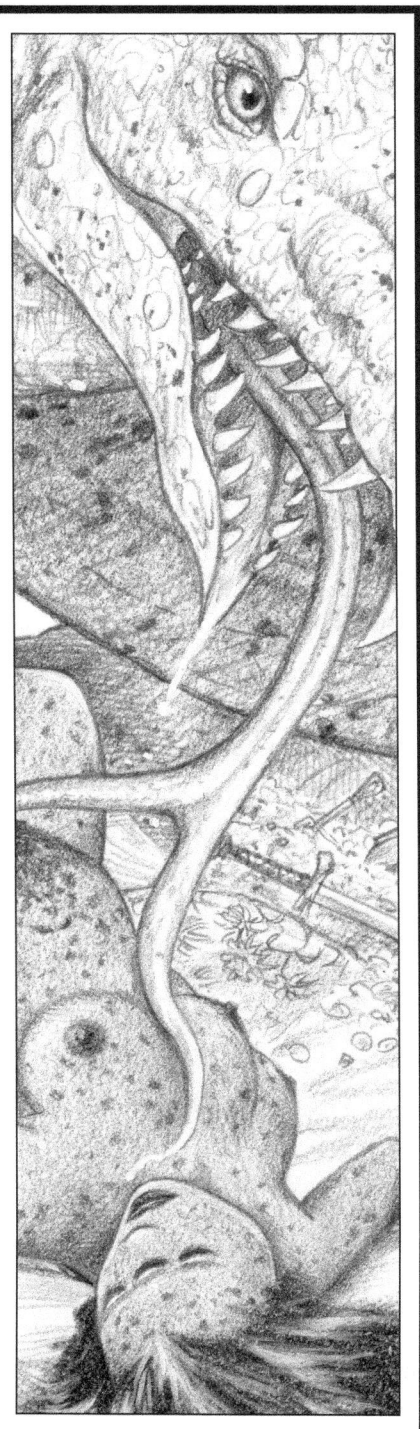

Dragons kidnap princesses all the time. This dragon's taefling captive longs to be rescued, but dreads having to marry the brave knight who rescues her — because her heart belongs to someone else. Yet their love was so taboo that her father, the king, wouldn't stand for it. And now this taefling princess knows that it would be better to live in fear of a dragon who molests her, and die by his maw if she must, than to live without her true love.

Fantasy
Sword & Sorcery
Heterosexual sex
Lesbian sex
Dragon/woman cunnilingus
Nonhuman physiology
Forced sex
Romance
Incest

The dragon Skrebulorius towered high above Saffil on massive legs, its reptilian eyes glowing red in the dark, cavernous lair. Powerful arms ended in giant white claws that menaced her, always looking ready to reach out and grab her again. Immense leathery wings stretched wide behind him, beating about Skrebulorius like those of a giant bat. He leaned his armored head forward on a long, green-scaled neck until he was eye to eye with the blue-skinned woman. She recoiled in terror, but there was nowhere to go on the oversized pillow-bed on which the dragon had placed her. She was almost tangled up in her long, flowing dress, and there was nowhere to run anyway. She could only look up, her three yellow eyes wide with panic.

"Sweet Princess Saffil," Skrebulorius said in a deep voice, booming down like that of some mountaintop deity, his reptilian lips curling back into a sinister smile. "We're a matched pair. I'm a most resplendent dragon, magnificent even for my own kind; and you're a woman whose beauty is not easily matched by any other taefling."

This close, she felt his body heat, and it was as if she were standing next to a blacksmith's forge. His head was massive; all she could do was stare with her three wide eyes at the rows of white daggers in the beast's mouth, and she knew he could eat her in one bite. "Please don't hurt me," she pleaded for the hundredth time since the dragon had snatched her away from the celebration.

He laughed, low and long, and his breath stank of rotting meat on a hot desert wind. He furrowed his heavy brow and leaned in closer, until she could see faint tendrils of smoke curling up from his plate-sized nostrils. "I've not harmed you yet, princess. I took you from your father, in the midst of your grand engagement parade, without so much as scratching you. Now you're mine—forever."

She felt bold for the first time, and she cried out, "My father will send his best champions to rescue me!"

Skrebulorius let out a bellowing laugh, throwing his head high above her on his long neck. "Foolish taefling! The champions of a hundred kings have fed my glorious belly. I've roasted a dozen of your father's finest. Perhaps the thousand helpless taeflings I scorched today will give him pause for thought."

Saffil closed her three eyes tightly and tried not to remember the scene, but it played behind her eyelids like a never-ending nightmare. Soldiers, men and women, children and infants... innocent people, there to join in the celebration of a cursed betrothal that was against her will. Many had died as the dragon had swooped down over the screaming crowd, breathing hellish jets of flame; many more were burned and injured, scarred for life. She could still hear the distant sounds of their agonized screams fading away as the dragon, holding Saffil prisoner in his big claws, winged away from the kingdom with his prize.

She snapped her eyes open as the terrible creature rose to his full height above her. He backed away on big legs, fanning the air again with his wings. "I'm off to find supper for Your Highness. When I return, I'd best see your beautiful nakedness, My Lady—and if I don't, then I'll roast you alive and find a new taefling wench!"

He dipped his head suddenly down and exhaled, and Saffil screamed and threw up her arms. But two flames shot from his big nostrils, flaring to either side of her, and just a black puff of smoke burst from his mouth. He pulled back, laughing jovially as Saffil hacked and coughed amidst the sooty cloud.

"The next one will be real," he said, "if you're clothed when I return."

He turned, lumbered through the cavern, and leaped out the cave's mouth. Momentarily, he came into view, his massive form held aloft by the giant wings. She watched him fly towards the sun, which was setting beyond nearby mountains, until he was out of sight.

Saffil knew that the situation was grim. She was his prisoner, and the dragon was unlikely to fall to any champion her father sent. She struggled amidst her gowns to get off the big pillow-bed and, holding her skirts, hurried to the cavern's mouth to get an idea of what she was up against. It was a sheer drop straight down, probably several thousand feet; above her, it went straight up for hundreds more. There were no ledges nearby. There was no escape.

In despair, she turned back to survey her prison. The cavern was huge, dominated mostly by a massive pile of treasure towards the back. The dragon had no need for the gold and silver and jewels, and plundered it simply because he knew people valued it. Her own taefling race had had little trouble with dragons for centuries, but Skrebulorius was the biggest, baddest, meanest dragon anyone had seen in a dozen generations. Rumor had it he'd been enhanced through magic gone awry; whatever the cause, he was practically invulnerable. He'd been marauding through her father's kingdom for months, and had finally grown angry at the king's retaliatory attempts to destroy him.

There were other things in the treasure pile, too—priceless paintings, ancient vases, elegant crowns, ornate scepters, and steel-banded wooden chests full of more treasure. Staves, pikes, halberds, swords, shields, and other weapons were strewn everywhere, along with endless remnants from suits of armor: steel chainmail, shining breastplates, gilded helmets, studded leather cuirasses, battered shields with various coats of arms. There were tapestries thrown haphazardly on the pile. A bust of some human queen sat askew towards the back, and the head and shoulders of a statue of a great taefling wizard protruded from the mounds of coins and jewels. Near her pillow-bed, a full-length mirror leaned precariously against the cave wall. It was framed in mahogany and edged with decorative copper that was turning green with corrosion. There was a long crack across the lower third of the dusty glass.

Saffil caught her reflection in the mirror and stepped closer. Her elegant silken dress, although a bit dirty, was typical of taefling royalty: soft yellow, lined with white accents, sleeveless and backless. The skirts, studded with small gems, were pleated, with a ruffled hemline. The neckline curved deep and wide over her three ample breasts, revealing plenty of pink-speckled blue skin and dual cleavage. Atop her head, subtly pinned into her mint-green hair, was a silver tiara adorned with a large oval ruby. She'd been dressed for her unwanted engagement to Prince Rastun, heir to the throne of a faraway taefling kingdom. The wedding was in two months, and the engagement parade had been a celebration for her father's kingdom. She thought again of her bird's-eye view of the blazing destruction the dragon had wrought as he'd rained sheets of fire across the helpless crowd. They'd tried to run, but there'd been nowhere to go.

Because of those innocent deaths, she felt tremendously guilty at lamenting her plight, but she couldn't help it when she beheld the pain and sorrow that painted her face in that mirror. The top of her taefling head was a bit wider than a human's, but her face sloped to a narrow, graceful chin. Her three almond-shaped eyes, entirely yellow save for cat-like pupils, were spaced evenly on her head; delicate, arched ridges protruded above them, with no eyebrows, and they looked tired and empty. Her wide, shallow nose flap had just one thin horizontal nostril, wider than her middle eye and nearly closed. She couldn't remember the last time she'd seen her dark-blue lips swell with a smile; now, they were thin and deflated. Even her hair, in need of washing and styling, hung limply about her face where a few tresses had been pulled from their combs;

the green curls looked lifeless, like fine seaweed flattened against her head. She was a wreck.

But she'd been a wreck for a long time; the dragon was just the latest disappointment in her life. On the one hand, she was Skrebulorius' prisoner; on the other, she was away from her father, away from his forced obligations, and away from his hatred of who she was. All she could think of was how much she needed the true love of her life—instead of that young taefling prince the king wanted her to marry.

She took a deep breath. As much as the thought of disrobing for the dragon disgusted her, she had to get the dress off. She had no doubt the dragon wouldn't hesitate to roast her alive if she refused. She reached up and unpinned the tiara, tossing it into the obscene pile of treasure. No loss there. It was just a silly decoration anyway.

She usually needed a handmaiden to help her with the dress, but she was on her own. She reached back with thin, four-fingered hands, her nails painted pink to match her speckles, and found the main knot. She had to work at it for a minute, but once it came free, she was able to loosen the back of the dress and shimmy her shoulders out of it. She shrugged it down over her arms and peeled it down her torso to reveal her white corset. She slid the dress down over her tiny waist and slim hips until it was on the cave floor and stepped out of it. Then she found the various pins and combs holding her hair in place, and it all let loose so that it tumbled about her shoulders.

The corset was like a vise, tightly wrapping her abdomen, and lifting and pushing her three breasts together. She reached back, arms twisting painfully, to find the main knot. It was a smaller cord than on the dress, but she managed to get it loose. A few moments later, she stepped out of the damnable thing. She kicked off the yellow shoes and turned to back to the mirror.

Her legs, arms, and face held small pink speckles, but her

torso was replete with them. They grew larger and more numerous towards her belly, until there was almost as much pink as blue there. She was thin but not bony, and of nearly perfect proportions for a taefling. Her waist was narrow, her slim hips seeming broad by comparison. There was a thick patch of curly green hair between her legs, much darker than the hair on her head. Her three swelling breasts were very large on her petite form, her three big areolas like targets with fat, bull's-eye nipples. Mint-green hair, cascading about her shoulders, mostly straight but slightly wavy, hung far down her back and tickled the tops of her breasts in front. It looked a bit more natural now.

She knew she was beautiful, but it wasn't vanity. Taeflings were generally considered a beautiful race, and humans sought after them mightily. It was said that taefling kings had such universally good relations with humans because of the beauty of the taefling women—who were, admittedly, exotic by human standards. And, Saffil knew, she was considered one of the most beautiful. It wasn't just because she was a princess, either; even if she'd been a peasant, she'd have been a knockout. But taefling law forbade those of royal blood marrying outside their race. That was half the reason the love of her life was such a problem for her father. But just half.

It was chilly in the cave, she realized, as the fine hairs on her body pricked up and her three nipples grew firm in the cold. She made a hasty retreat to the pillow-bed and wrapped the blanket about her. She'd no sooner gotten comfortable when she heard the beating of the dragon's wings, and soon his big form filled the cave entrance as he kicked his feet up, flapped his wings madly, and landed with a crash that seemed to shake the entire mountain. She sucked in her breath as the gargantuan beast lumbered forward, eyes glaring down at her.

"You're covered," he hissed.

"I'm very cold," she said, three eyes wide with fear.

He seemed to think about this, and then he took in a deep

breath and breathed on her. Once again, she thought she was about to get toasted, but he merely blew out hot air. It was almost too hot, and his giant lungs just kept providing more, as if from a bellows the size of her father's castle. And it stank as much as ever. But when he was done, the cave had noticeably heated up, and the very pillow-bed on which she sat was pleasantly warm.

"That should do," Skrebulorius said. "Now, show yourself to me."

It was weird, but he was a dragon, so it wasn't like it could be anything sexual. She took a deep breath and threw the blanket aside. She was on her knees, and she rested her hands on her thighs as the dragon's barrel-sized eyes crawled over her. It felt disgusting, as if his gaze were the hands of some drunken human sailor.

"Wonderful taefling," he said in a whisper that blew the hair around her face. "So beautiful."

He leaned in again, until his scaly nose was close, and he opened his mouth. A forked, serpentine tongue snaked out, flicking about her breasts. She tensed, held her breath. The twin tips danced about her chest, circling and teasing her trio of breasts before moving to the jutting nipple of her middle breast. She sucked in her breath in surprise as he twirled his tongue around there—and then he shot it over to her left breast and repeated the process, then to her right, and back to her middle. He alternated with the lightest of touches, and her nipples grew harder in response. Electric tingling sizzled lightly through her body. She tried to will her physical reactions away, but felt herself growing wet between her legs.

"Ah, those breasts like me," said the dragon, leering at her. "Now lie back and spread your legs."

Terror washed over her for a moment, and in that instant she knew she was going to scream at the dragon, tell him there was no way she'd let him violate her, and he could breathe fire on her all he liked. But as she drew in a breath and prepared to holler, something stopped her. The tongue had felt good on her nipples, and she couldn't help but wonder what it would be like elsewhere. There was nothing she liked better than a tongue down there, that was for sure. And it had been so long since she'd felt her lover's tongue...

She lay back and parted her thighs a little. Skrebulorius seemed to light up at that, and he leaned in closer, tongue snaking out of his mouth. It was a huge tongue, too, flatter than a taefling's but several inches wide. And it was damn long.

He licked up her thighs, teased around the bush of green hair that hid her lips, licked up to her twin navels. His tongue was wet and quite hot, and as he twirled it around it left a wet trail. Then he moved lower until it teased at the hairy edge of her mound. Her heart pounded madly in her chest, but she did her best to look disinterested and a bit afraid. But she was eagerly anticipating it.

He moved down to her knees and began licking his way aggressively up her thighs. She found herself parting her thighs as he neared her crotch, even though she wasn't consciously doing so, and by the time he made it there, she was spread quite wide. The dragon's tongue lashed about her labia with surprising delicacy considering its size, and she felt the wonderful feeling flooding through her. She willed the tight muscles that normally held her external vertical labia to relax, and they opened wide; the inner horizontal labia followed suit, opening like a mouth to expose the wet, teal-colored recesses of her pulsing vagina. It didn't take very long before she felt the familiar sensation begin building deep inside her, and she felt her hardening clitoris, hidden behind those four lips, growing and presenting itself, ready for the friction of what nature expected would be a thrusting penis, but would be the exciting feel of a tongue.

But she couldn't shake the reality that this was a dragon, with a forked tongue and stinking breath, who had killed many of her people and maimed many when he had stolen her away, so she closed her eyes and let her mind wander to another time…

*　　*　　*

Furious with her father, Saffil had returned to her rooms, her handmaiden Averlin with her, after a long and shocking royal function. Averlin was one of the few humans in the employ of her father's court. It wasn't uncommon for humans and taeflings to work for each other when kingdoms and nations had alliances, and Averlin had come there after her parents, traveling traders who Saffil's father had befriended, had died several years before. With no surviving human family back home, Saffil's father had taken the girl in.

"I can't believe my father had the nerve to offer me like that!" Saffil cried as Averlin began helping undo the dress.

"I'm sorry, My Lady," Averlin said. She was dressed in the plain, peach-colored garb of the serving staff, with her blond hair pulled back into a tight braid. She was pretty, for a human; her skin was pale, and in stark contrast to Saffil's blue skin. And Saffil was always intrigued by the girl's yellow hair, a color that would never be found on a taefling. Averlin was barely out of adolescence, while Saffil was a bit older. Saffil could remember the innocent young girl who had first come to tend to her six years before.

"Choosing my husband!" Saffil spat, pounding her fist against the wall. "It's unacceptable."

"I'm… I'm sure that King Toranno just wants to marry you to a prince," the handmaiden said as she hurriedly worked at the dress.

"One would think I should be able to at least *approve* of the prince before my father awards me to the highest bidder, like a whore at auction," Saffil snapped as Averlin released the knot and helped pull the dress down. "Even taefling prostitutes have the final decision as to whether they'll have sex with someone, for Caylor's sake!"

"I'm sure he loves you, My Lady," Averlin said in a small voice as she loosened the corset and helped Saffil struggle out of it.

"I sometimes wonder," Saffil said. "He knows I want to choose my own lover, but he doesn't approve of my choices."

She kicked off her shoes and waited as Averlin worked to get the tiara and combs and pins out of her hair. Averlin didn't say anything, and in that silence Saffil knew why. She'd wanted to ask the girl for so long, and now seemed the time. As soon as her hair fell free, Saffil spun about to a surprised Averlin.

"I know the servants talk," Saffil said. "I know the rumors are out there. What is it they say about me?"

Averlin looked like a dog caught with the rump roast in its mouth, not knowing quite what to do. "I'm sure I... I don't know what you mean, My Lady."

"Averlin—please!" Saffil said, reaching out and placing her hands on her handmaiden's pale shoulders. "You've tended to me for six years. I'd like to think we're friends. Please, what do they say? I'll never tell anyone you told me."

Averlin avoided her gaze, gulping and trying to look anywhere else. But Saffil's three big breasts were exposed and pressing into Averlin's two clothed breasts, and Averlin seemed to be trying not to look at them or at Saffil's face. "My Lady, I hate to gossip—"

"Gossip away—not as my servant but as my friend." She gripped the girl's pale shoulders tightly, and then Averlin finally looked up and met her eyes.

"They say you don't want to marry any prince, or... or any man," Averlin said, her voice weak and trembling. "They say you want to marry... a woman."

Saffil stared at Averlin for several long moments, and then smiled. "Is that what they say?"

"Y-yes, My Lady."

She sighed and released the other's shoulders, went to her big bed, plopped down on it. "It's true, you know."

Averlin's eyes bugged out. "It... it is, My Lady?"

"Yes—there, I've said it!" she cried, throwing her hands up. "I like girls—and that infuriates my father! It embarrasses the family and hurts taeflings everywhere and offends the gods, or so he says. I say it's my choice, but he doesn't agree. Duty and honor and all of that. I'm not just being a rebellious daughter, you know; I just want someone to love, someone I can be happy with—but it must be a woman. And I could care less if she were a princess or a pauper."

Saffil was suddenly worried about her rant, and that Averlin would think she was making some kind of advance on her. She hurriedly added, "I'm sorry to tell you all this. I don't mean to make you uncomfortable. It's just that... you're the only person I can talk to about anything, because I know what I tell you won't leave this room."

Averlin slowly approached the bed and gingerly sat beside Saffil. "How do you know?" she asked in a small voice. "If you don't mind my asking, My Lady, how do you know you want women?"

"I'll answer if you stop calling me 'My Lady' when we're alone," Saffil said.

Averlin smiled. "All right, Saffil."

Saffil smiled back. "I've always known. When I was very young, I was excited by kissing girls. They kept taking handmaidens away from me. As I got older, the drives were just too strong. I've never been interested in men. And my father just can't handle that."

There was a long silence that got increasingly awkward before Averlin said, "But... have you ever... I mean, besides kissing... have you ever... been with a woman?"

"Just once. The handmaiden before you, a taefling girl named Velsa. We were the best of friends, and one night we were up late playing a card game and… well, I'm not sure what happened. We were having a good time, and somewhere in the middle of it all, I kissed her. She kissed me back, and we giggled, and the cards were forgotten. The next thing I knew, we were on the bed, embracing as lovers, and soon the clothing came off. We made love for hours, and it was the best night of my life.

"But the next day, Velsa felt shameful about what had happened, and she told the housemother—and *she* told the chief of staff, and before I knew it, my father knew, and he lost his temper. He had her reassigned to our country estate, and he punished me—he claimed I made Velsa do those things. But I didn't."

Averlin was looking at her with wide eyes. "I've heard about that from the servants. Some are afraid to wait on you alone, because they fear you'll… take a liking to them. It makes them nervous. I'm the only one who isn't nervous, so of course they tease me—they say I like girls, and they taunt me for it."

Saffil said, "You have nothing to worry about, Averlin—I promise you, after what happened with Velsa, I won't make that mistake again."

She met Averlin's eyes. Unlike taefling eyes, they were mostly white, with colored rings around dark pupils. Averlin's colored rings were the brightest, iciest blue; Saffil had always been intrigued by them, but she'd never really looked this closely at them before. They were truly beautiful.

And as she stared into those deep, blue pools for the long moments that followed, she suddenly wondered if Averlin were disappointed at what Saffil had just said—did she *want* her to make that "mistake" again? It had never occurred to Saffil that the human girl might be attracted to females. But Saffil couldn't be sure—perhaps her sexual desires and lovesick imagination were clouding her judgment—so she fought the urge to act. But she couldn't help but see Averlin in a completely new light. She'd never considered the girl a potential lover, but Averlin was truly the best, closest friend Saffil had. Suddenly, she seemed beautiful and sexy—and could she be the woman Saffil had always sought but thought she'd never find? Had the right woman been under her nose for six years?

She dared not act on her excited thoughts, so instead she only held her gaze on Averlin's. Presently, Averlin found the courage to speak.

"It wouldn't be a mistake," she said in her small voice.

"What are you saying?" Saffil whispered.

Averlin squirmed a bit where she sat, and seemed to be working to find the words. "I've served you since I was a girl, but I'm a woman now. I listen to what they say and how they shun you and disapprove of you, and it angers me. And I get so upset with your father that I want to cry, because I feel badly that you're denied what you want."

Averlin grabbed Saffil's hand, clasping it tightly in hers. Saffil, nude and exposed, turned on the bed to look at her. "It's wrong to force you to be something that you aren't!" Averlin suddenly blurted out.

"Is that all you want to say?" Saffil asked. Her heart was beating faster, whooshing blood in her ears, and she grew lightheaded. She felt the heat of Averlin's hand clutching hers, and the heat building between her legs.

Averlin seemed to be mentally debating whether she should do it, but threw caution to the wind. "When they taunt me and say I like women, I want to scream at them. I want to tell them that they're right, that I *do* like women—and that I like *you*."

With that, she dived forward, grabbing Saffil's head with her hands, pulling Saffil's face to hers, and kissing her. Saffil returned it, and soon the two were writhing on the bed together, their tongues intertwining, their hands exploring each other's bodies. When Averlin's fingers first found their way down to Saffil's soft bush of pubic hair, Saffil grabbed her wrist and stopped her.

"You have to be sure," Saffil said. "I don't want my father to send you away. I don't want you to regret it later."

"Oh, sweet Saffil, that won't happen," Averlin said. "You're the most beautiful woman I've ever known. I've watched your body every time I've seen you undressed. I've fought the urge to touch you in these places for years. I've longed to be with you, to bring you pleasure, and to feel pleasured by you. I've lain in bed so many nights, touching myself and fantasizing about being with you."

Saffil's three eyes widened. "You have?"

"Oh, yes. I can't tell you how many times I've—" Her face reddened. "I can't say it."

"Yes, you can," Saffil whispered, sliding her hand down the girl's face and to her chest, resting lightly on her covered breast. Humans only had two of them, just like their eyes, and that was an excitement in and of itself that Saffil had never before considered.

Averlin took a deep, shaking breath. "We don't use oil lamps in the servants' quarters; we have candles on our nightstands instead," she whispered in the private space between their close faces. "They're fat and long, and I have a special one. I... I use it inside myself, and I think of you. I slide it in and out, under the covers, when other girls are in their beds beside me, and I rub myself with my other hand. I rub so furiously, and I move the candle so fast, and I have to keep perfectly silent, but all I want to do is scream out your name—because it's you I want, not some candle, and because... because I'm in love with you, and I've been in love with you since the first day I met you. I was just eleven, and too young to understand, but I was drawn to you. When my parents died and I came here, I'd always get excited to wait on you. It's been six years, and I've grown older and come to know my body and my feelings, I've realized that I'm absolutely and totally in love with you—and I can't be silent about how I feel any longer."

Saffil was stunned, but only for a moment. This was what she wanted—and who she wanted. The girl had loved her in painful silence for years, and Saffil hadn't even noticed. In that moment, Saffil was overwhelmed with emotion.

"I love you too, Averlin," Saffil said, realizing then that it was the truth, and she kissed her newfound lover.

They got Averlin's clothing off, and they made love on that bed. It was bizarre for Saffil in one respect, because human women were different in many ways. Their labia were not clamped together, and they had just the vertical lips. There were smaller lips, but they were also vertical. Most excitingly, Averlin's clitoris was easily accessible, not as deeply concealed as a taefling clitoris was.

So it was overpowering on so many levels: the sex, the vast differences they found as they explored each other's bodies, the totally forbidden nature of their union, and the deep love they felt. Saffil made Averlin come first, working the girl's little pink clitoris before sliding one finger, then two, then three inside her. She brought the helpless girl to a shrieking orgasm, and when it was over, Averlin kissed her and told her it was her turn.

"I want to taste you," she whispered. "For so long, I've wanted to taste you."

She crawled between Saffil's legs and began to work her tongue up and down Saffil's tight labia. Saffil relaxed her outer labia as Averlin's tongue forced its way inside and began exploring the horizontal seam beyond. Those lips parted like eyelids opening, and the girl hungrily tasted Saffil's juices.

Saffil shuddered in response, and she felt her clitoris expanding even as Averlin found the throbbing nub. Averlin tenderly kissed the swollen organ, and the sensation drove Saffil wild with desire. She watched the yellow-haired head wiggling about as the girl tongued her, and she reached out to place her hands there, to gently hold Averlin as if afraid the girl might stop the wonderful thing she was doing. Saffil trembled as the girl licked her, and she was equally turned on by the girl's ass, up in the air behind her—it was such an exciting sight. Humans had more shapely, bulbous buttocks than taeflings, something else Saffil had never considered but that suddenly seemed utterly erotic to her.

She would later learn that Averlin had been with a girl once, a human servant traveling with a visiting human prince; they had flirted for two days, escalating their obvious excitement until they were sure of each other's desires, and they fled to the fields and made love under the stars. But despite that single experience with another woman, there was no doubt Averlin knew exactly what she was doing. Saffil thrashed on the bed, squirming and kicking and grabbing the sheets, and when Averlin slid her tongue up inside her, it was unbearable. She had found not only orgasmic bliss but an overwhelming physical connection with the truest love of her life. She screamed in ecstasy, screamed in happiness, screamed her way into paradise—

*   *   *

—screamed and wailed as the dragon thrust his tongue in and out of her. She didn't want to like it, but the memories of Averlin that night were all she was visualizing. The dragon's tongue was far larger than Averlin's, of course, although smaller than Saffil had expected for such a huge creature—but it still felt gigantic in there. It was hard to keep the fantasy going, but she did.

Before she knew it, she was in the throes of a gut-twisting orgasm. She screamed on that pillow-bed as Skrebulorius stiffened his tongue to a rigid pole and began madly fucking her with it. She thrashed her body through her orgasm until it ebbed, and then it returned again, and she screamed some more as she rode it out. When it was over, the dragon removed his tongue, then quickly licked her clean. She could feel her labial muscles completely relaxed, and felt herself lewdly exposed, as they had widened to admit him.

The giant beast sat back on its big haunches and laughed. "Beautiful and sweet," he said. "There's nothing like the nectar of a humanoid woman. And I knew you'd like having a dragon. You'll have the rest of your life to enjoy me. Now, here, I've brought you some food. I stole it from some picnicking humans. You should have seen their faces."

He was holding a big basket, which seemed tiny in his great claw, and he set it down. Inside was a fresh loaf of bread, some cold cuts, a block of sharp cheese, several pieces of fruit, a baking dish of apple cobbler, and a jug of honey mead. There was enough to feed her for several days. Saffil ate ravenously, and washed it down with a bit of the mead.

"I'm off to find my own supper," the dragon said. "Don't think about going anywhere. Even if you somehow managed to escape, I'd punish you by scorching your father's entire kingdom, and burning every last taefling in it alive."

He lumbered out of the cave and took wing in the darkening sky. Saffil found a soft, thick tapestry in the treasure pile to use as a warmer blanket on her pillow-bed, and she huddled under it, trying to forget what had really happened and thinking of that first night with Averlin. It had been such a wonderful night—so wonderful that she'd just been tongue-raped by a dragon and had handled it. And the subsequent nights had only gotten better. She missed the girl terribly.

Averlin hadn't regretted her choice like Velsa had; she'd told no one of their relationship. But of course Saffil's father had found out. Saffil remembered the night he'd come to see her in her chambers...

* * *

Their trysts continued for several months. Each day saw them falling more deeply in love; each sexual encounter saw

them more physically attached to each other. They knew they'd eventually have to flee the kingdom, because they could never be together otherwise.

One night, Averlin was due to arrive in her rooms — officially because Saffil had requested Averlin for a massage, and unofficially because she was really in the mood for love-making. She ordered all the servants away for the evening and instructed the housemother to retrieve Averlin from wherever she was working and send her up. Excited with the anticipation, Saffil donned the slinkiest nightdress she had — a sheer thing, see-through thanks to its fine mesh, barely coming to mid-thigh — and lay on her bed, waiting eagerly for her beloved.

But when her door opened, she was astounded at who appeared.

"Father!" she cried, surprised, because he almost never came to her rooms. She quickly came to her knees and pulled the bedspread up to cover herself.

"Good evening, my daughter," King Toranno said with a paternal smile. He was so big, towering above her next to her bed. His skin was a lot darker blue than hers, and his speckles were almost red. His long hair and full beard were a dark, mossy green. Angular, thick brow arches topped three yellow-orange eyes that seemed to blaze like fire. He was a muscular man with broad shoulders and rippling chest muscles beneath his evening tunic. "We seem to have a problem."

"What is it, Father?" she asked.

"The chief of staff came to see me today," he said. "It seems the servants have been talking about things they've seen and heard."

She grew cold beneath the covers, but managed a straight face. "What sort of things, Father?"

"I think you know," Toranno said. "You've continued to allow these urges you have — these unnatural, alien cravings — to control you. And they must stop."

Saffil's mind raced in panic. How had the servants known? She'd always been very particular about keeping their trysts secret. "Father, I don't know—"

"Don't play me for a fool, child," he snapped, and she shut up. "You've been having sexual relations with Averlin. Now, you're my daughter, and I love you, and Averlin is the child of departed friends—but you know my feelings about this. I'm sick of these deviant aberrations of yours."

There was no sense lying. "You don't understand what we feel. Our love is no aberration."

"You're confusing love with lust," he said. "I understand that. I'd be lying if I said I never strayed from your beloved mother, may the gods care for her soul. I had my sexual adventures with other women. I know what sexual needs are all about. And when you're married to a taefling prince from an allied kingdom, you can do as you will. You can engage in this immoral sex with a harem of women, whether they're taefling or human or nomiar or even arkorsh—whatever you want, as often as you wish. But you'd best be sure your husband doesn't find out. And there *will* be a husband, Saffil—a husband from a royal line. That's your obligation to me, to this family, to this kingdom—to our very race. Do I make myself clear?"

She nodded, fighting back the tears and the anger that boiled within her. She wouldn't let the hateful bastard see her cry. She'd agree with whatever he said, but soon she'd leave the kingdom with Averlin and never return.

And then a cold chill washed through her as she remembered what he'd done to Velsa. "Where is Averlin?" she asked.

"She's no longer your concern," King Toranno said brusquely, his triple eyes burning into her. "I've sent her to where she'll be of better use."

Saffil rose up high on her knees on the bed, face to chest with her father, and screamed, "Tell me where she is!"

He glared down at her. "I've sent her to Oyzel's Grand

Academy. She'll be there for three years—long enough for you to forget about her and marry a man."

Saffil fell back, shocked. "The... the *military* academy? You can't send a woman there!"

"She's hardly the first woman to attend Oyzel's. Many have, and some have become capable warriors. We've even had humans graduate—although never a human woman, so far."

"But Averlin isn't a warrior!" Saffil cried. "She's a servant girl—she'll never make it there!"

"Then, either way, our problem will be solved," he said in the coldest of voices.

She screamed, leaping up off the bed, intending to keep screaming in his face until she deafened him or he saw it her way—but he smacked her down with a backhand. She felt as if he'd hit her in the head with an oaken club. Her world spun, and she almost lost consciousness. She came back to dizzied awareness, flat on her stomach, face in the pillow, and her father was roaring at her.

"You'll stay away from her!" he hollered. "You'll stay away from all women, and all humans! You'll marry a royal taefling prince and become his wife! You'll do this family and this kingdom proud!"

He leaped onto the bed, grabbed her hair, and hauled her head up so sharply she yelped. He got in her face with his.

"Now you listen to me, you disgraceful whore," he snarled, brow furrowed tightly above his three glaring eyes, his lips bulging out, inflated with anger. "You do as you're told, and I'll be sure Averlin is safe. But if you transgress just once, I'll send her to the front lines in the war against the arkorsh in the Western Badlands. If you have sex with another woman, if you kiss another woman, if you hug another woman, I'll send her to battle. If I even think you're looking at a woman with lust in your eyes, Averlin will be gone. And if she survives that, I'll go to the academy and kill her myself!"

He threw her head back to the pillow and climbed off the bed. "Don't defy me again, daughter. Ever."

And then King Toranno walked out, and Saffil started bawling—

*   *   *

—she bawled on the pillow-bed as she remembered it. It had been unbearable, and still was. That had been three years before.

From then on, the chief of staff or a male servant accompanied female servants whenever they served Saffil in private. It was embarrassing to change when they were in the room, even though they turned their backs. And it was embarrassing that the female servants never again looked her in the eye. But Saffil never complained. She wouldn't do anything to risk Averlin's safety.

Oyzel's Grand Academy, named for an ancient taefling military genius, had been established as a cooperative effort of all taefling kingdoms on the continent two centuries before. Only the best of the best were sent there, to learn even better ways of becoming the finest warriors. The all-encompassing training regimen was brutal, and sometimes students died.

But there were exceptions to "best of the best." Oyzel's was also used as a place to send people that monarchs wanted to go away. Usually, they were non-criminals who had privately angered royal families; the monarchs couldn't jail or execute them, so instead they'd publicly grant them Oyzel's commissions. Anyone would welcome such a great honor.

Except those folks didn't want to go there, weren't even soldiers, and rarely survived the ordeal. And just sending a woman was bad enough; he'd sent a human woman. Averlin was the most prime target for harassment or worse while she was there. Rumor had it that women sent there against their wills were frequently relegated to little more than sex-servant status to cater to the men. Saffil always shuddered at the thought, and that kept her behaving for her father—so that his protection of Averlin would remain in place.

King Toranno had his daughter right where he wanted her. Saffil suspected he would honor his promise to keep Averlin safe, because he likely knew that if Saffil heard of Averlin's mistreatment, she'd not care about her father or his kingdom at all. Plus, he owed a debt of honor to her dead parents, whose child he'd taken in, so his claim that he'd kill Averlin was probably just for show. The solution was to play along for now, and later hire human mercenaries who could pull off an incredible rescue and escape—and then flee the land with the one she loved.

It all seemed pointless now. Saffil had been kidnapped by a dragon, held in his lair atop some distant mountain, and her father would never find her. If he did, how many champions would die trying to rescue her? Even with magic, fighting a dragon's fire was difficult.

She was lost forever. And Averlin was lost to her forever.

At least she wouldn't have to marry a man.

She counted the days by tearing out threads from her dress and knotting them together. Skrebulorius wasn't there much, surprisingly; he'd been a pain in the ass to a dozen kingdoms, and enjoyed setting croplands ablaze, eating cattle, burning villages, and so on. No champion had lasted long enough to even have been considered a nuisance. So he spent most of his days away, and some nights as well.

But when he was at the lair, he liked to look at her, and bade her lie naked and exposed on the pillow-bed. Sometimes he'd have her stand and strike various poses, or prance around, or even sing and dance for him. His tastes were bizarre. And, frequently, he'd lick her with that tongue, tease her breasts and tickle her thighs and arouse her, and she had a few orgasms that simultaneously excited and repulsed her. With every one of them, she kept Averlin firmly in mind, going to a place where she could imagine making love with the girl. Still, she knew it was the dragon's tongue, and she couldn't ignore how good it felt. If only the beast would do something about his horrid breath.

One day, about two months into Saffil's enslavement, Skrebulorius returned, landing in the cave with a resounding THUD and waking her from a dead sleep. She sat up to see him holding something shiny and silvery in his clawed hands.

"Behold this fine toy!" the dragon roared, and he threw the silver thing forward. It clattered to the stone, rolling towards her before scraping to a stop. It was a man, without a doubt, clad in full-plate armor. His gauntlets and helmet were missing, and she could see by the blue skin he was taefling. The disheveled young man was alive and well. He looked groggy, and his forehead was scraped and his face bruised. He came to his knees, saw her, and his eyes widened.

"My Lady!" he cried.

"Rastun!" she cried in surprise. It was her betrothed prince.

"He's come to rescue you!" the dragon bellowed with a laugh. "As you can see, he didn't do such a good job."

Rastun looked to her with three pleading, bright-green eyes. "I'm terribly sorry, My Lady," he said. "Your father dispatched me to rescue you, and I've failed." He was very young, and he looked a little frightened. His spots were yellow, his hair a darker blue than his skin. He was a good-looking taefling man, but he still didn't appeal to her.

"It's all right," Saffil said. "Thank you for trying." She pulled her blanket close. She didn't need anyone else seeing her naked — not even her supposed husband-to-be.

"I thought we could have a little fun," Skrebulorius said gleefully. "Princess, drop that blanket. Prince, remove your clothing."

Neither of them moved a muscle. The dragon growled, and black smoke shot forward, billowing about the pair. "I won't say it twice," he said.

Saffil dropped her blanket, exposing her beautiful taefling body. Rastun, to his credit, kept his gaze locked firmly on her eyes.

"Do what he says," she said. "He'll kill you. We'd have seen each other naked anyway."

Rastun nodded, then stood and removed his breastplate and backplate, then the chainmail shirt beneath it, then his greaves and chainmail leggings. His padding came next, and soon he was down to just his underclothes. He shed them and stood there, as naked as she.

She had to admire his form. He was muscular and well-defined, from his toned biceps to his strong pectorals to his rippling abdominals, which were almost yellow where the spots grew thick. His blue penis hung flaccid between his legs. She'd seen naked taefling and human men before, and appreciated the physique of the taefling male; they didn't have those wrinkled, dangling sacs human men did, as taefling testicles were inside their bodies. And there was no foreskin at all. Taefling penises were shorter than human penises, but the heads were bulbous and enlarged, much like Averlin's special candle. Rastun seemed ashamed as she scanned his body, but she smiled at him, willing him to be at ease.

"Well, what are you waiting for, prince?" Skrebulorius said. "Take your princess. I want to watch."

"I'll never do that," Rastun said, spinning to face the dragon with a steel jaw and icy stare. "Not until we're properly wed. You might as well kill me now."

Saffil saw by the look on the dragon's face that the beast was ready to do just that, so she leaped off the pillow-bed, crying, "No! Please, don't hurt him!"

"Then he'll do my bidding," the dragon snarled.

"He will," she said, grabbing the man's hand and pulling

him towards the bed. Then she whispered in his ear, "It's all right. He's done terrible things to me. This will be wonderful by comparison, really. I know it's not how we pictured it, but it'll be fine."

She wrapped her arms about him and pressed her three soft breasts against his hard chest. He said, "I'm nervous, My Lady, but I've been nervous since we were officially betrothed. I've heard that you... well, that men aren't your interest."

"Right now, it's you or a dragon's tongue," she said. "I'd rather have you. And it doesn't matter what I prefer. Like I said, we'd be doing this eventually anyway."

Rastun returned her smile and pulled her close to kiss her. She felt no sexual attraction at all. He did, however, as she felt his penis hardening, rising up and poking against the furry thatch of hair between her legs. It throbbed steadily as she kissed him, until it sprung free and upward. She'd never been with a man before, so she convinced herself it was a worthwhile experiment—especially since, if they managed to escape, she'd be having wedded sex with him until she could find a way to rescue Averlin and flee the kingdom.

She reached down and wrapped her hand around Rastun's erect penis, the first time she'd ever touched one. She felt clumsy, as she didn't know quite what to do, but she began stroking it with a firm grip. He wrapped his arms tightly around her as she worked, and he kissed her again. It didn't take long, and he was completely into it.

It wasn't sexually exciting for her, but it was mentally exciting; having sex with a man was something she'd never done, so she figured the adventure was worth it. Sensation was sensation, after all, and maybe she could learn to enjoy it. She was planning how to touch him, where to move, what to whisper in his ear, when he picked her up and carried her to the pillow-bed. She was surprised, but realized that it was the male way to take control. It was very different from being with a woman, which was soft and relaxed and comprised of giving and sharing, and less about domination and submission. But she understood, and she resigned herself to letting him direct the encounter. It was a given that the prince had enjoyed his father's concubines since about his tenth year, when his penis had begun growing outside his body, lengthening quickly during the first few months of puberty in preparation for adulthood. Young taefling males were encouraged to have sex with taefling women, and with a court like his father's, he'd probably screwed a thousand of them. He wouldn't be without plenty of experience directing the sex.

Rastun laid her on the pillow and climbed between her legs. She was hoping he'd start with his mouth and tongue, which could excite her no matter who did it. She looked forward to clamping her thighs about his head, pretending he was Averlin, and coming in his mouth. That would be a nice precursor to the sex act.

But without prologue, she felt the bulbous head of his penis shoving roughly against her tightly sealed vertical labia. She wasn't turned on yet, not at all, and she knew she'd have to work hard to get there, but without any foreplay, he was trying to force himself into her. She was so dry, and it wasn't comfortable, but before she knew it, he was grunting and straining—and she felt her outer and inner lips pop suddenly open. She held back a yelp of surprise. He'd hit the perfect spot, splitting her vertical and horizontal labia apart and jamming up inside her.

He started working back and forth, but not much of it was inside her. It chafed her, because she wasn't remotely ready and barely lubricated, but he picked up the pace and moved his hips faster anyway. After a minute of that, she started juicing up, but she still wasn't turned on. Even the dragon turned her on better than Rastun was doing.

Rastun supported himself on his hands and knees, and her hips hurt the way her legs were splayed. With more of her juices flowing, he sped up his hips and began pounding into her. It didn't hurt so much as it was overwhelming. Her heart wasn't in it, but it did finally start feeling good. She felt her reluctant clitoris, at the upper part of her vagina and behind the top inner lip, begin to stir. Blood pumped into it, and the friction from the fat knob of his penis began strumming the half-asleep nub awake. Yes, that was better...

He pounded harder and faster, and she gasped and took the strange, alien invasion, all the while conscious of Skrebulorius towering above them, watching every stroke. The prince worked his hips like a machine, banging his penis inside her and grunting with every thrust. And as he bored in and out of her, it felt even better — that familiar tingling sensation began burning in her clit, which had grown almost to its full size, and her insides began to burn with ecstasy. Maybe it wasn't so bad after all.

Even still, she thought of Averlin and her candle. Averlin had brought her favorite candle to Saffil's chambers one night, to show what she'd been talking about...

*   *   *

The candle was made of red wax. It was a good ten inches long, and the bulging base, wider than the shaft and designed to wedge into a holder, had been smoothly rounded to form a bulbous tip not unlike the head of a taefling's penis. Averlin had stripped down and was lying back on the bed, her legs spread.

"Watch this," she said with a sexy smile.

She fed the fat end in between her labia, which glistened with her juices, and her face strained a bit as she worked the red shaft inside her. Once the end disappeared inside, she began working it back and forth in a slow, jiggling motion. A few dozen short strokes yielded lewd sucking sounds, and then she went deeper. Saffil was excited by the act, and by the breathtaking visual of the crimson shaft sliding between creamy, white thighs and fluffy, yellow pubic hair.

Before Saffil knew it, the girl was driving the candle deep inside her pink pussy so that nearly two-thirds of it vanished. When she pulled it back, it came almost all the way out, save for the bulb. She built up a good speed, hanging onto the end of the candle with both hands and fucking herself hard and fast.

"Oh, this feels so good," Averlin whispered. "Do you want to try it?"

Saffil, who was also naked, was staring at her with three wide eyes and an open mouth, and nodded stupidly.

Averlin pulled the wet candle out and pushed her lover back onto the bed. Without warning, she swung her leg up and over Saffil's head and lowered her pussy down. Saffil's tongue met the pink pussy, wet and dripping from its candle adventure, and she began lashing at the exposed human clit. Averlin settled back so her wet vagina seemed to suction onto Saffil's energetic mouth, nearly suffocating her, but it felt wonderful. The aroma was heady and exciting, and the taste like nothing else—a bit like the caviar of the rare Eastern Mountains land shark, only better. Every whiff of it drove Saffil wild with desire and made her own blue vagina churn with excitement.

Between her legs, she felt Averlin feed the fat end of the slippery-wet candle between her four wet lips, and the fat knob popped inside her. She pulled her mouth off Averlin's pussy, sucking in a breath in surprise as she felt the wax phallus sink deep into her soft insides, until she didn't think it couldn't possibly go in anymore. Then she felt it slide almost all the way out of her—and then plunge smoothly back in again. Averlin started slowly at first—nice and easy in, just as relaxed out—but seemed to know when to speed things up. And before Saffil knew it, the girl was fucking her as hard and fast with the candle as she had been fucking herself with it. The sensation of the shaft sliding across her clit was incredible, and the fat end filled her up in ways she'd never imagined. In response, Saffil pulled the girl's pussy back against her face and ate her out hard, matching every thrust with a lashing, probing tongue.

They stayed like that for what seemed like hours, until Averlin leaned down and began licking inside Saffil's relaxed labia, where she stimulated the subtle nerve clusters there that a penis could never find. Averlin knew just how to make her come. She felt her body begin to tremble and shudder, even as she felt Averlin begin to shake above her, her pussy sliding madly across Saffil's face. Saffil knew they were going to come together.

She went crazy with her tongue, flicking Averlin's clit, licking up and down her slit, and she moved her hands up to help out. Averlin began to cry out, even as she fucked Saffil harder with the candle and sped up the tonguing she was giving the insides of Saffil's lips.

And then Averlin was wailing in ecstasy, shaking uncontrollably, coming all over Saffil's face. The candle-fucking already had Saffil just about there, but hearing Averlin crying out in pleasure, and tasting her hot juices soaking Saffil's mouth, was all it took to send Saffil over the edge. She came too, screaming into her girlfriend's pussy, and she rode a wave of perfect pleasure forever.

Then they held each other, and Saffil knew she'd never love anyone like she loved Averlin...

*   *   *

It wasn't like that with Rastun.

Saffil was just beginning to head towards the hope of an orgasm when the prince suddenly stiffened, jerked, and grunted like an animal. His hips hitched, and hitched, and spasmed, and with every movement, Saffil felt the prince coming. It was like someone was shooting spurts of hot water up inside her, sort of like having a douche. It felt bizarre. She thought that if she'd been coming too, it would have been something of a turn-on. But she hadn't, and it wasn't. If she could just have had even a weak orgasm, it might have been worth it.

But Rastun stopped and collapsed on her, dead weight forcing air out of her lungs. He didn't move, no longer thrusting his penis inside her.

"What's the matter?" she said.

"Nothing," he said, breathing heavily. He forced himself up on shaky arms and looked at her. Sweat poured down his face. "It's okay—I came."

She felt his penis shrinking inside her, and she realized he hadn't just come—he was done. It was over. No orgasm for her. Before she knew it, she felt his soft penis sliding right out, dragging what felt like a quart of semen with it. She felt it ooze down her butt crack, like gooey slime, and it just felt gross. The whole experience had been a worse disaster than she could have imagined. She realized Skrebulorius' tongue was a better experience than this guy. At least the dragon made sure she came, and his tongue didn't spew disgusting slime inside her.

He must have seen the troubled look on her face. "Are you okay? Is something wrong?"

She realized then that it didn't matter how many concubines he'd bedded in his young life: He was an inexperienced young boy who didn't have the slightest clue what a woman's body needed or how it worked. The concubines certainly were never going to complain, and would never tell him he was bad in bed. He probably thought he was the greatest royal stud a taefling woman could hope to have—and the concubines had probably told him such for years, even if they laughed about it amongst themselves later. Rastun just didn't understand, and could hardly be blamed for how it had gone down.

She managed a smile, reaching up and touching his face. "No," she said. "You were great."

Rastun smiled back. "I'm glad."

And suddenly, he was yanked away from her in Skrebulorius' great claw. He hollered in surprise, but before anyone could do anything, the dragon flicked his body back as if tossing aside a piece of garbage—and the young prince flew out the cave entrance.

Saffil screamed and came up on her knees, even as Rastun's scream echoed down the mountain as he fell. The dragon roared with laughter.

"I'm no expert, but that looked like a lousy lay," the dragon said. "Now I'm off to retrieve him. He'll make a tasty supper."

And with that, Skrebulorius headed for the cave and dived out. Saffil stayed on her knees, frozen in shock, for several minutes, as her dead fiancé's semen continued to ooze out of her and drip onto the pillow-bed.

A few days later, the dragon flew her to a pond on the side of a nearby mountain, where he let her clean herself. He did this about once a week, and she relished the short time she got to spend in the cold waters. He always left her to her bathing, flying off to hunt for food.

She scrubbed herself down with a scrap of cloth from her engagement dress until she felt almost new again, and then enjoyed swimming about the sparkling pond that reflected the brilliant blue of the sky. Eventually, her heart fell when she saw the distant form of Skrebulorius as he winged his way back towards the mountain. She got out of the water and dried off with the blanket she'd brought, and stood there letting the sun dry her blue body as she waited for the dragon's arrival.

He was nearly there when the blast of blue hit him from out of sight beyond the mountainside. The dragon screeched at the magical blast, and Saffil gasped in shock. Skrebulorius wheeled about in mid-air and flew evasive maneuvers to Saffil's left. She watched in awe as the attacker came into sight.

It was another would-be rescuer, this one bedecked in a

full suit of armor—helmet and gauntlets included—and riding a black, winged horse. The horse galloped through the air, in pursuit of the dragon, even as the mounted knight extended his golden lance ahead of him and let loose with another blast of powerful blue magic. This one slapped Skrebulorius right in his ass; the dragon howled in pain and tumbled downward. The knight spurred his mount on; big, feathered wings flapped hard, and the pair dived after the dragon.

Saffil hurried towards the mountain's edge, wrapping her blanket around her as she ran, in hopes of seeing what was happening—but, just as she reached the edge, the dragon swooped up before her. She screamed and threw herself back, and felt the rush of air as he passed over her. She recovered in time to see the winged horse fly over, and she clambered to her feet and spun around.

The dragon whirled about in mid-air above the pond to face the champion, who was bearing down on him, lance extended. Skrebulorius let loose with a tremendous cone of fire from his mouth. It flared out, ever wider, and the knight and his winged horse looked like goners.

But the knight had come with magical protection. The fire broke around the knight, as if he were surrounded by an invisible sphere, and horse and hero escape even a singeing. He was still bearing down on the dragon, and he let loose with another blast from his magic lance at close range. The blue bolt exploded in the dragon's still-open, fire-breathing mouth; Skrebulorius few backward, end over end, and crashed into the cold pond and went under.

Saffil screamed and leaped into the air with excitement. Certainly this dragon had never faced so formidable an opponent! The battle appeared to be over.

The knight reined his winged black horse about, and the pair circled the pond. Saffil cheered from below, even as the knight made a second pass. Skrebulorius had been under awhile, but the knight was clearly making certain that his foe was dead. After a third pass, the knight flew in for a landing, and his flying horse's hooves hit the rocky ledge and clopped to a quick stop nearby. Saffil went running to her rescuer as the man dismounted.

Then the dragon suddenly broke the surface of the pond, rising up like a sea serpent and roaring his anger across the mountaintops. The knight spun about, bringing his lance to bear and letting another blue bolt fly.

The dragon was half out of the water when the blast arrived — but, this time, he held up a claw and easily deflected it.

"Foolish little man," the dragon growled. "How long did you think you could last with but one magical trick? You're lucky it took me this long to adapt to that weak enchantment."

The knight dropped his lance and drew his sword, and as it cleared the sheath, Saffil could see that the long blade glowed a brilliant red. The knight held it up before him as the dragon advanced out of the pond. Water steamed off the fiery body of Skrebulorius, and indeed the pond around him steamed like a pot ready to boil. The knight glanced back to check on Saffil's position, then moved to put himself between her and the dragon.

And in that moment, Saffil realized what an utterly selfless thing that was to do. Sure, the knight had thoughts of riches, and maybe Saffil's hand in marriage if he were a taefling prince, but he had to know how futile his attempts were. He was going to die — and for nothing.

In that moment, Saffil knew then that if the man somehow succeeded against all odds and slew the dragon, and if he were in fact a prince... she'd marry him. She'd do it. He'd have earned it. She'd never be able to be faithful to him, because she'd use every resource to get Averlin back, and if Averlin were gone she knew only another woman could ever make her feel right. But she knew she'd marry him, be good to him, bear him children, and satisfy her father's obligations. She owed everyone that much.

Skrebulorius breathed again, and the incredible wave of flame was like a growing fireball that obscured the dragon as it advanced on the knight. He held his crimson sword before him, standing his ground, and like before the fire broke harmlessly around him and away.

The dragon roared in anguish when the smoke cleared, and lumbered out of the steaming pond and headed towards the knight, who charged to meet his foe. Skrebulorius was fast, reaching out with both massive claws even as his head dived down, his maw full of teeth gaping wide. But the knight was faster, spinning, ducking, and swinging his sword—and lopping off one of those big claws.

The dragon howled in agony, but the knight spun about, swung again, and lopped off the other claw. The handless dragon reared up and back, roaring in pain, and the knight rushed forward and plunged his sword deep into the dragon's belly. Skrebulorius howled once more and doubled over, and when his head came down low, the knight swung wide and cut a long slice up the side of the dragon's neck.

Without a sound, the dragon fell, black blood spraying from the wound. His massive head hit the rock, and the knight backpedaled quickly to avoid getting hit. The dragon rolled sideways on the ground and thrashed violently. With every jerk of his immense body, the ground shook. His tail flailed mightily about, splashing in the pond. His head flopped on the rock as blood sprayed everywhere, and his rear claws dug madly at nothing. Finally, the dragon stopped moving forever.

Saffil couldn't believe it. The dragon was dead. She'd been saved. She staggered forward as the knight sheathed his glowing blade and turned to face her. His shining armor was splattered with dark dragon's blood; it dripped off his helm, and so much poured from his magic sword that the blade itself seemed to be bleeding.

"Brave knight," she said as she stood before him. "You've earned whatever treasure my father has promised."

Duty. Honor. Obligation. It all flooded through her mind. She'd never understood it, and really didn't now—at least, not as far as it applied to family and kingdom. But she understood it on a personal level. She'd made a promise in her mind, and it was sacred and unbreakable. She'd never stop trying to find Averlin, would never stop trying to be with the woman she loved, but she'd be this man's wife if he indeed were of royal taefling blood. Still, she hoped against hope that he was just a knight—and not a taefling prince.

The knight took a final step forward, dropped to one knee, and bowed his head to her. She reached down and placed her hand on his armored shoulder. "Rise," she said.

But the knight didn't. Instead, he reached up with gauntleted hands and lifted his helmet off. His head was encased in a chain-mail coif, and he turned his face to look up at her, with his pale face and stunning blue eyes.

And high cheekbones. And broad smile. Saffil gasped as the knight reached up and pulled his—her—chainmail coif off. A pile of blond hair cascaded down around her shoulders.

"Averlin!" Saffil cried.

Averlin came to her feet with a broad smile and excited eyes. "You didn't think your father sending me to Oyzel's would stop me, did you?"

Saffil screamed with joy and leaped into Averlin's arms.

Averlin had surpassed everyone's expectations at Oyzel's, excelling better than any woman ever had, and better than most of the men. She had a knack for the warrior arts, and soon earned the men's respect. She'd been determined to show King Toranno up and one day return for Saffil. She'd just graduated from the Academy, and had been named a true warrior, when word arrived of Saffil's kidnapping. She had resolved to rescue Saffil, but knew she needed help.

She'd journeyed to the Northern Mountains and sought out the aerolarr people, a peaceful race who lived on high peaks and flew their winged horses, called the krysaor. They'd never allowed a krysaor to leave their possession, but she lobbied hard in the name of love for another woman. That's where she had an edge. The aerolarr were hermaphroditic; they required two to reproduce, but each aerolarr had male and female sex organs. They mated for life, had no concept of infidelity, and considered the love between two mates the highest form of love. As such, they couldn't fathom why Averlin and Saffil had been so hatefully prevented from being together, and why someone's genitalia mattered. They agreed to train her to ride a krysaor.

She then flew beyond the human kingdom of Zandor to the south, where she pleaded with a good dragon to help her. The good dragon served as protector of several kingdoms, and while he refused to destroy his dragon kin, he provided her with the magic lance from his treasure trove. That dragon was displeased with Skrebulorius' out-of-control behavior, and admitted that it was time someone put him in his place. But he warned her that Skrebulorius was very skilled in the magical arts, and it wouldn't take him long to defend against the lance. Averlin had better be a damn good warrior, the dragon told her, and also recommended she seek certain protection.

So Averlin followed a rumor the dragon related to her and searched for an old fire wizard, a recluse living in the Forgotten Forest, a wooded island that was an oasis amidst endless miles of swamps, bogs, and salt lakes. The ancient taefling sorcerer, once the court wizard for Saffil's great-grandfather, asked why he should help her. She told him her story, and the old man completely understood. After all, he'd been banned from the kingdom for similar transgressions ages before. Now he lived in the Forgotten Forest, in an old stone tower, with his lifelong companion—who was a human male.

"They'd been lovers since before my father was born," Averlin said. "Seeing them together, holding hands—blue skin against white—reminded me even more of you. He enchanted

the very sword I'd been awarded at Oyzel's, and ensured I'd have the greatest protection from the dragon's fire. But he warned me that, even with the sword, the lance, and the winged horse, I wasn't likely to survive."

"But you did—because of your amazing skills!" Saffil cried with a laugh. "Without them, all the magical aids in the world wouldn't have helped."

"It was more than that," Averlin said. "I love you, Saffil. My love for you is all that has kept me going these three years. When I heard of your kidnapping, I couldn't bear the thought of losing you. It was that love that defeated the dragon."

They embraced again, and Saffil said, "We can never go home again, you know."

"Then we'll find a new land," Averlin said, blue eyes flashing with excitement.

"Perhaps we should start a bit closer to home," Saffil said.

They flew to the dragon's cave, and Averlin was impressed. It needed to be cleaned up, the big entrance needed to be mostly closed off, and they needed some more blankets, but it was a good start. The riches alone would enable them to start their own kingdom, if they chose. "It will make a fine home for the time being," Averlin said, and she hugged her lover again.

"The armor is a bit cold," Saffil said with a smile. "And I'd really like to feel you instead of all that steel."

On the big pillow-bed, they made the most passionate love two people ever could. They were voracious, kissing and fondling each other all over. They massaged each other's breasts, slid their hands down abdomens and across hips, teased each other's thighs. They touched each other and worked their fingers steadily until they brought each other to powerful orgasms. Then they kissed some more, and when they had rested a bit, Saffil dived hungrily between Averlin's legs, even as Saffil threw her leg over Averlin and settled herself onto Averlin's mouth. They attacked each other fiercely, with hands squeezing buttocks and mouths making each other tremble with uncontrollable desire. And when they plunged their tongues deep inside each other, they held on to each other for dear life as they rode the most explosive orgasms they'd ever experienced.

*   *   *

King Toranno never saw his daughter, nor the finest female warrior Oyzel's Grand Academy had ever produced, again. Years later, he heard a rumor that a human female and a taefling female were the rulers of a small kingdom thousands of miles away, on the other side of the vast continent. The human was a warrior, known for flying her winged steed, and the taefling was a student of the magical arts, specializing in fire magic. She reportedly had two male wizards as her teachers — one taefling, one human. Of course, it was just a rumor.

The kingdom survived, and with his new wife Toranno fathered another daughter. Her name was Fymno, and she grew into a beautiful taefling woman who eagerly married the first prince the king brought to her. The wedding was lavish and finally bound together two taefling kingdoms, just as Toranno had always wanted.

It came to pass that Fymno visited her father while her husband was away on a diplomatic mission to Brodur, on the ocean coast to the south. He went to see her late one evening; her rooms were Saffil's old chambers, and as he topped the stairs near the door, he heard familiar sounds coming from within. Quietly, he moved to the door, which was slightly ajar. Near the hinges, he peeked through the small gap and beheld the sight on Fymno's bed.

Fymno was on her back, her legs in the air, and a male human servant was giving it to her. He was on his knees, hanging on to Fymno's ankles, powerfully thrusting his brown hips. Dark thighs slapped Fymno's blue ass, and her cheeks jiggled mightily. And the angle was perfect; the king could see the human's big penis disappearing into her blue vagina, then reappearing, covered in her juices. Fymno moaned with every thrust, eyes closed, swaying her head to and fro, orange hair flying about as she enjoyed the ecstasy.

King Toranno sighed and pulled his handkerchief out of his pocket. "Here we go again," he whispered.

He unbuttoned his pants and pulled out his stiffening blue penis, and he began stroking, his eyes focused on the scene. The last time he'd done this was when Saffil had engaged in sex with Averlin. He'd masturbated dozens of times watching them before his values finally took over.

This time, it was different. Fymno was married, and the king knew a human couldn't impregnate a taefling.

Fymno's moans increased, and the excited servant picked up his pace. He pushed against her ankles, forcing her ass higher off the bed, changing his angle of penetration. Fymno immediately began to wail in pleasure with every thrust of his big tool. The king stroked his own cock faster in response. And finally, when his daughter launched into a long, drawn-out, screaming orgasm, and when the human grunted and lurched against her as he came, the king ejaculated into his handkerchief. It was all he could do to keep his mouth shut.

Then he hurried away. Thank goodness she was married to a prince. Toranno would make sure she came to visit more often, and make sure she had a rotating supply of male servants when she did.

But first things first: He'd order the brown-skinned human servant who had been screwing his daughter to report to his private quarters later that evening. Someday, Toranno's values would take over, and he'd feign disgust with himself, but until then — well, it had been a long time since he'd enjoyed the feeling of making sweet love to a human servant boy.

He felt a twinge of hypocrisy, but then he remembered that he was the king.

About the Authors

J.T. Beckett ("Obsidian Phage") is the pseudonym for a psychologist specializing in sexual dysfunction. J.T. believes in erotica and pornography as a healthy extension of human sexuality, but J.T.'s peers wouldn't quite understand J.T.'s interest in writing erotica, thus the pseudonym and the ambiguous gender. J.T. has dabbled in fiction but J.T.'s publications have mostly been in poetry under J.T.'s real name. This is J.T.'s first published work of erotica, but J.T. hopes to pen a few more. J.T. lives in the American Northwest.

Milena Benini ("The Sea Bride," "Night in Berlin") published her first story at 14 in the SF magazine *Sirius*. Her stories and articles have appeared in print and online in Croatia and abroad, including *69 Flavors of Paranoia, Neverwhere, Axxón*, and *InterNova*. She contributed chapters to *The Complete Guide to Writing Fantasy* and to *The Complete Guide to Writing Science Fiction*, which won the 2008 EPPIE award for best self-help book. Her Croatian awards include four SFERAs (best novel, novella, short story, and related work) and the tastiest SF award ever: a whole Istrian prosciutto, won for "most-Istrian" short story in 2009. She also translates SF, working with authors from Douglas Adams and Charles Stross to N. K. Jemisin and Terry Pratchett. Besides SF, she enjoys genre literature of all kinds, feminism, politics, and random furry animals. She blogs in Croatian at nosf.net, in many languages at milerama.nosf.net, and in English at milenab.tumblr.com. She's on Twitter as @Milerama.

Julie Dixon ("Desperate Measures") has been an avid *Star Trek* fan since she saw the show as a young girl in the 1960s. She has always loved adventures on alien worlds. She also has a fantasy she'll never really act out, much to her husband's relief: being gangbanged. With her husband's encouragement, and the help of a pseudonym so she won't have to explain it to her kids and family, she has lived that fantasy, as an alien-world adventure, with her story in this anthology.

David M. Fitzpatrick ("Succors for Incubation," "Always a Prince, Never a Princess") has had over 50 short stories published in magazines and anthologies in the U.S., UK, and Canada. He has edited several anthologies, including *Salacious Tales* and *Atheist Tales*. By day, he writes for a newspaper and is also a freelance writer. He teaches an adult-education class on writing short fiction, firmly disagreeing with the old saw that "those who write, write; those who don't teach writing"; he feels a writer can do both—and perhaps *should* do both. He lives in Brewer, across the river from Bangor. He keeps hoping Stephen King's errant Muse will accidentally land on his house on the way to King's. No luck yet.

Jane Gallagher ("Virgin's Sacrifice," "Just a Toy") spent her youth afraid that someone would discover she didn't believe in gods, find her hidden erotica novels, and figure out that she liked girls. She's fine with all these things now. Her most recent short story appeared in the anthology *Atheist Tales*. Her two stories here are her first attempts at erotica, and she's excited to merge that theme with speculative fiction, which she loves so much.

Janix Jenn ("Love Thy Neighbor") is a writer of erotica in many genres. Her name is also a pseudonym; she writes non-erotica under her real name, where she has written in every fiction genre and on every nonfiction topic imaginable.

John Grant ("I'm Running") is the author of some 70 books, of which about 25 are fiction, including novels like *The World, The Hundredfold Problem, The Far-Enough Window, The Dragons of Manhattan* and *Leaving Fortusa*. His book-length fiction *Dragonhenge*, illustrated by Bob Eggleton, was shortlisted for a Hugo Award in 2003; its successor was *The Stardragons*. His anthology *New Writings in the Fantastic* was shortlisted for a British Fantasy Award. His novellas *The City in These Pages* and *The Lonely Hunter* have appeared from PS Publishing.

In nonfiction, he co-edited with John Clute *The Encyclopedia of Fantasy* and wrote in their entirety all three editions of *The Encyclopedia of Walt Disney's Animated Characters*; both are standard reference works in their field. Among his latest nonfiction has been the loosely linked series *Discarded Science, Corrupted Science, Bogus Science,* and *Denying Science.* He has just finished a huge encyclopedia of film noir and "a cute illustrated rhyming book for kids about a velociraptor."

He has received two Hugo Awards, the World Fantasy Award, the Locus Award, and a number of other international literary awards. Under his real name, Paul Barnett, he has written a few books (like the space operas *Strider's Galaxy* and *Strider's Universe*) and for a number of years ran the world-famous fantasy-artbook imprint Paper Tiger, for this work earning a Chesley Award and a nomination for the World Fantasy Award.

To learn more, visit www.johngrantpaulbarnett.com.

Amy Judkins ("The Perfect Woman") edits erotica, although she admits that quality in that genre is often lacking. She also enjoys reading and writing science fiction, and admits that its quality can also be touch and go in the small-press world. Her story in *Salacious Tales* is her first SF/erotica story. She thanks her boyfriend for his insight into making her male protagonist think and act like a man, and for several of her male friends for proofing the story and letting her know that her boyfriend knew what he was talking about.

Holly Knight ("Primal Urge") loves men and loves being a woman, but admits to having some very male qualities. Most notably, she has a very strong sexual desire, more like that of the men she knows who seem always interested in that one thing. She's okay with that, and feels that she understands the idea that men think about sex all the time. She has written fiction since she was a teenager, but she never considered submitting for publication until she heard about *Salacious Tales.* It seemed a perfect match of two of her favorite things. If her extremely religious family ever found out, they'd lose their minds, which has made this experience all the more satisfying.

E.W. Lee ("Tommy's Adventures in Gloryland") is a freethinker, librarian and writer living in Kansas. He is the author of numerous books, articles, and stories, including the short story "The Screwletter Tapes" which appeared in the anthology *Atheist Tales.* Raised in a Southern Baptist family, he married a lapsed Catholic and now has three lovely children who are also secularists. Read into that what you will.

 **William Markly O'Neal** ("Blood of Bacchus," "Flattery Will Get You Nowhere") is a Hoosier whose stories have appeared in the *Cover of Darkness* anthology and *Weird Tales* magazine, and featured in podcasts at www.TalesToTerrify.com. A collection of his horror stories, *Fishing in Brains for an Eye with Teeth,* is available on Amazon.com. He's currently seeking a publisher or agent for his Roaring Twenties horror novel *Cold Dead Love.* William is a proud member of the Horror Writers Association. Follow @WilliamMarklyON on Twitter, or find him on Facebook at www.facebook.com/WilliamMarklyONeal.

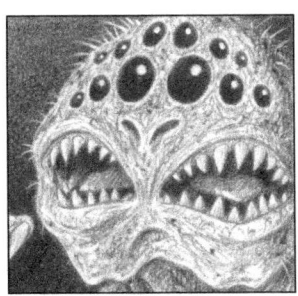 **Corwin Merrill** ("Call of Cunthulhu," "Stranglehold") isn't afraid of anything, including writing an erotica story with "cunt" in the title or one where a man inexplicably wants to screw and then strangle a helpless victim. He's written cheesy erotic fiction for adult magazines, but his real love is science fiction, fantasy, and horror, and he jumped at the chance to write serious erotic fiction for *Salacious Tales.* By day, he's a Web developer, programmer, and graphic designer, which is more than enough reason to need to write sex stories.

 **Robert M. Palmer** ("Dinner and a Peepshow") is a freelance copywriter living in coastal Maine. His love of fiction stems from a deeply ingrained paper fetish and a need to see his name in print. His shorts have appeared in *Peeks & Valleys, Midnight Times,* and *Thuglit,* ranging in theme from sexy dead girls to antisocial button men. In his "free time" he plays with dead animals. His pen is for sale at www.TheRealRobertPalmer.com. You can stalk him on Twitter: @TheRobertPalmer.

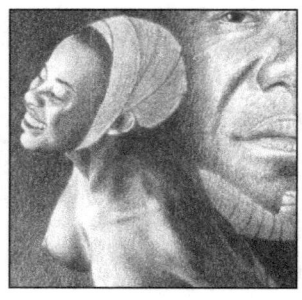

Frances Pauli ("Opal Heart") writes speculative fiction, usually with touches of humor or romance — which means, of course, that she has trouble choosing sides. She's always been a rabid fan of things outside the box — odd, weird, or unusual — and that trend follows through to her tales which feature aliens, fairies, and even, on occasion, an assortment of humans. Frances eats far too much chocolate, drinks far too little wine, and does her best to get the stories out and on paper before they drive her completely insane. More information on her work and upcoming releases can be found at www.francespauli.com.

Dalibor Perković ("Hi-Tech Sex Lib") is a Croatian science-fiction writer, born in Mali Lošinj and now living in Sesvete, Zagreb. In the late 1990s he was a member of the *Studentski list* editorial staff and was a co-founder of another student newspaper, the *SL Revolt*. He started working for the at-the-time opposition daily *Novi list* in 1998. He returned to college in 2002, earned a physics degree, and works as a teacher. He has written a collection of science-fiction stories, as well as one novel. He received SFERA awards for the best Croatian science fiction novellas (*Banijska praskozorja*, "The Banija Dawns," in 2000 and *Preko rijeke*, "Across the River," in 2004) and one for the best novel (*Sva krv čovječanstva*, "All the Blood of Mankind," in 2006). He was a long-term editor of the *SFeraKon Bulletin*. In 2012 he was a co-founder and the first president of "Nastavnici organizirano" ("Teachers Organized"), a non-government organisation whose aim is the development of the Croatian education system.

 **Aleksandar Žiljak** ("Argosy," "Days of Orgone," and all the illustrations for *Salacious Tales*) was born in Zagreb, Croatia, in 1963. He graduated on Electrotechnical Faculty in Zagreb in 1987, and got his Master of Computer Sciences degree in 1990. After working for five years as a high-school professor, he became a freelance illustrating artist, working mostly for children's magazines, newspapers, school textbooks, and illustrated books, and also producing book-cover art. He specializes in wildlife illustration, but also does science fiction, mystery, and similar subjects. He is a member of Croatian Freelance Artists Association and Croatian Applied Arts Artists Association and the Croatian Writers Society.

Žiljak also writes science fiction, fantasy, and horror, starting with short horror stories in 1991. Some of his early stories appeared in the now-defunct *Futura* magazine. Since then, he has been a more or less regular contributor to various anthologies published annually in Croatia, most notably those produced by the SFera SF club from Zagreb. Currently, his stories appear in places such as *Grifon* fantasy magazine and *ABC Tehnike* technical culture magazine for young people. In the mid-1990s, Žiljak also wrote two SF screenplays; one of them was recently resurrected into a new development cycle.

Žiljak's first story collection was *Slijepe ptice (Blind Birds)* in 2003. In the same year, he published a popular science book *Cryptozoology: The World of Mysterious Animals* under the name Karl S. McEwan. His second story collection, *Božja vučica (The Divine She-wolf)*, was published in 2010. Both collections drew considerable attention, while his interest in cryptozoology resulted in numerous TV appearances in Croatia.

In 2012, he published a somewhat controversial political SF novel *Irbis,* in which a Croatian soldier (reincarnated as a snow leopard), his cyborg bodyguard, a deposed Chinese gangster-princess, the lord of the Croatian underworld, and a clone of a notorious terrorist all get involved in a world revolution some time in the nanotechnological future. The novel received considerable critical acclaim outside of Croatian SF circles.

In 2003, Žiljak started translating his stories into English and submitting them for publication worldwide. They have appeared in Germany (*Internova* and *Nova* magazines), Denmark (*Phantazm* webzine), Serbia (*Politikin zabavnik* youth magazine, *Art-Anima* webzine, *Omaja* magazine, and several anthologies), Argentina (*Axxón* webzine), Greece (*9,* weekly comics, and the SF supplement of the *Eleftherotypia* newspapers), People's Republic of China, Italy (*Futuro Europa* magazine), France (*Station Fiction* magazine), Poland, USA (*The Apex Book of World SF* (2009), edited by Lavie Tidhar; *Apex Magazine; Extinct Doesn't Mean Forever* (2011), edited by Phoenix Sullivan; *Gears and Levers,* (2012), edited by Phyllis Irene Radford; *World Literature Today*), UK (*You'd Better Watch Out!* (2012), edited by Kevin G. Bufton), Bosnia-Herzegovina, Bulgaria (*Irin Pirin* literary magazine), Romania (SRSFF, the Romanian Science Fiction and Fantasy Society Web site) and Ukraina (*Ukrainian Fantastic Observer* magazine). More stories are currently awaiting publication in several English-language anthologies.

For those interested to learn more about the Croatian SF scene, Žiljak's article "Science Fiction in Croatia" is available in English on several Web sites worldwide.

Žiljak is also an SF editor. He edited several story collections by some of the most prominent Croatian authors. He also co-edited (with Tomislav Šakić) *Ad Astra,* a 640-page anthology of the Croatian SF story 1976-2005. Today, Šakić and Žiljak edit an SF magazine *UBIQ,* voted the best European SF magazine on Eurocon 2011 in Stockholm.

Žiljak has won four Croatian SFERA Awards for best SF stories (in 1996, 1998, 2000, and 2011), two for best SF art (in 1993 and 1995), and one for his editing work on *Ad Astra* (2006), with Tomislav Šakić).

www.ingramcontent.com/pod-product-compliance
Lightning Source LLC
Chambersburg PA
CBHW071337020726
47502CB00001B/129